VIOLENT SHADOWS

BIANCA K. GRAY

To those who don't believe in themselves.
Here's to hoping that you someday will.

CONTENTS

CHAPTER ONE

June's legs dangled in front of my face before accidentally kicking my head.

"June!" I cried as a sharp pain ran through my body. I ducked my head as I rubbed my forehead with my hand, squinting up at my redheaded friend.

"Sorry, sorry," she muttered as she hoisted herself up onto the branch that was above me. I leaned back against the base of the tree, wrapping my arms around my knees that were curled into my chest.

"June," I started hesitantly, leaning my head backwards to look up at her. Her feet dangled off of the thick tree branch as her arms were wrapped around the trunk of the fake tree. She looked down at me, her green eyes appeared even greener with the leaves surrounding her face.

"Yes Z?" June asked, blinking her eyes once.

"Are you nervous?" I asked, looking down at my hands. I heard her shift on the tree branch.

"Of course I'm nervous. Everyone's nervous when it's

their turn to take the Test," she said with the confidence of someone who never had to worry about Preparation. Sometimes, I wished that I believed in myself as much as June did. Unfortunately, I never could quite muster that much self-confidence.

"But, you've always been number one during Preparation," I pointed out. And that was the truth of it all, wasn't it? She never could doubt herself because she had always been praised, validated in her belief that she would pass any test that came her way. Unlike me.

June sighed as she jumped from the tree branch, narrowly missing my legs. She turned to face me and crossed her arms as she sat down across from me. I hugged my knees closer to my chest, resting my head in the small gap between them.

"Zinnia," which was my full name, "Preparation and the Test are two *very* different things." What she said was true. It was what the adults had always said to us. But, I've always found this hard to believe.

"Why? Are *you* nervous?" she asked. I looked up at her through my lashes as she sat there staring at me, waiting for my answer. It wasn't that I was *nervous* about it, necessarily. The thought of *taking* the Test didn't make me want to throw up. Just the thought of what would come after it. Though, I had accepted my fate the moment Preparation had begun.

I was five years old when I started Preparation. I remember I was extremely excited to start it. Preparation leads to the Test, which leads to the rest of your life. However, it never occurred to me what would happen if you didn't pass the Test, that you *could* fail the Test. It didn't occur to me until I was five and was faced with preparing for it, for the Test that I was to take eleven years from then.

The moment I walked in, the Instructor placed a paper maze in front of me and the other students. She told us that when she counted down to one, on one we were supposed to take our pencils and go through the maze to find the outside. She said if you came to a dead end, you had to put your pencil down, and couldn't go on anymore. I guess I didn't quite understand what she meant. So when she counted down to one, I picked up my pencil and went through the entire maze until I reached the outside. She was surprised that someone was able to complete the maze, and I felt extremely proud of myself. However, when she looked at my paper, her face had darkened. I remember frowning as she frowned, wondering what I did wrong. She handed me back my paper and said because I didn't listen to directions, I got a zero. That if I did that on the Test, I wouldn't pass.

I had hit every dead end but looped the single line to keep going, never taking my pencil off of the paper until I was outside of the maze. She told me that I had hit a dead end right at the beginning, and I was supposed to put my pencil down then. I told her that I didn't hit a dead end because the line didn't die. I had looped around so it would keep going. I remember her frown got so deep that I thought her face would turn inside out.

There was a conference with my makers after that. They sat down with the Instructor, and I sat outside of the room with the door slightly ajar. She told my makers she wasn't confident that I would pass.

"She can't follow directions, at all," the Instructor had said. I remember my makers were silent after her words. The silence bore such seriousness that I was almost brought to tears. She told them she would monitor my progress and let them know if there were any positive changes. But for now, they should prepare for me not passing the Test.

On the walk home, I had asked my makers what would happen if I didn't pass. My father stopped walking and looked over at my mother. They exchanged a look that I didn't quite understand. He, then, squatted down in front of me so that we were eye-level, with his large hands clasped onto both of my shoulders. He held on so tightly that his knuckles were white and that my shoulders started to ache. I scrunched up my face from the pain.

"Zinnia," he said, barely above a whisper, "The people who do not pass the Test... They don't... We don't know *exactly* what happens to them. But, they never come back. So you must try your best to pass it." His eyes wandered side to side before locking onto mine. "Do you understand?"

"Not really," I had stated. My mother grabbed my hand and started walking forward as my father stood up and walked behind us.

"Zinnia, you have to pass the Test. Do you know why?" she had asked. She faced forward and her lips had barely moved so I wasn't sure if I had heard her correctly. Plus, she was walking so fast, my little legs could barely keep up.

"So I can start the rest of my life," I said, repeating what was always said to me.

"No, Zinnia, so you can *live*," she whispered, her voice heavy with a seriousness I didn't quite understand until I got older. Her eyes met mine for a second, but I could see her pain there. The unknown. The fear. The caution. But most importantly, the warning.

Even though I had tried to progress positively throughout my time at Preparation, unfortunately, even if the outcome was the same as everyone else's, the way I seemed to get to the answer was always wrong. So I continuously got zeros. To the point where, because my name started with a Z anyway, my nickname was Zero.

At the age of fifteen, now, my parents seemed to have accepted my fate. Just as I had. I wasn't going to pass the Test. What came after that was a mystery to me.

"I'm not nervous, per se," I said slowly, finally answering June's question. "I kind of already know what the outcome is going to be." June gave me a slight pout, her wild red curls creating a sort of halo effect.

"We don't know that for sure. Who knows? You may be pleasantly surprised," she said. I snorted.

"Pleasantly surprised? If I pass the Test, June, it would be a miracle."

"We're talking about Zero passing the *Test*? June, your optimism will be the death of me," spoke Forest, his voice coming from behind us. He sat down next to me and flicked my forehead once he was settled.

"Ow," I said, rubbing the mark that he left.

"There's nothing up there in Zero's brain. And we all know what happens to people who eat a lot of air," Forest said, clicking his tongue, snapping his fingers, and then making finger guns at June.

"Don't say that, Forest," June pouted, pushing his shoulder with enough force to make him fall over on his side.

"We all know it's true," he defended. I hesitantly nodded my head.

"The stupid people, like me, we don't pass," I have told June this a million times. Yet, she continued to plan our life out afterwards. What we were going to do together once we became a part of society, how we will beg to be placed in houses next door to one another, how even our children will be the best of friends. Every time she did this, I had to remind her that my nickname was Zero for a reason.

"What happens to the people who don't pass the Test?" June asked after a while. It was a question she avoided asking for most of our lives. Forest shrugged and looked at me, as if I would have the answer. All I could remember was what my mother said once in a hushed intense whisper when I was five.

"They're not allowed to live," I repeated what I was told in a matter-of-fact tone. June frowned and turned to look at me as Forest raised his eyebrows, staring at the grass.

"That can't be true," she said. I shrugged.

"It's the only thing I've been told," I said.

"I'm sure they just say that to scare you into trying harder," June said, starting to stand up.

"Yeah. Zero's always so dramatic," Forest laughed, slightly awkwardly, as he stood up as well. His brown eyes didn't meet mine.

"You're probably right," I said, referring to June's comment as I elbowed Forest in the side for his. He gave me his famous wild smile as he elbowed me back.

"They must go somewhere, though," Forest mumbled, glancing over at June as if waiting for her to agree. She nodded her head as she stepped in line with us, linking arms with me.

"They must. Even though no one we know has never not

passed, if it's even *possible* to fail it, they must do something with them," she said. I involuntarily scrunched my nose up at the comment. She was wrong. There *was* someone we knew who didn't pass the Test a couple of years ago. But, for some reason, everyone had forgotten about him.

"I heard they go and do the jobs that no one wants to do," Forest said.

"Who told you that?" I asked.

"Female Maker," Forest said immediately. June giggled at his wording.

"That could be true," June said, her eyes looking up as she thought. She frowned suddenly and her steps slowed.

"What is it?" I asked, noticing her face was twisted into something I would call her 'thinking face.' She shook her head and looked at me.

"It's just... I wonder why they've never told us what happens after someone fails the Test."

CHAPTER TWO

I sat in Preparation listening to the Instructor drone on and on, my head in my hands as I zoned out. It was our last class before we had to take the Test, and she was lecturing us on how to prepare properly for the millionth time. If I had to hear, "Clear your head the night before" and "Remember to give thanks to the Nation" one more time, I would probably throw myself off the top of the Preparation building.

"Now after you take the Test, you may return to your families before the results are announced. Once you pass the test," they never said '*if*' because passing the Test was always a definite thing, "You will be assigned a job within the community, and you will forever be a citizen of this great Nation." My eyes glanced over at the man in the framed picture above her, Benjamin Adams's eyes watching me as I started to tune her out.

This speech wasn't directed towards me. Everyone in the Adams Community already knew I wouldn't pass the Test. I could always feel their pitying glances when I walked around town. What would happen to me was a mystery to everyone. Maybe they would all somehow forget about me as they had forgot about him.

I turned my head to look out the window. It was raining today, which meant I'd have to put on protective gear to keep from getting burned. My mind started to wander as I thought about the one other person that I knew failed the Test and that everyone else seemed to have forgotten about.

His name was August, named after the calendar month. He was born in summer, and like a summer baby, he was very open and free. He was a couple of years older than us, and he had only failed a couple of times during Preparation so everyone automatically assumed he would pass the Test, when it came time. No one thought someone would fail within our community. To their knowledge, no one ever had. The only person who would fail in this community, everyone thought, would be me. The little girl with auburn brown hair and a tiny pale face nicknamed Zero was a sure candidate to fail. August wasn't.

It's said that he argued with his Preparation Instructor a lot, that he had trouble with authority and following directions—which was a comment I would always receive at my end of the year Instructor commentary. But, he still continued to pass Preparation nonetheless.

Everyone *loved* August. It was hard not to. He gave candy to the little ones, and when he smiled at you, you felt like you were the most special person in the whole entire world. He somehow made everyone feel like they were worth something.

I remember the day before his time to take the Test. I

was on the swings, only thirteen almost fourteen young at the time. He walked up to me and stared as I ducked my head to hide my seemingly always-present tears. Sitting down on the swing next to me, we stayed silent for a moment. After awhile, I felt him shift as he turned towards me.

"You're called Zero, right?" he asked. It was the worst time to call me by that horrid nickname considering I had just gotten another zero in Preparation that day. I sighed, wiping my tears quickly and angrily before twisting my swing to face him, my eyes flashing. I could feel my chest burn, as it always did when I felt this way.

"It's what they call me. Why?" He smirked at my sudden flash of anger.

"I've never seen someone have such a strong emotion," he said, his blue eyes bright on his sun-kissed face. My emotion started to bay as my small rounded, yet slightly narrow eyes widened at his words. No one had ever said that to me with such fascination before. Then I scowled, hiding my face, slightly.

"Yeah. I have to take the pills to keep it stable. Though, I hate how it makes me feel, so sometimes I skip it," I was surprised at what I was saying, but I almost couldn't stop myself. He nodded knowingly.

"I hate it, too," he whispered, a glint in his eye that I couldn't quite name. As I scrambled to think of what else to talk about, to think of a question that would connect us even more, he interrupted my thoughts.

"So, Zero, what's your given name?" he asked, leaning back into the swing, his legs parallel to the ground.

"Zinnia," I answered. His smile reached his eyes as he turned to look at me.

"Zinnias must've been in full bloom when you were born," he smiled. He sat up in the swing and held a large hand out to me.

"I'm August," he said. My hand looked tiny and ghostly pale compared to his as his hand seemingly engulfed mine.

"I know," I said, my lips twisting into a small smile. I bit my lip to stop myself from saying, *"Everyone knows you."* He seemed slightly surprised, but he smiled back at me, making me feel like everyone else he had flashed that smile to, like I was the most special person in this whole universe.

I had gone home thinking I would see August again, praying I'd have the courage to speak to him. But that day, after he took the Test, he never came back home, and no one remembered he ever existed. Including his own makers.

There were a few people every year that never came home, but their makers would proudly say they were gone working in the Capital. A great achievement. But, after saying their kids were gone in the Capital, they would never talk about them again, like they were somehow forgotten, too.

My eyes blinked as I realized that the last Preparation was over. I grabbed my bag and slipped on my protective boots as I rushed to get out of the classroom as soon as possible. As I slipped out of the classroom, I looked outside the window, and the hologram of a nice meadow that Forest, June, and I were sitting in was gone, replaced with reality. Cracked dirt and nothing else for miles, only the shadow of the Wall lay in the distance. *If only the rain didn't come*, I thought bitterly. The fantasy that life was better here was only a lie that was always shattered by the rain. I pulled the heavy protective jacket around my shoulders and placed the helmet onto my head before trudging towards home.

When I opened the door to my house, Happy greeted me. Her dark brown hair flew out behind her, as she was about to hug my legs. I held up a hand to stop her, mumbling something about wearing protective gear, as I took it all off. Once it was hanging in the metal closet next to the door, did I then hug my little sister.

"You're taking the Test tomorrow, right?" Happy exclaimed as she wrapped her arms around my legs. I smiled down at her and nodded as she beamed up at me, brushing her hair out of her face.

My makers weren't allowed to have another child. It was told that they were going to have one and that was I—unlike June's family which was allowed to have six for some reason, but that's beside the point. However, after I turned nine, the Nation told my makers they were now allowed to have two children. My makers always denied this, but it's because I was a sure-to-fail-the-Test child, so they let them have another one just in case. And when I was ten, Happy was born. She was named Happy because instead of crying, my mother says, she let out giggles. I personally think my mother was too drugged up to hear the difference, but Happy was named Happy nonetheless, and happy she was.

Happy was five now and had just started her Preparation this year. Like me, she was extremely excited her first day. Unlike me, she passed and didn't get a zero. It was proven that, most likely, I was just a bad egg, and it wasn't the combination of my makers' genes. Hopefully, this will let them have another child… when I'm gone.

"Who's there?" my mother called out from the kitchen. There were smile wrinkles around her small hooded, dark brown eyes. Her high cheekbones seemed even higher as her smile widened upon seeing me. Her black hair was tied up in a neat bun at the nape of her neck as she wrapped her arms around my middle, hugging me.

"Mom, you're choking me," I managed to get out.

"I thought you might have forgotten your protective gear and…" My mother worried a lot. I think she'll never stop worrying. Sometimes, I liked to think she'd still find a way to worry about me somehow, even after forgetting my existence.

"It's fine. I didn't forget it. I'm not a *complete* idiot," I muttered. My mother's lips straightened into a thin line.

"Now, I did not say a word like that," she frowned. "If you judge a fish by its ability to climb a tree, it will live its whole life believing that it is stupid."

"Albert Einstein," we said at the same time.

"I know," I groaned.

"It's true, you know," my mother said, shaking a spoon at me before returning to the kitchen to continue making dinner.

"Mom," I said, coming into the kitchen with Happy in tow.

"Yes?" she asked as she added a whole bunch of garlic into the pan. I narrowed my eyes at the amount but didn't say anything.

"We never talked about Albert Einstein in Preparation," I stated, leaning against the counter. My mother looked up and then looked around the room before slipping her hand underneath the counter and pressing down on a harmless knob. That harmless knob played a video to the Nation that was pre-recorded every month whenever my mother wanted to talk about something she didn't want the Nation to overhear. I never figured out how she was able to make it with just a few items around the house, and I always thought my mom was extremely paranoid for making the device. Why would the Nation be upset at hearing what we're talking about?

"Well, you wouldn't learn about Albert Einstein in Preparation, now would you?" she said, a look of disdain on her face.

"I don't think I understand what you mean," I said slowly.

"Albert Einstein was a genius human within his time. He came up with the Theory of Relativity. He was a brilliant scientist. But, Albert Einstein would not have passed 'the Test,'" my mother was being short. It was a sign that her anger was about to boil over. I never understood why she had to emphasize when someone in history was a human. We all were humans.

"If Albert Einstein was a genius within his time, why wouldn't he have passed the Test? The Nation is trying to cultivate geniuses. That's why the Test was put into place because if the world was full of smarter people, the stupid people wouldn't have ruined the world like they did. The Test is designed to weed out the stupid people," I said, not understanding my mother's conspiracy theories. I never did. She never made any sense, and it always contradicted the things I have been told about the Nation.

"The Nation is not trying to cultivate *geniuses*, Zinnia," my mother looked like she was about to say something more, but the door to the house opened. Immediately, my mother pressed down on the tiny knob and resumed cooking our evening meal.

"I'm home, Nabi," my father called. Nabi was my mother's given name. She was from a different, smaller part of the Nation. Her name in her community's original language —before any language that wasn't English was banned— meant Butterfly. When my mother was born, *her* mother said that a butterfly had landed on my mother's head. My grandmother secretly taught my mother the community's original language—the little that she knew—but learning other languages was strictly forbidden. The only time any other language was allowed to be used was only for the naming ceremony. Other than that, it was forgotten by most people, with even my mother only knowing a few random words that my grandmother taught her. My mother would always try to teach me these words, to keep the culture alive is what she would say, but I tried my hardest not to listen. I didn't want to get into trouble like my mother had. And, I was already different enough in Adams.

"What's for dinner?" my father asked as he put away his protection gear. My father was a tall, big man with light auburn brown hair, like mine, and large light amber brown eyes. I took after my father in his coloring, but I had my mother's face shape, and my eyes were smaller than my father's, a characteristic inherited from my mother. Happy took more after my father, except with dark brown hair and dark brown eyes, my mother's coloring. She had his deep-set, downturned eyes that made it seem like she was always thinking, wise, like him.

I was immediately envious of Happy when she was born. She looked mostly like everyone else within the community that we lived in, while I stood out and looked slightly different. It was bad enough that I was called Zero all my life, already different from everyone else since I wasn't going to pass the Test, but also I *looked* different physically, which was always pointed out to me when I was younger. No one in the Adams Community looked like me or my mother. And I was a little glad that Happy would almost never have to deal with that.

My father sat down at the table, his freckles seemed to glow under the light.

"Were you out in the sun all day today?" my mother asked, setting down the meal in front of us. My father worked in the community greenhouse. He helped grow the plants that the community ate. He didn't always work there. He used to work as something else before I was born. He never talks about it, and no one in Adams dared talk much about my father for some reason. Though, I've always heard he was a brilliant man.

He did something that caused him to be punished, to marry my mother from a different community—who was being punished for reading books apparently, among other things—and he got demoted to working at the community greenhouse. However, he always tells me it's a very important job, and even though marrying my mother was a punishment, he loves her very much. I didn't know if I *completely* believed this, because I had heard a rumor that marrying my mother was a punishment for him because he was in love with someone else at the time, and love marriages were forbidden. Forest was the one who told me that—after begging him to tell me what he knew—and although I didn't trust Forest normally, it was a rumor that made sense.

"It did rain midday," my father answered my mother's question. The meal that my mother put out in front of us was spicy pork with a lot of garlic. My mother always cooked with a ton of garlic. She said it was something people in her community did. The pork was paired with short grain rice that stuck together that also came from her community.

The Nation sometimes would send us food that was made from the Shin Community. I always thought it was nice of them, since she seemed to miss her home, but my mother would get angry every time the package arrived. I was never sure why.

I had always felt special because of this. I got to eat food from a different community while others don't. No one else had this experience because it was unusual that my mother isn't from Adams. Normally, you stay in the community you were made in and marry someone from that same community. No one ever really was able to leave, unless your job required it.

My father smiled as he scooped out a large helping of the pork and rice. He loved it when my mother made food from Shin. It was always something different, and he enjoyed it immensely, even if it *was* a lot of garlic.

"What were you guys talking about when I came in?" my father asked nonchalantly, but my mother stiffened.

"Albert Einstein!" exclaimed Happy, her mouth full of

food. My father's face darkened, and he slowly put down his spoon as he turned to look at my mother.

"Nabi," he warned.

"Yes, Winter?" she asked, still chewing her food as if nothing was happening. She slipped her free hand under the table and pressed a knob.

"You can't *talk* about things like that. She—the Nation will hear," he hissed. My mother put down her spoon and turned to face my father. I chewed slowly as I watched them go back and forth.

"The *Nation* will hear nothing. Besides, even though I said nothing to put them in danger, your children deserve to know the truth," she said back. My father sighed.

"Nabi," he said in his exasperated tone that he used when he didn't want to fight.

"Winter," she mocked him.

"Nabi, the Nation is in the middle of deciding where to put you next. Must you always cause trouble?" my father asked, his eyes closing as a vein bulged from his forehead. He took a deep breath as my mother continued.

"The Nation shouldn't *have* to decide where to put me. They thought I belonged in the 'library—'" For some reason, my mother always put air quotes around the word 'library.'

"They didn't think you'd read the *books* that you were supposed to be *organizing*," interrupted my father.

"—And then once I had learned the truth about our 'great Nation,' they removed me from the 'library,' moving me to do work that a mindless person could do. Cultivating geniuses they say? Ha!"

"Technically, your original job *was* mindless work. You were supposed to be just putting away the categorized books," my father said, rubbing his temples with his fore-fingers.

"But, I read them!" exclaimed my mother. "What a horrendous crime!!" I quietly continued to eat my dinner as I listened to their conversation. Every time they argued in front of Happy and I, it always felt like they were talking in some kind of code.

"You're *supposed* to follow directions. You know, because of *your* genes Zinnia can't pass Preparation. What do you think is going to happen to her tomorrow, Nabi, hmm?" my father asked, throwing his hands down as he looked at her, in a calm manner. My mother glared right back at him. It was as if they had forgotten Happy and I were sitting right here.

"I don't know," she said. "You tell me, since you're apparently 'all knowing.'" Her fingers formed air quotes as she spoke. My eyebrows knitted together in confusion as I looked back and forth between them. My father stared at her for a moment longer as she glowered at him.

"You didn't take your medication today," he pointed out.

"Neither did you, I take it," she said right back. Her nostrils flared as she stood up and began taking the dishes off of the table.

"But Mom I didn't—" I started to say as she took my half-full plate away.

"Both of you, go upstairs into your rooms," she ordered. Happy frowned before getting up from the table.

"Well, if we're done talking about this now, you might as well push your button again before the Nation starts to wonder what is up," my father called from the living room.

My mother scowled and scurried over to the kitchen table to press the button.

"How did you even—"

"I'll rip these out like I did the last ones," was all my father said to my mother's half finished question. Her scowl got deeper.

I ran up to my room and closed the door, the floating light turning on as I walked in. Sitting down on my bed, I looked out the tiny window, out into the darkness of the night. The holograms were back up and running since the rain had stopped. I had always wondered if other communities had holograms, if the fire rain reached their parts of the Nation, too. My mother said that in her community there wasn't any fire rain, at least there wasn't before she left. She says that the fire rain here just solidifies the fact that this place was horrid. I guess it made sense that there wasn't fire rain anywhere else. Our community's nickname *was* the Fire.

My mother always complained about how the Adams Community was absolutely horrible. I didn't know whether to agree with her or not, though. I had never been anywhere else. This community was home to me. And if I pass the Test, this place will be home forever.

If I pass the Test...

I turned away from the window and laid down on my bed. Why did I continue to torture myself with all of these ifs and daydreams? I wasn't going to pass the Test. And whatever was going to happen to me after that...

I turned to look back outside again and opened the window. Hot air blew in and with it carried dust that wasn't in the mirage I saw, but I didn't care. In the distance, even with the hologram playing, I could see the Wall. It loomed higher than any of the buildings I've ever seen. I learned the Wall was built around the whole Nation. It was 796 meters tall, so I've been told. Whether someone actually went up to measure it or not was a mystery to me. I learned, though, that the only building taller than the Wall was in the heart of the Nation. It was called the Pencil, and it was over 800 meters tall. A blue light shone from the top.

Sometimes, I imagined I could see the small light from my window. The President lived in that tower. Probably so did the rest of the Senate. Although people say it's the safest place, I've always felt they were wrong. Something that noticeable, if there were anything outside the Nation—although I've been told that there's not anymore—it would be the first thing I would target.

I shook my head as I leaned my head out of the window and breathed deeply. Tonight may be my last night, and all I had were questions I knew would never get answered. What happened to people who failed the Test? What happened to August? What is the Wall for?

Preparation taught me that the Wall was put in place when the Nation was first formed, to keep out those that were evil and morphed and had gone wrong during the Last Days. Animals and such. The stupid people as well. But, it has been hundreds of years since the Nation was formed. Those things would've died out there by now, considering land has gotten significantly smaller, and the land that there is doesn't grow what it used to. The Nation made sure to build on the best land. So, if the Nation has the best land, and if there isn't much land to begin with anyway, that means all the creatures out there—that the Wall is protecting us from—died. And if that's the case, why is the Wall still up?

I had asked this question in Preparation. The Instructor told me the Wall was still up because it held historical significance. It reminds us what happened, what us humans did to ourselves because of stupidity. That the Nation keeps it up to encourage the citizens and keeps it as a monument of what the Nation stands for. I didn't question the Instructor after this. But, inside, I didn't believe her. I felt like the Nation was keeping us in, instead of the other way around. We were caged. We were trapped.

The window shut forcefully, and at first I didn't know what had happened, until I realized my hands were on the sill, pressing down. My hands flew to my face as I lay back down on my bed. I shouldn't have those kinds of thoughts. I shouldn't. No one *normal* does. June doesn't. Forest doesn't. It's just because of what my mother has whispered into my ears. Lies about the Nation. *I had faith in our great Nation*, I tried to convince myself.

Turning on my side, I heard my bedroom door open. My father sat down on the edge of my bed as I sat up and looked into his familiar amber brown eyes.

"Zinnia," he started.

"If you're going to talk about the Test, don't bother. There's no use," I said, lying back down on my side. My father didn't leave. He sat there quietly for a moment.

"I know you're going to fail the Test," there wasn't a whisper of doubt in what he said. I winced. "And I know you're not going to be a Citizen of our great Nation," the word 'great' sounded slightly twisted in his mouth, "But Zinnia, if I know you, you'll still get through it all."

"I don't think I understand what you mean, Dad," I said, facing my bedroom wall.

"Whatever happens after the Test, that we don't get to know about, I believe you'll get through it." I sat up and frowned at my father.

"You know what happens. Mom has already said it. I don't get to live. If I don't pass the Test, I don't get to live. What do you think that means?" I snapped, tears starting to wet my eyes. My father's seemed to glisten under the moon-light, but no tears fell.

"Your mother has read a lot of books," my father started, trying to force a small smile onto his lips.

"So, she may know what the rest of us don't. Don't you think that's why she got punished? Why would she get punished for reading a couple of books, if they were harm-less?" I asked.

"You're starting to sound like her," my father said sternly, "If she—I mean, the *Nation* overhears—"

"What does it matter?" I interrupted. "I'm going to fail the Test anyway. But, we all already knew that." I waited for my father to say something, but he fell silent. I turned away and lay back down on my side, facing away from him. He sat there for a while longer.

"Do you think after the Test, when I fail, that I'll get to come home and wait for the results like everyone else?" I whispered, after a long while. I didn't dare speak too loudly or my father might hear the tears balled up in my throat.

"Have you heard of anyone coming back home after failing the Test?" my father asked me after a moment of tense silence. I shook my head quickly. The bed shifted as my father stood up.

"Then... I suppose not... Good night, Zinnia," he whispered. He stood there for a moment longer, as if he wanted to tell me something more, but then he left.

"Good night, Dad," I whispered to the empty room. And then I started to sob.

CHAPTER THREE

"You look like an absolute mess, Zero," was the first thing out of Forest's mouth the next morning.

"I didn't get much sleep," I muttered.

"Why?" Forest asked. I thought he was being a friend for once until he said, "I mean it's not like you were studying." I turned to face him.

"You know, Forest, one of these days I'm going to gouge out those beady little eyes of yours with only my thumb," I spat. His eyebrows raised so high I thought they were going to fall off of his forehead.

"Wow, you *really* didn't get much sleep," he muttered. Soon, June joined us on our walk to the Test hall.

"Happy birthday!" she yelled into my ear. I held a finger to it as I winced. A part of me wished my sixteenth birthday wasn't on the day of the Test because my mother had looked like I was about to walk towards my funeral rather than celebrate the day I was born. I don't think she even uttered the words. Instead, she met me at the door and tucked a lock of hair behind my ear.

"Who's daughter are you?" she had asked. It was a question that she asked periodically, though I never really understood why.

"Your daughter," I had answered, as I always did. My mother had given me a small, sad smile as she nodded, waving me off. I turned towards June who was beaming at me.

"You seem... chipper," I muttered. She turned to look at me and gave me her infamous pitying look.

"Didn't get much sleep?" she asked.

"She was worried about the fact that if she passes, how will people still call her Zero?" Forest joked. I elbowed him in his side. He elbowed me back, a smile on his face.

"Forest, I swear..." I started to threaten him again. But, June put herself in between us, linking arms.

"Now, now, you two. Will you ever stop teasing each other?" she asked, a small smile on her face. "You guys can bicker *after* you pass the Test. And then we can celebrate your sixteenth all night!" I looked over at her, but she wouldn't meet my eye.

"June..."

"*After* you pass the Test," she said more forcefully, making eye contact. I stared at her for a moment. There wasn't any harm in playing along, was there? I smiled back at her.

"Of course," I said softly.

"Are you both crazy? She's *Zero*. She's not going to—" June put a hand over Forest's mouth and smiled at me. I tried to smile back, though it faded as I hoped June and

Forest were going to be okay without me. *Wow, gosh, Zinnia could you get any more depressing?* I thought. *It's not like you're dying or anything.* Or, at least, I hoped I wasn't dying.

I stopped in front of the Test Hall before we walked in. It was the biggest building in the community and was at the center of town hall. It was made completely out of white marble and had gold detailing all around it. The Test Hall was the most beautiful building I had ever seen, and I had always stared in awe at it whenever I walked by.

"C'mon," June said, grabbing my arm as she pulled me into the Test Hall. A pit settled into my stomach as I tried to swallow the feeling of death as I passed the threshold. We walked into the center of the building and sat down with the rest of our class. There were twenty of us.

My eyes surveyed the room, and I saw people biting their nails and their legs shaking. Lily, who was second in the class, appeared calm. Her hair was tied back into a tight ponytail, and her eyes flashed like a predator's would. She was dressed in all black.

"Well, Lily looks prepared," muttered Forest. I nodded to him.

"She looks like she's at a funeral," I whispered. June scoffed.

"Her own," she smiled. I rolled my eyes. June and Lily always fought for the number one spot in Preparation. Lily won a couple of times, but June more often than not came out on top. Today would determine, forever, who was really number one.

"Welcome to the Test," our Preparation Instructor that we've known since we were five announced. Her voice echoed throughout the Test Hall.

"Today is a very special day. Today is the day where you all, hopefully, become Citizens of this great Nation!"

"May the gods bless this great Nation," we replied in unison.

"The Nation was created after our ancestors burned our home to nothing. We rebuilt to keep our species alive, but one thing was certain. We needed a change. The Nation thought up a Test that would determine whether or not a person was smart enough to follow the Nation and to make sure we wouldn't make the same mistakes that our ancestors did. This Test separated the geniuses from the mediocre, in hopes that by doing so, the Nation will last for eternity. This great Nation cultivates geniuses."

"This great Nation cultivates geniuses," we repeated. I looked around and saw that everyone looked excited. It was almost the start of the Test which led to the beginning of their adult lives. *But,* I couldn't help but think, *this marked the end of mine.* I bit the inside of my cheek and slumped down further into my seat.

"We are the only ones left on this Earth," our Instructor continued, "As Citizens, we must protect it."

"Protect this great Nation from the mediocre," we replied in unison, my voice a beat late.

"I wish you all luck on the Test. We'll celebrate after you have become rightful Citizens of this great Nation," she said, leaving the stage with a smile.

"May the gods bless this great Nation!" we exclaimed, standing up. We lined up according to our rank in class. I was last, of course, but Forest was in front of me.

"Are you nervous?" I asked Forest. He turned around,

and he did that thing with his eyes where it seemed to vibrate. Then, he smiled my way.

"Scared shitless," he said. Afterwards, he turned back around. I looked down at my feet.

"Me too," I whispered. He didn't respond. The line started to move, and I stood there for a second before following, slightly out of step with the others. The Instructor frowned at me for that. I looked down at Forest's feet as we walked, trying to match my pace with his.

Forest's feet suddenly stopped, and I looked up to see a hallway of different rooms. The doors were as white as the marble on the walls. We were separated into different rooms, each in a room of our own. June winked at me from the end of the hallway before grabbing the door handle and walking in. I felt the smooth metal in my hands, taking a deep breath, before turning the knob. The room I walked into was brilliantly white. It gave a Hospital feel to it. A clean feeling, but not necessarily safe.

"Zinnia?" the lady sitting next to a bed asked. She also wore all white, her dark curly hair loose around her shoulders provided extreme contrast to her clothing. I straightened my shoulders and raised my chin slightly.

"That's me," I said, my eyes narrowing at her. She smiled slightly.

"I'm Blue. I'll be your Test Instructor today," she said. She gestured for me to sit down. Her hand led to the bed next to her that was also white. I frowned at it and then turned back to look at her.

"You mean *only* for today. We take the Test once in our lives, right?" I asked. She smiled slightly again, but her arm remained raised, pointing to the bed. I glanced over at it and then shifted my weight onto my right foot and then back to my left.

"If I'm taking a test, why are you gesturing me to a bed? To sleep? That's hardly a test, is it?" I said, crossing my arms. Her smile did not waver, but her eyes narrowed slightly.

"I've heard you were a... curious one," she said. Blue lowered her hand and put it down to her side. She took a step forward. She was shorter than me by a few inches, but there was something about her that terrified me. I took a step back.

"The Test is inside your head. It's not... exactly what your Instructor said it would be. Though, you will use a skill that is important to the Nation within it. It's a scenario—rather than a usual paper test—that plays in your head," she said, turning towards the bed. "You will be given a shot that will administer the Test into your brain and make you fall asleep, which is why there's a bed. When the Test is done, you will be able to return to your family to wait for the results. Most people don't remember a thing." She picked up a syringe and flicked the dark brown liquid that was inside of it, causing it to bubble up slightly. I looked over at the bed.

"Even if you fail?" My gaze shifted to her. She looked slightly taken aback. The gloved hand holding the syringe lowered slightly.

"I'm sorry?"

"If I fail, will I be able to return to my family and wait for the results?" I asked slowly. A small smile appeared on her face. It sent chills up my spine.

"No," she said, just as slowly. It seemed like she enjoyed telling me this. "We know right away when you fail. There's no need to wait for results." It felt like the breath had been knocked out of me. My mother... My father... Happy... I would never see them again. I took a deep breath and closed my eyes before opening them. What a birthday.

"Right," I breathed. I walked over to the bed, took off my shoes, and crawled into it. I laid down on my back, my head resting on the softest pillows I've ever rested upon. My heart was pounding in my head as Blue walked over to the side of the bed. She grabbed my arm and wiped it down with disinfectant. I turned away as she pulled out the shot. My chest felt like it was on fire.

"Breathe, Zinnia," she whispered. I let out the air that I was holding, slowly. I felt the needle from the syringe puncture my skin and the liquid being forced into my bloodstream. It didn't hurt, but it was uncomfortable. Extremely uncomfortable.

"Relax," she whispered. And suddenly, I started to feel groggy. My eyelids felt like a hundred pound weight. Soon, I couldn't keep them open anymore, and all I could see was darkness.

CHAPTER FOUR

In the darkness, it felt like I was falling. A circle of light appeared, and slowly it got bigger and bigger until it took up my whole vision. I braced myself for the landing as the hard floor of a darkened arena came closer and closer to me. Looking down at my body, I was wearing a white gown, my hair pulled up into a ponytail. In my hand was a knife. My memory felt foggy, and I held my head as I took in my surroundings.

"While this is a scenario happening in your head, what you experience and feel are very real," I heard Blue's voice say.

"What?" I exclaimed. "How am I hearing you?" I could tell that Blue smiled by the tone of her voice.

"In order to administer the Test properly, I am asleep next to you," Blue's voice said in my head. "Good luck." Her voice echoed in my mind as a dark figure appeared from across the room.

"What am I supposed to do? Why do I have a knife?" I asked Blue's voice.

"The Test is not the kind of tests you would take during Preparation," I heard her repeat into my mind.

"What does that even mean?" my voice shook as a figure stepped forward into the light.

"It's a loyalty test," Blue barely breathed into my mind as my heart dropped from seeing the familiar face filled with fear. This was not what everyone said the Test would be like.

"Forest?" I asked. His eyes lit up at the sound of his name, and he looked up at me.

"Zero," he said. He was holding a similar knife in his hand, and wore a gown like mine, like we were both sleep-walking or in a weird dream.

"What is going on? Why are we here? Although," he said while looking around, "it kind of looks like the gym, huh?" I didn't understand how he could joke in this kind of scenario.

"Weird test," I awkwardly laughed.

"Kill your friend," I heard Blue's voice say in my mind. I watched as Forest's eyes widened, most likely hearing the same phrase being uttered into his. Our eyes locked.

"You said my experiences and feelings are real, even though this is happening in my head," I said out loud. Forest looked confused at me speaking to my Test Instructor.

"Yes," Blue responded after a while.

"Are you saying he's really in front of me?" I asked, my voice shaking. She stayed silent.

"If I do what you say, will he really die?" I asked again, a little louder. Forest stared at me, his jaw tensed.

"Kill him," Blue said in response. "He has committed a terrible crime. It is for the good of our Nation. Our great Nation."

"May the gods bless this great Nation," I heard Forest say under his breath, hearing the same instructions as me.

"I can't," I whispered, taking a step back as Forest took a step forward. His knuckles turned white from gripping his knife, hard. I swallowed.

"I'm not going to fight you," I told him. His eyes didn't meet mine.

"You're a criminal, Zinnia," he said, for once using my real name. My eyes felt hot.

"Don't you want to know what I've done?" I asked him. "Aren't you going to ask what terrible crime I committed?"

"The President wants you to kill the criminal," Blue said, the same phrase being echoed into Forest's mind.

"If you don't, you'll fail," Blue threatened.

"The President wants me to kill you," Forest said, still not meeting my eyes. *A good enough explanation,* I thought sarcastically.

"Forest, that doesn't make any sense," I pleaded with him. "It doesn't make sense for us to kill each other."

"I won't fail, Zinnia," he muttered, his eyes flashing at me. I took another step back. He wasn't going to listen to my words. He would do anything to survive. Failing was worse than death. I knew that better than anyone.

"This isn't real anyways," he convinced himself. My eyes looked around the arena searching for some kind of escape. When I zeroed in on some kind of an exit, I turned around and started to run. I heard Forest pick up speed behind me, his steps heavy and thundering. There was a tunnel where I entered from, and I ran for it as fast as I could. This was all in my head. I needed to wake up.

"*Please* I can't kill him," I pleaded with my Test Instructor. This test didn't make any sense. We never learned how to fight in Preparation, let alone how to kill someone. Why would they *want* us to kill someone? As I got closer to the tunnel, the heavy stone door started to close from the top. I tried to pick up speed, but the arena seemed to get longer and longer the faster I ran. By the time I got to the tunnel, the door was shut. I banged on the door, tears covering my face as Forest caught up to me. He was never athletically gifted, and I heard him breathe heavily from behind. He pulled my ponytail without hesitation, bringing me to the ground.

"Kill him," I heard Blue's voice say.

"Kill him," a chorus of voices said. "It's for this great Nation." I didn't know where the voices came from, and I winced as my vision blurred.

"Screw this Nation," I coughed as I tried to get up. Forest kicked my ribs, and I felt a gush of air fly out of me.

"You won't remember it," Blue's voice was clear in my mind. "Everyone will think that he just went to work in the Capital, and eventually no one will remember him or what you did." I could tell that Forest was hearing the same message as he looked suddenly inspired, straddling me to the ground. *So that's what happened to those kids,* I weakly thought.

"Forest, please," I managed to get out as he raised his knife into the air. I felt this burning sensation build up in my chest and churn through my blood. It was something that I had felt often as a kid, but there was something in me that knew if the burning feeling traveled further throughout my body instead of just building in my chest, something terrible would happen.

I stifled the feeling and felt the air move around me as he brought down the knife, aiming for my chest. I put up my hand, the knife splitting it into two as I pressed against the hilt of the knife. Forest's eyes widened as I pushed up, my hand on fire from the pain as I tried to keep the knife from my chest.

"This isn't real," Forest said to himself.

"It's real," I nearly shouted back to him, my own blood dripping onto my face.

"I *have* to kill you," he whispered, beads of sweat dotting his forehead. His hands were starting to tremble and the force behind the knife was lessening a little.

"You don't have to," I reassured, grunting as I pushed it up more. My hand was becoming numb. He stared at me for a moment.

"The President," he muttered.

"Screw the President," I angrily whispered. His brown eyes filled up with tears as he stared at me.

"I can't kill you," he finally said, his voice morphed from the tears in his throat. "You're one of my best friends, Zinnia." As his lips pulled back into a smile, I heard the air move around me, and as I blinked, a knife appeared in the middle of his chest. He looked down at it, stared at some-thing behind my head, and then fell to the ground, blood slowly sputtering out from him as he gasped for air. I pushed his legs off of me and frantically looked at him, my hands shaking over his wound.

"Forest?" I cried out. "*Forest?*" My voice was shrill. The glow in his eyes slowly started to fade.

"Oh, get over it," I heard a familiar voice say. "Neither of us will remember him anyways." I looked up into familiar emerald green eyes.

"June?" I mouthed. She shrugged.

"You two were always at the bottom of the class," she said. I stared at her, my knees becoming soaked with Forest's blood. My mind froze as I took in the unfamiliar expression on her face, unable to comprehend what was happening.

"What?"

"They brought me from my first test to here because you two were being so pathetic," she explained. "You two are too strong minded."

"Strong minded?" I said, softly, as the anger started to build up. "You just *killed* one of your best friends because 'the President' asked you to." I gestured towards Forest's dead body, trying to keep my breakfast from rising.

"And you wouldn't? You know, if you two had just *listened*, maybe the two of you would still be alive," she hissed angrily. *Still be alive?* She walked over to where Forest's body was as I continued to gape up at her. She pulled the knife from his body, a sickening, squelching sound came with it and then a gush of dark red blood poured out from the wound.

"If I just listened," I said slowly. If we fought each other, would they have ended the Test? Would either of us had to have died?

"You're both so dumb," June muttered as she walked away from me, "And dumb people will ruin this Nation." She then suddenly turned around, her knife cutting through the air towards me, the same way that Forest had died.

The knife rotated in the air, the silver metal glinting, and I felt the burning in my chest escape at the sight, flowing down my arms and legs, and then out of me, as if water was pouring out of every inch of my body. Suddenly, fire erupted all around me, disintegrating the knife and everything that was in its way. All I could see were the heat waves from the explosion. Forest's body was gone, and June's was as well. Before I could process what had happened, it was over. Everything had turned to ash. My heart stopped as I looked all around me, the leftover heat from the explosion washing over my body.

"June?" I whispered. As I went to look at my hands, my eyes widening at the sight of flames, the arena suddenly changed in a blur.

Somehow, I was outside in the town square, and everything was on fire. I watched as the flames licked towards the feet of Happy, who was standing in the middle of the town, crying. Flames that seemed to be attached to me.

"Zinnia!" she cried. It was a scene I had seen before. A recurring nightmare that I had as a kid. My heart pounded as the flames got closer to her, and my chest began to ache. I could feel the pull of the fire as I tried to bring it back into me.

"Happy!" I cried out as she started to scream from the pain of the flames. It started to encase her little legs, whirling around her like a tornado. The fire was searching for something, and sweat rolled down my forehead as I tried to bring the fire back into my chest. However, the flames wouldn't listen.

"This isn't part of the procedure. Her sister isn't supposed to be here. This isn't even supposed to be a part of her task. I don't understand what's going—" I heard Blue's voice say before cutting out, panicky, as if she were talking to someone next to her, and not me. But, I hardly listened to her words. All I could think about was that I had to save my sister.

"Zinnia," her cries were getting weaker. Those deep set eyes of hers became glazed over. I closed my eyes and took a deep breath, calming my beating heart. As I calmed down, I looked around at the fire that was previously engulfing the town. The fire was dying down. I blinked a couple of times, as I couldn't believe what I was seeing. *I* was doing this. I could feel the fire being sucked back into me. A weird burning sensation hovered around my chest, and it continued to grow and grow until the fire was completely out. This wasn't just a task. This was... me. I couldn't explain it, but this feeling wasn't in my head. That fire was... inside of me, constantly moving in my bloodstream.

"What's happening?" I asked, my voice shaking. And then all I could see was black.

The circle appeared again, and I fell in, landing on my feet in a completely white room.

"Where am I? Did I pass?" I asked, desperately. *I must've*

already taken the Test, I thought to myself. I couldn't remember what had happened before entering this room, but there was a part of me that knew the Test had already taken place. I just couldn't remember it no matter how hard I tried.

An empty silence filled the room. A door opened on the other side of it, and a woman with short white hair walked in. She was smiling, but there was something sinister about it.

"Hello Zinnia," she said. Her voice was as chilling as her smile. There was something about her. Something that seemed... forced.

"Who are you?" I asked.

"I am President Eclipse," she said, a seemingly permanent smile etched onto her face. Her smile was wide, almost unnaturally wide. Her voice had an air about it, as if she had the confidence of someone who had lived for hundreds of years.

"Why are you here?" I asked. Her eyebrows rose at my demanding tone.

"Hm," she said walking around me, as if I were her prey that was about to die and she was the vulture circling, flying lower and lower...

"No wonder you're failing Preparation. You don't even know how to greet your President?" she asked, her white eyes finally having some life to them.

"You seem to already know my name," I muttered. Her smile disappeared from her face, suddenly, unnaturally. A chill crept down my spine, and I took a step back. This room was too white. There was nowhere to hide.

"My name is Zinnia Winterschild of the Adams Community, currently in Preparation and not a part of society. It is a great pleasure to meet you, President. May the gods bless this great Nation, and you as well, President Eclipse," I said, quickly. Her eyes narrowed at me as she stopped her circling. She leaned towards me, her eyes almost as white as her hair.

"You failed your task, child of Winter from the Adams Community," she said, her voice staying at that same chilling note. I refrained myself from shuddering.

"Unfortunately, though, for you Miss Zinnia of the Adams Community, there were some... technical difficulties."

"What do you mean?" She smirked.

"What did you do back there?" she asked, ignoring my question.

"I don't understand what you're asking."

"What did you do in your task?" she asked, standing up straight.

"I..." I thought back to try to remember my task, "I can't... I can't remember."

"Can't you?" she said, echoing my tone of confusion. "You overrode the system, the liquid in your bloodstream. You overrode it, slightly. Was it on purpose? A dream, perhaps?" She seemed genuinely curious.

"I—"

"Your mother is Nabi of the Shin Community, yes?" she asked, interrupting me, her voice becoming bitter. A file suddenly appeared in her hands.

"Y-Yes, that's right."

"She was punished and sent to the Adams Community

for not doing her job, yes?" she asked, even though she seemed to already know what happened.

"Not for not doing her job, but for reading the books—" She leaned forward suddenly, her smile completely disappearing.

"Reading? What do you know, Zinnia?" she whispered.

"I don't know what you mean..."

"Do you know *what* your mother is?" she demanded. I shook my head.

"No, I don't know what you mean," I repeated.

"What happens when you fail the Test?"

"I don't know."

"You don't know what's beyond the Wall? Beyond the Nation?"

"*I don't know*," I insisted. She glared at me.

"You're not telling me something," she accused. She grabbed my head and pushed it towards the ground as she leaned towards my ear. I felt pathetic tears start to prick at the corners of my eyes. I tried to swallow them down.

"You must tell me what you know," she hissed. I flinched from her voice. There was something in my head urging me to tell her everything my mother had ever told me, though I didn't feel any of it would help me here. I closed my eyes and pushed back against it as hard as I could.

"I know nothing," I lied through my teeth. I could feel what she wanted to know at the tip of my tongue, but even my own memory wouldn't dare whisper it. Her eyes narrowed for a second, and then she released my head, letting me stand back up straight.

"This Nation isn't built on those with minds like yours. Though, a treasure like you... such a pity," she said, her smile back as her eyes started to look dead. I frowned as I looked at her more closely. It was as if there were scales on her face instead of skin. I gasped and took a couple of steps back.

"We're not going to let people like you ruin everything again," she hissed. I started to scream. And then everything went black.

CHAPTER FIVE

When I woke up, I was on a moving hover train. I tried to sit up, but manacles around my arms and feet kept me from moving.

"Don't bother," a voice from across the carriage said. I craned my neck to look over at the person the voice belonged to. It was a boy about my age. He had short, tight curly hair and the color of his skin was unfamiliar to me.

"Where are we going?" I asked, unable to hide my panic. He laughed, but it sounded hollow.

"Where do you think? We're going towards the Wall," he said, without energy.

"Why would we be going to the Wall? Why are we tied down?" My anxiety was rising. I didn't like being unable to move.

"We failed the Test. We're tied down so we can't try to escape. I've heard stories that when you fail, you get sent to the Wall to die. We're probably heading towards our death sentence," he said, laughing without humor.

"We're going to die," I whispered. It was something I had already expected. I had expected it my whole life. But the reality of it... It was something else. The anxiety overwhelmed me, and I started to hyperventilate. Black spots clouded my vision and sweat dotted my hairline.

"Hey," the boy whispered, "It's okay."

"I," I gasped, "I can't breathe."

"Just hold your breath," he said. I laid my head back onto the metal table that I was tied down to and looked up at the carriage's ceiling.

"What's," I gasped, "Happening. To. Me."

"You're having a panic attack," he said calmly. "Just hold your breath. Just—hey, what's your name?"

"Zinnia," I barely got out. There was something heavy on my chest. I couldn't breathe, I couldn't breathe, *I can't breathe.*

"Zinnia, listen to my voice, okay? Just concentrate on my voice," he said. I'm going to die, I'm going to die, *I'm going to die.*

"Everything's going to be okay," he lied. "It's all going to be okay. I just need you to hold your breath and count to ten. Okay, Zinnia? Can you do that for me?" Hold my breath. I need to hold my breath. I took my last gasp of air that barely filled my lungs and held it. One. Two. Three.

"My name's Lightning by the way," the boy said. Four. Five. Six.

"I'm from the Du Bois Community," the boy continued to talk. Du Bois, the community named after one of the first Senate members Frederick Du Bois. Seven. Eight. *What a weird name,* I couldn't help but think. But, all the original Senate members were named strangely. Nine. My heart rate slowed, and the weight on my chest started to lift. Ten.

"I'm Zinnia," I finally said. The taste of blood wouldn't leave my mouth. "I'm from the Adams Community."

"Ah. Benjamin Adams," Lightning said, a bit under his breath.

"I've never seen such white skin before," Lightning said, a little louder. "It's weird. Like a skeleton or a ghost or something." I laughed.

"You think I'm kidding. When they rolled you in, I thought you were a goner," he said, laughing along with me.

"I've never seen such dark skin before," I spoke, honestly. "I've never seen people like you in person."

"Me either," he said. "We learn about people who look like you during Preparation. I've just never seen one in person. Though, you look a little different."

"My mother's from the Shin Community. She looks different from the people in the Adams Community," I said.

"You're community-mixed?" he asked, his eyes wide. I laughed, hearing the unfamiliar term.

"Yeah, I guess I am." The train suddenly stopped, and anxiety closed my throat.

"You probably took pills every morning right?" he asked, whispering quickly.

"Yeah," I whispered hoarsely. *Well, most mornings.*

"Listen, the rush of emotions is going to hit you soon. If you don't take the pills, they can overwhelm you, especially if you're not used to the emotions," Lightning said quickly as we heard people talking outside of the train carriage.

"I used to... I used to skip taking them sometimes, but this feeling—"

"It's fear. You failed the Test for being strong minded, right? Use it now," Lightning said before the door opened. I tried swallowing the lump that was growing in my throat. The men came in and unlocked the manacles around our arms and legs. They tied our hands with rope and made us walk one in front of the other. I was behind Lightning. And as I looked up at him, I couldn't help but think that he was unbelievably tall. My head came to his shoulder blades.

I looked around him to see where we were going. There were four men, and they were wearing protective helmets, so we couldn't see their faces. They led us towards the Wall, which was a lot whiter than I thought it'd be, and a door opened up, as we got close enough. The Wall wasn't just a wall... it was a building? I started to question everything I had ever been taught.

"Where are these ones from?" asked the man who had opened the door. He was holding his mask underneath his arm, and his ironically kind brown eyes looked me up and down before closing the door behind us.

"One from Du Bois, the other from Adams," one of the masked men up front said. The other man narrowed his eyes at me. He reminded me of my mother.

"Adams?" he asked, looking over me.

"Yeah, the girl's from Adams," the masked man said. He took off his helmet, and I gasped. His eyes were like a cat's, vertical slits. He smiled at my response, revealing sharp canines. The other masked men followed his example, but he was the only odd looking one. Ears popped up from his black hair. The other man was still eyeing me.

"She looks kind of like the people from my community," he muttered.

"Where'd you say you were from, Yun?" asked the cat man.

"Wu," Yun said. Wu Haoyu, the man that the community was named after, was said to be a hero in the war that led to humanity's downfall. Anyone from the Wu Community was always proud of their namesake, at least that's what they told us in Preparation. The two men led us to a cage, and then closed the door behind us, not bothering to untie our hands.

"Where are you from?" asked the cat man, turning towards me. I blinked as I tried hard not to let the fear overtake me. His yellow eyes stared, unblinking. I swallowed the lump in my throat.

"A-Adams," I managed to get out. The cat man gestured towards me as he turned towards Yun.

"See? I told you. She's from Adams," he said. Yun narrowed his eyes.

"Where are your parents from?" he asked.

"Yun, if she's from Adams, her family's from Adams. No one marries outside of their community. That's not a thing—"

"Let her talk, Jag," demanded Yun. Jag narrowed his yellow eyes, as his pupils enlarged for a split second before returning to their normal slits.

"Fine," he said, shrugging. Yun looked at me, expectantly.

"Um, my dad's from Adams. My mother is from Shin," I said quickly. Jag suddenly turned his head towards me and walked over, much like how a cat stalked towards their prey.

"Shin? Your mother's from Shin?" he asked. I nodded my head quickly and glanced over at Lightning for help. Unfortunately, his eyes were closed, and he looked like he was trying to stay as invisible as possible.

"You're community-mixed?" asked Yun.

"Not unheard of, especially in the Capital," Jag muttered.

"But in Adams?" asked Yun. "That place is so far off the map..." He looked at me, as if almost pityingly, "What'd your parents do?"

"Whatever it is, it's obviously genetic considering she ended up at the Wall," Jag said, shrugging it off.

"I just feel kind of bad for her. Living community-mixed in a place where it's unheard of. She should've grown up in the Capital," Yun lamented. They started to walk away and as they did, they turned on a switch, causing the cage to become electrified. I jumped back from the bars.

"She could've lived in the Capital if she didn't fail the Test," Jag told Yun.

"Still," Yun said, looking back at me. I scooted towards Lightning. He was a big man, considering I was taller than most of the girls back home. But, for some reason, I felt safer being next to him.

"Who else is on our list?" asked one of the men to Jag. It seemed like Jag was in charge.

"We got one coming from Shin, one from Washington, one from Bakshi, one from Rizal, and," Jag paused and groaned, "one from the Capital." Lightning's eyes opened so quickly that I almost screamed from being startled. He leaned forward to hear the conversation better, careful to not touch the electrified bars.

"Don't forget the two from Khaldun," Yun yelled from across the room. Jag pointed towards Yun and nodded.

"Also the two from Khaldun. No humans this year," Jag said, closing the cover of the tablet. *Humans?*

"Well," I heard Yun mutter, "They normally die, don't they." I tore my gaze away from the two as I glanced over at the boy next to me.

"What is it?" I whispered to Lightning. He was biting the inside of his lip, chewing it.

"They're kids from around the Nation," he muttered.

"So?" I asked.

"That's a lot of kids that failed for the Nation to never mention what happens after failing, don't you think?" Lightning said, turning to look at me. Then, he looked over at the men who were laughing and talking. Jag was staring right at us, smirking, his ears upright on his head.

"Though, I do wonder why someone from the Capital failed," Lightning whispered, his eyes on Jag. Jag's smirk disappeared, and he narrowed his eyes before turning away.

"Anyone can fail," I said. Lightning looked over and laughed a little.

"When the one from the Capital comes, then you'll understand," Lightning said. He proceeded to lie down on the metal ground, his head facing away from me.

"I'm going to get some sleep before whatever they're going to make us do happens," he said. "You should get some rest, too. It's going to be a while until the kid from Rizal gets here. It's from the opposite end of where we are." I wanted to ask how he knew that, but he seemed to fall asleep right away. How he could be calm enough to do so, I didn't know. He also didn't seem that surprised at seeing Jag, despite the fact the dude looked like a giant humanoid cat.

CHAPTER SIX

I must've drifted to sleep because I woke up to the loud noise of the cage being opened. Sitting up, I noticed Lightning was already awake.

A girl who was smaller than I was, with black hair that reached her hips; and a boy, with short red hair and copper freckles dotted all over his pale skin, stood at the entrance of the cage. They were slightly pushed, and the boy fell in, unable to catch himself due to his tied hands. I scratched mindlessly at the rope around my wrists as the men closed the doors. Jag winked at me with his cat-like eyes before the electricity started back up again.

"Are you okay?" I asked the boy. He pushed himself up into a sitting position and smiled at me.

"Peachy," he said. The girl kept staring at me, her head turning side to side, as if trying to figure out where she knew me.

"I'm Zinnia," I said, breaking eye contact from the girl who looked eerily like my mother, in order to look at the redheaded boy. "This is Lightning." Lightning nodded his head as a greeting. The newcomers both didn't seem fazed. Neither of the boys seemed fazed either at how different the girl looked. I suddenly felt bad for being fascinated with how different Lightning looked from me. I guess I was the only one who had never seen people who didn't look like my dad or this redheaded boy, besides my mom. Or they were better at hiding it than me.

"Uh, I'm Freckles, er, my nickname back home was Freckles. My real name is Ash," he said.

"What do you want to be called? Freckles or Ash?" asked Lightning, his voice low. Ash shrugged.

"Whatever you want to call me I suppose."

"Well, I guess it doesn't really matter," I said, "Considering." *Our imminent death*, I finished in my head but didn't dare speak aloud. I turned towards the girl who continued to stare at me.

"What's your name?" I asked, a little weirded out from her staring.

"I'm Jangmi," she said, her eyes studying me. "Where are you two from?" She finally broke eye contact with me to look at Lightning. Lightning shifted under her stare. I guess I wasn't the only one slightly intimidated by her gaze, despite her size and stature.

"I'm from Du Bois. Zinnia here's from Adams," he said. She whipped her head back at me and narrowed her eyes.

"She's community-mixed," Lightning finished, seeming to guess what was on Jangmi's mind. I remembered where Jag said the other kids were coming from. Shin Community.

"You're from Shin, right?" I asked Jangmi. She fixed her

eyes on me and nodded, a ghost of a smile creeping onto her face.

"You're Nabi's kid, correct?" she asked. My eyes widened. How... How could she possibly know that?

"I'm your cousin," she smiled, widely, not seeming to catch my surprise. But before I could ask her anything else, two more people came into the Wall. I couldn't see past the electricity rippling around the bars, but it looked like two boys. They turned off the electricity, opened the doors, threw them in, and turned the electric barrier back on.

One was significantly taller than the other, perhaps even taller than Lightning. The other was skinny, but not necessarily small. They both had black hair, but the smaller one's hair covered one side of his face while the other's hair was cut short, close to his head. Both looked determined and not at all scared. I scooted closer to Lightning. I could feel him looking at me weirdly, but my gaze was fixed on the two newcomers. I had never seen anyone that looked like either of them before. Ash decided to take charge in this instance.

"Hey ya," he started off. "Ash," he said, placing a hand on himself, and effectively choosing a name. "Washington Community." The shorter one looked him up and down. His skin was dark but not as dark as Lightning's was.

"Rohit," he stated, shortly. "Bakshi Community."

"I'm Agwe," said the tall one. "I'm from Rizal." He flashed a smile in my direction, as I glanced over at Lightning who looked slightly shocked.

"I thought the kid from the Capital would be here before the Rizal one," Lightning muttered under his breath, so quiet only I could hear.

"Well it's nice to meet you," Ash said. We continued to

introduce ourselves, and as we did, Jangmi moved closer to me. She linked her arm with mine and smiled. I had a cousin. My father was an only child, and even though I knew my mother had more siblings, I thought it'd be impossible to meet them. Sadness filled me as I realized we had to meet in these conditions, but I swallowed the feeling down and smiled back at her.

"I wonder why the electric barrier is up though. As if we'd be able to escape," Agwe said, looking through the bars. Ash scoffed.

"I mean, who knows? One of us might have the ability to walk through solid wall. This barrier would stop them from doing that," Ash shrugged. "Although, even if we *did* manage to escape, I don't doubt that those men," he pointed at the five men outside the cage, "probably have abilities that would trump us all, so," he shrugged again, "I guess it'd be pointless to escape." Rohit and I leaned in, looking at him with wide eyes. His head moved back as he looked at us.

"What?" he asked.

"Abilities? To walk through walls?" I asked.

"And you're saying that those men out *there* have abilities?" asked Rohit. Ash furrowed his eyebrows together.

"You didn't know?" he asked, genuinely confused. Agwe shrugged and Lightning looked away.

"Some communities might not talk about it," Agwe said.

"Most communities don't. Even if they did, it would be in secret conversations," Lightning clarified. He looked over at Agwe and narrowed his eyes. "But considering how far Rizal is from the Capital, it's surprising that you know anything about it." Agwe grimaced.

"It's discussed in... secret conversations, as you say," Agwe said.

"Most Asian communities have those secret conversations. They are stories that we grow up with, passed from generation to generation," Jangmi piped up, seemingly to defend Agwe. Rohit seemed to relax after Jangmi's explanation.

"Oh, you mean those stupid bedtime stories," Rohit mumbled. Jangmi's eyes flashed at him.

"Asian?" I asked. Rohit sighed and blew his hair from his eyes.

"You're from Adams right? The most ignorant place in the Nation," he rolled his dark eyes. "There are many different races of people: the Asian race, the Caucasian race, the Black race, and Indigenous race. Though, the Nation is not split up by those races, but by ethnic groups. Which is a completely different thing. However, the ability thing, *that* I've never heard about. At least about it really being true. So I guess I'm just as ignorant as you," he looked me up and down, "Snowflake." I narrowed my eyes at the remark and tried to hide the glance I took at my skin color. I wanted to know more about the different races and ethnicities, and what they meant—and where I fit in within the races—but I didn't dare ask.

"So what's the ability thing?" I asked, turning towards Ash.

"Some people have special abilities. They're able to... *do* things that normal people can't. I've heard different things as to how it came about. Some people say that it was the radiation from World War III; others say that people with abilities were around before that, and this is just what's naturally happening. Either way, those kids, the ones with special abilities, they're weeded out from the normal ones. And they get sent away," Ash said. He shrugged, "I don't know much about it. But, I do know if you fail the Test—and survive—you probably have some kind of evolutionary ability, considering the nature of the Test." *She could've lived in the Capital if she didn't fail the Test,* Jag's earlier words bounced around in my head.

"You already knew it was a loyalty test?" Lightning asked. I wrinkled my brow at the conversation. I couldn't remember the Test for the life of me. Ash frowned.

"Everyone in Washington knows. Everyone in the Capital knows, too. It isn't hidden," Ash explained. Lightning leaned forward to ask another question, but was interrupted.

"Why do they get rid of the kids with these abilities? Wouldn't it just help the President to have kids like us around?" asked Rohit, leaning back against the only solid metal wall that didn't seem to have an electric barrier around it. I guess behind the wall, there wasn't any other room, so if someone could walk through solid walls, they wouldn't get very far, especially if they had just realized their own abilities.

"Is it possible for kids with abilities to pass the Test?" I asked. Ash shrugged in response to Rohit's question.

"I live in Washington, not the Capital. Washington is great and all, and the Capital resides in the middle of us, but I don't know everything. However, yeah, of course kids with abilities pass the Test. They pass it all the time, I'm assuming. That's why there's so many strange people in the Capital. I just don't know why they let kids with abilities fail,"

Ash shrugged again, and then looked sadly through the bars of the cage.

"What's going to happen to us?" he barely whispered. No one could meet his eyes.

Jangmi stayed suspiciously silent. She seemed to be having a staring contest with Jag. They both refused to look away from each other, his ears in an upright position. They twitched slightly as the door opened, and finally he turned away.

Three kids walked through the door of the Wall, lined up. My eyes widened, and I couldn't help but lean forward as I looked at the girl at the end of the line.

She had completely white hair that was cut at her chin, but that wasn't the most striking thing about her. Her eyes were a bright blue color, almost purple, and her pupils were practically non-existent. Her ears were large and pointed, also completely white. Her skin was also incredibly pale. But, she wasn't wearing any clothes. Or rather, there was fur growing in place of clothes. A white long fox's tail swished out behind her. Her chin was pointed as she held it up, and her big inhuman-like eyes stared at me. When our eyes met, she let out a snarl, smashing her sharp teeth together.

"That one's from the Capital," Ash breathed. They opened the door to the cage, but they kept the animal girl, locking her up in a separate one. She glared at us from the opposite end of the room.

"She's a handful, isn't she?" said one of the newcomers. He had a charming smile, light brown skin, and short, but layered, full head of wavy black hair. His light green eyes stood out on his brown face. They were large and wide, surrounded by long, dark lashes. His smile was crooked and almost playful, reminding me of Forest. He was also possibly the most handsome person I've ever met.

The girl next to him wasn't without beauty either. Her eyes were also green, but a more emerald color, reminding me of June, and were also large and wide with dark, full lashes. Her skin was slightly darker than her brother's, but her black hair was longer and was wavy, almost curly, framing her small face nicely. I could tell they were related. They basically looked like mirror images of one another.

"Anubys is being presumptuous. We hardly talked to the... girl on our ride here. Though, we do assume she is from a strange place," the girl spoke. There was an elegant sort of air about her, and she spoke very formally.

"Where are you guys from?" I asked, trying to keep my jaw dropping from looking at them. Jangmi hadn't finished her staring contest with Jag, and the boys were so beauty stricken from the girl that they couldn't even wipe the drool from their chins, so how could they possibly form words in her presence? Her eyes turned towards me.

"My brother and I are from Khaldun. The Golden Community," she said, her eyes not blinking. I had to keep from drooling myself. Her eyes were so easy to fall into. I blinked.

"Ah," I said, "I'm from Adams," and then continued introducing everyone else in the cage. No wonder why they held such proper posture and manners. Despite being possibly one of the furthest from the Capital, Khaldun was known for their wealth. I had learned their cities were lined with golden buildings. The people in my community who had assigned jobs that took them around the Nation would tell tales about Khaldun. That they would move there, if it were allowed, despite the unbearable heat. That the people were beautiful, and the community of Khaldun was almost unreal. Well, they were right about the people being beautiful.

"My name is Eset, and this is my brother Anubys. We're quite pleased to make your acquaintance," Eset said, nodding to each of us and flashing a smile. Her smile wasn't like her brother's. It was straight and impossibly perfect. Her brother's smile held more mischief. Lightning silently counted everyone who was in the cage, including the animal girl who was pacing inside of her own, snarling at the guards that would come close. Nine, in total.

"That's all of us," he whispered. Jangmi looked up at him, breaking her staring contest with Jag.

"It's time for us to leave then," Jangmi said, almost excitedly. I gave her a look. The rest of us had gloom on our faces, although Agwe looked surprisingly calm. Why was she so excited? We were about to face death. And if we somehow managed to escape, who knew what was behind this Wall, or if we'll even be able to go past it? I did wonder why they were waiting for us all to gather, however.

The electric barrier was turned off, and the men brought us to our feet, lining us up one after the other. The animal girl was at the back of the line, muzzled. She narrowed her inhuman eyes at me, her whole eye that impossible purple-blue. I was placed in front of her, and I tried hard to keep my fear at a minimum. At the front of the line was Agwe. Turns out he was taller than Lightning. The back door opened, and in front of us laid a forest.

"I thought the War left the world in ruin. I thought there wasn't anything else past the Wall," I whispered.

"Shut up," a man said from beside me. They walked us towards the outside and then retreated back into the Wall, guns pointed at us so we couldn't follow. The door shut, and suddenly, it was just the Wall. It didn't look like there was ever a door.

"HEY! Wait! Aren't you going to untie us??" yelled Ash, running towards the Wall.

"They're not going to," Lightning said, scowling.

"Well, they *do* expect us to die, don't they?" Anubys smirked. Lightning looked him up and down and then glared.

"I don't see how *you're* so pleased about this arrangement," Lightning retorted. Anubys slightly looked up to him; they were almost eye-level, but not quite.

"I'm not pleased. Let's just say I'm amused and leave it at that," Anubys taunted, his voice a decibel above a whisper. The animal girl was desperately trying to take the muzzle off of her head.

"Why aren't they shooting us?" I asked. "I mean, why go through all this trouble if we're going to die anyway?" The expression on Lightning's face told me he was thinking the same thing.

"Maybe to make it more merciful," shrugged Rohit. "Though that does give us the option to survive."

"No, they must know we're going to die. There's no point to any of this if we don't end up dying," I said, shaking my head. Eset blew hair out of her face as she squatted down and grabbed a pointed rock in front of her with her bound hands, starting to cut the rope that kept her hands tied.

"They know there are animals out there that can and

will kill us. They just like to see the struggle," Eset said, halfway through cutting through her rope. "Why do you think they tied us with rope instead of using metal?" She held up the frazzled ends of the rope as her hands got free, an eyebrow raised.

She made a good point. It was odd the guards had used rope. No one used such tired methods of restraint anymore, not when they could use other, less breakable material. I had never even seen rope up close before they tied my hands with it. It was itchy and hurt when my skin rubbed against it.

"They don't want to watch us get shot; they want to see us struggle," Eset continued. She got up and walked over to me and started to untie my rope. Her eyes were focused as she furiously rubbed the sharpened rock against it.

"They won't see us do anything," I said, though my voice lilted slightly. "There's no cameras around." Eset shrugged, a small smile threatening to grace her full lips.

"Maybe not," she said, her emerald green eyes starting to glint like her brother's, "But when they find our bodies, they'll see the struggle." I rubbed my wrists where the rope was tied before going towards Jangmi and untying hers with my fingers. Eset went to her brother, and we continued to untie the rest of them. Jangmi glanced over at Agwe, and Agwe looked away before she looked back at me.

"We... Agwe and I have something to tell you," she said. I furrowed my eyebrows together slightly. Agwe and Jangmi? They barely talked or even looked at each other inside of the cage. How did they *both* have something to say?

"But not here," she said. "We have to get away from the Wall first."

"Where can we go? Nothing exists outside of the Nation," Rohit muttered. Lightning's eyes unfocused as he looked beyond the trees.

"Actually, there *is* something ahead," Lightning said, his eyes glazed over, as if he were looking at something that wasn't there. Jangmi frowned, irritated, and lightly hit Lightning's arm. His eyebrows rose as he looked at her. She shushed him and started moving forward, beckoning for us to follow her. The animal girl was still struggling with her muzzle, but she immediately followed after Jangmi. I looked over at Ash and he shrugged, but started forward.

"What could possibly be ahead? Mutants? *Great*, we're all going to die," Rohit groaned. Ash scoffed.

"If they're mutants, wouldn't *we* fall under that category?" asked Ash, gesturing towards the animal girl. She glared at him.

"I... Well I mean... Well aren't we... I don't know anymore," Rohit struggled to say but gave up. The twins shared a meaningful look towards each other, communicating some unspoken message. What it was, I couldn't begin to understand. We all followed after Jangmi.

"Do nine people usually fail?" I asked finally, after we walked in silence for a while. We were far enough from the Wall that I was, at least, 96 percent sure no one was listening to us. And 99 percent sure Jangmi wasn't going to shush me.

"Maybe. No one would know though. The failures aren't counted so there isn't really a statistic," Ash answered, coming to walk beside me. Lightning had taken the lead from Jangmi, walking at the head of the group. But, he turned his head slightly to respond to Ash.

"If you knew it was a loyalty test, why did you fail it?" Lightning asked. Ash stared at the back of his head for a long while, taking in a shaky breath.

"Would you have been able to do it? Even knowing ahead of time what it was?" Ash asked in response. Lightning was quiet.

"How do you know so much?" I asked him. He shrugged. He seemed to do that often.

"I lived in Washington. The Barrier as they call it. It's closest to the Capital. You hear a lot of stuff on the streets," he said. James Washington was someone who protected many people during the end of the world. Some say he gave his life to save thousands, others say he lived until he was over a hundred years old and was a member of the first Senate. No one seemed to know for sure.

"You guys would openly talk about that kind of stuff?" I asked. "About abilities and the Test?"

"Not openly, I wouldn't say that. I've been to the Capital. I've seen people that can do amazing things. It's just kind of common knowledge," he said.

"You've *been* to the Capital?" I was shocked. Normally if you didn't have an assigned job that took you around the Nation, you just stayed in your own community, never leaving. He laughed at my reaction.

"Yeah. There's not really a separating line between the Capital and Washington. There are guards, sure. But, it's easy enough to slip past them. All you gotta do is offer them something they can't refuse," Ash said, winking. I looked at him confused, and then he rubbed his pointer and middle finger against his thumb. The universal sign for money.

"Ohhh," I said, dragging out the one syllable into three.

"How do you know where we're going?" I heard Rohit ask Lightning up front.

"I just do," said Lightning.

"Okay, but *how*?" Rohit pressed. Lightning stopped walking, and his glazed over eyes slowly focused onto Rohit.

"Remember how we were talking about abilities?" Rohit nodded. "Mine is I'm essentially a giant human map." Rohit's eyes widened as Anubys started to snicker.

"*That's* your ability?" Anubys asked, biting his lip to try to keep from full-out laughing. Lightning glared down at him.

"Why? You think it's funny?" asked Lightning, his whole body stiffening as he glowered at Anubys.

"Chill, big guy," Anubys laughed, putting his hands up as he took a couple of steps back. I stepped in between the two of them, hoping that it would break up the tense eye contact that the two were having. Lightning's eyes were full of distrust as he looked at Anubys. His eyes weren't angry, rather it seemed like he was measuring what kind of threat Anubys was in his head.

"How do you know what your power is?" I asked, looking up at him. His eyes were still focused on Anubys as he answered me.

"When I stopped taking those pills, I found out about it," he said, tearing his gaze away from him. Lightning glanced down at me, and then started walking forward. "Du Bois... Du Bois's nickname is Steel, you know?" I nodded. "There's a lot of factories and a lot of mines. It's essentially just the place where the Nation fucks the earth up so that the rest of the Nation can have essential stuff. The air is terrible there, and once you're sixteen and have passed the Test, you start working in the factories or in the mines. There aren't really a lot of different assigned jobs for us in Du Bois." I nodded along as I tried to keep up with his pace, two steps equaling about one of his. He was right though. Everything that I learned about Du Bois made me feel like Adams was maybe a somewhat better place. At least the air wasn't so terrible all the time, as it was in Du Bois.

"My brother was working in the mines one day. I had stopped taking my pills for about a month by then. I just didn't see the point in them. I would pretend to swallow the pill and then hide them somewhere, make them disappear," he looked over at me. "Well, you know how it goes." I nodded. I did the exact same thing sometimes, though never for longer than a few days. I always felt guilty about it. But, I guess I wasn't the only one who didn't do as I was told. Probably all the kids here didn't take their pills at some point. It was weird to know that. I was used to being surrounded by people who never broke the rules. It was kind of relieving to be around these people, even if we did end up dying.

"Anyway," he continued, "One day the mine my brother was working in collapsed. No one knew where he was within the mines. No one knew where anyone was. There wasn't really a map drawn out as to where the mines led to or how deep they went. And I had never felt the suffocating feeling that I did then, in my whole life. Knowing that my older brother was going to die. It hurt. My chest started to hurt. And then, that's when I knew. I saw where he was. It was as if a map was put into my head. I could *see* him, Zinnia. It was the oddest moment of my life, and I thought I was dreaming it, at first. But, I could see he was dying, and I didn't hesitate. I told some people my brother had told me where he might be working within the mines. And they dug them out, all of them. I saved my brother and a whole bunch of other people with this ability. So, I never took my pills again." Anubys was walking behind us, listening to the story.

"Do you think it'd be easier if your brother was like you? Had a special ability?" asked Anubys. Lightning glared and Anubys backtracked, "I'm not trying to poke fun at your ability. I'm genuinely curious what you think."

"It might've been easier for him if he was like me," Lightning mused, after a while. He shrugged. "I don't really know. I guess it would depend on what kind of ability he had." Anubys nodded while Eset glared at him. Anubys just mouthed 'what' at her.

The sun was starting to set, and Lightning said it was getting harder for him to see where we were going because of the amount of energy he was using, so we stopped and sat around on the ground. The air had started to have a biting chill to it, still being the middle of spring, and I wrapped my arms around myself to generate a little bit of warmth.

"Should we build some kind of shelter?" asked Rohit.

"Do you know how to?" asked Ash. Rohit sighed, dramatically.

"No," he said sadly. Ash shook his head, tsking, while Rohit made a face at him. They both started to lightly push each other as they cracked a couple of jokes. I wished I was able to feel just a bit as carefree as the two of them seemed to.

"Honestly if we're going to die, what's the point, right?"

I said, sitting down in the grass, looking away from the two of them. Agwe looked at me with wide eyes and then chuckled.

"Well, aren't you the optimist?" he laughed. I shrugged. I just felt so apathetic to the whole thing. My whole body was on high alert, ready for anything to attack us. I had never felt so paranoid before or more exhausted in my life. Maybe it was because of the lack of drugs in my system, maybe it was my instincts telling me I needed to be ready to run or fight, or maybe it was the fact I knew I was going to die.

"What were you and Jangmi going to tell us anyway?" I asked him. "We're pretty far from the Wall now." Jangmi and Agwe exchanged a look with one another, and then Jangmi started talking.

"The Asian communities have been told generation after generation about the people with abilities," Jangmi started. Rohit sighed loudly, anticipating what was going to come out of her mouth, but nodded along.

"It's pretty much a folk tale by now," Agwe interrupted. I stared at him confused. They were from different communities, yet they're told the same folk tales?

"Yeah," Jangmi agreed, "Much like tall tales."

"Myths," Agwe said, giving another word.

"Fables!" Jangmi exclaimed looking at Agwe. He nodded, excitedly agreeing with her.

"Okay, we get the point, go on," Rohit said, gesturing for them to continue.

"Anyway, Wu, Shin, Rizal, Musashi, Bakshi, and many other communities have these tales. They are stories from before the Nation was created. About World War III," Jangmi started. She looked over at Agwe. He looked back at all of us. We all leaned in, focused on what they were saying; even the animal girl stopped pulling on her muzzle to listen.

"In these stories, it's said there were great warriors, warriors that could live through explosions, warriors that radiation could not affect," Agwe paused for dramatic effect, "Warriors with unimaginable gifts."

"These warriors were the cause of great discussion throughout the old world. They could do things most humans could not. Some could move things with their minds. Others could control people or nature. There were such a variety of different gifts. But, the problem was that these people were a threat to humans in such a big way. There was only a small population that were able to do these things. Maybe ten percent or so?" Jangmi asked Agwe. Agwe chewed on the question before answering.

"Yeah, that sounds about right," he said.

"So, countries fought over the most powerful people, but not just to have and use, but also sometimes to kill. They fought over what regulations they should put on them. Some countries slaughtered them by the hundreds. Others saw them as weapons. People with abilities, they were not safe from harm's way," Jangmi continued.

"As we all know, North Korea attacked first, which is what caused the domino effect of the War. And they did, this much is true. But it wasn't *just* an attack. All the soldiers were people with abilities. The governments in place were trying to wipe out those with abilities with the cover of a war. Unfortunately, it backfired, ruining the earth in the process. Millions died. Not only people with abilities, but normal humans as well," Agwe said sadly.

"Okay... What does that have to do with anything? So it's a different story than the one we're told in Preparation. So what?" said Rohit, obviously not wanting to continue the conversation. He turned to the rest of us, "It's just a tall tale that grandparents tell us before bed. It's not true. I just thought it was a weird bedtime story before all this happened."

"A tall tale? More like Preparation is covering up the reason as to why a whole species was almost wiped out," Anubys retorted. He looked annoyed by Rohit's apathy to the whole situation.

"Why are we told a different story during Preparation? I mean, if what Ash said earlier was true, then wouldn't the whole Senate be people with abilities? The President?" I asked.

"Maybe there wasn't enough written down about it," Lightning answered.

"No," Jangmi said. "They know what happened. They are just hiding it."

"Why though?" I asked.

"Think about it. You wipe out a generation that knew of those with abilities and people who had abilities themselves. Brainwash the ones that were left that all the people with powers died. Give them a false sense of security, and then strike later. But, the problem is they're not striking, so what's the point? I mean, it's not like people with abilities are trying to wipe out the human population of the Nation," Ash said. That's when the animal girl tried to talk. We all looked at her, and she looked incredibly frustrated.

"Someone take the muzzle off of her. Why hasn't anyone done that yet?" asked Lightning, looking around. We all didn't meet his eyes. It probably wasn't the best time to say I was terrified just by looking at her. How could I possibly get close enough to be able to take off the muzzle? Lightning walked over to her and tried to take it off of her. After a long while of concentrated silence, the muzzle came off, and the animal girl looked at all of us before speaking.

"I know you guys are afraid of me. I can *smell* your fear," she sneered. Her voice was rough, a voice that knew of struggle. "My name is Volplie." Suddenly her appearance turned more human-like, almost in a blink of an eye. Her ears and tail were gone, her teeth turned more normal, but her eyes still stayed in their inhuman like state.

"You were talking about the Nation and the President, right?" she asked. We nodded, staring at her with wide eyes. She could change her appearance...

"President Eclipse has not forgotten what the humans have done to us," she revealed. "It may have been hundreds of years since the war, but President Eclipse has not forgotten."

"What do you mean?" asked Lightning. I glanced over at Eset who was shifting uncomfortably. I caught her glance over to her brother, almost as if she were worried.

"She's a cold-blooded *snake*," spat Volplie, "who only cares about her own well-being."

"Okay..." Ash said slowly, confused.

"She's experimenting. On humans," she finished quickly, as if she didn't want to explain further despite the fact that her statement alone was only going to provoke curiosity.

"So the Senate and the President do all have abilities," Lightning mused.

"Experimenting?" Rohit asked. She sighed and suddenly

she was back in her weird animal-like state. Her eyes flashed at Rohit.

"Yes. She takes human babies and tests them."

"Where does she get these human babies? Surely if they're *human* wouldn't the other communities know about it? Babies going missing?" Eset asked. Volplie looked over at Eset and her ears twitched the longer she looked at her.

"Don't play dumb," she muttered, her nose twitching, as if Eset was exuding a smell that the rest of us couldn't pick up. "Not every Evolved couple in the Capital produces Evolved children. A lot of the time, they have human children, normal children. They offer those normal children up for testing." *Evolved?* It must be a term used in the Capital.

"What is the testing for?" asked Rohit. Volplie looked angrier with Rohit as he kept asking questions.

"I don't know. All I know is that hundreds, maybe even thousands of babies die from it. And over half of the ones that survive turn out to be monsters. They're not human anymore, and I *don't* just mean by how they look," Volplie said. She started to look shaken as her eyes glazed over, as if she were remembering something horrible.

"Are you... are you one of those children? The children that were tested on?" I asked. Ash looked at me with surprise, as if I said something I wasn't supposed to. Volplie's eyes narrowed at me, looking more predatory as she did.

"Do I *seem* like a monster to you?" she snarled. I blinked quickly.

"No, no that's not it. It just seemed like you were remembering—"

"I am a *born* shapeshifter, not one of those monsters," Volplie spat.

"She's from Adams. You know how those kids can be," placated Rohit. Her gaze cut to him, and she growled.

"You're no better," she hissed. She climbed the nearest tree, sitting down on a branch high above us. There was silence as everyone looked over at Rohit and I.

"I didn't mean to insult her. I just thought..." I let my sentence drift off. It didn't matter what I thought. The fact of the matter was I had originally thought of her as a monster. I shouldn't have said anything.

CHAPTER SEVEN

"So they tell you that story, the real story about the War," Anubys said, turning towards Jangmi. There was something off about his questioning. There was something off about both him and his sister Eset. Especially since apparently Eset smelled differently than the rest of us, according to Volplie. I looked up and saw her glaring down at me and, quickly, I looked away.

"Yes," Jangmi answered.

"Why?" Anubys questioned, crossing his arms.

"Like Volplie said, the people with abilities, they haven't forgotten. Like Jangmi and I, they're told the same stories generation to generation. Because they live in the Capital, those stories are better known. The Test isn't put into place to weed out the smart people from the stupid ones, it's there to figure out if there are still more people outside of the Capital that are still evolving. And whether those people will follow President Eclipse or not," Agwe explained. He looked over at Jangmi, and she continued, like they were taking turns in telling what they've been told.

"Those people that follow President Eclipse believe the humans should suffer, more than they already have. We are already separated by race and ethnic groups, caged in our own communities, never having the chance to leave it. We are already being suppressed. I do not know much about the human testing, however it does not surprise me. We have been told, a generation ago, that there are groups outside of the Nation, a rebellion rising up against her," Jangmi said. I frowned. *A rebellion against the Nation?*

"During the Test, in the past eighteen years or so, we've been told that if something changes in it that wasn't supposed to happen, we have an ability. If we have an ability, we are told to fail the Test, purposefully, in order to find the rebellion and join it," Agwe finished.

"You're trying to tell me you guys purposely failed the Test because there's a *rumor* of a rebellion? Against the Nation?" asked Rohit, voicing my thoughts. He scoffed, "That's ridiculous."

"It's the truth," blinked Jangmi. Lightning just frowned at their words as he stared at the ground, processing.

"We're told those who fail the Test get taken to the Wall and then get shot," Lightning piped up. His voice was low as he spoke. "That's the story my community tells, but you're saying you were told you were able to *survive* failing the Test?" Agwe nodded in response.

"Yes," he said. "We've always been told it's possible to live and find the rebellion. Although, not all of us believe it." He gestured towards Rohit as an example. Rohit scoffed at the motion as Lightning shook his head.

"That just doesn't make sense," he mumbled.

"What's interesting is you guys keep saying 'we' when you mention humans," voiced Anubys, a ghost of a smirk on his face, "Or have you forgotten you two have abilities as well?"

"Just because we have an ability doesn't mean we're not human. Our families are human, our friends. There's no reason to fight against each other," Agwe reasoned.

"Yet the humans wiped out millions of the Evolved to protect themselves," Anubys retorted, using Volplie's unfamiliar term. It flowed off of his tongue as if it were a normal part of his vocabulary. Ash's head turned suddenly to look at Anubys as he said it, frowning.

"People are scared of what's different. This is a new world, Anubys. There's no point in living in the past. And there's not a justified reason to do the same to humans as they did to the... Evolved, as you say, of the past," Agwe said. He looked at Anubys weirdly.

"I wonder why you failed the Test, though, if you agree so strongly with President Eclipse's cause," Agwe pondered. Anubys flashed a crooked smile.

"I'm a bit too much to handle for anyone," he smirked. The sun had gone completely down now, and a shadow was cast across Anubys's face, causing his smirk to look more sinister. It was as if the night brought out a darker side to him, a side that couldn't be seen during the day. Yet, I couldn't stop looking at him.

"Hey, guys? We should probably find shelter or something. You know what they say, creatures stalk in the night... or something along those lines," Rohit said, standing up and looking around. There were only trees surrounding us. I squinted into the budding darkness, trying to look for anything that we could use for shelter, but there was none.

"We're not going to find any shelter now, Rohit. It's already night," Ash yawned. He settled onto the ground, essentially making up his mind about where we were going to sleep as he laid down in the grass.

"Lightning, the giant map, might be able to help," teased Anubys, resting his elbow on Lightning's shoulder while grinning up at him. Lightning glared down at Anubys in response. Anubys was either oblivious to the look or was actively ignoring it, that silly crooked smile still present on his face.

"He makes a good point," I agreed. Lightning turned his glare to me before softening his gaze.

"Fine, I'll check," he said. He looked down at Anubys, incredulously, and then said, "Get off of me."

"Oh, right," said Anubys, stepping away from Lightning. Lightning's eyes glazed over as he searched through his map to see if he could find any shelter. His eyes focused back on me after a few moments, and he sighed. I knew the answer before he spoke it.

"The only place I can see is the place I saw earlier. But, it would take another day to get there," Lightning said.

"It's a group, isn't it? The rebellion," Jangmi excitedly asked. Her little body could hardly contain her excitement. Lightning shrugged.

"It could be. It looks like a makeshift community of some sorts. There's people there," Lightning said.

"No shelter? At least it's not raining, am I right?" asked Ash, lifting his head from the grass to smile at everyone. No one responded to him. "C'mon guys, you gotta think positively."

"So if everything the Nation has ever told us has been a lie, then do you think the morphed, messed up animals that the Nation said the Wall protected us from don't actually exist?" asked Rohit, almost hopefully. He looked over at me, and I shrugged.

"Maybe they don't," I said.

"And maybe they *do*," Anubys teased, a glint in his eyes, looking at Rohit as if he were something to eat. Rohit scowled at him and hugged his scrawny knees to his chest, looking around.

My eyes caught sight of the moon that rose in the sky. My dad had always said the moon was like a silver coin. That no one could grow poor as long as they looked towards the moon for guidance. It didn't really make any sense to me, but tonight the moon really did look like a silver coin. I could see the stars from out here as well. Better than I ever could in the Fire.

I leaned back and laid down onto the grass. It wasn't soft and itched my arms and legs like crazy, but it was real. It wasn't a hologram. This was *all* real. I never thought I'd be able to see trees in person before, let alone grass. I propped myself up with my arms and looked at everyone here. They were all so different, coming from completely different places in the Nation. And yet, we all shared something in common. We were special. I craned my neck as I looked up at the stars in the violet sky, trying to hide the smile that was about to bloom on my face. The stars were almost like glitter in the night.

My whole life I had been told I wasn't special, that there

was something wrong with me. I was told I was too stupid to continue in society, that I couldn't fit in. But, as I looked at the companions around me, I realized we *were* special. *I* was special. Maybe more special than anyone back home. We just simply didn't fit into the Nation. And maybe, maybe that was okay.

Lightning leaned back and looked up at the sky while breathing in deep.

"I've never seen stars before," he muttered, next to me. I looked over at him, surprised.

"You haven't?" I asked. He shook his head.

"The smog in Du Bois is so bad that you can't really see the stars," he said. I nodded in agreement. It was hard to see the stars even in Adams.

"Yeah, it's definitely easier to see them out here," I said.

"They're really beautiful," he breathed. Ash scoffed.

"You would think that if the Nation was really a Nation cultivating geniuses, they would've figured out how to combat pollution," Ash called from where he was, still laying down in the grass. He added, sarcastically, "Wow, what a great Nation we have."

"May the gods bless this great Nation," we all mocked and then started laughing. Volplie stood up suddenly from her branch. The sound caused me to look up at her, and it looked like she was staring off into the distance, her ears upright and twitching. Her eyes fixated on something.

"What is it, Volplie?" asked Rohit, nervously.

"Maybe it's a morphed animal," Anubys said, putting his hands up in claws while pretending to pounce towards Rohit. Rohit flinched while Anubys laughed. Eset put a hand on Anubys's arm and shook her head slightly, as if to say stop.

"I apologize for my brother. He doesn't know where to end his excessive teasing," she said softly to Rohit. Rohit's brown eyes grew wide as he looked at her, and I stifled a laugh as we all watched him try to coolly play it off.

"Nah, I mean, nah, it's whatever you know, it's chill. It's all good," Rohit said, obviously bewitched by Eset's beauty.

"Dude, stop, you're embarrassing yourself," whispered Ash next to him. Rohit clamped his mouth shut as his ears started to flush red. He untucked his semi-long black hair in order to hide them. Volplie shushed us down below when we started snickering over Rohit's embarrassment, her eyes glowing in the darkness.

"Something's coming," she hissed. "I suggest climbing the trees." She looked back into the darkness, and for the first time since we started this journey, she looked terrified. Whatever was coming, she knew what it was, and she wasn't telling us. We paused for a moment, as if processing what Volplie was saying. And then, as if we were one, we all started to scramble towards the trees. Agwe helped Jangmi reach a branch, since she was too short while the rest of us struggled to climb them. Anubys and Eset, however, took their time.

"Are you coming up?" asked Lightning, concern shone in his eyes. Anubys smirked up at him.

"I think we'll be fine. Although, Eset, you should probably get up there," he said to his sister. She rolled her eyes.

"I think I can take care of myself," she said, a hand on her hip. Anubys mocked her eye roll.

"Just go up there, but stay within range," Anubys

warned. *Within range?* She sighed and then turned to climb the tree that was nearest to where Anubys was. He cracked his fingers and looked up at the treetops. When his eyes met mine, he flashed a crooked smile. *What was he doing?*

"What's coming?" asked Lightning to Volplie. She was on a branch above him. She didn't turn her eyes away, and her body tensed, as if ready to run.

"I can't describe it," she whispered. That's when we heard them. It sounded like garbled speech, or hunting calls. And when they came into view, my jaw dropped. There were about twenty of them. They were humans but they weren't... right. They all looked like they were mixed with some kind of animal. And when they saw Anubys in the clearing, they screamed. It sounded so human, with so much rage. But, they weren't human, not anymore. A few of them had wings and started to fly towards the trees, spotting us in the branches.

"Oh dear Nation, what do we do?" I cried. That same fear from earlier was starting to twist in my stomach. It was almost familiar now, but it was still like a knife piercing through me so that I couldn't quite breathe fully. I quickly glanced down at Anubys, and it was as if he were counting down. To what, I wasn't sure, but even Eset had a look of concentration on her face.

Suddenly my branch started to shake, making me almost lose my balance, and standing in front of me was a bird human. But, it wasn't human, and it wasn't like how Volplie was either. Its mouth was in a twisted beak, its eyes uneven. Its back was curved into a perfect C as it stalked forward with not feet, but rather talons. It had arms, like a human's, but it was attached to giant bat wings. It opened its beak revealing rows of weirdly sharp teeth as it screamed at me, as if trying to talk to me. I backed up against the tree trunk, my heart hammering in my chest.

"Zinnia!" I hardly heard Jangmi cry. The former human's eyes didn't hold anything in them. It was soulless. It wasn't supposed to be alive.

I couldn't help but glance down at Anubys, who was surrounded, as the creature slowly stalked towards me. We were doomed. And then before I turned back to look at the thing that was staring at me as if I were something to destroy and eat, I saw a smile creep onto Anubys's face. However, this smile was different; it wasn't his usual mischievous smile. It was something... sadistic.

His face and stature relaxed, but his smile stayed. And suddenly, the humanoid creatures all started screaming at the same time. The thing in front of me fell from the branch and dropped to the ground as it screamed out in pain. The sounds brought tears to my eyes. It was like a thousand humans were screaming, as if they were being tortured, with Anubys standing right in the middle of it. His smile grew as their screams grew louder and louder, piercing the quiet of the night. And then abruptly they stopped, falling to the ground. They were dead as quick as they came.

"Oh gods," Ash breathed. I couldn't get Anubys's sadistic smile out of my mind. It was him. He somehow killed them without even moving a finger. And he enjoyed it.

"I knew I heard the name Anubys before," Lightning whispered. "The old Egyptian god of death." Once every last of the humanoid creatures were dead, Anubys almost collapsed, but he caught himself as he started towards the ground. He had sat down in the middle of the circle of dead corpses that lay before him. Twenty morphed humans, dead in a blink of an eye. Eset quickly climbed down from the tree and ran to her brother, grabbing his arm.

"Anubys? Anubys, are you okay?" she asked, worriedly. He gave a lazy smirk.

"I'm fine," he panted.

"I should've been standing next to you," she argued.

"It was better that you were up there, Eset," he retorted. She twisted her lips before taking in our surprised faces. Her face then became like stone.

"Anubys and Eset. Considering everyone's named after something from their birth, I'm guessing you guys have some explaining to do," Lightning said, crossing his arms. Eset narrowed her eyes at him.

"My brother saves *all* of your lives and the first thing you want to do is *interrogate* us?" she countered. She took a step forward, as if challenging Lightning.

"*I don't trust you,*" Lightning hissed, taking a step forward towards her, accepting whatever challenge she was going to bring him. "And I especially don't trust your brother."

"Lightning makes a good point," treaded Agwe slowly. "Considering he can make twenty... beings drop dead just from a look, we have to make sure he won't do the same to us."

"Especially since it doesn't seem like it was his first time," Ash pointed out.

"Also, his name is Anubys. Literally the old Egyptian god of death," Lightning repeated. Anubys chuckled.

"If I was named after the Egyptian god of death, wouldn't my name be Osiris?" questioned Anubys.

"The god of death before Osiris was considered Anubys. I know the Ancient histories, don't test me," Lightning spat. Anubys shrugged.

"We can kill all of you and bring you back a thousand times over before we'd bow to your questions," hissed Eset, suddenly losing her cool. I stared at her, confused. *Kill all of you and bring you back.* Suddenly, it hit me. He may have the curse of death, but she gave the gift of life. No wonder they were twins.

Lightning narrowed his eyes at her as Anubys grabbed his sister's arm back, as if to calm her. His grip was strong, though his face was the perfect expression of weariness. My eyes narrowed while Eset's held fire in them, instead of their usual iciness.

"We'll answer your questions. But, probably not here, yeah?" said Anubys, gesturing to the dead bodies around us. "I don't know about you, but *I* don't particularly like the stench of death, despite everything." Eset looked down at him in disbelief, and Anubys gave her a meaningful glare back. She quickly turned away, but she still looked angry. Anubys slowly got up, and I had to grab my arm from going to help him to his feet. He tiredly smiled at the group, and then led the way deeper into the forest. As we walked further, it was almost as if a switch turned on inside of Eset. Her face became its usual stone, icy self: unreadable.

Once we got to a clearing, Lightning looked around and then sat down. We weren't too far away from the bodies, but there wasn't really anywhere else to go in the dark.

"How were you able to kill twenty people without batting an eye?" asked Lightning, getting right into it. Anubys smirked.

"Obviously, I am one of the Evolved," he said, the light sheen of sweat still present on his brow. His attitude, though, made it seem like he had already recovered from using his ability, if it even was a difficult task for him at all. Lightning narrowed his eyes, glowering at Anubys.

"You knew you were able to do it, though," Agwe said, slowly. "How are you able to have such control over it?" Anubys smirked, but shrugged in response, not elaborating further. Lightning made a noise of frustration.

"Everyone's named after something that has to do with his or her birth. My name is Lightning because when I was born, there was a bad lightning storm. Zinnia is probably named after the flower because they were probably in season when she was born," Lightning demonstrated, trying to keep his cool although his anger was starting to build. While he always seemed so calm around everyone else, I noticed Anubys seemed to irritate him the most. "It doesn't make sense to me why you're named after the Egyptian god of death and your sister after an irrelevant goddess."

"Irrelevant?" smiled Eset, but it didn't quite reach her eyes. "That goddess you're talking about is the Egyptian goddess of life. A goddess holds a bit more significance than a passing lightning storm, don't you think? Maybe you don't know much about the Ancient histories as you say you do." Lightning's face darkened, and Eset's smile grew.

"Why are you guys trying to keep it a huge secret? Lightning knew he had his ability before the Test. It's not that big of a deal if you guys did too," Rohit pointed out.

"The difference is that Lightning is just a giant map while I can kill multiple people at once before they even touch me. You all just want to know if I've killed before, although I'm guessing you've already assumed I have," Anubys said, a crooked smile on his face. It was as if he were amused by the whole conversation. All I could see in my head was Anubys with that sadistic smile from when he was killing those monsters.

"Have you not?" I asked, my gaze settling onto him, pointedly. Anubys looked at me and blinked while his smile started to disappear.

"No, you're right. I have," he admitted bluntly, seemingly without emotion. He looked over at his sister, and she seemed to refuse to return his gaze. He sighed and then flashed another crooked smile at me.

"Okay, so here's the long-winded story everyone seems to want to know. When I was born, our mother died temporarily with Eset still inside of her. They thought she died from childbirth, but when they got Eset out, our mother magically came back alive. They realized then we were 'bewitched,' as they put it. I was able to put people to death while Eset was able to bring them back. Pretty cool, huh?" No one responded and he rolled his eyes.

"So, they named us accordingly. Me after the old ancient god of death and Eset after the ancient goddess of life. Essentially that's what Eset does. However, she doesn't necessarily give you life, just brings you from the other side to the living. Our names are... fitting." He said the word 'fitting' sarcastically, as if he disagreed with it. Or maybe he just disagreed with the abilities they were given. The curse they were given. He looked around at everyone and then laughed a little.

"So have I killed people? Yeah. I've killed a lot of people," he grimaced. For a split second, he looked haunted, but it was gone as quick as it came so I wasn't sure if I saw correctly.

"Are you happy now?" Eset calmly inquired, but her tone held quiet anger towards us for making her brother retell a story they both didn't want to relive. Though, I had a gnawing feeling in the back of my mind that there was something he was leaving out. Lightning leaned back.

"So you can control it," he stated. Anubys cocked his head from side to side before giving a smirk.

"Most of the time," Anubys joked. Jangmi patted his hand and nodded to him.

"It's okay," she said. "Thank you for telling us." He patted Jangmi's hand back and seemingly genuinely smiled at her.

"It's okay. I didn't *really* have a choice," and then I realized he was mocking her so he was still a major jerk.

"We should probably get some sleep. We're all going to need enough energy tomorrow to try and find food," Agwe mentioned. Anubys pointed a thumb behind him, in the direction of the dead bodies.

"I mean there's dead carcasses right there and they're practically animals," he said, somewhat seriously. Ash looked at him in disgust.

"What the fuck is wrong with you?" he barely whispered. Anubys's smile just got bigger from the remark.

CHAPTER EIGHT

"Mom?" I shouted into the darkness. "Mom?!"

"Zinnia?" I heard my mother's voice cry out. I tried to follow the sound of her voice, but my eyes wouldn't adjust to the darkness surrounding me. Anxiety choked me, as my vision wouldn't give way. I blindly searched for her in the dark, my hands poised in front of me.

"Zinnia, you have to run. I made a mistake. You can't be a part of this," I heard my mother whisper from every direction.

"What do you mean? Mom, where are you?" I asked, frantically looking around into the darkness, in hopes that I would see her. "I miss you," I whispered.

"You have to run," she hauntingly whispered. "It's not safe."

"What's not safe? Mom, what are you saying?" I yelled. Her face suddenly appeared in front of me, streaked with blood. Her eyes were rolled to the back of her head.

"Trust no one," she hissed. And then I started screaming.

I woke up, drenched in sweat, as I gasped for air. My hands fluttered over my heart in order to stop it from beating so hard. What was happening? What was *happening* to me? My eyes frantically searched my surroundings, not recognizing where I was at first. Anubys sat up, staring at me.

"Are you okay?" he whispered from across the area. And then, uncontrollably, I started to cry. He looked so shocked by the emotion that it was almost comical, and it was obvious he really didn't know what to do as his hands were held up, frozen.

"I don't know what's happening to me," I whispered as my heart continued to pound through my chest. His eyes glanced around the clearing before crawling over to where I was.

"Well, I can't say I really know either. You were whimpering while you were sleeping," he said, not really comforting me. His hands hovered over me, as if he wanted to touch me, but then they settled back into his lap.

"I feel so tense all the time. Jumpy," I explained, wiping the sweat from my forehead and face.

"You're probably feeling fear." I gave him an incredulous look.

"I already got that, thanks," I said sarcastically as I hugged my knees into my chest. He looked at me curiously. His eyes were so green and hypnotizing. I felt myself almost get lost in them.

"Did you have a nightmare?" he asked after a while. I looked at my hands and nodded.

"Yeah," I said, not wanting to elaborate more. He cocked his head to the side, as he studied my expression.

"I have nightmares, too," he whispered, an admittance that seemed to not come easy to him. I glanced up at Anubys, meeting his eyes.

"I used to have only one nightmare; even if I took the pills, I'd have it. The town would be burning and, somehow, it would be my fault. In some way, I would cause the whole community to be set on fire," I whispered, lost in the memory. There were other weirdly vivid dreams I always used to have. Dreams of me fighting with a sword in my hand, but I didn't mention those to him. A small smile played on his lips.

"Ironic, considering the Adams's nickname," he said. I laughed a little. It felt good to laugh.

"Yeah, I guess." He looked at me seriously for a second, and it looked like he was thinking hard about what I had just said, as if he realized something. And then he looked away, a sly smile on his face.

"What was your nightmare about tonight?" he asked.

"My mom," I admitted.

"What about your mom?" he asked, leaning forward a bit. He seemed genuinely interested in what I had to say. I would've thought he was just being courteous, just asking to be polite, but I honestly felt like he was truly invested in the conversation. I rubbed my hands against my bare shins.

"It was weird. She kept telling me to run, and then she told me to trust no one," I said. Anubys's smile was wiped from his face.

"Huh," he said, "Interesting."

"Weird, right?" I nervously laughed. He pressed his tongue to the inside of his cheek before turning back to me.

"You know," he paused as he thought, "dreams are usually how your subconscious warns you. I wouldn't take it lightly," he said, weirdly serious. "You should probably heed your mother's advice." I looked at him sideways. Granted, I didn't know Anubys for very long, for barely a day, but I hadn't seen him be so... genuine before. If that even was the right word to use. I narrowed my eyes at him.

"You know why I'm up, so why are you?" I questioned. He smiled slightly at me and then leaned back on his arms, looking up at the stars. He rolled his head towards me.

"I don't sleep well," he said, his nose scrunching up a bit.

"What do you mean?" I asked, looking back at him. He winced for a second and shrugged, sitting back up right. We were sitting right next to each other, our sides lightly touching. I shifted uncomfortably as I felt my whole body seem to sing from his bare leg being close to mine. He licked his lips nervously before continuing.

"I... I didn't tell the whole story earlier," he whispered, glancing at me to see how I would respond. He almost looked... vulnerable.

"I figured," I whispered back. He smiled slightly.

"It's true I killed my mother and Eset brought her back. But, there's a catch. When Eset brings someone back, a part of them goes missing. And she... well... wasn't the same, but that's a story for a different day," Anubys muttered.

"When the doctors saw what happened, they thought we were demons, but our father paid them off so they wouldn't tell anyone. My father was pretty wealthy," he lightly bragged. I rolled my eyes in response.

"When Eset and I were five, one of the doctors had gone bankrupt and wanted our father to keep paying him off. Our father refused, saying that no one would believe the ramblings of a mad man. And no one did. Not until a kid in my Preparation class started teasing me about it. Stupidly, so *childishly*, I wished he would disappear, and before I knew it, he fell to the ground screaming at the top of his lungs. He was holding his head as if it were about to burst. And then he died," shrugged Anubys. He said the phrase nonchalantly, as if he were unfazed by the death. He looked over at me, his eyes glazed over from the memory.

"I knew it was me. I knew I killed him. And part of me found some pleasure in it. Some kind of sadistic rush. Eset didn't know how to control her ability then—neither did I for that matter. She didn't know how to bring the kid back. And so, we proved the ravings of a mad man right. Soon a riot came to our house. They..." he glared at the horizon, his jaw clenched angrily, "They brutally slaughtered my Mom and Dad. But, before they got to me and my sister, I made sure they all felt pain before they dropped to the ground, lifeless." I held still for a moment, silence stretching out between us, and then I reached over and gingerly touched Anubys's arm. He looked over at me and then relaxed a little.

"Word about what happened traveled, and after that, President Eclipse came looking for us. She made us do her bidding. I would kill whomever, and Eset would bring them back. And we would keep doing it over and over again as a form of torture..." Anubys paused, his eyes widening for a moment as he glanced quickly at me.

"*Anyways*. I've done a lot of things most people wouldn't necessarily find moral. So I can't really sleep at night," Anubys thought for a moment, "Or ever really." Unknowingly, or maybe purposefully, Anubys admitted that he and Eset worked for President Eclipse as torturers, before being able to take the Test. My mind raced as I realized they were given assigned jobs before the age of sixteen. Who knew how long they had been torturing people. It might've been the only thing they knew.

But, I couldn't help but wonder why they took the Test in the first place then, if they already had an assigned job? And how in the world did they fail, if President Eclipse was all they ever knew? More questions filled my mind, but I didn't voice my thoughts or concerns to Anubys. It was clear he didn't mean to tell me that much, and a part of me was a little afraid of him. He laughed a bit.

"I think I'm a little too comfortable around you," he slightly whispered, looking over at me with those hypnotizing eyes. His voice was slightly menacing, as if he were warning me. He ran a hand through his short black hair, almost as if he were irritated that he found me comfortable. Comfortable enough to tell me too much.

"It's not a bad thing. It just means we can trust each other," I said, hopeful. He raised an eyebrow at me. I knew what he was thinking. I didn't trust him, and he, in turn, didn't trust me. We didn't trust each other and yet there was some pull that made us feel as if we could.

"Do you feel that?" he asked as if he had heard my thoughts, grabbing my wrist. It was magnetic.

"Why?" I asked hesitantly. He leaned forward, looking me deep in the eye. Underneath his iris was an ever present white that showed, unlike any other eye I had seen before.

"It means that our abilities are very similar," he purred. "It means that your ability is just as destructive as mine." I blinked rapidly at his words and then ripped my wrist from his grip.

"I think we should go back to sleep," I suggested quickly, not being able to hide the shake in my voice. He shrugged, leaning his head back against a tree.

"I can't. But, you do as you wish," he said. He continued to look up at the stars as I made my way back to where I was sleeping. I couldn't stop visibly shaking.

What Anubys said hit a nerve. He could kill people with just a look, a wave of a hand. And I had a gnawing feeling I could too. That I carried around the shadow of death as well. I hugged myself together as I tried to slow my breathing. I didn't want to kill people. I didn't want that to be who I was. I didn't want to be... destructive.

Suddenly, I felt something on me. I looked up and saw that Anubys had taken off his light jacket, placing it on me. My shaking stopped as I looked over at him. His eyes were closed, and he looked unbothered, as if he didn't just cover me with his jacket. He must've felt sorry for how we ended our conversation. And I don't know why, but a warm feeling washed over me. I cuddled into his jacket, subconsciously, and sleep came quickly afterwards. Surprisingly, I was able to dream without any disturbances.

"WAKE UP!" someone shouted into my ear. I instinctively reached up and hit the person in the face.

"Ow, Zinnia. Thanks," said the voice. I opened my eyes, and Ash was kneeling in front of me, holding his nose. I immediately sat up, holding his hand back so I could look at it. It was gushing blood.

"You didn't need to punch me so hard," Ash joked. "We could've just talked it out."

"I am so sorry!" I exclaimed, covering my mouth with my hands.

"It's cool," Ash said, muffled by his hand as he leaned his head back in order to stop the bleeding. "It's not broken, is it?" I took another look at his nose.

"No," I said, shaking my head. Ash smiled slightly.

"Well, thank the Nation for that," he said.

"What happened?" asked Lightning, holding a dead bird by its legs. I looked at the bird, my nose wrinkled.

"What?" he asked in response to my facial expression. "We have to eat."

"Zinnia here punched me in the face this morning," Ash said, answering Lightning's question. Lightning looked at me, incredulously.

"Why'd you punch him?" he asked. He turned to Ash, "What'd you do?"

"Why do you assume I did anything?" Ash asked defensively, pouting at Lightning. Lightning rolled his eyes.

"Are you okay?" he asked him.

"Oh yeah, peachy!" Ash said, putting up a sarcastic thumbs up.

"Zinnia, you gotta stop attacking people," Lightning

teased, placing the dead bird down on the ground as he started to pluck the feathers off of it.

"You're not as funny as you all think you are," I muttered, laying back down on the grass. Ash laughed. Afterwards, he looked over at me, puzzled.

"Hey, isn't that Anubys's jacket?" Ash asked, nodding his head towards the jacket that I was currently using as a blanket. Lightning glanced over at it, his eyes studying it curiously. I looked down at the the dark blue jacket and immediately took it off.

"Yeah, it is. I woke up from a nightmare last night, and he was awake and gave it to me," I almost stammered. Ash gave me a knowing look and before he could say anything, Jangmi ran to where we were with Agwe following close behind her.

"I got more birds!" she exclaimed. She was holding three birds in both hands. Ash's jaw dropped.

"Where'd you get that many dead birds?" he asked, warily.

"Oh, when Lightning was throwing rocks up at them, I realized they were not flying away because I was hoping they wouldn't. So, then I tested that thought out and told them to kill themselves and they all flew straight into the ground!" Jangmi said, excitedly. She smiled up at Agwe.

"I discovered what my ability is!" she exclaimed. Agwe nodded.

"I know, I saw," he said. Ash grimaced and leaned towards me without taking his eyes off of Jangmi.

"She's so excited that she just told a bunch of birds to go kill themselves," he whispered.

"At least we all have one bird to eat," I whispered back. He nodded, agreeing.

"True." Volplie, Anubys, and Eset walked towards us, holding firewood. Volplie was still in her half human half weird animal-like state. They dropped the firewood at Lightning's feet. He looked up at them confused.

"I mean since you were barking orders this morning, we just kind of figured you were in charge of everything," Anubys smiled. He mock-saluted him before walking towards me, holding out his arm. My eyebrows furrowed together in confusion. He laughed slightly as I gave him my arm. I didn't realize that he had dimples before. How did I not realize that?

"I meant my jacket, but thanks," he teased.

"Oh," I said quickly. I felt my face flush as I took my arm away, handing him back his jacket. He slipped it on and then turned away. Eset narrowed her eyes slightly at the exchange, but in a second, her face was like stone once again. She helped Lightning try and get a fire going so we could cook the birds Jangmi made commit suicide. Ash looked around, silently counting everyone that was here.

"Hey, has anyone seen Rohit?" he asked. Agwe looked around and shrugged.

"Wasn't he with you, Lightning? Before you met up with us," asked Agwe. Lightning looked up, his expression perplexed.

"Uh," he said slowly, "Um, I think he was at first. But, we split up while trying to look for food. Just a second, let me see if I can locate him." Lightning's eyes unfocused as he looked into his mind map to try and find Rohit. Eset continued to keep the fire going while Jangmi and Agwe were unplucking the birds so we could eat them. I was frozen, waiting for Lightning to say something. He looked even more puzzled when his eyes focused again. He frowned slightly.

"I can't... I can't see him," he said slowly. Anubys snorted.

"You can't see him? I thought you were a giant locator that can locate any place and anything. You know, like how a map can," Anubys pointed out.

"Not the best time, Anubys," Eset murmured. Anubys shrugged.

"I'm just saying," he told her. Eset's hand mimicked a throat slash, telling Anubys to cut it out. He scrunched up his nose, rolling his eyes.

"Why can't you see him?" asked Ash, starting to sound worried.

"I don't know. I can see all of you, I can see the village thing up ahead, I can see some animals, but I can't see him. I don't know why I can't see him," mused Lightning. The look in his eyes told me he was about to start panicking, however.

"He's probably one of those freaks that's on a different wavelength," Volplie remarked, eyeing the birds that Jangmi was plucking.

"A different wavelength?" asked Ash. Volplie nodded, not taking her eyes off of the birds.

"Some of us are on different brain wavelengths or something. They work differently. Those few people are pretty much invisible to other people who have abilities that have to do with the brain," Volplie explained.

"So I can't see him?" asked Lightning. Volplie shrugged.

"Unless you work on the same wavelength as he does, probably not. Same probably goes to the shadow of death over there," Volplie nodded in the direction of Anubys. Anubys chuckled.

"My ability doesn't have to do with the brain. It's a physical death, not a mental one," Anubys said, matter-of-factly. Volplie looked over at Anubys, and her purple-blue eyes looked him up and down.

"Disagree with me all you want," she said, "but I bet if you tried to kill Rohit, you wouldn't be able to." Anubys narrowed his eyes.

"You're saying my power is mental," he said slowly.

"It starts with the brain waves, yes," she said back, just as slowly. Then, she whipped her head to look at the bird Agwe had started to cook.

"Well, he couldn't have gotten far. Rohit, I mean," Agwe mentioned. Lightning nodded.

"We should split up and look around," ordered Lightning. "Even if one of you gets lost, I'm able to see everyone here, so I'd be able to find you." We nodded and went off in different directions. Lightning, Jangmi, Agwe, and Eset stayed behind to cook the food, while Ash, Volplie, Anubys, and I all went to look for Rohit.

As I walked, I looked up at the sky. It was so blue. The leaves on the trees were unbelievably green, and when the sunlight hit the back of it, it looked like it was glowing. A light—almost golden—green. The color reminded me of—My thoughts were interrupted by something coming towards me from behind. I froze, wide-eyed in fear as whatever it was got closer and closer. And then, they burst out from the bushes, and I screamed before turning around, momentarily recognizing the figure in front of me. A hand immediately covered my mouth.

"Anubys?" I asked, through his sinewy hands. He let go of me.

"Yeah, it's me. Why for the good of the Nation did you scream?" he asked, exasperated.

"I thought—Well, I thought that you were one of those morphed people. I didn't know what was happening," I argued, defensive. Anubys laughed as he looked at me in disbelief.

"You're kind of a weird person," he said. I furrowed my eyebrows.

"I'm not weird. Anyone would've screamed if they were scared like that," I pointed out.

"Not in my experience," Anubys shrugged. I squinted my eyes at him and then turned around, continuing to walk in the direction I was going. Anubys followed me. I looked at him, puzzled.

"Why are you following me?" I asked. "We're supposed to split up to look for Rohit."

"Well, considering you're the scaredy cat that you are, I figured I'd come with you," he replied, a completely serious expression on his face. Though, there was a ghost of a smile playing on his lips.

"I'm *not* a scaredy cat," I argued.

"Seem pretty scared to me," Anubys teased. I frowned at him and then pushed him slightly.

"It's just because of the lack of emotion-controlling pills. Fear is just at the forefront of my mind. I can take care of myself," I explained. Anubys raised his eyebrows.

"Okay then," he said, "I'm sure *with* the pills you're the most badass community-mixed girl from Adams."

"I'm the *only* community-mixed girl from Adams," I pointed out. "Well, besides my little sister."

"Oh *really*?" Anubys said, feigning ignorance. I rolled my eyes. Before I could retaliate, we both heard a yelp coming from the left.

"Rohit," I whispered. We ran towards the direction of the sound, far away from the others. And in a clearing, there was Rohit with a giant spider crawling in his direction.

"Oh thank the Nation... Zinnia! Anubys!" Rohit cried out, half anxiously and half relieved.

"What happened?" asked Anubys.

"I was looking for things to eat, but I got lost and then this thing—" Rohit screamed as it crawled faster towards him. He was throwing little berries he had gathered in his hands at the large spider, whose height hit Rohit's knees.

"Ah," said Anubys, lazily hanging back.

"Aren't you going to do something?" I asked him. He looked over at me and then clicked his tongue.

"See the thing *is*, I can't," he said.

"What do you mean you *can't*?" I asked him slowly. "You literally can kill anything without moving."

"Yeah, see, I can't do that unless Eset is within range," Anubys explained. "And *unfortunately*, Eset isn't anywhere near us." *Just make sure to stay within range,* I remembered Anubys had told Eset when the morphed humans had attacked. *Shit.*

"You don't think it's poisonous, do you?" I asked, nervously.

"Whether it's poisonous or not, I'm pretty sure it's going

to eat him," mused Anubys. "I mean, unless *you* do something." I thought for a moment.

"What about Rohit? Couldn't *he* do something?" I asked. Anubys shrugged.

"If he was going to do something, he would've done it by now," said Anubys. "Maybe all he can do is turn invisible. And I don't think that would help him with a giant spider."

"Guys??" Rohit said, his voice shrill. I knew what Anubys was trying to get at. It was up to me. I took a couple of steps forward before throwing a stick at the giant spider that was crawling towards Rohit. I didn't know if I was going to be able to release whatever was inside of me. But, I could still feel it, like how it felt in my dreams. A fire inside, churning through me, building in my chest.

The spider stopped and turned around, facing me. I tried not to look at its eight beady eyes as I breathed deeply. I can do this. I can do this. I closed my eyes and concentrated.

My heart started to race as I began to let go of the fire that was within me. It ran down my arms and towards my feet. I opened my eyes and the fire started to spread. It hit the grass and suddenly, the fire was everywhere. It burst out of me, turning the spider into dust. However, I couldn't get it to stop.

My heart started to beat faster and louder as it continued to eat up everything in its path. I couldn't stop it. I didn't know *how* to stop it. It was like my nightmare, but instead of it being a bad dream, it was actually happening. I felt like I couldn't breathe as Rohit screamed when the fire started to eat him up too. I closed my eyes, trying to drown out the sound of Rohit's cries as he was being burned alive.

Frantically, I combed my memory of my dream. How did I stop it before? What did I do?

I looked over at Anubys, worried, and fire was consuming him as well. His whole lower half of his body was aflame, but he didn't scream. He just looked at me, curiously, as if I were some kind of wonder.

Closing my eyes, I tried to slow my breathing. I needed to calm down. I couldn't kill these two people. I couldn't have their blood on my hands. I shut my eyes tightly as I focused on the beating of my heart. Slowly breathing in and out, I felt my heart start to beat in accordance with my breath. I felt around for the energy of the fire, trying to bring it back inside of me as it continued to search for the flame of life within Rohit and Anubys. Slowly, I could feel it being sucked back into me, settling into my chest.

Once I opened my eyes, I realized all the greenery around me was gone. Everything was burnt and dead. Glancing over at Anubys, I saw he was somehow still standing there, already regenerating the burned skin that he lost. In a few seconds, he was the same as he was before. He smirked at me as he walked over to where Rohit was whimpering.

"I'm so sorry," I cried. My eyes were burning as I took in the sight of Rohit's body. "I couldn't control it. I didn't know what I was doing. I was just... I was just trying to help." I felt the tears roll down my cheeks as I looked at Rohit's barely alive body. His skin looked like it was melting off, the muscle being shown underneath. The skin was blackened, charred around the edges of where the skin was falling off. It was everywhere. However, his head was still okay. His face still looked normal, despite the pained look on it. He was whimpering as he looked up at me, but I could tell he wasn't really seeing me. The pain was blinding him. It looked like he passed out with his eyes open. Fear and pain clouded his eyes, which were unfocused and glazed over due to the immense agony he was probably feeling, or lack of it. I looked away.

"I'm so sorry," I sputtered. Anubys looked over at Rohit, as if he were just an animal that was caught up in this mess and not the person we had been traveling with for a day. He picked up one of the berries—one that wasn't burnt into a crisp—that Rohit had dropped and popped it into his mouth.

"Yeah-h-h, you didn't kill him. But, he's not going to end up surviving this," said Anubys, matter-of-factly. "So, I guess you'll end up killing him, when he dies." I looked over at him in disgust. He looked morphed in my vision, due to the tears filling my eyes. I blinked, letting more of the hot liquid fall. Anubys's face softened slightly at the sight.

"Don't worry," he said, "His blood won't be on your hands." As if *that's* what I was worried about. As he said this, he was holding Rohit's head. With a flick of his wrist, he broke Rohit's neck, putting him out of his misery.

"It'll be on mine," he finished, his expression somber. I let out a breathless gasp, as if someone had just punched me in the neck. Falling to my knees, I looked at Rohit's dead body, sobbing relentlessly.

"No," I sobbed, "No, no, no." I crawled over to Rohit, cradling his head in my lap, as Anubys moved away. Rohit's dark brown eyes looked up at me, lifeless.

"I'm so sorry, Rohit. I'm so, so sorry," I wept. "I didn't mean to. Please know that I didn't mean to."

"Come on, Zinnia, we have to go. Before Lightning realizes we stayed in one place for too long," Anubys whispered, lightly touching my shoulder. I flinched away from his touch and met his eyes with contempt.

"No," the word sounded morphed, "No, *you* did this to me." Anubys's face froze, and he narrowed his eyes, taking his hand away from me. He crossed his arms.

"How?" he asked, barely moving his lips. "How did I *do* anything to you?"

"*You* made me a killer," I seethed. He shook his head slightly and let out a small chuckle, but it sounded hollow.

"I didn't do that to you, Zinnia," my name sounded like a curse in his mouth, "You did that to yourself."

"I didn't know how to control it, and you *knew* that," I pointed out, wrapping my arms around my legs that were curled into my chest to keep from shaking.

"It's not my fault you couldn't control it. I knew you were destructive, but I didn't know you were *that* destructive," said Anubys, his face close to mine.

"I'm not—"

"Look around, you little spitfire," he gestured to the area surrounding us, "You burned down an entire field in a matter of seconds. Not to mention the fact that you—" he stopped himself when he saw my face. He cleared his throat and looked away, standing back up straight. "You're destructive. And now you know just how much." I furrowed my eyebrows, and looked down at the charred grass around me, my eyes moving back and forth rapidly. We were just talking last night about how I was like him. How I was the same as him. How I was as destructive as him. I slowly looked back up, my eyes narrowed.

"You *wanted* this to happen," I said slowly, putting the pieces together. He looked taken aback and laughed, hiding the anger that was rising in him.

"How do you figure that?" he asked, with so much contempt I was almost scared. But, fighting that fear, I stood up and looked up at him, stepping closer.

"You wanted to make me see how destructive I could be. How destructive I *really* am. You wanted me to realize I was *just like you* so you wouldn't feel so godsdamn alone. And when you realized Rohit was lost out here, you knew some animal or creature in these godsforsaken woods would go after him. You sought me out, followed me, so you could be with me when I found him. So you could create some kind of lie as to why you couldn't kill the creature yourself, despite the fact that you're a walking, breathing grim reaper. You purposefully convinced me to try and do it. You *knew* Rohit was going to die. You *knew* that I would—that I would... kill him," I breathed in a shaky breath. "And you knew that you would be left untouched because you can't die." Anubys's face looked darker as I kept talking, his lips in a taut line.

"But you know what? I may have been the cause of death for one person. But at least I've never been used to torture hundreds of people, for probably no reason. At least what I did was an accident and at least I never wanted to kill or actually killed a little boy. At least *I* wasn't the cause of death for my *makers*," I attacked. Anubys clenched his jaw, angrily, his green eyes flashing at me.

"Are you done?" he said through gritted teeth. I blinked and backed up, finally looking away from him.

"Yeah, I'm done," I whispered.

"Good," Anubys hissed. My eyes glanced over at him,

and he looked like he was going to say more but then stopped himself, shaking his head. He clenched his jaw as he looked at me, no, *glared* at me, before walking back the way we came. He didn't look back, not once. And I started to quietly sob.

CHAPTER NINE

I stood there for a moment longer, tears falling down my face. For a minute, I let myself wallow in self-misery and self-pity. And then I wiped my face with the back of my hand and looked towards the direction Anubys disappeared to.

I didn't understand him. I didn't understand how he thought killing Rohit would save me from guilt, as I knew that was probably the reason why he broke his neck. Even though Anubys was the one to give him over to the other side, *I* was still the cause of Rohit's death. I burned him so badly that he was going to die anyways, if Anubys didn't kill him. It was still all my fault. No matter how much I wanted to blame Anubys for it, I knew he wasn't entirely at fault. He didn't kill him. *I did. But, I'm not sorry for what I said*, I thought defiantly, as some form of self-preservation. *Okay... maybe I was a little sorry.*

Aimlessly, I kept walking. I didn't know which way was which. I also didn't know where I came from. Every tree looked the same. That, and I wasn't really looking. I just thought about what Anubys had said to me. I had only known him for a day. I've only known any of them for a day. I couldn't say I really knew him. Or that I knew Rohit for that matter because I didn't. I didn't know any of them. Even so, I knew the people in Khaldun murdered Anubys's mother and father. I knew Anubys and his sister Eset worked for President Eclipse. I also knew Anubys felt so guilty about everything he's ever done that he can't even sleep at night. I knew a lot more about Anubys than I thought I did.

Suddenly, the guilt started to eat away at me. Not for Rohit, but instead for Anubys. For blaming him, for not trusting him. Except, it was hard to trust him. How could someone who has killed hundreds of people from the moment they were five years old be trustworthy? How could a person like that possibly be a remotely good person? How could a person not be messed up from that when I was messed up from just one person's blood on my hands?

"Zinnia?" I heard the familiar voice and turned around, facing Lightning. He looked distraught. The bags under his eyes looked more pronounced, and his eyes looked haunted, worried. I looked over at him, the sight of him bringing tears to my eyes.

"I saw smo—What happened to you?" he asked, looking at my clothes. They were slightly charred.

"Th-There was a fire," I blubbered as I rested my forehead onto his chest. After a little while, he wrapped his arms around me, hugging me tightly. He petted my hair as I sobbed. I wasn't sure if he understood what I was saying. He might've just thought I was crying because I was so scared to be by myself. Or maybe he already knew everything, and didn't want to bring it up. Either way, he didn't respond to what I had said.

"Let's go," said Lightning. "I'll take you back to the others." I clung onto him as he started walking. Lightning had been there with me from the very beginning, *helping* me on that hover train. I felt that I trusted him more than anyone else. His eyes were glazed over as he was looking into his mind map to find the way. All I could hear was the wind rustling the leaves on the trees and the light sounds of our footsteps. And I was thankful to Lightning for the much needed silence.

When we got back to camp, Eset was sitting next to Anubys, in an obvious heated conversation. My eyes widened as I looked over at Eset. Of course, *Eset*. The anguish I had been feeling disappeared. I had never felt more relieved. I released Lightning from my grip and ran towards her. Her eyes widened in surprise as I took her hands into mine and looked into the same hypnotizing eyes her brother had. Though, they were different from his. Colder, somehow.

"You," I said, gripping her hands tight until my knuckles turned white, "You can help." She glanced over at Anubys, and they exchanged meaningful glances that I couldn't quite interpret.

"Help with what, Zinnia?" asked Lightning carefully, as if he were walking around eggshells. He had come up behind me. I looked up at him.

"With Rohit," I said, almost desperately. My eyes returned to look at Eset.

"You can help, can't you?" I pleaded. "You can bring

people back from the dead." Lightning's gaze fell on Anubys, crossing his arms as he realized what happened.

"You better start talking," Lightning said through clenched teeth, "Now." Anubys didn't even look the slight bit nervous at Lightning's intimidating gaze. He just smiled a bit.

"Right, yeah, Rohit's dead. Didn't I mention that?" he asked, as if it were just a passing thought.

"What. Happened?" Lightning pushed, his eyes flashing.

"Zinnia and I were searching together, aaaand we both found Rohit pretty far from here. He was in some trouble, but I couldn't help because without Eset nearby I'm *practically* useless. There was this spider that was going after Rohit," he paused as he looked at me. I started to hyperventilate as I remembered what happened. The fire. The unbearable heat.

"And I—" I started.

"And Zinnia provoked the spider and then the spider started spewing fire. It was *crazy*. We *barely* escaped with our lives. When we went back, Rohit was dead," Anubys finished quickly, looking away from me. Eset's eyes narrowed as she glanced at Anubys, but her confused look disappeared as soon as it came.

"But you," I said, still holding Eset's hands, "You can bring him back. It's what you do." She looked over at Anubys slowly. Afterwards, she glanced up at Lightning. She sighed, but something felt off about it. Like she was *acting* sad.

"I can't," she said. "I can't heal a body. I can only bring it back from death." Her tone felt... off. Almost as if she were lying. I blinked and let go of her hands.

"Rohit wouldn't be the same if I brought him back," she said, and that much of what she said rang true. Who knew what kind of person he'd be if he came back from the other side.

"But, you can—" I started to say she can indirectly regenerate Anubys from wherever he is. However, she interrupted me.

"I *am* really sorry, Zinnia. I wish I could help," she said. *No, she didn't*, I thought. She wanted Rohit to stay dead. For what reason, I didn't know. But, she looked over at Anubys, and I thought I saw a very small smile playing on her lips. Lightning's lips tightened.

"We shouldn't split up anymore," he muttered. Agwe stood up and wandered towards us.

"Where's Rohit?" he asked. Ash was standing behind him, looking over at us, almost desperately. As if Ash and Rohit were friends. Maybe they were becoming close, and I just never noticed it. A crushing feeling pulsated throughout my chest, and I desperately clawed at my neck. I needed to get out of here. I needed to release this pain somehow. Ash glanced over at me curiously. It was my fault.

I killed him.

I killed him.

I killed him.

I—Someone grabbed both of my hands that kept clawing at my neck with their larger one. I heard the low mumble of Lightning's voice as he explained to the others what had happened to Rohit. The *lie* of what happened to Rohit. None of them knew the truth. The light brown hand pulled away from my neck, both of my small hands still in its grasp. Its fingers were long and almost strangely delicate-like. The hand looked almost elegant in a way. I stared at it as if desperate to memorize every single line on it. The skin felt smooth, like the softest silk. Unlike how Rohit's skin looked on his burnt dead body, this skin looked very much alive.

"Zinnia," the voice that the hand belonged to breathed, "It's okay." I finally tore myself away from the long-fingered, golden hand and looked up into familiar green eyes. Anubys's eyebrows rose as he stared at me, his face a little too close to mine for comfort.

"I-I," I stuttered. He stared at me meaningfully. There were specks of gold within the green. How had I not noticed that before? His pupils were dilated, and I felt like I could fall into them, like little black holes, and disappear from this reality.

"If they find out what really happened," Anubys barely breathed, "They won't spare you." He didn't glance away, as if trying to bore what he was saying into my memory.

"None of us know each other. The moment they find out you killed one of them, they won't be able to trust you." *One of them*, as if I wasn't a part of the group anymore. I guess I wasn't. I killed one of us. One of them.

"Do you understand what I'm trying to say, Zinnia?" he asked, his voice still barely above a whisper. I nodded. He removed his hand from mine, releasing both of them.

"Okay. Good. Now, calm down." He finally looked away from me, and I realized then that I had been holding my breath. I let it out as I looked up and saw Ash staring right at me. His eyes bore holes into mine, as if he knew. As if he could tell I was lying about what happened.

"We're going to have to be more careful," Lightning said.

"Travel in a group, as one," Volplie spoke, standing up from her crouch-like position. "We are not the predators out here, yet merely the prey." Her violet eyes roamed the area before saying, "We're stronger as a group." Lightning nodded his head in agreement.

"How much further?" Jangmi asked, looking up at Lightning. His eyes glazed over as he looked into the map that was in his mind.

"A day's worth of travel, probably," Lightning replied. A day. A lot can happen in a day.

CHAPTER TEN

I lulled behind the others as we continued to travel. Lightning led the group, but his head would turn periodically, his eyes gazing at me quizzically.

Agwe and Jangmi were continuing to compare notes about what they were told growing up about the Nation. And while I tore my eyes away from Jangmi and Agwe's heads getting closer to one another, my eyes caught the back of Ash's mop of red hair. He was also dragging his feet a little, his head bowed slightly. I stared at him, a lump growing in the back of my throat. *Were Rohit and him close?* I swallowed as I looked away.

I heard Volplie jump from a tree branch above me, and looking up, I caught her curious gaze. I promptly looked down.

She knew. She knew. She *must* know, I thought. I wrung out my hands as I continued walking along. Someone sauntered up next to me, and I felt myself stiffen.

"You're kind of pathetic, do you know that?" Anubys

whispered. I looked up at him, my eyes burning from trying to hold back from crying. He smiled a bit, his dimple appearing.

"He's *dead*, Anubys," I whispered, falling back more. "And everyone knows it was *me*." Eset walked ahead of us, however I could tell that she was keeping tabs on our conversation. Anubys scoffed at my words.

"No one knows it's you," he muttered, "*yet*. If you keep acting like this, they'll figure it out pretty quickly." He walked in silence for a moment before lightly hitting my arm.

"Besides," he smiled, "You didn't kill him. I did." I furrowed my eyebrows at him and then focused back on the ground.

"You know that's not true," I barely spoke. "He would've died either way because of me." Anubys shrugged.

"Yeah, that's true," he said, confirming my thoughts. I held back a sob.

"But *please*, Zinnia," he said, slightly annoyed, "You're acting like this is your first time."

"It *is* my first time killing someone, Anubys," I hissed. Anubys sighed. A shadow flickered over his face for a split second, as if he knew something I didn't. But, he didn't elaborate.

"You didn't even know him," he pointed out.

"That's not the point," I whisper-yelled. Anubys grabbed my arm and stopped walking, pulling me to a stop as well. He paused, his green eyes boring holes into my face. He didn't seem to care if Volplie was close-by or not.

"This whole thing, this Rohit thing, I'll keep it a secret," he whispered, leaning close to my face. His usually mischievous face hardened. "As long as you keep mine," he threatened. My skin raised with goosebumps as my blood chilled. At my fearful expression, his relaxed, and he gave me another crooked smile before walking ahead of me.

I knew what he was referring to. What he had told me last night must be kept a secret. If I told anyone, he would tell mine. One thing was clear to me, at that moment. I would be a fool to ever trust Anubys.

I looked at the group that continued to get further and further away from me, and my eyes glanced up at the treetops. Volplie was sitting on a tree branch, staring at me, like she was listening to everything. I knew she knew. I closed my eyes and said a prayer to the old gods, any of them, to save me and then continued to walk forward.

The sun was beating down on us as we walked towards whatever it was Lightning saw in his mind's eye. Lightning said the community that was ahead was close, but I wasn't used to this much sun. Holographic sun, sure, but the real thing? It was a bit unbearable. Almost like... My mind wandered to the charred field and Rohit.

The shake of the leaves rustling next to me interrupted my thoughts.

"You look perplexed," Jangmi said, staring up at me. She had the same face shape as my mother. The same face shape as me.

"Rohit's death shook me up, but I'm fine," I lied through my teeth. Her eyes softened, and subsequently she grabbed my hand. We walked hand-in-hand for a while. It reminded me of my mother.

She would always want to walk with our hands together, although I would always refuse as I got older. No one else held hands with their mother walking down the street in Adams. Yet, as I looked down at Jangmi's hand in mine, I wondered if maybe it was normal in Shin. How even worse my mother must've felt about living in Adams when I refused her.

"You're not alone," Jangmi whispered. She gave me a small, comforting smile, and I tried to smile back, except it probably looked like I was in pain. I shook my head.

"I just miss my family," I said. That wasn't really a lie. I *did* miss them a lot. She nodded her head.

"I do, too," she paused for a moment. "You know, I've heard stories of your mom. Nabi ee-mo." While the word was the banned Shin Community's original language, I recognized it as the word for 'aunt.' I didn't know a lot of words, but it was how my mom would refer to her sisters for me.

"She's probably a disappointment back home, too, huh?" I asked. Jangmi stared at me, in confusion, and then chuckled a bit.

"She might've been a disappointment in the eyes of *your* community, but in mine, she is regarded as a hero," she disclosed. She looked... proud of my mother. My eyebrows furrowed.

"Us hanguk saram-deul," she paused and then clarified, "Us *Koreans* are never one to back down from a fight," she smiled. Koreans. It was a word I had only heard once, and it was from a conversation I probably wasn't supposed to listen in on.

"I am *Korean*, Winter," I had heard my mother crying to my father from behind their bedroom door.

"Nabi, I don't want to hear this again—"

"My children deserve to know their history," she had exclaimed.

"Do you want them to get in trouble with the Nation?" I could barely make out.

"They are Korean, too," she continued. Hearing my dad sigh and head towards the door, I ran from it and back to my room before my dad could open it and see me. I blinked as I focused back onto Jangmi.

"Why do you call yourself that?" I asked.

"What? Korean?" Jangmi responded.

"Yeah," I said. "You're from the Shin Community. Shouldn't you just say that?" Her almost black eyes looked confused.

"Your mom... didn't tell you anything, did she?" she asked, her face falling a little. I blinked.

"What was she *supposed* to tell me?" Jangmi chewed on the inside of her cheek. She contemplated whether she should tell me or not, and I stood in bated breath, waiting to hear whatever it was my mother so desperately wanted to tell me for so long.

"That's who we were, before the War," she finally decided to disclose. "All the communities were once a part of a different nation. Some nations survived better than others. That's why there's the Adams Community, Washington Community, Du Bois Community. You're all from the same nation. Other nations did not survive as well. Koreans are fighters. And we fought very well in the War. But, we were a small nation. And now, we are a smaller one."

"So all the communities are just the surviving nations from the world before the War?" I asked. She nodded her head. Her eyes glazed over as her face darkened.

"Yes, the Korean nation is now the Shin Community, named after *the* Shin Sung-ho, one of the *great* soldiers from the war," Jangmi laughed a little, only her smile didn't reach her eyes.

"The West, the ones who unfortunately won this war, chose him as our namesake, but we don't claim him as one of us. He was a traitor, Zinnia. Helped destroy us to preserve himself. Have you noticed how the communities are named? Adams, for Benjamin Adams. Washington, for James Washington. Du Bois, for Frederick Du Bois. We're told they're all warriors, soldiers that helped create this *great* Nation. But, they were all *cowards* who destroyed the rest of the world for their own gain," she scowled.

"I thought the War was really between the Evolved and humans," I said, using Anubys's word for what those with abilities were called.

"Well, yes and no," Jangmi answered. "It was a war orchestrated to get rid of the most powerful people. But, it also was between the East and the West. Power, control, whatever it was the nations fought for back then. They just used the... Evolved to fight it for them. Some of the Evolved were ruthless, only knowing violence due to their upbringing. It is why President Eclipse wants humans to suffer. Why the Senate encourages it." Jangmi seemed hesitant to use the word that Anubys used, and I wasn't sure why. I stayed quiet for a moment.

"Why aren't we allowed to know that history? About what nation our communities really came from?" I asked.

"Why are we split up by color?" Jangmi asked back, staring at her warm olive-toned skin before looking back up at me. "The nation that the Adams Community belonged to was a nation with many different people with different ethnicities. However, they split you all up. Isn't the answer obvious?" I shook my head no.

"It's to keep the masses placated, we think. That nation was full of hate at one point. Unable to unite. Hatred and violence would not be helpful to President Eclipse. And President Eclipse learned well not to make the same mistake. Although, it *was* a surprise when it was announced that Nabi ee-mo would go to a community of a different race," Jangmi mused. "Perhaps it was to make her hateful. Or to make her feel alone. Perhaps both."

"My mom wasn't a hateful person," I argued. Jangmi nodded, smiling to herself a bit.

"Then she survived well. Let's hope she continues to do so," she whispered the last part before squeezing my hand tightly. My mother's face streaked with blood from my nightmare flashed through my mind. *Trust no one.*

"I think we're close!" I heard Lightning yell from up ahead. Jangmi's eyes lit up, and she dropped my hand, running towards the front of the group. Volplie jumped down from the treetops, her eyes roving over my body before meeting mine. It was as if she were measuring up what kind of threat I would be in the future. I held my hands from shaking as she glared at me and continued walking towards Lightning.

His black eyes met mine as everyone gathered around to look past the cliff we were standing on.

"I knew it! I *knew* the Rebellion camp existed!" Jangmi exclaimed as she leaned forward to see it. Her arms were pumping enthusiastically as she stared at it, her body shaking from excitement.

I walked up to where Lightning and Jangmi were and looked over the edge. Down in a valley, surrounded by high mountains, was a little, makeshift town of sorts. From this height, it looked like an ant's village.

"You know, if someone pushed you, you'd die," a familiar voice said. The hair on my neck stood up as I backed away from the edge slowly.

"You *would* be the person to talk about killing someone so casually," I quipped, looking into those impossibly light green eyes. Anubys shrugged.

"Guess it's in my nature," he smirked. We stared at each other for a moment, my blood boiling just from looking at him.

"Okay, guys, I don't know what happened between you two..." Ash said, interrupting our staring contest. My heart jumped.

"Nothing happened," Anubys and I said at the same time. Ash's hands went up defensively.

"All right, I get it, nothing happened. Buuuut, can you guys *not* go at each other's throats right now? One of us already has..." he let his sentence drift off. Water started to well up in his light brown eyes as he shook his head. His freckles that dotted his cheeks moved upwards as he smiled slightly.

"We just have to stick together," Lightning finished for Ash. Ash looked up at him appreciatively.

"So, does that giant map in your head tell us how to get down there, big guy?" Anubys asked. Lightning's jaw clenched. He really didn't like him. *That makes two of us,* I thought to myself.

"I can only see people, really clearly. Some landmarks," Lightning begrudgingly replied, "Not paths, not entirely." Anubys nodded slowly, glancing over at his sister.

"So, you have no idea how to get down there then," he pointed out.

"I didn't realize there was going to be a cliff, no," Lightning answered.

"Let's just climb down it," Volplie interrupted. Eset scoffed, the first real emotion that I think I've seen on Eset's face besides feigned politeness and bursts of anger.

"Not all of us are a cat hybrid... *thing*," Eset said, looking down at Volplie over her tall, elongated nose. Volplie made a face.

"*Excuse me?*"

"Pardon my twin sister," Anubys stepped in between Volplie and Eset as it started to look like Volplie would lunge for Eset's throat. "It's getting late, and she's not really a people person, as you know." My eyebrow jumped at the last phrase. *How would Volplie know?* Eset crossed her arms at Anubys's excuse, obviously not agreeing with it.

"I am not a cat hybrid thing," Volplie hissed, looking around Anubys's body at Eset. "For the last time, I am a *fox* hybrid thi—I mean, shapeshifter." Volplie cleared her throat, "I'm a fox *shapeshifter*."

"Foxes can't climb trees," Eset muttered. Volplie slowly was turning more and more like an animal.

"I am a *gray* fox," Volplie growled.

"You're white," Eset pointed out. There was a twinkle in her eye that I had seen before, in the charred field after Rohit... I looked at Anubys who was taking a step back. Something was going on with those two.

"I have *albinism*," Volplie hissed. She poised as if she were about to sink her teeth into Eset. Taking Anubys's place as the mediator between them, I widened my eyes at Volplie, trying to convey a message of danger. It wouldn't be good for her to try and hurt Eset. Not with Anubys there. And some part of me felt it was what the twins wanted from her, from any of us. Her blue-purple eyes looked at me, confused, but that split second of confusion was turning her body back to her half-human half-creature form.

"Let's not fight," I said, turning my head towards Eset. If looks could kill, and if she had her brother's abilities rather than the 'gift' of life, I would probably be dead.

"It's stupid," I insisted. "Obviously she wouldn't look like a typical gray fox. She's a shapeshifter." Volplie nodded along with me, though she still looked wary from the look I gave her. I hoped she wasn't going to make me explain later.

"And honestly, it doesn't matter anyways," I said. I looked over at Lightning for help, any kind of help. He was just watching Eset, most likely in a trance. I rolled my eyes. "We just need to get down there. We shouldn't be fighting."

"I don't think we'll get down there tonight," Lightning finally muttered. The sun was starting to set. Agwe stared at the town in the valley.

"I'm not sure if we'll get down there ever," Agwe said,

uncharacteristically negative. We all turned towards him. He took a rock the size of his palm and dropped it down the side of the cliff. At a certain height, the rock suddenly disintegrated.

"A forcefield," Agwe waved his arm towards the sight.

"Well," Lightning said, "That's going to be a problem."

CHAPTER ELEVEN

While Lightning and Agwe discussed ways to get through the forcefield, Eset and Anubys whispered to one another in hushed tones. Busying my hands by pulling at the grass beneath my criss-crossed legs, I watched as Eset's eyes looked crazed, almost hungry in a way. She glared at Anubys, speaking in a language I didn't understand, before composing her face to the expressionless stone mask I'd become used to seeing on her. I tried hard not to gape at them. They were somehow able to speak in their community's original language to the point of having a full conversation. Even my mother, the rebel, wasn't able to do that.

"Volplie," Eset cooed, her head held high. Volplie scowled at her. I watched through my lashes as Eset saun-tered over to where Volplie was standing. Her violet eyes gave away her insecurity for a moment. It was hard not to compare oneself to the beauty that was Eset. She just looked so... alive. Her beauty glowed through every part of her, in her movements, her voice.

"I apologize for earlier," her faux apologetic face was almost undetectable. "I am *incredibly* hungry, and when I haven't eaten for a long period of time, it is difficult for me to remain... pleasant." Her lips pursed at that last word but still broke out into a polite smile. She placed her hand on Volplie's shoulder in apology. Volplie didn't seem to detect the disingenuous tone from Eset, completely enamored by the beauty of her face and voice. Even one with animal instincts wouldn't be able to resist her.

Volplie ducked her head and mumbled an acceptance of sorts as Eset broke into another poised, polite smile before turning away. Once turned, her face was ice cold once more.

"If you're hungry," Jangmi spoke up, "I can get us food." It seemed I wasn't the only one listening in on Eset's apology. Jangmi walked over to Anubys, placing a hand gingerly on his arm. He looked down at it, eyebrows knitted together.

"I will call the animals here," Jangmi explained, "However, I'll need your help to kill them." Anubys stared at her for a long while, as if unable to comprehend what she was asking.

"You *want* me to kill them?" he asked, slowly. Jangmi nodded her head.

"Of course. You can kill them quickly, can't you? And all at once."

"I don't..." Anubys struggled with his words, "They feel a lot of pain... when dying by my hand." Jangmi squinted her eyes in thought.

"No," she said, dismissing his concern, "I'm sure you can

kill them without the pain. Swiftly and painlessly." She brushed her hands together as she started to walk forward.

"I don't think you understand what I'm—"

"Practice makes perfect. Let us try," she said. She grabbed his arm and placed him in front of the group, steadying her hand to show him he needed to stay there.

"I will call a few animals here, and you focus on just wanting them dead. Not the torture part," she ordered. Anubys looked annoyed at being given orders, but I could see a bit of hope in his eyes. He cracked his knuckles and gave a lazy smile in her direction. His sister rolled her eyes, but it looked as if she were curious too. Would the boy who reveled in the torture part of his power be able to just kill and leave it at that? She sat down on a rock and crossed her arms.

"All right, whatever your name is—"

"It's Jangmi," she interrupted.

"All right, *Jangmi*," Anubys restarted. He cracked his neck before saying, "Let's do this." Jangmi sat a little further away, her eyes closed. Her eyebrows were scrunched up as if she were thinking about an answer to a test in Preparation.

"She just found out about this power," Agwe mentioned from next to me. I craned my neck up to look at him. He was incredibly tall.

"I'm guessing she's using this opportunity to practice as well," Agwe said. Lightning nodded from next to him.

"A lot of us still haven't found out what our abilities are yet," Lightning's low voice rumbled through the air. "It'd be good for those who know their power to practice with it more."

"But not me, I'm guessing," Anubys said over his shoulder. Lightning and I rolled our eyes at the same time.

After a moment, Agwe asked Lightning, "Do you see anything coming?" Lightning's lips curled into a slight smile.

"Yeah, I see a few animals coming this way." Just as he said this, two squirrels were scurrying towards Anubys, followed by a bunny. Jangmi's eyes flew open, fixed onto Anubys.

"Go!" she demanded. Anubys's face flickered with fear for a moment, and then it tensed with concentration. He stared hard at the animals in front of him. That same feeling washed over me when I saw him the first time he used his power. Normally, the white surrounding his iris made him look kind of lazy, maybe a bit mischievous, but when his power was pouring out of him, the whites of his eyes made his iris look more sinister, evil almost.

A smirk played on his lips, similar to the smile that bore his face when the mutated humans were attacking us. The animals in front of him whimpered and whined from the torture that was plaguing them. The smirk grew wider. I bit my lip as I watched him, waiting for him to stop. But, when it was clear he wasn't going to, I took a step closer, hoping I was in his eyesight.

"Anubys," my clear voice cut through the air between us. His name was all I could say. The smile was wiped off of his face at the sound of my voice as his eyes hardened. He slowly blinked, his green eyes moving towards me. And as they did, the animals lay dead.

"See! We knew you could do it without torturing," Jangmi exclaimed as she ran towards the dead animals.

"I still tortured them," Anubys stated, his eyes not leaving mine. I averted my eyes from his intense gaze.

"Yes," Jangmi nodded, "It's still a process. You're learning though, and it wasn't *too* much torture. Only slight." She smiled as her fingers showed how small the torturing was. Anubys smiled softly back at her. Eset got up from her seat on the rock. If she was proud of her brother's small achievement, she didn't show it.

"That's not enough to eat though," Ash pointed out, sighing a bit. "There's nine of us..." His voice drifted off.

Clearing his throat, he corrected himself, "Eight, I mean." Rohit's charred body flickered through my mind. My breath hitched in my throat as Lightning stared at me, concerned. I couldn't give away anything about what happened this morning. "*The moment they find out you killed one of them, they won't be able to trust you,*" Anubys's words echoed in my mind. I swallowed my guilt and tried to mimic the soft, quiet sadness around me.

"It's hard trying to get animals I can't see to come," Jangmi sighed, putting her hands on her hips. "Plus, I've only done this once." She held up her hands in frustration at the criticism.

"I'm tired. Everyone will have to eat a small amount. But, at least you'll be able to eat," she muttered.

"Should we find shelter?" Ash changed the subject. In the two days we had known Jangmi, she wasn't one to lose her temper. It looked like we were all hungry and tired of each other.

"If Anubys keeps watch, we should be safe," Volplie pointed out.

"I gotta sleep like everyone else does," Anubys remarked.

Staring at him with her unnerving eyes, Volplie shook her head.

"You don't really sleep though, from what I can tell." Anubys's eyes squinted slightly.

"What's that supposed to mean?" his voice dropped, menacingly. Volplie shrugged as she slowly looked away.

"There might be openings on the side of the cliff," I said in order to change the topic. If Volplie heard what we were talking about last night, then Anubys's and Eset's secret about President Eclipse wasn't really a secret anymore.

"Yeah, dens for animals maybe," Ash pointed out. Grateful for the change in subject, Anubys chimed in.

"Or mutated creatures," he joked. We all shuddered at the thought.

"It might be best to be out in the open," Lightning mused. "Better chance at finding a place to hide instead of being cornered in a cave."

"Are mutated creatures nocturnal?" I asked. We hadn't seen any in our journey here to the edge of this cliff during the daytime. But, last night... Anubys's sadistic face appeared in the forefront of my mind. I shook the image from my head.

"No one really knows," Ash said. "Only Volplie seems to have heard of them before leaving the Wall."

"It could be President Eclipse releasing them only at night to pick off the surviving people outside the Wall," Volplie muttered.

"You mean purposefully?" I asked. Volplie shrugged.

"She's a snake. I wouldn't put it past her," she growled. As Agwe started a fire for the squirrels and the one bunny to be cooked, Volplie walked over to a tree, poised as if about to climb it.

"There's just something that doesn't feel right about all of this. The Wall, the creatures... I've seen them before but not that subdued," her eyes made contact with mine. Chewing on her bottom lip in thought, she turned around and disappeared into the treetops.

"I'll take the first watch," Lightning said, sitting down. "I'll be able to see if anyone is coming before they get here." Anubys almost interjected, but Agwe gasped in excitement when he got the fire started as Jangmi hit his back in encouragement.

"Let's eat," she said, her eyes twinkling from pride.

I trembled as Forest walked towards me, blood pooling into his hands from the wound in his chest.

"Save us," he said, his voice sounding far away. "Save us, Zinnia." I ran towards him, hoping to save him, hoping to stop him from bleeding. And as he fell to the floor, his face morphed into the pained expression of Rohit's. I stifled a scream as his charred hand reached out to me, bits of burnt skin flaking off of him. White, ivory bone revealed underneath.

"You killed me," his voice hauntingly spoke. "You murdered me."

"I'm sorry," I cried, as I took a small step back. "I'm so sorry, Rohit."

"You killed us all," he said, his voice mixing with Forest's.

"Save us," Forest said.

"You'll kill us," Rohit echoed afterwards. I turned away from the grotesque scene, running into darkness. Into the arms of my mother.

"Mom?" I asked, my voice small as I smelled the familiar stench of garlic and old pages of books surrounding her.

"Let me tell you a story," my mother's voice said, disembodied from her. I looked up as she looked down at me, her growing taller as if I were a small child. Blood ran from her eyes.

"There once was a girl with fire in her heart. Born from the mind of one who knew all. Born from the hands that could create dreams. She came upon a crossroads of shadows," my mother's voice continued, but her mouth did not move.

"Mom?" my voice became smaller as I pushed myself away from her. Her arms held me tightly.

"Pray to Hecate, the goddess of crossroads. Pick one path to choose. Beware the shadow maker. Beware the silver-tongue," she whispered. "But most importantly, trust *no one*."

"Shadow maker?" I heard my voice repeat, though it lilted slightly, turning it into a question.

"You'll kill us all," she breathed, the blood running from her eyes. Forest's and Rohit's voice echoed hers.

"Save us," their voices said, intermingling with one another. It was as if their voices were all around me. I reached for my mother again. However, as I did, she disappeared. All I held in my hands was a handful of grass.

I sat up, sweat rolling down the sides of my face. I dabbed at my head with the back of my hand, feeling someone's eyes on me. I gazed up at Anubys who was staring at me intently. *Of course,* I thought to myself. Of course he was awake.

"What did you dream about?" he whispered once he crawled over to me. "Looked like a pretty bad dream." Lightning was next to us, leaning against the base of a tree. His head lulled to the side, his chin against his chest, fast asleep. *So much for keeping watch,* I couldn't help but think.

"It's my mom," I muttered, almost unable to stop myself from telling him the truth. "She keeps appearing in them." Anubys's eyes lit up at the mention of my mother.

"Nabi, right?" he asked. I nodded my head, curious as to how he knew her name.

As if knowing the question that was being formed in my head, he said, "I heard you and your cousin talking about her."

"Oh," I said, bringing my knees up to my chest. I noticed that, again, Anubys's jacket was around my body. I looked at him quizzically, but didn't ask the question that burned my tongue.

"Your mom... Jangmi referred to her as a hero to the Shin Community. Do you know why?" Anubys asked, his light green eyes seemed to glow in the darkness. I shook my head.

"No," I said. "I don't know why she said that." *Trust no one,* my mom's voice echoed in my head. I stared at Anubys for a moment, studying him, and then looked away. He seemed to want some kind of information from me. But, I knew I didn't have the information he wanted.

"What are you asking for?" I whispered, my eyes focused on the path that led to the woods we came out of. I heard Anubys breathe in sharply at my question.

"Why does there need to be a reason?" he asked, softly. Nevertheless, there was a warning behind his words: *Don't pry... or else.* I shrugged. And before I had time to answer, I heard a snap come from the entrance of the forest. My eyes widened as my back straightened. I stared into the darkness, looking for any kind of movement.

"Probably those creatures," Anubys said, stalking over to wake his sister up. He slowly shook the others awake, as I moved to wake up Ash and Lightning. Ash stared at me, sleep still in his eyes.

"What's going—" I put a finger to my lips and pointed at the entrance of the forest. Ash's eyes widened as he looked into the darkness.

"Spiders," he muttered. My blood ran cold as I looked over to where he was looking. Spiders were crawling out of the forest, a lot of them. And they were bigger than the one that was attacking Rohit earlier. I felt myself freeze as I felt Anubys's curious gaze on me.

"Anubys," Lightning ordered as the spiders came closer. They were the size of a human being, standing up. And who knew what kind of abilities they possessed?

"Anubys," Lightning hissed, his eyes darting towards him. Anubys rolled his eyes.

"Quiet, I'm concentrating," he said. He closed his eyes, and as the spiders started to writhe on the ground, they stopped.

I looked over, and just as I did, Anubys fell backwards off the cliff. I felt a scream escape from my lips as I leapt towards him in order to grab his arm. *Save us*, the voices whispered in my head. *Kill us.* My hand missed his as he fell over the edge. I desperately peered over the cliff as he fell, and a loud thud resounded throughout the mountains. He landed, luckily, on a ledge that stuck out from the side of the cliff. Blood started to pool on the rock around his head. I held my breath as I waited to see some kind of movement.

"I'm fine," I heard him groan, and subconsciously, I let out a sigh of relief. He was already starting to regenerate, the blood disappearing from the back of his head.

"My brother is *so* clumsy," I heard Eset say from beside me. She shrugged as she got up, clearly unfazed. A part of me had a wicked thought as I noticed the spiders were still alive, recovering from the slight torture they faced. Did he purposefully fall over so he would be out of range?

"What do we do?" I whispered. I didn't want to show the fire that was building in my chest. The uncontrollable fire that was sure to get them all killed.

Suddenly, the spiders were thrown back, an invisible force clumping them all together into a ball. I turned, looking for the source of the power, and I watched as Eset's eyes fixated knowingly on Ash. His brown eyes were slightly glowing, as his hands were outstretched from his body, controlling the ball of spiders. Sweat dotted his hairline, and he threw the group of spiders over the edge of the cliff. The spiders were still balled together by some kind of force, and we watched as the barrier around the spiders hit the force-field below. An explosion echoed around the mountain.

"Forcefields," Eset said, a small smile on her lips as she leaned down to help her brother up. Agwe walked over to the edge of the cliff, staring down at the community that lay below. Lights began to dot the valley and some noise drifted up towards us.

"I think the forcefield is down," Agwe said, bewildered,

as he looked over at Ash. Ash's face turned the same color as his hair.

"I guess that's my ability," Ash muttered. I glanced over at Anubys, who used his sister's arm to pull himself back over the cliff. She had used his jacket that I abandoned and tied it to her own to get him up. He dusted his pants as his eyes met mine. A part of me wondered if Anubys somehow already knew what Ash's ability was.

He looked away as he turned towards his sister, conversing quietly in—what must be—the original language of Khaldun. *You'll kill us all*, my mother's voice echoed. I shook my head, tearing my gaze away from Anubys. *Trust no one.*

CHAPTER TWELVE

A gust of air blew up from the town below, and suddenly, I couldn't move an inch. It was as if I were frozen to the cliff. A woman with curly brown hair and skin that matched it, stood on a platform of air that had raised her up onto the cliff. Her eyes were watching each of us, as if she were concentrating very hard. I tried to move my arm, but my body refused to listen, now under the command of someone else.

A man stood next to her with shoulder-length black hair and pale, white skin. His eyes were downcast, and his hands were strained towards the wind that was somehow holding them up. They both stepped onto the cliff, almost in unison.

The woman was shorter than him as they stared us down. I could barely move my eyes to look at them as they measured us up.

"Let them go," the man finally said. "They're just kids." The woman's gaze softened, and I finally had use of my limbs. I stole a look at Anubys as I flexed my fingers, and he looked pissed he was not in control of his body for a small period of time.

"How did you destroy the forcefield?" the woman asked, putting a hand on her hip. She was shorter than I was, but there was power in her gaze. Immense power. I gulped.

"Sorry, that was me," Ash said, timidly putting a hand up. She eyed him before looking over at the man. He seemed to be in charge.

"What do you think, Biao?" she asked. The man named Biao pursed his lips as he stared at us. His eyes were similar to Jangmi's, except smaller on his face and more downturned.

"You all are from the Nation, I take it?" he asked.

"Obviously," Anubys scoffed. Biao's thin eyes glanced over at him and examined Anubys, up and down.

"How did you escape?" the woman asked.

"What do you mean?" I responded. She stared at me, confusion filling her face for a moment.

"You... didn't escape?" she asked, slowly. She and Biao exchanged a look. Lightning took a step forward, in order to hopefully explain further.

"We all failed the Test," Lightning said. "They took us to the Wall and—"

"And let you go?" she almost stated, an eyebrow raised. Biao took in a long deep breath, as he seemed to think. I held my own as I watched him consider his options.

"Freeze them, Lidya," he barely spoke, and once again, I couldn't move at all. Lidya's eyes concentrated on each of us as she forced our legs to move towards the wind current. No matter how much I tried to scream at my legs to stop moving, they listened to whatever Lidya wanted. It wasn't necessarily painful, but it was a different kind of agony. All of us stepped onto the platform made of wind, and the wind moved downwards, like an elevator.

Eventually, we were standing on the ground in the middle of the town. The buildings were worn down and were all made from the trees that grew around the mountains that hid it. People came out of their homes, some half asleep, as they looked our way while our bodies forcefully led us towards one building.

"These kids are the ones who took down the forcefield?" a large man with blonde hair asked in shock as we walked by.

"They were *let go* by President Eclipse," Lidya said, her voice almost gossipy. The man's eyes widened.

"Devlin, get Tayen," Biao ordered as he marched by. Devlin's blue eyes almost fell out of his head as he quickly started walking in the opposite direction. Whoever Tayen was, they seemed pretty important. Lidya continued to have us walk into the building, and I winced when I saw the cage. I knew what was about to happen.

Against my will, I walked into it and was still unable to move until the cage was locked and electric currents hummed against the metal of it. It was just like the one inside the Wall.

Suddenly and all at once, I felt a release throughout my body and once again was able to move my limbs. I stretched my arms up as I looked at the faces of those around me. Anubys and Volplie looked pissed; Lightning's and Eset's faces were unreadable; and Ash looked downright terrified. Jangmi and Agwe just seemed positively elated, despite the circumstances.

"You're caging us up because we failed the Test? Shouldn't you be welcoming us into your ranks?" Anubys asked, getting as close to the bars of the cage as possible. Lidya glared at him.

"They let you go," she said. "They don't ever let you guys go." The words sent chills down my spine as I stared at Anubys and then glanced over at Eset. A thought filled my mind, but I quickly let it go.

"Sending *kids* to fight us? It just doesn't make sense," Biao shook his head, as he leaned against a desk. His arms were crossed as he curiously looked at us.

"But, for them to let go of eight kids? To give them to us instead of killing them?" Lidya argued. Biao shrugged as he took a step closer. He looked like he was going to say something else, but he went silent as an older woman walked into the one room building. Her gray hair was tied in a long braid down her back, and she walked as if she had all the time in the world. She was old. Older than I had ever seen anybody in Adams. Usually, the elders were put to rest after a certain amount of time.

"Tayen," Biao said, greeting her. Her brown eyes glanced over at him, and then she looked at the eight of us. Her eyes roved over each of us as she walked the length of the cage and then back again. They stopped momentarily on me, and I felt myself hold my breath. Finally, they looked away, almost as if she didn't just stare deep into my soul.

"They were the ones who destroyed the forcefield, Tayen. They also were let go for some reason by—"

"Ah yes," Tayen spoke, her voice holding years of wisdom in it. "This one has the power of forcefields." She pointed at Ash, and Eset's smirk and words from earlier echoed in my head. I turned to look at Anubys, who gave me a lazy look back. They knew. They both knew, somehow.

"How do you know that?" Ash asked, his mouth agape. Tayen laughed a little at the question, as if it had been a while since she had heard it.

"My own power can see what others have," Tayen answered. Anubys sneered.

"She's a siphon," he glared at Tayen. She flashed a small smile at him and then softly nodded her head.

"What's a siphon?" I heard myself ask.

"A siphon is someone who can take your power... after killing you," Anubys answered, his eyes not leaving hers. I felt myself involuntarily shudder at the thought.

"We are without power until we take, yes," she said in agreement. The fear of her killing me for my power flashed through my mind for a moment, numbing me.

"Though, I do not take powers anymore, my dear boy," she assured, as if she could hear the words that were in my mind.

"Who knows how many powers she has," Anubys muttered. Tayen smiled again at Anubys's words before waving down Biao.

"Turn off the electric current," she said.

"But—"

"Turn it off," she demanded, her voice lowering as she looked meaningfully at him. He bowed his head in submission and went to turn off the electric currents. The humming stopped.

"Their powers—" Lidya interjected, but Tayen put up a hand.

"None of them have the ability to walk through walls,"

she said. "And the ones that do have power so dangerous in their blood, they won't use them on us now." Her eyes glanced over at me and the image of Rohit flashed through my mind. Subconsciously, I wrapped my arms around myself and looked away from her gaze.

"Their powers?" Lidya asked, holding a clipboard in one hand and a pen in another. My eyes widened as I realized they must have a record of everyone's powers at the rebellion camp. Tayen stared at us and started to recite each of our abilities.

"The tall one, he's a healer," she said, referring to Agwe. "The quiet one, he is a map. Helpful, don't you think?" Lidya nodded in response. "The little one, she's a creature whisperer. Tricky power." Jangmi's eyes lit up at Tayen mentioning her.

"The redhead, he's a forcefield," Lidya nodded as she wrote these down. "The girl with ice in her eyes, she's a resurrector." I heard Biao's sharp inhale as his gaze looked towards Eset. She ignored it as she pointedly continued to look at Tayen. "The fox girl, she's a shapeshifter." Lidya's face looked like she wanted to say *obviously,* but instead she just pursed her lips. Tayen walked over to me, her eyes twinkling as she met mine. She pointed a wrinkly finger at my face as she turned to speak to Lidya.

"This one is hellfire," she said. She cocked her head to the side as she barely spoke, loud enough that only I could hear, "And perhaps something more." *Hellfire?* Biao's sharp gaze looked over at me, his eyebrows scrunched together. I shrinked in his exacting glare. Tayen then walked over to Anubys, who sneered at her. She smirked to herself.

"This one is a shadow maker," she said. "The grim

reaper." *Shadow maker?* My head turned sharply towards Anubys as I heard my mother's words bounce around in my head. *Beware the shadow maker.*

"I have a lot of names," Anubys responded, not meeting my frightened gaze. Biao's eyebrows raised as he walked over to Lidya. He looked over her shoulder at the list and bit the inside of his cheek.

"Some of these kids have very rare powers," he whispered. Even though he tried to keep his voice low, we all could still hear him. "A resurrector? The shadow maker? Hellfire, itself? Why would President Eclipse let any of these kids go?" I backed away from the front of the cage, not wanting to be seen after Biao mentioned me. Tayen said I was hellfire. Not that I controlled hellfire, that I *was* hellfire. Whatever that meant.

"Look at the other powers, too," Lidya whispered back. "They are all powers that could help them get to us." They shared a glance and then looked at Tayen who seemed to be studying me intently.

"Hellfire and shadow," she muttered as she looked at me and then looked at Anubys. "Hellfire's shadow." I watched as Anubys balled his hands up into fists at her words. Her wrinkled eyes gleamed as she looked back at me.

"Very dangerous together," she whispered to me. *Beware the shadow maker*, my mother's words repeated. Tayen then backed up as she waved towards Biao.

"Release them," she said. "They're all useful." Biao's eyes nearly fell out of his head.

"Tayen, some of these kids—"

"They won't hurt us now," she said. Biao stared at her,

frustrated. He eventually sighed and opened up the cage door. None of us moved. He looked at us, exasperated.

"Well? Get the fuck out," he said, gesturing for us to leave. We all quickly walked out of the cage as another person walked through the main door.

"Tayen, one of the soldiers wanted to talk to..." his words drifted away as his bright blue eyes met mine. A sigh of relief almost left my body, and it took everything in me not to throw myself at him in a hug. I knew him.

"August?" I heard my voice say. He blinked as he stared at me in wonder. He was taller than before. And his skin was more sun-kissed, probably from being outside in the Rebellion camp all day. I braced myself to hear the nickname I had heard my whole life, the one August called me the first time and only time he met me. And I waited for the ridicule that was bound to come out of Anubys's lips afterwards.

"Zinnia?" he said, surprised. I looked back up at him, shocked that he remembered my real name.

"What are you doing here?" he continued.

"I could ask you the same question. I thought you were dead," I pointed out. He took a small step towards me.

"I escaped," he said. "They all died... but I was able to escape." His eyes lowered as he spoke those last words, but darted back up to mine as if to gauge my reaction. I could barely process that he was in front of me, let alone what he was saying.

"The first in a couple of years," Biao said. "Lidya was the one before him."

"His story isn't nearly as exciting as mine," Lidya said, putting her hand on her hip. "All he did was *talk* his way out."

"A silver-tongue," Tayen said, giving me a knowing glance, as if she had seen the dream I had earlier. *Beware the silver-tongue.* "Very useful." She turned her attention back to August.

"Let's go. We must get the forcefield back up," she said, taking August's helpful arm. She turned her gaze towards Ash and beckoned him over. "You will be helpful." August continued to stare at me, shock filling his face as Ash swiftly walked over to her.

"You two can catch up in the morning," Tayen said, patting August's hand. "For now, they should sleep."

"I *hate* Aphrodite's children," Anubys muttered as Biao led us to our living accommodations.

"Aphrodite's children?" I asked, glancing over at him. He gave me a look before breaking out into a crooked smile. But, his eyes remained dead.

"Your friend," he jerked his thumb back over his shoulder, "They're called Aphrodite's children. So charming, anyone would do their bidding. That's their power."

"She called him silver-tongue," I said, the term sending chills down my back. Anubys shrugged.

"Some people call them that, too," he muttered. He stared at me, as if knowing what was on my mind.

"You guys were friends back home?" he asked. I shook my head.

"I only talked to him once," I said. He raised an eyebrow.

"You must've made an impression then," he said, referring to how August knew my name. I scrunched my face up in disagreement.

"It's just a small community. And I *am* community-mixed," I mumbled under my breath. Anubys stared at me for a moment longer, as if knowing the turmoil that was going on in my mind.

"Well, I'll see you tomorrow, *Hellfire*," he whispered, guessing at what I was intensely thinking about. My blood froze at the mention of that name. He flashed me another crooked smile, his hawk-like eyes meeting mine. Then, he turned and walked towards the boys' accommodations.

Eset rolled her eyes at her brother's antics as she led the way into our cabin. It was small, just one room with a bathroom attached to it. The beds were bunk beds, and I could see Eset's disgust with it.

"I will sleep on the bottom," she declared, choosing a bottom bunk. Volplie chose the top bunk of hers, to Eset's dismay. Jangmi slept on the bottom of the other one, and I climbed up to the top. I pulled the covers up to my chin as I stared up at the ceiling.

She came upon a crossroads of shadows. Pray to Hecate, the goddess of crossroads. Pick one path to choose. Beware the shadow maker. Anubys's face came to mind. *Beware the silver-tongue.* August's impossibly blue eyes flashed in my thoughts. I put my hands on my face as my mother's words echoed over and over in my head. *You'll kill us all. Save us.*

Pick one path to choose. But, both paths didn't sound all that great. I barely knew who Hecate was, having not paid attention during the Ancient histories portion of Preparation, but I clasped my hands together and desperately prayed to the goddess anyway.

CHAPTER THIRTEEN

"Put these on and meet us in the field in half an hour," Lidya ordered as she threw clothes at each of us. I woke up with a grunt as they landed on me. They were heavy and partially made of some kind of metallic-looking material. Eset held it up, her tall nose scrunched.

"Training armor," she said, putting it gingerly onto her bed. She looked impossibly beautiful, even though she had just woken up. Her black hair cascaded down her shoulders in perfect waves, and her face wasn't swollen from sleep in the slightest. I subconsciously rubbed my own face, hoping it wasn't too bloated.

"Training armor?" Volplie asked as she started to change right in front of us. As she put on the shirt of the armor, her fox ears immediately disappeared and so did her tail. Her eyes also went back to normal human eyes, however still that violet color. Volplie looked at herself in surprise as Eset smirked, her head angled up to watch her from the bottom bunk.

"They are as heavy as real armor, so you get used to the weight, and they nullify your powers so you can't rely on them," Eset said, getting up to go to the bathroom that was attached to the room. I turned around in my bunk to face the wall as I changed into them. The shirt settled heavily onto my chest, blowing out the fire that was coursing through my veins.

"How does she know so much?" Jangmi asked in wonder as she put on the armor.

"She's not like the rest of us," is all Volplie said. I wondered if Volplie overheard the conversation that Anubys and I had the other night. But, I wasn't about to try and figure out if she had, in case I would accidentally give too much away. And if I gave anything away... I thought about the promise I made with Anubys and shook my head.

Volplie jumped down from her top bunk, landing with a heavy thud due to the armor she was wearing. It looked like silver silk on her, and rippled over her like water. The clothes definitely didn't look like they weighed as much as a small person.

"Don't look at me like that," Volplie said, pointing a sharpened nail at me. I widened my eyes at her gesture.

"Like what?" I asked.

"Like I'm a normal person," she grumbled as she walked out the door. She did look completely normal, save for her white hair and abnormal eyes. Without her ears, tail, and fur covering half of her body, she looked like the rest of us. And not really much like a monster at all.

"I think she feels safe in her half form," Jangmi mused as I climbed down from the bunk. I nodded in agreement as she seemed to assess me.

"Do you want me to braid your hair?" she asked. "We have some time."

"Sure," I said, sitting down between her legs as she started to brush through my hair with her fingers.

Eset came out of the bathroom, tying her black hair at the nape of her neck, once Jangmi finished up my French braid. The braid hit the middle of my shoulder blades as she let go of it. Eset stared at us—in her cold, unfeeling way—and then walked by. Her silver armor made her look even more regal than usual as she marched out of the cabin.

"For someone with the gift of life, she always looks like she might wield death at any moment," Jangmi muttered.

"Maybe giving life takes away some of her humanity, bit by bit," I voiced my thought aloud. Jangmi nodded as she finished doing her own French braid.

"Are you hoping Anubys gets a little bit of *his* humanity restored bit by bit as he takes life?" Jangmi asked, softly. I turned my head to stare at her, my braid hitting the side of my face at the movement.

"Why would I hope that?" I asked. Jangmi shrugged slightly, but a whisper of a smile graced her lips. Without an answer, she walked out of the cabin, and I wondered if I spoke at all while I slept.

The nightmare I had was the same as the night before. My mother's eyes were bleeding as she held me, forcefully telling me a story about a girl who had come to a crossroads. Who had a path to take. But this time, I could see both paths. One had Anubys and the other had August, and they both had held out their hands.

Biao was tapping his foot in the field as the rest of us started to gather, all of us wearing that silk silver armor. Anubys was the last to walk up to the field, with Biao's sharp eyes noting the movement.

"Come earlier, tomorrow," Biao ordered, but Anubys just shrugged. He gestured towards the field.

"I'm here on time, aren't I?" he merely retorted. Biao just whipped his head back to face the rest of us as a response.

"You will be training while you're here. You'll have lessons in regards to controlling your powers later, but first you will be learning how to fight without them," he said as he paced back and forth. Lidya stood in the background, her deep set eyes watching us intensely.

"Scared of us using our abilities?" Anubys asked. His eyes always had this perpetual look to them as if he were looking up, almost like a glare. The glare one gives before they're about to rip out your throat.

My hand subconsciously fluttered to my neck, and Anubys's eyes seemed to dart over to look at the movement, hyper aware of his surroundings. He quickly glanced back at Biao. Biao's arms were crossed, his lean muscles rippling at the pose.

"Considering you're a shadow maker, we would rather you not use your abilities," Biao dismissed. Anubys raised an eyebrow.

"Terrified, aren't you," he said. Biao's face didn't move a muscle as he ignored Anubys once again. My eyes found and then followed August as he walked slowly onto the field.

"I have other matters to attend to, so August and Lidya will teach you the basics today," Biao said, gesturing towards them. "They're good fighters in the Shadow Army, so listen to them well. If I hear *any* of you gave them a hard time, or even *uttered* a sound of complaint, I'll order Lidya to freeze you for a whole day, do I make myself clear?" I shuddered at the thought of Lidya taking over my body once more, and I had a feeling the rest of the group agreed as they all nodded as well. August's eyes lingered on me as Biao left the field. He looked like he wanted to say something, but it was Lidya who spoke.

"If one of you is planning on bringing down this camp, we'll show you why we won't fall easy," she said, baring her teeth at us as she smiled. "We'll start with a run."

Running with armor seemed easier in my head. However, as we began doing the laps around the field, I felt myself fall further and further behind. My chest hurt with every breath I took, and the armor felt like it was trying to drag me to the ground at every moment. I also felt myself glance over at August as I would run by him and Lidya. He was standing next to her, recording something onto a clipboard every few minutes.

"You had a thing for him, huh?" an annoying voice appeared next to me. I almost jumped at the sight of Anubys jogging easily beside me. He didn't even look like he was breaking a sweat. When the shock of him being next to me passed, I just rolled my eyes at his words.

"Who? August?" I asked, panting heavily. I glanced over at Eset who was running behind Lightning. It also seemed like this was a breeze for her as well.

"Why aren't you two dying like the rest of us?" I accused, trying to ignore the burning in my legs. Anubys gave me a crooked smile.

"Whatever do you mean, Miss Barbecue?" he asked. I rolled my eyes, again.

"This was part of your training when you were young, wasn't it?" I muttered under my breath. His eyes hardened for a moment, at me mentioning him working with President Eclipse, but the anger left as quick as it had come.

"Perhaps," he merely said. An honest enough answer from him. But, he knew I wouldn't speak of his secret. Not as long as he knew mine.

"Didn't sleep well, huh?" he asked, as he ran backwards, slightly ahead of me. His eyes glanced down and then met my eyes once again. I blushed as I realized he was noticing my dark circles.

"It's whatever," I muttered.

"Another nightmare about your mom?" he asked. I didn't know if he was actually concerned or if he was fishing for some kind of information.

"Are you still working for President Eclipse?" I asked. "Are you planning on taking this Rebellion camp down?" His light green eyes roved over me, his face hardening as he contemplated his answer.

"No," he said, almost exasperated. "We escaped President Eclipse." He turned around as he said this, running faster with ease as he left me in the dust. I watched as he ran past Ash, who was heaving worse than I was, and settled in the middle of the group. Not too fast, but not too slow. And I didn't know whether I believed him. *Beware the shadow-maker*, the voices repeated in my head as I winced. And in order to stop hearing them, I ran a little faster.

I collapsed onto the grass once Lidya let us stop running. Training wasn't over, by far, but I didn't know if I was going to make it through the rest of it. A shadow crossed over me, and I opened my eyes to look at August handing me a bottle of water. I grabbed it and downed it in a second, some of it spilling out the sides of my mouth.

"It's nice to see you, Zinnia," he said, his voice a little deeper than it had been before.

"Everyone forgot about you," I said, putting down the empty bottle and getting right into it. "*Everyone* did, and I wasn't sure how."

"Yeah," he sighed as he sat down on the ground next to me, causing my body to involuntarily relax as he did. An effect from his powers, I knew that now. "The Test does that. If you fail the Test, everyone forgets who you were. It's easier to not ask questions that way, I guess."

"What about your makers?"

"Probably easier on the Nation if they don't have grieving makers rising up to try and overthrow the govern-ment," August muttered. His eyes shone on his face, like two sapphires. He stared at me, like he couldn't believe I was sitting right next to him and at any moment I was going to be ripped away from this world.

"I thought you would die, honestly," he said. I tightened my lips into a line at his words. I wasn't sure how to respond. He noticed my facial expression and back tracked quickly.

"Not that I think you're weak or anything. I just didn't think you'd be able to complete the Test. I thought you wouldn't be able to do it," he said. "And then, if you did fail, I wasn't sure if you would be able to escape." I frowned at his words.

"Do what?" I asked. He stared at me, realization clouding his face. The high points of his cheeks started to flush, and he ducked his head.

"Never mind," he said. "It's better if you don't remember." Before I could ask him another question, he quickly got up and walked back over to Lidya who was barking orders at us.

"We're doing a hundred push ups, right now. I want your back as straight as a board," she ordered as she started to walk around us. She hit Volplie's back with a stick as Volplie hissed at her.

"Straight. As. A. Board," Lidya repeated, meeting Volplie's eyes. Volplie glared up at her for a moment more and then dropped her gaze, straightening her back in the process. Lidya clapped her hands as she counted.

"Okay! Let's go!" she shouted. "One!" My arms screamed in protest as she had us drop and rise in unison. A part of me wished I died during the Test, like August assumed I would.

"Slow down, you'll choke," Anubys said as he dropped his platter of food onto the table I was sitting at. I was alone as I tried to inhale the food in front of me. Jangmi and Agwe wanted me to sit with all of them, even Lightning had the offer in his eyes, but I wanted to be alone. I wanted to remember what August thought I had forgotten. Obviously, Anubys didn't get the message.

"I want to be alone," I muttered, my mouth full. Anubys stared at my mouth in disgust as he settled next to me.

"Yeah, I can see that," he said. *So, he did know*. I rolled my eyes. In shock, I watched as he started to eat his food with a grace I would never be able to muster in my whole lifetime. Anubys saw me gaping at the delicate way that he was eating, and I swear he blushed slightly.

"Eating with President Eclipse's inner circle makes you like this," he said, as he continued to eat.

"I didn't ask," I retorted as I pursed my lips and then continued to eat my own food. We were sitting in a cafeteria of sorts. And the other members of the Rebellion camp were eating around us, but avoided the table that held our group and the table that Anubys and I sat at. Most people took to glaring at us as they walked by, caution lingering in their eyes.

"They don't like that we were let go," Anubys said, noticing where my gaze was falling. I looked back at my food, not responding to him. I wasn't sure why he was next to me anyways. Why he never left me alone.

"What's plaguing your mind?" he asked. "Besides the nightmares." His smile unnerved me as I studied him. Even though I didn't trust him, necessarily, he always seemed to at least partially tell me the truth. I chewed on my cheek.

"Do you remember what happened in the Test?" I asked. Anubys's smirk slowly disappeared from his face. He narrowed his eyes at me.

"Why are you asking?" he said.

"I—" I tried to figure out how I wanted to word it. "August said he was surprised I was able to complete the Test. He thought I wouldn't be able to do it. That I would've died."

"Some people don't remember the Test," Anubys said, turning back to his food. "Humans almost never remember, if they pass. But, some of the Evolved do. I think it depends on what exactly happened and how much of that liquid they put into you."

"I remember a little bit of it. It was like the recurring nightmare I used to have, where I would just set the town on fire and not be able to stop it," I whispered. Anubys didn't seem shocked as I relayed this information.

"That's not what the Test is," he said. I blinked, my food forgotten as I stared at him.

"What do you mean?" I asked, my voice small. There was a part of me that whispered I didn't want to know. To get up from this table and never speak about this again. But, my body didn't move.

"The Test is where you're forced to kill your friend," he said, nonchalantly. "Like Ash said, it's a test of loyalty." I felt my heart drop to my stomach as I stared at him.

"Forced to kill your friend?" I repeated, my mouth going dry. This is what August didn't want me to know. If I wasn't dead, then I must've...

"Yeah, people can fail the Test one of two ways," he put up one finger, "Either they get killed by their friend because they refused to fight, which makes you either weak or disloyal to her, both she doesn't want." He put up another finger, "Or, you refuse to kill your friend and instead use your power to get out of the Test. Although, even using your power, it can accidentally kill your friend anyways. It's the refusal part that President Eclipse fails you for, not for using your power." I stared at him as he looked generally unfazed about the whole situation.

"So, August thought I would refuse and not use my power," I said. Anubys shrugged.

"That can happen sometimes as well, if one doesn't know how to use it," he said. He looked me up and down, and then gave me a lazy smile, "But, you're hellfire. He should know better. Once you're in danger, it's just going to burst out of you, no matter what you do." My nose wrinkled at his comment.

"How do you pass?" I asked. Anubys gave me a curious look.

"The Test? It's easy. If you decide to kill your friend, you pass," Anubys shrugged.

"You don't... *actually* have to kill your friend?" I asked. Anubys smirked.

"While President Eclipse might hate humans, she doesn't want the population to dwindle *that* much. If you make the move to kill your friend, and they do as well, then you both pass. No one dies. But, if the other person doesn't want to kill you, then she does let you kill them, since they failed," Anubys explained easily. "Most of the humans are easily brainwashed though, so most survive the Test."

"Thanks," I muttered after a long while, staring into my food. I wasn't hungry anymore, and I pushed it away.

Forest's face flickered into my mind, causing my stomach to turn.

"For what?" he asked, as he put a forkful of meat into his mouth. He chewed on it slowly, that forever smirk imprinted on his lips.

"For telling me the truth," I said, honestly, as I got up from the table and stalked back towards my cabin.

CHAPTER FOURTEEN

I couldn't stop thinking about what Anubys said to me in the cafeteria as I picked at the grass that lay beneath my legs. Staring at the mountainous terrain that rose like walls around the little colony that was here, Forest's face from my dreams flashed in my head. *Save us*, his voice echoed around me. *Save us, Zinnia.*

Closing my eyes, I shook my head slightly, trying to get the thought of him out of my mind. But no matter what I did, he still stood there, holding his chest as blood spilled out of him. *Did I kill him?* Did I kill him like I killed Rohit? I barely noticed the sound of someone settling into the grass next to me and jumped as a hand barely tapped my shoulder.

"Sorry," Lightning said, as I looked up at him, terror clouding my eyes. He frowned as his dark eyes analyzed my facial expression.

"Every time I see you I feel like you have fear clutching your heart," he muttered as he leaned forward. He didn't look at me as he said this, so I settled my gaze onto the Rebellion camp, watching as others went about their duties.

"You always catch me at a bad moment," I muttered. But, the fear had dissipated. Even though Lightning wasn't one of Aphrodite's children, his presence for me had always been calming, since that day on the hover train. His dark eyes glanced my way.

"Do you want to talk about it?" he asked. I shook my head as I sighed. I knew he noticed the dark circles under my eyes, his own eyes had wandered there a second earlier, but he didn't mention them. If he knew of my nightmares, he knew not to ask about it.

"I don't," I answered, after a while. I continued to pick at the grass, thinking. I didn't know why I talked so freely with Anubys when I knew I didn't trust him, but didn't with Lightning. Especially since my whole body was always at ease next to him.

"Maybe you shouldn't hang out with Anubys by your-self," Lightning said, monitoring my reaction. I looked over at him, surprised by the comment.

"Why?" I asked.

"Because every time you talk to him, lately, you seem to retreat further and further into yourself," he pointed out. *Do I?*

"He's honest," I said, truthfully. I caught Lightning's frown and laughed a little to myself. "He's honest, but he's also terrifying."

"He's the scariest person I've ever met," Lightning admitted, as I laughed harder at the comment. I knew Lightning would never admit it to Anubys's face, and I could see his mischievous antics if he ever found out. Lightning's own dark eyes shined with amusement.

As we mentioned Anubys, we watched his sister march across the camp towards the cabin she and I were staying in. Lightning sucked his teeth as he watched Eset walk, fire in every step.

"No, scratch that. Somehow, *she's* the scariest person I've ever met," he said. I nodded quickly in agreement. Eset was probably the most bone-chilling person I've come across, despite her power being a warped version of the gift of life. Lightning started to get up, brushing the grass off of his silver pants.

"We probably should start making our way back down to the field," Lightning muttered. "Round two of training is starting." I felt my muscles groan in protest as I picked myself up from the ground, the armor weighing me down.

"I wish we could take this off," I said, pulling at my shirt. Lightning shrugged as he started to walk down the hill.

"They don't want us using our powers," he said. He turned to stare at me, for a moment longer, as he contemplated whether he should say his next words or not.

"Out with it," I sighed. The tips of his ears reddened as he looked down at me.

"You know, if you ever want to talk, I'm here for you," he mumbled. I smiled at his words.

"I know," I said, touching his arm. "You're a good friend." And I meant it. He gave me a small smile and nodded in response before turning to walk back down the hill. I followed him as we walked towards the field together.

"This is Devlin," Lidya said once we were all gathered at the training field. Devlin's blue eyes made contact with each one of us, as if he were getting a read on us. His short blonde hair was pushed back out of his face, and he wore the same armor that Lidya was wearing: black skin tight, long-sleeve, silk shirt and dark pants. He was a large man, his muscles bulging through his armored shirt.

"He'll teach you all how to meditate," she said. My eyebrows raised at the words. *Meditation?* This large, warrior-looking man was going to teach us how to *meditate* instead of fight?

"I'm a terrible fighter," he muttered, as if he knew what we were all thinking. Lidya smiled at his words as she clapped a hand onto his shoulder. He winced at the impact.

"Devlin here is only good because he can't seem to die," she said. "He regenerates lightning quick. Even so, he is the most unlucky person I've ever met." She smiled up at him as he pursed his lips at her words.

"One time, we were attacked by those stupid Nation goonies, right? And somehow Devlin came up to me without *any* limbs. He was just staring up at me, with those big blue eyes, being like 'Lidya,'" she mimicked his voice and pretended to cry, "'my arms and legs were cut off by some guy and I lost my weapon,'" she started to fake cry louder, "'Do you think Biao will ki-i-ill me?'" Lidya roared with laughter, doubling over, as Devlin's frown became deeper.

"It was the funniest moment of my life," Lidya sighed, wiping away a tear.

"Yeah, anyways," Devlin said, stepping slightly forwards as he side-eyed Lidya, "meditation has helped me be a better fighter." She nodded her head, trying to keep a straight face as the hair gathered into a puff on the top of her head bobbed along with the motion. She crossed her arms over her chest.

"So, you lot better listen to Devlin or I will punish you accordingly," she said, glaring each of us down, the earlier amusement gone. I tried to not swallow in fear. None of us questioned her as she walked off the field to go do whatever was more important than meditation. As she reached the edge of the field, she burst out into more loud laughter. Devlin sighed loudly.

"Please, sit onto the grass," Devlin said, gesturing towards the ground once Lidya was out of sight. We all slowly got down onto the ground, some of us groaning in the process. None of us were used to this much physical activity, except for the demon twins maybe. I was getting used to the weight of the armor, slowly, but my muscles still screamed out in protest. I didn't know how I was going to be able to move tomorrow.

"Now, meditation is really important when it comes to fighting. A lot of us get into our heads when we're faced with a life or death situation. And when fear comes up, our powers get out of control," he said, looking at us as he took in a deep breath. We all followed his actions. He breathed out, and we did too.

"Is that how you lost all of your limbs?" Anubys said, swallowing a snicker as he looked up at Devlin seriously. Devlin closed his eyes as he put up a hand.

"Please," he said. "Concentrate." He took another deep breath as I quickly glared over at Anubys. He just gave me an innocent look.

"Some of us, while fighting, might get put into a rage

and that's not good either. A rage will lead to more killing, unnecessary ones, and can cause a strain on one's mental health," he said. "So, learning how to meditate will balance your mind so your powers do not go out of your control, fear will not control you, and it will help you keep your head." *Fear would not control me.* I was sick of feeling afraid all the time. I didn't want to continue to have nightmares. And if learning how to meditate was going to fix that, then I was about to be the calmest person in this camp.

"Close your eyes," Devlin ordered. I closed them and faced the darkness of my mind. Forest's face reappeared in the forefront of it, and I felt my heart beat faster and faster, fear overtaking me.

"Clear all thoughts," Devlin said, his voice piercing Forest's face and causing him to turn into smoke. *Clear all my thoughts?* I thought to myself. *How am I supposed to do that?*

"If you can't clear your thoughts, imagine yourself in a place where you have felt very peaceful. Think about this place, think about all the details that make this place memorable. Make it real inside of your head," he said, his voice being softly carried on the spring breeze. My bedroom back at Adams came to the forefront of my mind.

The memory of how I would always look out the window as the acid rain fell, the ever-present hologram gone due to it, materialized. I thought about the sound of the rain hitting the window, sizzling as it touched the cool glass. I felt myself touch the window, wanting to feel what it would feel like if the acid were to touch me. If it would be like the fire that was in my nightmares, the fire that was coursing through my veins. Then, the image shifted suddenly. My mother's eyes rolled to the back of her head, dried blood on her face as she turned towards me.

"*Born from the mind of one who knew all. Born from the hands that could create dreams. She came upon a crossroads of shadows,*" she repeated. The word 'shadows' echoed all around me as I frantically scrambled towards my mother.

"*Be careful, Zinnia,*" she whispered, her voice sounding like it was almost on the verge of tears.

"*Be careful and trust no one,*" she warned as I reached for her. Just as my hands touched the arm of my mother, she turned into air, and I could feel someone shaking me.

"Zinnia?" a voice called out to me, but all I could see was darkness as I kept trying to find my mother.

"Mom?" I called out into the darkness. "Mom?" But, I couldn't see in front of me. All I could see was inky blackness as I desperately tried to search for her. My body screamed at me that she was in trouble. An image of my mother's dead body flashed through my mind. *You'll kill us all,* the voices around me whispered. *Save us.*

"Zinnia!" the voice cried out, bringing my mind back into the present as I opened my eyes. I stared up into light green eyes, the color of jade. The blue sky was behind him, setting him in an almost soft glow.

"Anubys?" I asked as he breathed out a sigh of relief.

"You got trapped in a dream," he snapped as I sat up, holding my head. Why did it seem like he was mad at me?

"What do you mean?" I asked, using the same tone he used on me. Devlin was standing next to Anubys who was sitting on the grass, one knee raised like he was about to get up. Devlin stared at me, his blue eyes assessing me for something.

"How did you know she got trapped in a dream?" Devlin asked, making eye contact with me, though he was asking Anubys. Anubys looked up at him and then rolled his eyes.

"I've seen it before," he muttered. Devlin didn't move his gaze from me as he breathed in sharply.

"You need to see Tayen," he said. Then he looked over at Anubys, adding, "Both of you."

Tayen closed her eyes, the veins on her bronze skin visibly raised on her eyelids. She felt around my scalp as she thought. I stood as still as possible, not daring to move a muscle.

Anubys was outside of the room, waiting for his turn as Tayen dealt with me first. He didn't say anything to me as we walked towards Tayen's cabin, which was abnormal of him. He seemed to always be talking my ear off. I wondered if he would tell the truth to Tayen. As I stared at her with her eyes closed, I wondered if it were even possible to lie to her. She opened her brown eyes, staring at me thoughtfully.

"What is it?" I asked.

"You were sent a dream, last minute," Tayen said as she walked back to sit at her desk. Piles of papers sat in the corner of her mahogany desk and a cup of pens were on the other side. It was neat and orderly. She sat back in her chair as she faced me, her eyebrows furrowed in thought.

"I was sent a dream?" I asked. Tayen nodded as her eyes glazed over.

"It was rushed, not well thought out. There are some parts of the dream that are... traumatic, due to what was going on," she said. "The whole warning might not be there as well." *She saw my dream.*

"Who sent it to me?" I asked, leaning forward. "I've been dreaming of it for a few days now. What does it mean?"

"Your mother was a dreamer," Tayen said. "It was her power, but not her only one it seems." My heart stopped as I stared at Tayen. Pieces of her gray hair had fallen out of her braid and were resting on her forehead.

"My mom had powers?" I asked, softly.

"A dreamer and a creator," she said. "An inventor. That's what she's talking about in the beginning, I believe. Born from the mind of one who knew all. Born from the hands that could create dreams. She's talking about herself." I winced as I heard the phrases I had heard in my nightmares.

"I didn't know she had any powers," I whispered.

"My guess is your father does, as well. But," Tayen pursed her lips as she thought, "I don't think your mother wanted you knowing." *Wanted.* I felt a chill run down my spine as I started to realize Tayen was talking about my mom in the past tense.

"You said parts of the dream are traumatic because of what was going on when she was sending it to me," I said. Tayen's eyes focused on me, the glaze over her eyes disappearing. She twisted her lips, trying to keep them from pitying me.

"The blood from her eyes..." I said, slowly. The realization came like a slow moving fog. It wasn't until it enveloped me entirely did I realize.

"My mom is dead?" I asked, my voice thick with the tears that were collecting in my throat. I tried to swallow the lump, but my mouth had gone dry.

"I would ask your cousin," Tayen said, "about the stories of your mother." And with a wave of her hand, I was dismissed. She didn't want me to ask anymore questions, not wanting to answer them herself. But, I knew she knew more.

"What happened to my mom?" I asked, before leaving the room. "How did she die?" Tayen looked up at me, pity clouding her eyes which made the pit of my stomach twist in fury.

"By the hands of President Eclipse," Tayen said, with a voice that knew of death, a voice that had lived with loss and grief for most of her life.

I felt the fire that coursed through my blood trying to find some way to escape, to turn me into a living flame. But, the spelled armor wouldn't let it out, making it just churn through my system, over and over. I felt myself start to sweat as I pivoted quickly and walked out of the cabin. It was so hot, so blindingly hot. I squinted as I walked outside, the sun hitting my face. Anubys's hypnotizing eyes stared at me, studying me as the sweat rolled down the sides of my face. I wiped my mouth and my nose as it started to pool around it.

"You're about to explode," Anubys said as he studied me. Tears welled up in my eyes, boiling hot tears, as they spilled over, burning my skin. His face twisted into concern, an expression I hadn't ever seen on his light golden-brown face.

"The armor is keeping the power inside, but I think it's going to make you sick," Anubys whispered as he took a small step forward. His facial expression was enough to have me screaming. The boy who could make anyone drop dead with just one look was afraid of *me*.

"You think I don't know that?" I snapped. Anubys's eyebrows raised, but his lips curled into a small smirk, as if he were amused.

"Don't worry, little Pyromaniac." Before I could snap at him to not call me that, he put a cool hand on my forehead. He brushed it down my face and then took both of his hands and grazed them down my arms, cooling the skin as he did. The fire in my lungs and veins started to settle, until I could breathe normally again. I wiped the remaining sweat off of my forehead as I stared at him in wonder.

"How did you do that?" I asked. He flashed me a crooked smile as he leaned against the cabin door, waiting before he went to see Tayen.

"The shadow of death can put out any light," he said, winking at me as he walked into Tayen's cabin. I stared at his lean back, watching as the door closed behind him. I turned back around, remembering the feeling of Anubys's hands running down the sides of my arms. It was as if the heat was being sucked into him, cooling me down. Death was like a black hole. Nothing living could remain. And, my mother was lost into that vortex, forever.

CHAPTER FIFTEEN

When Anubys emerged from Tayen's cabin, his normally bright green eyes looked cloudy. I pushed myself off of the cabin wall and hurried after him as he strode past me.

"I was waiting for you because I have a question," I explained, as I got within hearing distance from him. For some reason, I felt embarrassed that I was waiting for him. But, Anubys didn't turn to look at me, his wavy black hair slightly being messed up from the wind.

"I don't really want to answer any more questions, Zinnia," he muttered, his voice like ice. His tone froze me to the ground, and he continued to walk to his cabin without one look back at me. I heard Lidya's laughter from next to me as she walked by, lightly kicking Devlin's thigh as they walked.

"I told you those kids would've thought you were a fighter not a lover," she laughed.

"They just looked *so* disappointed," Devlin groaned.

Lidya's light laughter burst out of her again as they continued past me.

"I can probably answer it for you," a voice said next to me, startling me out of my frozen state. "Your question." I looked over at Eset who was still staring at her twin's shrinking back, Lidya and Devlin slightly covering the sight.

She turned a bit to look at me as I gaped at her unearthly beauty. I never knew if I envied her beauty or wished to covet it. Her eyebrows scrunched together slightly at my gaze, and I coughed as I tried to bring myself back to reality.

"Do you know much about Anubys's powers?" I asked, my voice small in the presence of her. She smiled slightly, her green eyes that resembled Anubys's darted over to him as the sound of his cabin door slamming made its way back to us.

"I know everything about him," she said, "Especially when it comes to his powers." Her eyes rested back onto me, and I had to keep myself from shuddering.

"Earlier, he told me I was going to explode, after leaving Tayen's cabin. My power was trying to come out, but it couldn't because of the armor. He touched me and was able to... kind of... get rid of it," I explained. Her eyebrow raised as she listened to my rambling.

"You want to know how he was able to do it if he's wearing the same armor as you," she guessed. I nodded my head, watching as some people walked by us. Eset waited until they were out of earshot to continue.

"Anubys's power is too great to be completely contained by this armor," she said. "He is not a normal Evolved. *We* aren't normal." *We.*

"My power wasn't able to get out," I muttered, wanting

to separate myself from those two. She smirked, almost looking like a mirror of Anubys.

"If you gave it time, it would've," she stated, looking back at Anubys's cabin. "He knew it and didn't want to risk the damage." She rolled her head back over to me, meeting my eyes as her hair fell to the side. Her gaze unnerved me, as if she were studying every bit of my soul.

"Don't think he did it because he cared about you though," she said, causing my heart to stop. "Anubys can't care about anyone."

I couldn't stop the words from tumbling out of my mouth: "What do you mean?" She shrugged as she stood up straight, starting to walk away from me.

"He's unable to. Neither of us are," she merely said, the words barely reaching my ears. Once again, I found myself unable to move as I stared at the cabin Anubys disappeared into. I wondered what was discussed between Tayen and him. And a part of me couldn't help but wonder if what Eset said about him was true.

I sat on the couch in Tayen's office, exhausted and covered in sweat. Training was the same as it was yesterday and the day before that. Just strength building, but no combat yet. I was starting to get used to the weight of the silver armor they made us wear, but my budding muscles still screamed out in protest at every exercise.

Tayen strode into her office, followed by Biao and a girl I recognized but didn't know the name of. Her black hair was cut short to her high cheekbones, making her face look even more angular. Her black eyes studied me as she walked into the room.

"This is Mikazuki," Tayen said as Mikazuki stood in front of me. She kneeled down as she studied my face. I shifted uncomfortably in her gaze as Biao closed the door behind him.

"She's also a dreamer, like your mother," Tayen explained as she circled over to her desk. She sat down in her chair and leaned forward onto the mahogany surface, her hands clasped together.

"Mikazuki is someone I'd trust with my life," Biao said, crossing his arms across his muscular chest, "She and I escaped death together. She saved my life more than once." Mikazuki rolled her eyes at Biao's words as she sat down on the couch next to me.

"He's exaggerating," she said, waving his words away. She stared at me intensely and then gestured for my hands. I hesitantly put them into hers, and she quickly grasped them, closing her eyes.

"Why are we doing this?" I asked, looking over at Tayen as I found myself getting sleepy.

"We need to piece together your mother's warning," Tayen explained as I started to feel myself drift away. "We need the information that will..." Her words became garbled as I fell into blackness.

All I could see was my mother coming and then disappearing. At one point, she had blood dripping from her eyes. At another, inky blackness filled them where eyes once were. She was smiling in one flash and crying in another, tears of blood. Beheaded, and then suddenly, as large as a giant with arms wrapped around me, too tight. And in every single version of her that Mikazuki replayed over and over again in my mind, she spoke the same words: *Let me tell you a story... Came upon a crossroads of... Beware... Trust no one... Pray to... Beware... Beware... Beware.*

By the time Mikazuki let the dream fade away, I was covered in sweat. Opening my eyes, I felt my hands trembling as I tried to sit back up. Biao's strong hands gripped my forearm as he helped me steady myself.

"I can't make any real sense of it," Mikazuki said, sweat glistening on her own olive-toned skin. She looked just as shaken as I felt. "It's a warning, a deliberate one, but there isn't any real substance to it."

"I know," Tayen said, her head in her hands. Her neat braid looked slightly undone, as if she were also affected from seeing my dream replay over and over again in my mind. Perhaps she *had* seen it, somehow. I didn't know what kind of powers Tayen accumulated over the years as a siphon.

"I had hoped you would be able to sense if there was anything more behind the dream, any fragments missing," Tayen explained, standing back up. I wiped the sweat off of my forehead and the tears off of my cheeks as Mikazuki shook her head, her black hair flying out of her much like how a helicopter seed falls to the ground.

"The message is purposely vague. She might've thought President Eclipse would get to her and wanted to make sure another dreamer wouldn't be able to piece together what she was trying to say," Mikazuki said.

"Why would she think President Eclipse would want to know this message?" I asked, turning towards her. Her dark eyes stared blankly at me, but her eyebrows scrunched together as if she were confused.

"Your father can tell the future," she said, plainly, but her voice almost lilted like she had asked a question.

"My father?" I choked. Mikazuki blinked.

"He would be called a fortune teller by those who have abilities from my community, but in others, he's called an oracle or a seer," Mikazuki explained.

"There hasn't been one in many years. They're very rare," Tayen whispered, and then repeated the words that my mother had said in my dream, "Born from the mind of one who knew all... I thought she was referring to herself. She had the gift of inventing as well as dreaming."

"No," Mikazuki said, shaking her head, "No, I felt the imprint of the father behind those particular words. She meant him." *My father... could tell the future?* I thought back to everything I knew about him.

He was a gentle man, a quiet one. He never really talked out of place, and I never knew if he really loved my mother or not. But, there was never any indication that he was able to tell the future. He didn't know what would happen to me, he even said so right before I took the Test. Then, my eyes widened as I remembered his words. *"I know you'll fail the Test... But Zinnia, if I know you, you'll still get through it all."*

"My father could tell the future..." I muttered, almost under my breath. "And those words are my mom warning me of it."

"She's conveying what *might* happen in the future," Tayen nodded as she glanced over at Biao. He crossed his arms.

"What's mentioned in this dream regarding our situation?" Biao asked, turning his attention towards Mikazuki.

"In regards to us, her mother says, 'Beware the shadow maker. Beware the silver-tongue,'" Mikazuki repeated. Biao put a tongue into his cheek as he exchanged a look with Tayen.

"The shadow maker has to be that little sh—" Mikazuki gave Biao a look as she darted her eyes at me and then meaningfully stared at him. He coughed a little. "I mean, that kid Anubys."

"I know cuss words, for the record," I muttered. "I'm sixteen. Not eight."

"Still," Mikazuki responded. "It's not good manners. *Is* it, Biao?" He shrugged in response.

"The silver-tongue... Well, there are many of Aphrodite's children that exist. She could mean any one of them," Tayen said, directing the conversation back to my dream. Biao made a noise of agreement as Mikazuki shook her head.

"It would have to be in relation to her. And, fortunately or unfortunately, we *do* have a silver-tongue here. And he is a party of one at this camp," she said, giving Tayen a look that she was purposefully ignoring.

"I know you have a soft spot for August, Tayen," Mikazuki continued, getting up from the couch, "But, we *have* to watch him just as much as we watch the other boy. He's involved in her future, somehow. Involved in the vision the Fortune Teller once—" Tayen shook her head, vehemently disagreeing.

"The Oracle foretold that vision long ago. It could've changed by now. And we trained August. He's on our side. The boy—"

"We should talk, *privately*," Biao said, his eyes cutting towards me. I took that as my cue to leave.

"I'll get going," I said as I got up from the couch. Before I walked out of Tayen's office, I caught a bit of what the three were whispering about.

"His mind... a wall... He was an executor... His sister and him..." And then I shut the door behind me.

CHAPTER SIXTEEN

"Today we're going to start doing a little bit of hand to hand combat," Lidya announced once everyone gathered on the training field. August looked up from the clipboard he'd been writing in during training sessions every day for the past couple of weeks, meeting my eyes. My own quickly studied the ground to avoid those sapphire eyes that seemed to glow on his sun-kissed face.

For the past couple of weeks, I barely had time to think or feel anything about my mother's death. The nightmares had even disappeared due to the constant training and the muscle fatigue. A couple of weeks wasn't nearly long enough for us to gain enough muscle to be warriors, but a part of me knew we had to be combat ready sooner rather than later.

"Devlin and I will demonstrate the moves for you all, and you will follow along with your partner," Lidya said, breaking my thoughts. She stared at us expectantly, as we all stared back at her with blank faces. Lidya sighed and then gestured towards us.

"Find a partner," she ordered, exasperatedly. I turned to see if Jangmi wanted to be partners, but she had already picked her match in Agwe. They had become increasingly close the past few days, so it didn't really surprise me. I looked over at Lightning, hoping we could be partners, but Volplie walked up to him instead.

"Fight to the death?" she asked him. His eyebrows raised at her. Afterwards, he shrugged, as if used to Volplie's antics. I bit my tongue as I looked around for someone, memories of being left out in Preparation started to flood my mind.

My eyes met Anubys's, but I looked away swiftly. For one, I was avoiding him. If my father sent me a hint about my future through my mother before her untimely death, then I was going to heed it. There were two paths I could take in the sent dream. Anubys or August. There wasn't another path. And I wasn't about to trust the person that even Tayen couldn't fully see the mind of.

Turning away from Anubys left me without any partner as Ash was feeling under the weather today. August's gaze met mine, and without a word, he set the clipboard down on the ground and walked over to me. His black, silk-looking armor moving with him.

"Do you want to do the combat moves with me?" he asked, softly. A feeling of relief washed over, and I had to remind myself that it was just how August made everyone feel, due to what he was.

"Sure," I said. Lidya's eyebrow was raised as she looked

over at us for a moment, and then she turned back towards Devlin to show us a series of moves.

"Now you do it, over and over, as Devlin and I will check your form," Lidya said. "Once everyone has this down, we'll move onto the next move." I copied the moves that Lidya and Devlin did, trying to block August's slow-moving punches. I felt like a baby horse just beginning to walk. August laughed a little, his laugh reaching the darkest pieces of my soul and lighting them up. *His nose scrunches when he laughs*, I couldn't help but notice.

"No, here," August said, finishing off his laughter. He came behind me as he moved my arms into position. "You have to do it like this." He straightened my arms and pushed them forward, in the blocking motion. I felt heat start to rise into my cheeks and jumped away from him. If he noticed, he didn't seem bothered by it.

"You have to put more power into it," August explained. His blue eyes twinkled, but in a different way than Anubys's always seemed to.

"Let's try it again," he said.

I sank into the bench seat in the cafeteria next to Jangmi, Anubys taking up the seat across from me. The past couple of weeks, he seemed to respect the fact that I was avoiding him, as he was clearly also avoiding me, but I guess that was done now. My eyebrows scrunched together as he met my eyes, but he didn't seem to register my confusion.

"Hey Ash, where were you this morning?" Anubys asked as Ash, almost gray, sat down next to him with a large bowl of soup. The steam rose up and enveloped his face, making it look even more ashen.

"I'm sick," Ash said, his nose obviously stuffed.

"Didn't you hear him throwing up this morning?" Agwe asked, taking the seat next to Jangmi. Her eyes sparkled up at him as he did.

"I *heard*, but I didn't know that was an excuse for missing training. We started combat," Anubys said, taking a large bite of his food. He seemed to have lost the grace he had when he first came here, adopting the way the other boys seemed to eat, pretty quickly. Like a chameleon, I couldn't help but think.

"Don't be a dick, Anubys," Lightning said, taking the seat next to me. Anubys rolled his eyes as he chewed.

"I'm just saying. Inferno, here, had to practice with," he made a face, "*August.*" I scrunched my nose up at his nickname for me.

"She seemed to enjoy herself," Eset piped up, sitting on the other side of Anubys. I watched as Anubys seemed to stiffen as he looked up at me, his eyes unreadable.

"I don't know what you're talking about," I muttered, feeling the heat rise to my face once again.

"You had a crush on him back in your community, I'm sure," Eset responded, a small smile on her face. A growing homicidal urge rose within me, as I gripped my fork. I imagined stabbing her in the face with it.

"He *is* pretty handsome," Jangmi mused as Agwe shot a glance at her.

"I didn't have a crush on him," I lied. *Everyone* had a crush on August back in the Adams Community. And now that I knew what his power was, how could they not?

"You seemed pretty adept with combat," I accused, trying to get the attention off of me. The smile was wiped from her face.

"Everyone already knows where Anubys and I trained. We escaped," she said, repeating the falsity to anyone who would listen. The rumors spread fast after Tayen peeked inside of Anubys's mind. She didn't see a lot, but she saw enough. Enough to know that Anubys and Eset worked with President Eclipse since they were young.

"I thought you failed the Test," Lightning pointed out. Eset shrugged.

"We did fail it *and* we escaped," she said, not missing a beat.

"I'm sure," Lightning said, slightly under his breath. Eset glowered at him, the polite composure melting from her face. A second passed between them, Lightning not even realizing that Eset was giving him a death glare. She then got up and stalked away.

"Eset," Anubys whined after her. "He's probably just joking. *Eset!*" He then turned towards Lightning. "You're just joking, right?" Lightning looked shocked as Eset walked away. She slammed the cafeteria door as Lightning sighed and slowly pushed himself up from the table.

"I'll go talk to her," he muttered.

"It might not be a good idea to do that when she's like... Never mind," Anubys said as Lightning stalked out of the cafeteria after her. He sighed and ate another spoonful of food. Ash coughed into his arm as we all made a face at him.

"Why are you here?" Volplie asked, seemingly out of nowhere. I whipped my head around to look at her. I didn't even hear her walk up to the table. "Aren't you sick?" Ash gave her a pitiful look.

"I still need to eat," he whined. She rolled her eyes at him.

"Why was she so upset?" I asked, referring to Eset. Anubys glanced up at me. "I mean, it *is* true. You guys *did* work for President Eclipse, and no one knows if we can really trust..." I let my words drift off as Anubys's gaze hardened. Even if everyone now knew his secret, he could spill mine at any second. I immediately shut up.

"*Well*, Flamethrower," Anubys said, swallowing his food, "She's upset for precisely the reason you stated. People can't trust us because we were kidnapped by President Eclipse as children. We were raised by her. You don't think we hated what she did to us? And now, we have to live with everyone thinking we're here just to do her bidding?" I bit my lip from asking the obvious question: *Aren't you?* He seemed to recognize the question that was written all over my face as he gripped the sides of his tray.

"We're not," he answered. And then he got up and left as well.

"Now I see why he's been avoiding you," Jangmi muttered. I stared at her in disbelief.

"*You* trust him?" I asked. Jangmi shrugged.

"He could've killed us. He still could. He hasn't yet, so innocent until proven guilty," she declared. Agwe made a face, indicating he didn't necessarily believe her either. She caught the gaze and frowned slightly.

"We can't judge him for who raised him. It's not his fault he and his sister have highly desired powers. And considering their names, they weren't able to hide it when they were born. Word of a power like that, most definitely caught the president's eye," Jangmi explained. "They could've changed. No one is like those who raised them, really." Volplie stole a potato wedge from my tray and ate it quickly as I glared at her.

"If they truly *did* escape President Eclipse's manipulation," Volplie said, as she chewed on the stolen wedge, "then they are stronger people than I would give them credit for. The trauma that's inflicted on President Eclipse's inner circle... It's hard to recover and be your own person after that."

"You speak like you know from experience," Ash pointed out. Volplie shrugged.

"I was given my own traumas by the snake. Being an orphan in the Capital would do that to you," she merely said. I didn't know what to say about how Volplie grew up, and it seemed Ash didn't know either as he turned his almost-dead face towards me.

"You've met with Tayen a few times since getting here. What's that all about?" he asked, changing the subject. Volplie placed her unnerving purple-blue gaze on me, her iris somehow taking up her whole eye, even with the power-suppressing armor on. I suddenly turned towards Jangmi as I remembered what Tayen told me.

"Jangmi, you know the stories about my mother?" I asked. Jangmi nodded, slowly, shocked by my sudden outburst.

"I was sent a dream by her," I said. Her eyes widened as she gestured for me to go on.

"I want to know everything you know about her," I finished. She chewed on her lip and then nodded.

"It's time you knew more about Nabi ee-mo," she said.

Jangmi sat down on her bed, ducking her head as I leaned against the ladder that led up to mine. She stared up at me, her dark brown eyes studying my expression.

"What do you know about your mom?" she asked. I thought to myself as I tried to remember everything I knew about her. However, I couldn't help but wonder if everything I was told was just a lie.

"My mom... she was punished for reading books in the Library. My father would bring it up a lot. She read books, and she figured out information about the Nation. As punishment, she had to marry my father and was sent to a different community. My father did something as well, but I'm not exactly sure what it was. All I know was he might've been in love and that wasn't allowed," I said. Jangmi nodded along with my words. Love marriages were forbidden in the Nation. It made way for the opportunity for 'stupid' children to be born. Marriage was used to create an optimal child. So they said, anyway.

"Your mom wasn't punished for reading books in the Library. I think that might've been some kind of code between your parents as... she did *kind of* read, in a way. It is true she did figure out what was going on with the Nation. Your mother was someone who was gifted with two powers, which isn't normal. She could create a device out of pretty much anything," Jangmi explained. I remembered the many knobs that were in our house, made so the Nation couldn't overhear any conversations. I never knew how they worked, and now I guess I knew why.

"She also could create dreams and send them to people, even while they were awake. Kind of like... illusions, I suppose. She could trap you in a dream, and you wouldn't be able to leave it until she dictated. Like how Lidya can trap us in our own bodies," Jangmi said. She paused, seemingly for dramatic effect. "Your mom, Nabi ee-mo, she not only could *send* dreams, but she could watch yours as well. Many people's dreams are just them replaying memories of things that happened throughout the day. Sometimes, it's embellished. Sometimes, it's your greatest hope or your worst nightmare. But, she could step into them. Your mom, she read President Eclipse's dreams. And she found out *everything*." My breath froze in my lungs as I stared at Jangmi, waiting for her to go on. But, she didn't.

"What did she find out?" I whispered. Jangmi shrugged.

"I don't know everything. But, from the stories, she said the folk tales we were told as children were true. That President Eclipse was doing something sinister and using people like us to do it. It was all she could tell our halmoni before she was taken away," Jangmi said, using the old Korean word for 'grandmother.'

"Do you know anything else she might've found?" I asked. Jangmi twisted her lips.

"She used to send dreams to our grandmother, jumbled though because she didn't want President Eclipse to ever suspect she was feeding us information. Winter, your dad, he was in President Eclipse's inner circle before he was punished. He fell in love with a human experiment. Protected her. It cost the human her life. And he was sent away, though President Eclipse forces him to tell her the future every once in a while."

"A human experiment?" I asked. Jangmi shook her head as she closed her eyes.

"We don't know. We never figured out what they were experimenting for. After the last one, one after you were born, she didn't send another one for a long time. Not until a few months before this year's Test," she said, meeting my eyes before averting them, as if she had said too much.

"What did she say in the last dream? The one after I was born?" I asked, my mouth going dry. I convinced myself I needed to know. But, a part of me told me to stop prying.

"I can't," she muttered.

"Tell me," I pressed, grabbing her shoulders in order to make her look into my eyes. Her dark brown eyes looked conflicted as she glanced up at me. After a moment, she sighed and stared at her small hands.

"In her dream, all halmoni was able to figure out was your mom said President Eclipse made her... made her and Winter... create a monster. A monster that would destroy everything. She said she saw Winter's vision, the future he saw when... you were born," Jangmi said, quietly. I dropped my hands from her shoulders and backed up, away from her. I looked down at my hands. They were trembling. I put them behind my back, to hide them from Jangmi.

"She said I was a monster?" I finally breathed. Jangmi's eyes looked up at me, concern enveloping her face.

"She didn't know *what* you were. All she knew was President Eclipse knew this would happen—" she stopped talking as she looked at my face.

"Zinnia..." she whispered. I shook my head. My own

mother thought I was a monster. Rohit's charred body and terrified eyes flashed through my mind.

"I have to go," I muttered, pushing my way out of the cabin. She thought I was a monster. And a part of me, the part I had always pushed down deep within myself, knew it to be true.

CHAPTER SEVENTEEN

I hit the wooden sword against Ash's as he stumbled back. I didn't give him a moment to breathe as I swiftly lunged forward to attack him again. He barely blocked it as he fell to the ground.

"Gods, Zinnia," he muttered under his breath as I stopped with the blunt sword pointed towards his face. He wiped the sweat with one hand that was gathering on his freckled forehead as he grabbed my hand with his free one to bring him back onto his feet.

"You've gotten really good at sword fighting," he said. Ash had been my partner during combat training for the past week. While I picked it up quickly, he was slow going. I felt the weight of the wooden sword in my hand as I contemplated the training we had been doing.

"It feels familiar to me," I muttered under my breath. "Like, I've been practicing my whole life." Ash frowned at my words as he got his bearing.

"What do you mean? You've been practicing in your

sleep?" he joked. I shook my head. I couldn't tell him I had been having dreams of fighting with a sword my whole life. I was a hero in those dreams, the dreams that countered against the nightmares of me burning down the whole town square of Adams. But, those dreams were just sent by my mother; I knew it now. The dreams where I burned through every living thing as swiftly as air filling one's lungs were the real me. The dreams that showed I was truly a monster.

I shook my head again, trying to keep the thoughts out as I lowered into a stance, feeling the smooth wood in my hand. The weight was too light, not like the ones I used in my dreams as a kid.

"Let's go again," I said, as Ash blew his orange-red hair out of his eyes.

"I thought I'd find you here," August's low voice commented as I looked up at him through my hands. I was sitting on the top of the hill, far away enough from the camp. It was the best spot to observe everyone going about their day, but it was also a great spot to just mindlessly let yourself drift with the wind.

"What is it?" I heard myself say, the words harsh, but I had already begun to relax as he sat down next to me. A part of me wanted to scream at August for always making me feel at ease around him. But, it was what I needed, a break from the tensed shoulders and locked jaw that I had been sporting for the past week. I just didn't like that it was against my will.

"You're struggling with something," August pointed out.

He brushed his brown hair back, his blue eyes observing the rest of the camp.

"I'm fine," I lied. He sucked on his lips as he thought, suddenly turning towards me. His ocean eyes stilled me, kept me from breathing.

"Jangmi told me," he admitted. I turned away from him, as I pulled on the grass that was lying beneath me. "She thought maybe I could help." *Why? Because we had one conversation one time before all this mess happened?* I thought bitterly to myself.

"I don't want to talk about it," I muttered.

"Hellfire is a really rare power, Zinnia," he said. "It's normal to be scared about your child wielding such a gift."

"It's not a gift," I said, without thinking. I stopped myself before I let the rest of the words tumble out. No one could know. Not even August. He studied me and then leaned back onto one of his arms, the rest of him still twisted towards me.

"It *is* a gift. Such a great gift that even President Eclipse wanted you as a weapon," August said. Part of me wanted to believe him, and that part was starting to be convinced by his words.

"I don't *want* to be a weapon," I said. "I want to be help-ful. Like how Agwe can heal others, or how Jangmi can speak to animals. I wouldn't even mind if I was a shapeshifter like Volplie." My hand motioned towards Volplie as she walked through the camp, Jangmi eagerly talking her ear off next to her. *At least they're all harmless*, I stopped myself from saying. August was quiet for a moment, and then his fingertips touched the tips of mine in an effort to console me. There was a slight magnetism there, and I frowned as I looked at it. I knew what that humming meant. He slowly pulled them away at my expression.

"You don't have to be a weapon, Zinnia. But, your power could help a lot of people. It could help turn the tide," he said. I looked up into his eyes, his voice almost convincing me.

"Help the Shadow Army, you mean," I said, referring to what the rebellion warriors called themselves. He laughed a little.

"You *have* become a pretty great warrior. Your sword skills are way more advanced than I would've thought," he teased. I brushed a stray auburn lock of hair out of my face.

"I've had dreams," I answered honestly. "I've always had dreams of me wielding a sword. Being a hero."

"Dreams?" he said, his eyebrows raised. "Tayen did say your mother was a dreamer. She trained you then." I shrugged.

"I'm not sure why," I admitted. He glanced over at me, his eyes roaming my face as he studied my expression, careful to say the right words.

"She wanted to make sure you had a choice. That you would be able to fight for yourself," he said, and I wanted so badly for his words to be true.

"What's this? A lover's meeting?" an annoying voice interjected. I glared at Anubys as he walked up the hill, hands in his pockets. He smiled lazily at August, and I could feel him stiffen next to me.

"I'll get going," he muttered as he stood up.

"So soon?" Anubys asked, feigning disappointment.

"Anubys, stop being—"

"I just have duties to attend to," August answered, interrupting me. He waved goodbye, departing with a smile that didn't quite reach his eyes, and then bounded down the hill. Anubys sat down next to me despite my protests.

"Why are you bothering me?" I asked, a breath of irritation escaping my lips.

"You felt it, didn't you?" Anubys asked, his light green eyes making eye contact with me. I felt myself unable to look away.

"Felt what?" I lied. Anubys scoffed as he leaned forward a bit, his elongated fingers creeping towards mine. The magnetic feeling between them as the distance slowly started to close was almost dizzying.

"I saw him touch your fingers. You must know now," he said.

"Know what?" I spat. He pulled back his hand, the feeling dissipating as he did.

"How destructive he is," he barely whispered. His eyes eventually broke eye contact with me, and I finally felt like I could breathe.

"He's not destructive," I argued. "He's only a silvertongue." Anubys looked at me with disappointment clouding his eyes.

"Your blood hummed along with his. I know you felt it," he said. I could hear the unspoken words he almost said. Only powers that are alike one another were drawn to each other like that.

"It wasn't as loud as it is with you," I mumbled. Anubys's lips broke out into a crooked smile as he pushed himself off of the ground.

"Nobody's is more destructive than mine," he merely answered as he stuffed his hands back into his pocket. He gave me an unreadable look before turning away. I watched as he walked down the hill, my thoughts silent until he disappeared into his cabin, causing them to roar inside me once again.

CHAPTER EIGHTEEN

Jangmi had a huge smile on her face as I walked up to the training grounds. I rubbed my swollen face as I looked up at her, my lips twisted at her excited expression.

"What's going on?" I asked, my voice still coated with sleep. She started pumping her fists as she looked up with bright eyes.

"Lidya said we're having a showdown today!" Jangmi exclaimed. "A sword fight." I looked up at Lidya who was talking Eset's ear off. Eset looked positively murderous.

"When did she say this?" I asked. I looked around at our little group. Anubys still hadn't arrived, as per usual. But, Ash wasn't there either.

"She said it when Eset and I walked up. She really wants to see Eset fight with someone other than Anubys," Jangmi explained. Then, she locked eyes with Agwe and hurriedly flitted over to tell him the news. Just as I was processing this showdown, Lidya clapped her hands together.

"Now that everyone is here," she pointedly glared at Anubys who was still walking up to the training grounds, his black hair tousled. He just yawned in response as Ash ran ahead of him at the sight of Lidya's glare.

"Today we're going to do something a little bit differently. I'm going to make you guys have a sword fight with one another," she beamed. A small smile appeared on August's lips at Lidya's enthusiasm.

"Well, *I'm* going to die today," Ash muttered next to me. His breathing was slightly heavier from running, and I just gave him a sympathetic smile.

"You're not that bad," I placated. He rolled his eyes.

"Please don't," he said, holding up a hand.

"Are we doing this with our usual partners?" Lightning asked, a hand raised. Lidya smirked as she crossed her arms.

"Nope," she said, smiling. "Only the best of you will be fighting against one another today." Ash breathed out a sigh of relief.

"Thank the Nation," he whispered under his breath. I chuckled at his liberation. He elbowed my side as his eyebrows wiggled.

"You'll probably be one of them," he said. I winced at the gesture.

"I hope not," I muttered just as Lidya called my name. I looked up, startled. She stared at me for a moment longer.

"Zinnia," she repeated.

"Yes?" I asked. She sighed as she took a step closer to me.

"You'll be demonstrating with Anubys," she said. I felt a pit settle itself into my stomach as I looked over at Anubys. His face was unreadable as he stared back at me.

Anubys and Eset during combat training were almost a

blur of wooden swords every time. The only time they weren't clashing swords was when they were glaring at each other, sweat dripping down their faces. And then they were at each other's throats once more. I swallowed the anxiety that threatened to build up in my throat.

"But, first," Lidya said, pushing August forward. He stumbled slightly as his fingers gripped the clipboard in his hands a bit more tightly. "August will fight with you."

"Why August?" Anubys asked, almost leaning into the air behind him.

"Because it's a good warm up," she said, smiling. Her face relaxed as she looked at me more seriously, adding, "If you can beat August, I'll feel more comfortable about you going against Anubys." *Why put me against Anubys in the first place?* I couldn't help but think. She turned towards him.

"And you'll go against Eset first," she said. "Afterwards, Eset will go up against Agwe." Anubys rolled his eyes and threw out some sort of complaint, but I couldn't hear as my heart was pounding in my ears. It was true that I was *somewhat* good at sword fighting, at least against Ash who could barely lift it in his hands. However, I wasn't at the same level as Anubys, or even August for that matter.

Jangmi excitedly pushed me forwards towards the front, not noticing my hesitation. And Lidya thrust a wooden sword into my hands as she grabbed the clipboard from August's. His eyes seemed to twinkle as he looked over at me.

"This'll be fun," he said, feeling the weight of the sword in his hands. *Why did I have to go up against one of the instructors?* I groaned inwardly.

"So much fun," I muttered sarcastically as I lowered myself into a familiar stance. Once Lidya clapped her hands, August went on the offensive.

I uncomfortably parried his attacks. It wasn't like how it was with Ash, who was normally countering my own attacks. But, once I got the hang of August's advances, it almost felt as easy as breathing, like moving through water. Neither one of us had hit the other in the few minutes that passed, and I could almost see the frustration that was building in August's eyes. I had never seen any kind of negative emotion on August's face before, and the sight of it made me almost laugh. I didn't expect him to be competitive.

August picked up speed in his attacks, trying to overwhelm me. I breathed in deeply as I tried to keep up with his attacks. Once I was used to the pace, I managed to throw in my own offensive maneuvers. I thrusted forward as he quickly hit my sword away. And it went like that for a while. It was easy, fighting with him.

Finally, I saw an opening and thrust forward, hitting his side with the wooden tip, and he immediately stopped moving. His fierce eyes softened as he lightly panted, smiling at me.

"Good job," he said as Lidya narrowed her eyes. She announced me as the winner of the fight, but I couldn't help but feel off about it. August clearly wasn't winded, and I felt he left the opening on purpose. I shook the thought out of my head as Jangmi and Volplie congratulated me.

"That was insane!" Jangmi exclaimed as Anubys and Eset started to fight with one another. They moved lightning quick. So fast that I didn't see how Lidya could watch with human eyes whether one won or not. Her eyes darted back and forth rapidly as she watched the fight go on with hyper focus.

"I wish Lidya would let me fight Eset," Volplie muttered next to me as Jangmi rehashed what happened in my fight with August. I made eye contact with him as Jangmi spoke. He lowered his eyes after a moment.

"How was it?" Jangmi asked, lightly hitting my shoulder. I frowned as I looked away from August.

"It was easy," I muttered. "Almost like... breathing."

When Eset and Anubys's fight was announced as a draw, Anubys glowered at his sister, sweat glistening off his skin.

"I could've gone on for longer," Anubys growled.

"So could I," Eset hissed. They glared at each other until Lidya stood between them. She held her hands up and motioned for them to lower their swords.

"My gods, you guys are *twins*, aren't you?" she murmured as Anubys was the first to let go of his sword. At Anubys's release, Eset finally dropped hers and stalked back to the group. Anubys rolled his eyes at the action. Neither of them answered Lidya's question. She clicked her tongue against her teeth as she backed away.

"Okay," she said, mostly to herself. "Zinnia?"

"Shouldn't we give Anubys a rest?" I asked. Anubys's eyes glinted at my words as his gaze met mine.

"I can go all day," he said, flashing me a smile. My lips tightened into a line as I stood across from him. I picked up the sword that Eset had just used and weighed it in my hand. The handle was drenched in sweat, and I imagined Anubys's was as well.

"Don't worry," Anubys smirked. "I'll go easy on you." My competitive nature, that I really didn't know I had, flared.

"Don't bother," I snapped. Anubys's smile grew bigger. At Lidya's behest, I jolted forward, desperate to be the first to attack Anubys. He countered the advance easily and then started moving at that lightning speed that he would with Eset. *Going easy on me?* I thought, bitterly. *Yeah, right.*

If fighting with August was like moving through water, fighting against Anubys was like I was walking through fire. It was hard and painful, the way I had to move to fight him off. We clashed our swords together, with him pushing down on it for a second, his face close to mine. I felt his hot breath on my skin, and then he was gone in an instant. I rapidly tried to recover as I parried his attack, but I felt myself back up a few steps. He was overpowering me. And quickly.

Breathing heavily, I desperately looked for an opening in his flurry of attacks, but I didn't find one. I barely could see him, and his attacks were unpredictable. I didn't know where his sword was going to go next until the last possible second. It wasn't like breathing, fighting with Anubys. It was the feeling one gets when they're trying to fight against sleep. The end is coming, no matter what you do, but you try your hardest anyway.

As soon as it started, the fight was over. Anubys jabbed me in the chest, causing me to double over in pain. I gasped for breath as he dropped his sword in front of me.

"Good try," he said, patting my back as he walked past

me. I coughed as I choked on my breath. I could still smell his sweet scent in the air as I glowered at the ground. I knew one thing: I was going to make sure to never let Anubys beat me again.

CHAPTER NINETEEN

I woke up to the sounds of commotion and screaming. An alarm was blaring, shaking the walls of the cabin. Eset was peeking through the slightly ajar door as the yelling drifted in, and then she closed it, muffling the sounds.

"What's going on?" I asked her, rubbing my eyes. She shook her head, her shiny black hair in a single braid down her back.

"The force field is down," she said. She stared at me, her eyes dead. "Something has gotten inside."

"Probably creatures," Volplie said, sitting with her knees against her chest on her top bunk.

"We should do something," I said, climbing down the ladder.

"Do what?" Eset asked, arms crossing her chest. "Our powers are useless with these stupid clothes on." She pulled at the weighted armor we had gotten used to over the past month.

"We can't just *sit* here," I said. "There's *children* living in this camp." There were only a few families that were started here, and I caught glimpses of the kids around the camp. I knew I wouldn't be able to live with myself if anything happened to them. Jangmi nodded her head in agreement, standing up next to me.

"Zinnia is right," she said. "We can't just sit here and do nothing." Eset rubbed her temples as she closed her eyes.

"You'll be more of a hindrance than an asset," she muttered. Nevertheless, she put on her shoes. Volplie, Jangmi, and I exchanged looks and then did the same.

"Don't get killed," Eset said as she opened the door. Across from us, the boys' cabin door opened as well with Lightning leading them out.

"You guys decided to help?" he asked as a building nearby went up in flames. I swiveled my head around, trying to see what we were up against, but I couldn't see anything. Eset shrugged in response to Lightning.

"I told them they would die doing so with this armor on," Eset muttered. Anubys snorted.

"We sent Agwe to find some weapons," Lightning stated.

"The other Shadow members are all trying to fight whatever it is out there," Ash piped up.

"You sent Agwe?" Jangmi said, her reaction belated due to shock.

"He'll be fine," Lightning assured her. She stared desperately down the street, hoping to catch a glimpse of him.

"Since you want to save the children so badly, you should go to them," Eset said, coldly, as she turned towards me. I felt taken aback from her attitude, and I saw Lightning sigh behind her. She turned to look at him.

"Splitting up might not be good. We're not well trained," Lightning explained. She shrugged.

"We should split up," she muttered. "We don't know what we're up against."

"I'll go with the Torch here," Anubys piped up. I grumbled at his new nickname for me. Eset's normally cool gaze looked furious at his response.

"You shouldn't. You should come with me because..." her words drifted off as Anubys came to my side. There were more screams from down the street.

"I'll be fine," he merely said. I knew what she was referring to. Anubys wasn't able to use his power if he was out of range from her. When he first told me, I didn't know if it was a lie or not, but judging from Eset's reaction, I knew it to be true now. I wondered if it also meant she wasn't able to use hers as well.

"You should stay with Es—"

"I'll stay with you," he said. His tone was demanding, and I shied away from arguing with him any further. My eyes glanced over at him, curiously. Despite myself, I felt my heart skip a beat.

"Agwe," Jangmi breathed. She looked visibly relieved as she half ran to meet up with him. He was carrying with him some swords. Volplie ran over to Agwe and grabbed the biggest one, smiling widely as she did.

"Let's fuck these clowns up," she said, and then ran down the street, laughing maniacally.

"I'll go after her," Ash said, grabbing a smaller sword

from Agwe's hands as he took off in the direction that Volplie went.

"Volplie!" I heard him shout desperately. "Please wait up!"

"You couldn't get guns or something?" Anubys asked, leaning on his elbow that, unfortunately, rested on my shoulder. Agwe shrugged.

"This was all I could find," he said. I shrugged Anubys off of me as he gave me a smirk.

"There's not enough swords for everyone," Eset spat. Agwe stared at her, his face unmoving.

"I only have two hands," he pointed out. She made a noise of disappointment as Lightning handed her one.

"You're better at it than me," he said. She pursed her lips, snatching it from him.

"Let's go," she said, not looking behind her as she walked towards the commotion.

"Agwe and I will stick together," Jangmi said as Agwe handed me a longsword. I grabbed it, and the weight felt familiar as I felt it with my hands.

"We'll go find the children. You find those who can't fight and bring them to safety," I said. Jangmi and Agwe nodded as Lightning finally resigned to following after Eset.

"Just you and me now," Anubys said as Jangmi and Agwe walked down the street, a sword in Agwe's large hands. Jangmi almost looked like a child next to him due to how tall he was.

"Are they a thing?" I asked him as he stared at me incredulously.

"Z, please. You haven't put that together yet?" he asked, throwing his hands up as he walked towards the cabins that housed children. Before I could respond, a scream pierced the night, coming from the direction of one of the cabins.

"Let's hope you know how to use that sword now," Anubys quipped as we started running towards the sound. I couldn't admit that I hoped I knew what I was doing too as my mouth turned to cotton. But, I sure as hell wasn't going to give it to Anubys.

CHAPTER TWENTY

I entered the cabin, the sword held out in front of me as Anubys walked in behind, checking down the street for any other commotion. The cabin was bigger than the one I was staying in. Almost like a full house, with stairs next to the door and a small living area with a kitchen attached at the back wall. It was dark in this part of the camp, with no floating lights to illuminate it. Or they were destroyed.

My heart thundered in my chest as I heard another scream, coming from upstairs. Anubys gave me a look, his green eyes looking almost gray in the dim light.

He motioned for us to go up the stairs, and I nodded as I felt the panic start to settle in. I closed my eyes for a moment, trying to clear my mind like we practiced in our lessons with Devlin in the afternoons.

"We need to hurry," Anubys barely breathed. I nodded, opening my eyes as I walked up the stairs slowly, looking around once we were at the top. There was a small hallway and two rooms, the doors broken. I glanced into one of the bedrooms and suppressed the gasp that almost left my mouth. Two bodies, mangled, with their organs littered on the floor were lying near the foot of the bed. A man and a woman. A couple.

I let out a shuddered breath as I forced myself to walk as fast as I could to the other room. There, a human with its back towards us was standing in front of me. I heard squelching and ripping, like it was eating something as it stood there. In front of it, hidden behind a bed, was a small girl.

Her dark eyes focused on me as Anubys slipped from behind me and walked slowly towards the girl.

"Attack the creature," he whispered by my ear before he started running towards her. The creature turned towards him due to his movement, and without a second thought, I whipped out the sword and lunged towards the creature with all my strength, stabbing it in the back. It let out an unearthly scream as it turned towards me. Its eyes were gray, almost like a film was over them, and black liquid poured from the wound and from its mouth. It was a human. Or, it was once a human.

Its veins were puckered and just as dark as the liquid coming out of it. It tried to come closer to me as it dropped an organ to the ground, bright red blood staining its pale hands. I pulled the sword out of it and more of the black liquid spilled out of the creature, hitting my shoes. I resisted the urge to cover my nose, the stench of rotting flesh causing my stomach to turn. It reached towards me, and I quickly ducked from its grip and stabbed it once again, for good measure.

My blood was burning, I could feel the fire churning within me at the sense of danger and for the first time, I was grateful for the heavy armor we were forced to wear. The creature fell to the ground, gurgling on the liquid that was coming out of its mouth. And then suddenly, it went quiet. I looked up at Anubys, who was holding the little girl in his hands. He stared at me, almost in awe, as I felt my hands start to shake.

"We're not in the clear yet, Wildfire," he whispered, walking over the creature and out the door. "We need to go, now." I nodded as I followed him out, knuckles white as I held the sword in my right hand, black blood staining it.

"Keep your eyes closed, okay?" he told the little girl. She was all too willing to oblige as she squeezed her eyes shut as we walked past her makers' room.

"Did you see any more?" Anubys asked her as we hurried down the stairs. I looked around the cabin, trying to see if there were more of those cursed creatures. The child shook her head, her eyes still closed. We walked out of the cabin, and I felt like I could take a full breath of air as I started hurriedly down the street.

"Zinnia," I heard Anubys hardly say, and I whipped around to see one of those creatures grab him. He tried to fight against it as he held onto the little girl tightly. I saw him try to put her down so he could fight properly, but the fire inside of me was burning. Burning my skin, trying to find a way out as sweat drenched every part of me. The skinny creature ripped Anubys's arm open, with an inhuman strength. All I heard was his scream, and I couldn't control the fire that erupted out of me as I ran towards him. His green eyes turned wide.

"Zinnia, don't," I saw him mouth, but it was too late. I felt myself explode as the fire within me burned my body and the armor that was supposed to keep me from using my powers, turning me into a living flame. The fire escaped me, somehow stronger than before, as it crawled down the street towards him and the creature. It ate up everything in its path, including the little girl who had just gotten out of Anubys's arms. Her dying screams pierced the night, but it was too late for me to do anything. I couldn't bring the fire back into myself.

I was the fire, and it was me. And I felt myself engulf her, distinguishing the flame that was her life while another tendril of me reached Anubys and the creature. I felt Anubys's flame within his soul, and felt it wasn't easily consumed. The creature, however, was almost too easy to destroy. It had no flame within it. Nothing to fight the licks of mine; its body disintegrating easily.

"Zinnia," Anubys said, as I was jolted back into where my body used to be. He was burning, the smell of his flesh stinging my nose, but his face didn't portray any semblance of pain. The fire started to creep its way back towards me, but I glanced at the body that lay at his feet. A small, blackened corpse. *Did I...?* My flames flickered, trembled, and then my fire started to explode more out of me, engulfing it again so I couldn't see it. And I felt the tendrils of it snake around the town, burning the cabins near us. *I killed her. I killed her.*

"She's out of control," I heard a voice behind me say.

Please tell me she isn't dead, I wanted to scream. My flame eyes made eye contact with Devlin whose legs were burning. An Immortal. His flame was also too strong to engulf. But some wicked part of me wanted to feel it, wanted to consume his strength to add it to my own.

"You need to do something," he said to August who was behind him, Devlin using his body as a shield. I felt myself fall to the ground, my fire trying to find anything and everything to consume, to feed my growing grief. I was screaming inside of myself. Screaming wordlessly as the flames held me captive.

"Zinnia, control yourself," August said, and there was something behind his words that made me want to listen. "Trap your fire back within your body. Breathe it back into you." I involuntarily followed his order, and I felt the tendrils of the fire snake its way back towards my body.

"Create your body again. Trap your fire within you," he said, taking a step forward from behind Devlin who was already starting to regenerate his charred legs. I couldn't help but note that his healing was slower than how Anubys seemed to heal. I felt myself start to become solid, again, my skin reforming.

"Let the skin of yours soothe the fire of your soul," August said, taking another step forward. I started to cool down, but I was in pain from being forcefully contained. So much pain. August took another step towards me.

"Let the fire be distinguished outside of you," he said, and his voice held more weight than I had ever heard it before. It was charming, twinkling, but it had a weight to it that chilled me to the bone. Any fire that was left outside of me immediately went out, and I felt the ground that was beneath me again. I looked at my trembling hands, not a blemish on them, and as the sun started to rise, I started to sob uncontrollably. Nobody touched me as my hands covered my sight, letting the hot tears soak them. I was a monster. My mother was right. I was an absolute monster.

I felt my arms get raised as a shirt slipped over my head and covered my naked chest. I kept my eyes closed, the tears still slipping through, as strong arms wrapped around and lifted me. My head rested on their bare chest, their heart hammering in my ear, and I just let myself sob until there wasn't anything left of me.

Their voices overlapped one another as they discussed what to do with me. Luckily, according to Mikazuki, her parents were dead so there wasn't anyone that was grieving in that horrible sort of way. In other words, there was no one who really wanted consequences for me. But, it didn't make it any better. A child was dead. Another person was dead... because of me.

"Zinnia," Tayen's discombobulated voice said. I rolled my head towards her, barely seeing her face. She clapped her wrinkled hands close to my nose, bringing me back to the moment.

"Yes?" I asked, my voice dead.

"Do you think you can control it?" she asked. It was the one thing they were arguing about. If I could control the hellfire, then I could be useful. If I couldn't, what should they do with me? I shrugged in response, knowing I deserved a fate worse than death.

"She doesn't even know if she can control it," Biao said, gesturing towards me in anger as he turned back to the others. Lidya shook her head and argued against my inevitable execution.

"She hasn't been given the *opportunity* to control it," Lidya said, all for using me as a weapon against President Eclipse when the time comes. "Everyone doesn't know how to control their powers at first. That's why we're going to teach them."

"The armor doesn't work on her," Biao argued. "It's too dangerous. Tayen. We'd be putting all the people here in a danger we're not even sure we could save them from." The little girl, who I learned was named Dandelion, wasn't the only person to get hurt that night. Luckily, no one else died, but many people had burns that were slowly being healed by the few healers—like Agwe—the Rebellion camp had.

"The armor doesn't work on her because she *is* hellfire, Biao. Her human body is just a cage she has put it in. It's not a power, it's who she is," Mikazuki pointed out. "But, I'm with Biao, Tayen. She's too dangerous. And if she ever got into the hands of President Eclipse—"

"That won't happen," Tayen said, shaking her head.

"You see how close she is to that kid, Tayen. I mean, for the Nation's sake, he carried her across the camp back to her cabin. And can he really be trusted to put her on the right path?" Devlin said, crossing his large, muscular arms across his chest.

My mind became conscious for a moment as green eyes flickered through my mind. Anubys? *He* carried me? I had woken up that morning wearing nothing but an armored shirt as tears continued to pour out of my eyes, uncontrollably. I was tucked into Jangmi's bed, and I remembered I was carried there, but I didn't dare open my eyes to look at the person.

"Who? The boy with the sanpaku eyes?" Mikazuki asked, using an unfamiliar term. Biao closed his eyes and nodded towards her.

"Yeah, the one with the small irises," Biao answered. Did they mean how his eyes always looked like they were looking up at you?

"Her powers seem to listen to me. If anything happens during training, I can easily keep them at bay," August piped up, leaning against the wall near the door to Tayen's office. They turned towards him, and Biao made a face of disagreement.

"I saw him bring her back to normal," Devlin said, nodding his head. "It's possible August can keep her from destroying anything." *And from hurting anyone*, his unspoken words drifted into my mind. I winced as I remembered the pain of being forced back into my body by August's words.

"If she gets a handle on her powers, we can easily use her against them," Lidya said, almost gleefully. A weapon. That's what they wanted me to be for them. But, I didn't have the energy to beg them to just kill me. To tell them I didn't deserve to breathe the same air they once did. Rohit. Dandelion. And who knew who else.

"Tayen, I still think that it's—" Biao started to say, but Tayen put up a hand, interrupting him. She turned towards August.

"If you think you can control it for her while she trains,

I'll allow it," she said to him. August nodded, his eyes glancing over at me for a moment. "Lidya is right. She will be useful when the time comes." With Tayen's word, the conversation was done. I was going to be trained to control my powers, whether I wanted to or not.

CHAPTER TWENTY-ONE

Eset leaned against the tree, with Anubys not too far from her, sitting on the edge of the hill. I walked over, wearing regular clothes. It felt like I was nearly wearing nothing as I had gotten used to the heavy armor they had us wear for weeks. But, I couldn't wear it in case I turned into a living flame once again. There wasn't enough armor for me to waste just for training. Eset and Anubys were also both wearing regular clothes, in order to use their powers as well. I frowned at August as I reached him.

"What are *they* doing here?" I spat. The memory of the other night flashed through my mind from staring at the back of Anubys's head. Anubys didn't turn at my words, his gaze focused on the ground. If Eset was offended by what I said, her cold face didn't show it.

"Eset has the unique ability to resurrect creatures," August said, as if I didn't already know. "And her brother needs to be nearby in case anything happens." My head whipped over to him in horror.

"You want me to practice on *living* beings?" I asked, aghast. August made a face and glanced over at Eset who sighed.

"The being I'll resurrect isn't really alive, not like you and I. Besides, does it really matter? I didn't figure you cared much for life and death," Eset said, picking at her nails. Her eyes roved over me, "Considering." I felt the anger inside of me grow.

"What's that supposed to mean?" I growled, my voice dangerously low. She shrugged, a smirk on her lips. The fire inside me flared. I turned towards August, hellfire burning in my eyes.

"I'm not doing this, August. I'm not," I said, backing away. August put a hand on my arm as I pulled it back swiftly, as if his touch burned me. He stared at me for a second, his expression unreadable, and then cleared his throat.

"You won't actually ever reach them. I'll make sure of it. It's just to have the stakes be real. You have to *feel* like you're in danger. It's the easiest way to get the power to come out of you," he said. His blue eyes seemed to wash over me, calming me. The fire within me dimmed. I chewed on my cheek as I thought.

"I don't know," I said. "You think my power is linked to fear?" August glanced over at Anubys, whose back was still turned towards us. He seemed to freeze at my words, though. I couldn't get Anubys's scream as the creature tore open his arm from the other night out of my head. My eyes subconsciously glanced down at where the open flesh once was, but it looked like nothing was ever there in the first place.

"Based on what I've learned, I do," August said, turning back towards me. I didn't know if I was just being convinced by his presence, or if I really agreed with what we were doing, but eventually I nodded my head. *Curse that silver-tongue*, I couldn't help but think as I gave in. August nodded towards Eset, who pulled a body out from behind the tree, and I couldn't control the breathless scream that escaped my lips. It was one of those creatures from the other night.

"What is this? You're going to resurrect *that*?" I asked, frantically looking over at August. He nodded. I shook my head, backing away once again.

"No, you can't. What if nothing comes out of me? What if I can't kill it?" I asked. August shook his head at my assumption.

"I don't want you to kill it. I just want you to practice letting it out and then bringing it back in. It won't get to you. Anubys will make sure of that," August said. Anubys, without turning around to look at me, raised a hand as if he were greeting me. I stared at him for a moment, a pang in my chest ringing. His wavy, black hair moved slightly with the breeze and a part of me wondered why he continued to avoid me since that night. *Because you scare even him, the boy with death in his lungs*, the darkness whispered into my soul. I shuddered and quickly looked away.

"Fine," I said, resolving to my fate. "I'll do it. Whatever." August gave me a tentative smile. He motioned for Eset to reanimate the creature. It was missing an arm and as Eset stared at it, a smile blooming onto her face, its eyes flickered open. It snarled at me as it got up off of the ground, coming towards me almost immediately. I tried to concentrate on the fire that was starting to churn through me. It had an outlet, and I could feel that I could let the flames grow towards the creature, but something was stopping me from doing so.

My heart thundered in my chest as the creature made its way towards me. With its other arm, it grabbed my neck, and pulled me towards its mouth. Its nails dug into my skin, my breath becoming restricted. I closed my eyes, resigning myself to my fate. *This is what I want*, I thought. *This is what I deserve*. And then suddenly, the creature started to scream as it let go of me and fell to the ground. It held its head with its one hand and just as suddenly as the scream started, it collapsed. Dead.

Anubys was standing next to Eset, glowering, not at the creature, but at August. His jaw was clenched, a muscle feathering.

"I told you she's not ready," he said, his casual voice not matching the fury that was on his face.

"I didn't tell you to kill it yet," August replied, coolly.

"She was going to—"

"She wasn't," August stated. They glared at each other for what felt like ages. I cleared my throat, hoping to say something to ease the tension, but Anubys's gaze flickered over to me, softening a bit, before looking back at August.

"*You* don't understand, Silver-Tongue," Anubys said, a smirk playing on his lips once again. "She wants to die. After what she did, she's so *disgusted* with herself, that she *wants* to die. The hellfire isn't going to protect her if she doesn't want it to." His words cut me deeper than any sword could.

I knew it was how he saw me. I knew, deep down. He

was disgusted with me. Just as disgusted as I was. I lowered my head, unable to look at him any longer. *He* was disgusted with *me*. He, who tortured who knows how many people at President Eclipse's whim. He, who could take the life from anyone he looked at. *He* felt that way about me. That's the only reason I could think of as to why he knew what I felt about myself.

"If she doesn't want to protect herself, then we'll get it out of her by having her protect someone else," August declared. *Someone else?* My head jerked up to look at him, horrified at his words. He wouldn't *dare*. August looked like he was in pain as he avoided my gaze.

"If that's the only way, I'll do it, Zinnia," he said, without looking at me. "I have to." Anubys scoffed, and my eyes flickered towards him for a moment before looking away once again.

"Well, I'm done for today," he asserted. "I'm not going to sit here and watch her try to kill herself again." I felt his glare on me before he turned away. I watched as his feet started to walk down the hill, unable to lift my head to properly look at him.

"Anubys," August called out, but his feet didn't stop moving. I watched them until they disappeared from my sight.

"This was fun," Eset said, smiling as she turned to follow her brother. August sighed, a hand to his temple.

"I'll try harder next time," I whispered. "Please don't bring anyone else into this." His blue eyes softened, and he sighed again, putting his head into his hands.

"Don't worry, Zinnia," he said. "I know how to get you to... *want* to let out the fire. But, it'll be invasive." He didn't look at me as he said this, and I nodded, assuming how he was going to do it.

"Do whatever you need to," I said. "But, don't bring anybody else to these training sessions." He paused for a moment. The silence stretched out for a while, and then he looked up at me, almost curiously. He nodded.

"I promise," he whispered.

CHAPTER TWENTY-TWO

"You're going to let him into your *head*?" Anubys asked as he sat down next to me in the cafeteria. No one would sit with me anymore. Sometimes, Lightning would eat silently with me but besides him, everyone left me alone.

"Are you insane?" he said. "You really hate yourself that much?"

"I'm not going to let him into my head... I'm just going to let him convince me everything is okay. That's what he does, isn't it?" I asked, not looking at him. His words from earlier in the day still stung.

"Zinnia, you don't understand. You allowing that is letting him—" he hissed but then stopped as Eset sat across from me.

"What are you guys talking about?" she asked, pointedly staring at Anubys. He met her glare, and my eyes traveled to his hand gripping the food tray. His knuckles were almost white.

"Nothing," he said, and then he got up and walked away, throwing out his uneaten food. Eset's smirk resembled Anubys's, but there was something about it that intimidated me.

"He's been different since that day with the girl," she merely said before she started to rise out of her seat. I looked at her for a moment as the fear that Anubys thought of me as a monster rose into my throat, the taste of blood in my mouth. I swallowed as I held my hands together, tight, underneath the table.

"I thought you said he couldn't care about anyone," I said, meeting her eyes. Fury flickered in her cool gaze for a second and then disappeared as soon as it came.

"He can't," she said through her teeth, and then she followed after her twin.

"Zinnia, don't," Anubys's frightened voice echoed into my brain as I sat up in my bed, panting. I put my head into my hands as I tried to slow my breathing and cool the blood that was boiling underneath my skin.

"Beware the silver-tongue," I heard Volplie whisper to me from across the room. I raised my head quickly as I turned towards her, her purple-blue eyes almost glowing in the dark. The flickering light from outside hit her white hair, almost blinding me

"What did you say to me?" I asked, my blood pounding in my ears. She laid back down and stared up at the ceiling.

"Be careful," she said. "Silver-tongues are tricky."

August's kind blue eyes flashed through my mind as I shook my head.

"How would you know?" I snapped.

"I've met a lot of Aphrodite's children," she muttered. "And they're not the nicest." She turned over on her side.

"I know August," I said. Volplie stayed silent, but I knew what she was thinking: *Do you?*

Anubys's sword hit mine with a force that almost knocked me back. I blew a piece of hair out of my eyes as I glared up at him. He continued to push the sword towards me until I pushed it back and jumped out of the way.

"What's your problem?" I hissed. His light green eyes almost looked fiery.

"You can't let him use his power on you," he said. "Not in that way." I rolled my eyes as our swords clashed against each other again. This was why he was adamant that he was my partner for today? To try and convince me to not let August help me?

"You said yourself I wasn't ready," I grunted as I blocked his attack.

"I meant that you needed more time to get your head on straight, not for him to *manipulate* you," he said, nimbly avoiding my counterattack. He wasn't going as hard as he normally would, and I paused, staring at him exasperatedly as I leaned against my sword.

"Why do you care what I do?" I asked, finally. He stopped, his eyes flashed as he looked down at me. He was only a head and a half taller, but sometimes, it felt like he was towering over me.

"What?" he said, caught off guard. I blew a lock of auburn hair out of my eyes.

"What does it *matter* to you? You don't even know me. And you're disgusted by me, aren't you? About who I am?" I said, waving my sword around. His eyebrows knitted together as he watched me. Realization flooded his face as he took a small step forward.

"Zinnia, I'm not—" My heart stopped at hearing my name on his tongue.

"Less talking, more fighting," Lidya yelled out. Anubys had said my name plenty of times before. But, never like that. Never with that much... Taking a deep breath, I steeled my gaze as I lunged forward, and Anubys's gaze hardened as he easily countered it.

"You don't know what you're doing," he muttered.

"What? With this or with August?" I asked. He stared at me, before knocking my sword easily out of my hand. He leaned against his and smirked, but it felt more like Eset's.

"Both." Then he dropped the wooden sword in his hands and walked away with Lidya yelling after him. I blew the hair out from my eyes as I glared at his shrinking back.

"What's his problem?" Jangmi asked, curiously, leaning towards me. I shrugged as Lidya gestured for August to step in with my training.

"I don't know," I said, focusing on the next set of moves. August's ocean-blue eyes washed over me, releasing any anger and stress that was residing in my body. And I eagerly welcomed it.

"Are you sure you want to do this?" August asked, my hands in his as we sat on the hill that overlooked the Rebellion camp.

"Why does everyone keep asking me that?" I muttered. His eyebrows raised at my response. "Is there something I should know?" August thought for a moment to himself before shaking his head.

"No, it's just... It's invasive. I'll be... in your memories... your thoughts. It's not quite like mind-reading. But, it's more like... manipulating what happened. It's similar to lying to yourself," he said. In my memories?

"In *all* of my memories?" I asked. August gave me a look as he assessed what I meant.

"Yes. Nothing would be hidden," he said. I let out a shaky breath. Well, he already knew I killed a little girl. Does him knowing I killed another person matter?

"You'll only be manipulating that one memory of the other night though, right?" I asked. August's eyes were unreadable as he met my gaze.

"Of course," he responded.

"Fine," I said. "Let's do this." Lying to myself would be better than having the truth haunt me every day of my life.

August stared at me for a moment longer, his blue eyes piercing into my soul, and I swear my heart almost stopped. He really was handsome. It was no wonder why everyone loved August, even with his silver-tongue powers.

He gripped my hands and bowed his head. My blood hummed along with his, the sound that showed his power wasn't quite as harmless as I might think it is. It hummed louder and louder the longer he held them. I fidgeted as the pull started to become uncomfortable, as if my whole body was screaming at me for being near him. I heard him whisper something, but I couldn't quite make it out. And suddenly, I was thrust into my own mind.

I was going through my memories. It was as if I were reliving bits and pieces of moments from my life, but in every moment, August was in the corner of my eye. Once I would try to see him, the memory would shift, and I would suddenly be in another one.

Me, seeing Happy after she was born. My mother talking about nonsense as she cooked. Hanging out with Forest and June before Preparation would start. And August was somehow in each of them. Walking by, or watching, or participating. If I tried to question why he was there, or take a good look at him, I would suddenly forget what I was going to ask. Rohit was burning, and August was there somehow, watching, trying to help me. But, Anubys killed him. That somber expression turning into a sinister crooked smile on his face. Then, Dandelion.

Dandelion was in Anubys's arms, and the creature grabbed him. The fire reached towards them, but it wasn't Anubys putting her down, it was August. August was burning. August was saying, "Zinnia, don't," before I exploded. And August was the one who talked me back into myself. Dandelion's corpse wasn't there. I didn't see her blackened, hardened skin from the burns of myself. Did she die? Was she dead? Did I kill her? Or did she get away?

"How do you feel?" August asked, as his hands released mine. I looked up at the familiar blue eyes. Those blue eyes that had been watching me all my life, and I repressed the urge to blush.

"I'm fine," I said, shaking my head. I felt fine, but something was off. I couldn't put my finger on it.

"So you went through with it anyway," Anubys's voice said, interrupting what August was going to say next.

"Went through with what?" I asked. Anubys frowned and then glared at August. His green eyes flickered over to me, and I blinked as his face flashed in my mind next to Dandelion's, immediately replaced by August's.

"Do you remember everything?" he asked.

"Remember what?" I asked, confused. August tried to deter him from having this conversation with me, but Anubys pressed on, getting down on his knees so we were eye to eye.

"Do you remember what happened to the creatures and the little girl?" he asked. I frowned as I glanced over at August, my eyebrows knitted upwards.

"Yeah, I remember everything," I said. "August saved me." I remembered the feeling of August's arms around me as he carried me back to the cabin.

"What?" Anubys asked, his eyebrows raising. "You mean he forced you back into your physical body?" I nodded.

"Yeah, and he saved the little girl from myself," I said, slowly. I rubbed my neck as I closed my eyes, my head starting to hurt.

"Wait, I'm sorry. Let me get this straight," Anubys said, straightening up as he glared at August before turning his gaze back towards me. "You think that Dandelion survi— Wait," he stared at me for a moment. His eyes betrayed the hurt he felt, but his face hardened. "Who was *with* you that night?"

"What do you mean?" I asked, taken aback from his sudden anger.

"Who. Was. With. You?" he asked through gritted teeth. I leaned back from him as I glanced over at August, my eyes begging for help. August just calmly stared at Anubys, like he was watching him.

"August was with me," I answered. "He was with me that night." Anubys stared at me for a long time, and my lungs burned from not being able to breathe. His eyes froze me to the ground, drowning me with the pain that was hidden behind them.

"Of course," Anubys finally breathed. He turned towards August, "Did you manipulate *every* memory she has with—" August shook his head.

"Not all, but... you know I had to," August whispered. I looked from Anubys to August, the conversation confusing me.

"I'm sorry, I don't understand what's going on," I said. Anubys's light green eyes darkened as he glared at me.

"Yeah, you chose not to," he muttered, looking me up and down with disgust. He closed his eyes and then smirked at August before putting his hands into his pockets. Slowly, he turned away and started walking back down the hill.

"Anubys," I heard myself say. I didn't know why I wanted to stop him, to comfort him. I *hated* him. I could feel in my soul how much I hated him. That smile when he broke Rohit's neck flashed through my mind. Even still, I couldn't help but call for him. He paused when I voiced his name, but didn't look back at me. And then, when he realized I didn't have anything else to say, he continued to walk down the hill back towards the camp.

"Don't worry about him," August said coolly, brushing his chocolate, brown hair back with his hand. His other hand rested near mine, and I could feel the magnetism that wanted to bring them together. He followed my gaze and stared at our hands, centimeters apart.

"Do you remember what I told you? About this feeling?" he breathed. I nodded my head as the memory quickly came to the forefront of my mind. In it, he had grabbed my wrist and explained why it was that our blood called to one another.

"Because we're meant for each other," I whispered, smiling as I met his eyes. He held my hand, making my blood sing in harmony with his. But, I didn't have the heart to tell him that every part of me screamed out for Anubys when he was merely feet away.

CHAPTER TWENTY-THREE

August's head lifted as I exited my cabin, his half-smile making my heart beat quicker. I ducked my head as I met his eyes that looked like the glistening sea.

"Good morning," he said. I smiled in response as I gingerly placed my hand into his sun-kissed one. Every time I did it, it felt unnatural.

"We're going to skip combat training this morning," he said, as we walked towards the hill, hand in hand. "You need to start learning how to control your powers." I groaned as he nagged me.

"I knowww," I said, dragging out the word. As we neared the hill, I saw Anubys and Eset standing next to one another. For some reason, I felt myself try and take my hand out of August's before Anubys turned around, but August held onto it tighter.

Anubys's eyes glanced down at our intertwined hands, promptly looking away afterwards, his face expressionless.

Could he tell? Could he see how strange it was for us to be holding hands? I shook my head. Why did I care if he could tell how unnatural it felt to me? And why was it unnatural? I had a crush on August for half of my life. Shouldn't I be... elated?

"Finally ready to practice?" Eset asked, her eyes twinkling in a way they hadn't before. I nodded my head, hesitantly. I looked around the hill, at the lone tree that sat on the top.

"I see why you like this place," August said, quietly, next to me. "It's so similar to where we would hang out with June and Forest, isn't it?" I saw Anubys stiffen at his words. But, I laughed as I remembered the times where we would all meet and talk before Preparation began.

"It *does* remind me of that place," I said. Although, that place was just a hologram. Not a real one, not like this.

As if knowing my thoughts, August said, "Don't worry. I won't let you destroy it, if that's what you're worried about." I nodded as August squeezed my hand. It felt like bugs were crawling around in my skin, and I closed my eyes to quiet my mind. Finally, he let go of me and took a step back.

"Let's start," he said, nodding his head at Eset. She smiled brilliantly at him as she raised the creature again from the dead. It stalked towards me, its black mouth open as its pale, white arm reached out. I felt myself freeze as the fire started to churn inside. Glancing over at August, I saw him whisper something I couldn't quite hear, and then the fire jolted out of my body.

It wasn't like how it normally was. I didn't explode. Fire didn't come out of all of me, but rather in a straight line from my chest, down my arms, and out of my hands. It hit its mark, almost perfectly. The creature screamed from the flames and just as suddenly as it came out, the fire retreated back into my chest. I stared at my hands in confusion, turning them over and over as Anubys gave the final blow to the resurrected creature. I frowned as I stared at my hands, wondering why it had felt almost painful.

"That was great, Zinnia," August said. His smile lit up his whole face as he teased, "Not a Zero anymore, huh?" I blinked.

"I thought we weren't going to give any pain to the creature?" I asked, my head cocking to the side as the memory became foggy. His smile slowly faded.

"It was a mistake," he said. "I should've had you pull it back earlier." He and Eset exchanged a glance, and then he turned back towards me.

"Let's go again."

By the time lunch came around, I was covered in sweat from the unnatural way of the fire coming out and going back in me. I didn't dare tell August how painful it was when the fire was forced back into me, like a weighted punch in the chest. Or that it felt like my teeth were slowly being pulled out when the fire was forced out of me. I was doubled over, trying to catch my breath.

"Let's stop here," he said, concern filling his eyes. I put up a hand.

"I can... go again," I panted. He shook his head as he wiped a bead of sweat off of my temple. I repressed the urge to shy away from his hands.

"You have to eat," he said. "Keep your strength up." He smiled down at me as I collapsed into the grass, breathing heavily.

"I'll see you later," he laughed at my facial expression. "I have to talk to Biao." I nodded, waving him away. He smiled, and as he looked over at Anubys, his face contorted into something like guilt. He glanced back at me, softly smiling as he did, and then walked down the length of the hill.

"We should go," Eset said, pointedly looking at Anubys. I felt his stare on me, but I didn't dare meet it. I watched as his arm reached out, like he wanted to touch me. And then, his hand flexed as he pulled it back towards himself.

"Yeah," he said, putting his hands into his pockets. "Let's go." I watched as the twins walked down the hill towards the cafeteria cabin. I let out a breath as soon as he was far away enough. His presence was driving me crazy. I hung my head in my hands as I tried to convince myself I wasn't some kind of traitor to August.

"So you and August, huh?" Ash asked as he sat down next to me with a tray full of food. I didn't even know how he ate that much, considering how small he was. Where did he put it all away?

"I saw it coming from a mile away," Volplie muttered next to him. Ash raised an eyebrow at her. She shrugged at his look. "They're childhood friends, aren't they?" I nodded my head, but couldn't hide my confusion.

"How long has it been going on?" Volplie pressed. A

feeling of panic was rising in my chest as I thought hard to myself.

"I don't... I don't remember," I whispered. Jangmi gave me a worried glance before squeezing my shoulder.

"It's okay," she said. Volplie shook her head as she waved a fork at me.

"I told you. Silver-tongues are tricky," she muttered to herself, but I didn't have any recollection of her ever saying that to me. I held my head as it started to pound near my temples.

"Are you okay?" Agwe asked. I smiled and shook my head.

"Just hungry," I said, starting to eat my food. But, it all tasted like sawdust.

As I started to make my way back to the hill that overlooked the camp, I saw August and Anubys conversing with each other, heatedly. Anubys's thick black eyebrows were knitted together, as a smirk played on his lips. He scoffed. I couldn't see August's facial expression, the back of his head facing me.

"I *had* to do it, Anubys. Otherwise, she wouldn't trust me at that level. And the army needs her to..." I heard August say. I hid behind a cabin that was near them, and peeked around it to watch their conversation.

"You're playing with fire here, literally," Anubys hissed. "She's going to figure it out eventually. And she won't trust us at all."

"I'm stronger than you think I am," August said, his voice low.

"You had to make her fall..." Anubys pursed his lips as the sentence drifted away. Then he looked back up at August, his crooked smile looking as sinister as the day he broke Rohit's neck. *Make me what?*

"You're weirdly too close to the situation," I heard August mutter. "She trusts me more now."

"*Yeah*," Anubys scoffed. "I can see that."

"Just... Trust me," August said. "I know what I'm doing." I watched as Anubys shrugged.

"Trust a silver-tongue?" Anubys hissed. "Never." They silently glared at each other for a moment, before Anubys clicked his tongue and a smile that sent chills down my spine slithered over his lips.

"It's only a few more days now," I thought I heard Anubys say. "Better hope she's ready." Before I heard August's response, I quietly slipped away. I didn't want to be caught listening to their conversation.

Their words confused me. I didn't know what they were talking about. What was I going to figure out? Why wouldn't I trust them? Why did I *need* to trust them? A part of me believed I couldn't trust Anubys. I would be a fool to. But, August? Would I be a fool to trust *him*? I had known him all my life.

I sat under the shade of the tree on the hill, leaning against the rough bark as I stared at everyone walking by. Closing my eyes, I let my mind drift away.

A nightmare, a nightmare I knew I had before, but couldn't remember, plagued my mind. My mother's eyes were rolled back as she repeated the same words over and over again. I held my hands to my ears, pressing against them until I felt like my head was about to explode.

"Beware the shadow maker. Beware the silver-tongue," she repeated. The blood dripped onto my head. It dripped down my face, streaking it. It mixed with my own salty tears as my mother continued to berate me, getting bigger and bigger with each word.

"You'll kill us all," she said, her voice distorted. "Save us. Save us. *Save us.*" Her face morphed quickly into Forest's face, and then Rohit's, and landed on Dandelion's.

"You'll kill us all," all their voices said, coming out of little Dandelion's lips. "Save us. Save us, Zinnia." The fire inside me roared.

I felt myself choke as someone shook me awake. My eyes flew open, dark eyes staring back at me. I jumped at the closeness.

"Zinnia, are you all right?" Lightning asked. I held my hand to my chest, feeling my heart beat hammering.

"Yeah," I said, catching my breath as I leaned my head against the tree behind me. "I must've fallen asleep." Lightning's eyebrow rose.

"You had another nightmare," he pointed out. "I noticed you had them a lot when we left the Wall." He took a seat next to me, settling into the grass as he leaned against the tree. I cocked my head to the side as I tried to remember the nightmares he was talking about, my head pounding as I did. His eyebrow raised as he looked at me.

"Are you *sure* you're okay?" he asked, putting a

comforting hand on my shoulder. I shook my head and smiled weakly back at him.

"Yeah, I've just been having some headaches," I muttered. *You can trust him*, a voice screamed in my head. But, I ignored it. He wouldn't understand. He could never understand. Lightning was *good*. I lowered my gaze. He raised another eyebrow as he stared out at the people going about their day.

"This *is* a really peaceful spot that you've found," he said after a moment of silence. "It's too bad August is making you destroy it."

"He said he'll make sure it won't be destroyed," I said, somewhat defensive. Lightning didn't say anything, letting the silence envelope us.

"How does that work, exactly?" Lightning finally asked, turning his head slightly to look at me. "The whole putting your powers back into your body thing." I blinked as I tried to think.

"I'm not sure how it works. He just speaks, and it's like my body listens to him," I said. Lightning nodded in understanding.

"So, he's kind of like Lidya, except he just convinces you to do it." I squinted my eyes as I thought of the feeling.

"It's not convincing," I said, shaking my head. "It's more forceful than that. But, I don't know how to explain it."

"Ah," he responded. "Seems kind of dangerous." I turned away from him and stared out at the camp.

"Maybe. But, all of our powers are dangerous," I paused before saying, "Depending on who's using them." Lightning broke out into a grin.

"That's true," he said, chuckling a bit. Then, we let the

comfortable silence take the reins as we people watched for the rest of the afternoon.

"I can't believe we're eating fresh strawberries," Jangmi squealed as she picked another one and put it in her basket. We were tasked with harvesting the strawberries that were ripe enough to be picked on our day off from training.

"Who says we'll get to eat them?" Anubys piped up from a couple of rows away.

"There's enough for everyone, aren't there?" Jangmi asked, as she stared up at Agwe with wide eyes. He smiled at her forlorn expression and tucked a lock of black hair behind her ear.

"I'm sure we'll get to eat at least one," he said. She made an excited gesture as she picked another one.

"I hate strawberries," Volplie said as she sauntered by, behind us.

"Why?" I asked.

"They're too sour," she muttered.

"Shouldn't a fox like strawberries?" Eset asked, picking a fight. A ghost of a smile was on her lips as she continued to pick the red berries. She and Volplie still didn't seem to get along. Volplie made a face, part of her white hair pulled to the top of her head, much like the leaves of a strawberry.

"I'm a human that *shapeshifts*, Eset," Volplie muttered. As if karma was looking for vengeance, Eset made a noise of pain, holding her hand towards her face as she frowned at it. Lightning was by her side quickly, holding her wrist to look at her hand.

"What happened?" he asked, looking into her eyes as she haughtily pulled her hand back towards her.

"A bee sting," she mumbled. He stared at her for a moment longer and then went back to the bush he was picking strawberries from. Her eyes followed him for a bit before concentrating back on the wound on her hand.

"You think we'll get in trouble if we eat one of these strawberries?" Ash asked, his eyes lighting up as he came to our row. Anubys ambled after him.

"Lidya will probably punish the eater by having them watch her eat strawberries while frozen," he said, smirking.

"You'd like that, wouldn't you?" Lidya said, almost out of nowhere. Anubys wasn't fazed by her appearance, and his crooked smile got wider at her comment. He simply shrugged.

"Focus on the strawberry picking, kid. Lightning, Tayen needs you," she said, motioning her hand towards him. Eset stiffened as Lightning walked past her towards Lidya. Lidya linked arms with him before leading him away, her tongue sticking out as she looked over her shoulder at the rest of us.

"I wonder what Tayen needs a map for," Volplie said. Anubys glanced over at Eset before picking up another strawberry, dropping it into his basket.

"I wonder what his range is... for the little map in his head," Anubys muttered.

"What? You think he could locate someone anywhere in the world?" Ash asked, bewildered. Anubys shrugged a shoulder.

"Would be crazy, wouldn't it?" Anubys said. He leaned forward a bit. "By the way, has August been helping you with your powers lately?" At the mention of August, my ears pricked up.

"Yeah, he said he was going to. Just so I can help keep the forcefield running better, so nothing like... that night... happens again," Ash's brown eyes flickered towards me, and I looked away from their conversation. "Why?"

"Just wondering when he's going to start helping with my powers," Anubys said, snickering a bit.

"Like *you* need help with any of that," Eset said, rolling her eyes.

"They're probably afraid of you practicing," Agwe piped up. Anubys smirked a bit at his comment, as if he was proud of that fact.

"What? And they aren't afraid of the Bonfire exploding again?" he said, as I felt his gaze on me. I stiffened. "Pretty sure hers is way more destructive."

"They just want her to be able to control it," Jangmi said, coming to my defense, "*Because* it's so destructive. You already have a handle on yours. There's no need for you to practice." Anubys shrugged, his hypnotizing eyes meeting mine.

"Maybe there's another reason they want her practicing over me," he muttered. Before anyone could respond to him, he walked to another row to continue picking the fruit. I watched as he popped one of them into his mouth, dropping the leaves to the ground, and I couldn't help but smile to myself at the action.

CHAPTER TWENTY-FOUR

I woke up, covered in sweat. I wiped my auburn hair that stuck to my face out of my eyes as I climbed down the ladder of my bunk. I was so *tired* of nightmares. So tired of being berated by my mother night after night. It hadn't stopped since that day when I fell asleep under the tree. It was as if she were trying to sear the words into my head. Beware the shadow maker. Beware the silver-tongue. *I got it, mother*, I thought to myself as I slipped on my shoes and opened the cabin door.

"Where are you going?" I heard Jangmi's sleep-coated voice say.

"I just need to take a walk," I whispered. She seemed to accept my answer and turned over on her side, falling back asleep within a second. I quietly closed the door and breathed in the late spring night air. It was cooler at night, but the air was refreshing. It wasn't like how it was in Adams, or the Fire as we all not-so-affectionately called it. There, the air was thicker, and wasn't as refreshing. My mind wandered as I wondered what everyone was doing back home. What jobs they were assigned after the Test.

Walking down the street, the floating lights flickering as I did, I made my way around the camp. Ahead, in front of a burned down cabin, a figure froze in front of me. The shadow started running towards me and a breathless scream escaped my lips.

"Shh!" the figure said, putting a hand over my mouth, as if anticipating my impending scream. His light green eyes almost looked gray in the light. I blinked as I seemed to remember a memory. Him in a cabin, his eyes reflecting the color gray in the dim light. I shook my head. Anubys looked at me curiously, and then removed his hand from my mouth.

"What are you doing up?" he asked. I rubbed my temples as the flickering image of Anubys and August went through my mind. I squeezed my eyes shut and shook my head before opening them again.

"Nightmare," I said just as he said the same thing, but as a question. I raised my eyebrows.

"We seem to always talk when you get nightmares," he pointed out. I frowned. *Did we?* He motioned for me to follow him.

"The night air always makes me feel better," he said, leading the way. I followed after him, almost mindlessly. We walked side by side in silence for a moment, walking around the burned debris. There was someone in the Shadows that was able to move things with their mind and could easily rebuild these cabins, but they were recovering from the burns from that night. I closed my eyes, wincing as I remembered myself exploding.

"Your power feels different, doesn't it?" Anubys asked. I looked at his side profile as we continued to walk. His nose resembled Eset's, a slight bump protruding from the middle, and from the side, they almost looked like the same person. His eyes glanced over at me, and then he smirked.

"How do you know that it does?" I asked, quietly. How my fire came out of me earlier today versus the explosion it usually was, it felt like it was stifled, almost. Like a fist was wrapped around it, only squeezing a little bit of it out at a time. Anubys shrugged, but gave me a knowing smile as he slipped behind the old, iron gate that led to the gardens.

"I figured it would," he whispered. His eyes looked down almost mournfully. My eyebrows knitted together at his expression but didn't comment on it. He stopped, in the middle of the communal gardens. The moonlight illuminated the many flowers, though the usual brilliant colors were muted in the darkness.

"I come here, at night," he said. He smiled slightly, a glint in his hypnotizing, hawk-like eyes. "Nightmares." I felt my face soften as I looked up at him. He was leaning back, his head upturned to look at the night sky.

"It's almost the night of the full moon," he whispered, almost to himself. The magnetic pull that I felt emanating from him made me want to take a step closer, and it took everything in me not to. He seemed to contemplate something before turning towards me.

"You know, that day when we did that first training session with your powers," he paused, twisting his lips. My brow wrinkled in confusion. "I wasn't saying you were a monster, in case that's how you felt. I just... I just understand the feeling, is all."

"Oh," I responded. My head hurt as the partial memory came into my head. *"She wants to die. After what she did, she's so disgusted with herself, that she* wants *to die."* Anubys's words echoed around in my brain, but I couldn't remember why he said it. He gave me a sidelong glance before closing his eyes and shaking his head.

"What was your dream about?" he asked, changing the subject. I blinked.

"It was my mom," I said, before thinking. "It's always been my mom, lately."

"The dreamer." He flashed me a crooked smile. I tried to smile back but couldn't.

"Do you want to talk about it?" he asked. I shrugged. I shouldn't trust him. I knew it, deep down. However, I couldn't stop the words from spilling out of my mouth.

"It's her face, and it's like she's crying blood. Sometimes, she doesn't have any eyes. Sometimes, her eyes are rolled to the back of her head. And sometimes, she's squeezing me so tight I can't breathe," I whispered, trying to keep from shuddering. "She just warns me. Over and over again. Beware the..." I stopped myself, as I glanced over at him, eyes wide. He raised an eyebrow.

"She just says to be careful," I muttered.

"And to trust no one," he finished. I looked up in surprise. He smiled warily at me, his eyes almost like a predator's.

"What? You've told me that dream before," he whispered, his words washing over me. I frowned as I tried to remember the conversation. "But, this dream is a little different than that, isn't it?" He took a step closer, and I felt myself hold my breath.

"Her face changes. It becomes my friend Forest's face, and then Rohit's, and now... Dandelion's," I shook my head. "They all say I'm going to kill them. Then they tell me to save them. It's... confusing." Anubys sucked his teeth.

"Sounds like it," he said, taking a step back. He turned and continued to walk down the dirt path in the garden.

"I have nightmares about my past," he admitted. He looked like he wanted to say more, but instead said, "I wish they were as abstract as yours." I couldn't help but think his back looked sad, and I reached out, as if to touch him, comfort him. He turned, suddenly, and I pulled my arm back.

"I heard your dad is the Oracle." He spoke as if he met him before. I froze as I met his gaze. Something in his eyes was desperate.

"What does it mean if you were told you would be the undoing of—"

Just then, the sprinklers in the garden went off. I ducked from the cold water as I felt him reach back to grab my wrist. We ran to safety, and I started to laugh as I wiped the water off of my skin. There wasn't a lot of water on us, just a few droplets that stained my sweatshirt. I looked up, as he smiled down at me. His green eyes almost glowed in the darkness. His thumb gently wiped a drop from my cheekbone, the gesture warming every part of me. Water droplets clung to his dark hair, and in the moonlight, it looked like stars illuminating the night sky. I felt the smile start to fade from my lips as the magnetic pull brought me closer and closer to him, until we were inches apart.

His lazy smile was wiped off of his face as I started to lean in towards him. His eyes widened, and then he palmed my face. I blinked as my head was pushed away from his. And, when I realized what had just almost happened, my hands went up to my face in horror.

"Oh gods," I muttered, completely embarrassed. I felt the heat rise to my face. Anubys grabbed my chin, and his face looked amused as he tipped mine towards him.

"It's just because of the pull," he whispered with a tinge of regret. He grabbed my wrist, smiling playfully as he let go of my chin. "Do you feel that?" Our blood hummed along with one another, louder than I had ever heard it before. His smile turned dark, almost.

"It means our powers are similar," he murmured. Then, he let go of my wrist. I frowned as the memory came to my head. *Do you feel that?* It was almost like I was experiencing deja vu, but August's face was flickering with Anubys's. But, that's not what August told me. *It means we're meant to be.* His voice was loud in my head as I tried to recall the memory. I rubbed my temples, and Anubys's eyes watched me curiously.

"You should go back to bed," he whispered. I frowned up at him, my temple pulsating.

"Something's wrong with me," I muttered. He smiled, as if he enjoyed my pain.

"Go back to bed," he said, as he fingered the string on my sweatshirt. I closed my eyes, wincing, and then I turned away. My head turned slightly, looking at him as he still leaned against the iron gate.

"This never happened," I warned. His face lit up with amusement.

"Whatever you say, Sunshine," he breathed. I could feel the heat rise to my cheeks, and I turned away quickly, walking as fast as I could back to my cabin. I opened the door quietly and slipped back into my bed, my hands over my face as I thought about what just happened.

"Today, we're going to test out your teamwork," Lidya said after we all arrived at the training field. Biao was standing next to her, which was unusual. He normally wasn't at our training sessions. Lidya flashed a smile that unnerved me as she gestured towards August.

"You guys will be split up into two teams. It'll be capture the flag, essentially. Biao will take you guys up into the mountains," she said. "If you don't know what capture the flag is, the game is you have to defend your flag. Whoever steals the other team's flag, wins. Simple as that." Her smile got wider as Devlin revealed the eight folded uniforms they tended to wear. The silken black armor.

"*And*, you can use your powers," she said, almost gleefully. Then she frowned as she made eye contact with me and Anubys.

"Except you two," she said, pointing at us. "You can't use yours." Anubys crossed his arms as he feigned disappointment. I took a small step away from Anubys once I realized he was right next to me, the embarrassment from last night threatening to reveal itself on my face.

"Well, that's a bummer," he said.

"But, Eset can use hers?" Volplie piped up. Lidya looked excited as she turned towards her.

"Yes. She can resurrect whatever she thinks is necessary

out there," she said. "And you'll have to fight against it, I suppose."

"That's not fair then. Whoever has Eset on their team has the upper hand," Ash complained. Lidya shrugged.

"Jangmi can control animals. It's basically the same thing," Lidya pointed out. Ash pursed his lips as Jangmi seemed elated for being compared to Eset. Eset didn't look as happy about the comparison.

"Are we getting real swords then?" Anubys asked. Biao glared at him.

"No," he said. His word was final.

"Well, then how exactly are we supposed to defend ourselves against the animals and creatures those two throw at us?" Anubys asked, obviously annoyed. He gestured towards himself and then towards me as I struggled to not meet his eyes.

"That makes Firestorm and I vulnerable," he pointed out. I rolled my eyes at his newest nickname for me. August's eyes met mine at his words, concern for my well-being marring his eyebrows.

"Just stick with one," I muttered to him. He smirked.

"Firestorm isn't to your liking?" he teased.

"Miss Barbecue is preferable," I retorted, sarcastically. Anubys's eyes sparkled as a crooked smile spread across his face.

"The swords given to you should be enough to at least hinder the creatures for a swift getaway," Lidya responded to Anubys's comment, unconcerned. "Besides, you're supposed to *work* with your team."

"It does seem a bit unsafe," August seemed to mumble,

turning towards Lidya. His eyes met with Biao's, who shrugged in response.

"If they're going to be a part of the Shadows, they might as well get used to it," Biao responded. Lidya smiled smugly at August before gesturing towards his clipboard. He lifted it as he started to read out the teams. Jangmi, Ash, Anubys, and I were on one team. Eset, Lightning, Volplie, and Agwe on the other.

"Damn," Ash muttered once we gathered. "Eset and Lightning on one team? They're definitely going to win." We had changed into the black armor the other members of the Shadow Army wore. It was lighter than the other one, and I almost felt like I would float away into the breeze at any given moment. Anubys pursed his lips as he glared over at the other team. Eset smiled at him as she made a cutting motion over her throat. Anubys scoffed.

"Can we trade Ash for Agwe?" Anubys asked, raising his hand. Lidya made a face.

"No," she said.

"But, Agwe can heal people, and Zinnia and I might need to be healed," Anubys argued.

"No," she repeated.

"But—"

"The teams are final, Anubys," she snapped. Anubys slowly lowered his hand as Ash turned towards me and Jangmi.

"Am I really that useless?" he asked.

"Yes," Anubys answered.

"*Anubys*," Jangmi chastised.

"We don't need a forcefield," he pointed out. "They got a giant map on their team who will locate our flag immediately. And I can't use my powers at all. This is such a *bummer*. It's like they *want* us to lose." I couldn't help but laugh at Anubys's whining.

"I didn't realize you were *that* competitive," I laughed.

"I'll be damned if I lose to Eset," he muttered. Jangmi joined in with my laughter.

"A forcefield could be helpful to defending our team," Ash murmured under his breath. This made Jangmi laugh harder.

"I'm sorry," she said, gasping for breath. "You're right. You're right. It *would* be helpful." Ash made a face and turned away.

"We *could* put a forcefield around the flag. That way no one could get to it," I pointed out. Anubys put a hand to his chin as he thought. He was still glaring at Eset who was talking animatedly to her team. It was clear she had a plan and that she meant business. Her wavy, thick, black hair was pulled back into a tight bun. Anubys nodded once.

"Yeah, that could work. Until Ash gets beat to a pulp by my sister," he muttered. Ash's eyes widened as he looked over at Eset.

"You think she'd be the one grabbing the flag?" Ash asked.

"If I know my sister, and I know her better than anyone, she loves the glory of winning," Anubys grumbled.

"Okay," Lidya said, interrupting our conversations with a clapping of her hands. "Let's get going." She motioned towards us to grab a sword that was either blue or yellow. If you were hit by the sword in a vital spot, it would make a mark on you, and it meant you were out. We were team blue.

I walked over to Biao who started to lift us with the wind. I tightened my grip on my sword as I reminded myself not to use my powers during this exercise. But, as I glanced down at August whose blue eyes watched me as I was carried up, I had a feeling I wouldn't be able to use it even if I wanted to. At those thoughts, the fist around my fire seemed to grip it even tighter.

CHAPTER TWENTY-FIVE

"Take this pill," Lidya said, handing both Anubys and I a small white capsule. Anubys scrunched up his nose at the sight.

"What is it?" he asked. Biao had just dropped our team off at the spot where our flag was. The flag emitted a light into the sky that was still visible even during daylight. In the distance, I could see the light that was the other team's flag.

"It's to dull your powers for about a day," she said. "Just take it."

"You don't trust us to not use our powers?" Anubys asked with feigned surprise, a twinkle in his eye as he popped the pill into his mouth. He swallowed it down.

"I'm going to need some water," I muttered as I took the pill into my hands. Lidya pulled a water bottle out from the belt around her waist and handed it to me. Staring at the pill for a moment, I took a deep breath and then put it into my mouth, washing it down with the lukewarm water. Almost immediately, I felt this empty, cold feeling settle into my chest. Lidya took back the water bottle as she stepped onto Biao's concentrated air. She gave a wave as Biao looked us over disapprovingly before disappearing up into the sky. Anubys waited until they were out of sight before turning towards us.

"Okay, here's the plan," Anubys said, spitting the pill out of his mouth and throwing it onto the ground. I couldn't help but gape at him.

"You didn't take it?" I asked, incredulously. He turned towards me slightly.

"You *did?*" he said in disbelief. Then he sighed, as if he were disappointed in me before turning back to Jangmi. "You will take your animals and head towards their flag with Zinnia. Luckily, they have a light emitting from it so we don't have to do the work of trying to find it before fighting. They probably want us to finish quickly."

"We're not supposed to use our powers during this fight," I interjected. Anubys stared at the horizon for a moment, more annoyed than I had ever seen him, before turning towards me.

"I'm not going to give up my powers just to give someone peace of mind. I'm not going to kill anybody. It's just for the creatures my sister will resurrect. Do you know how many dead bodies that had powers when they were alive are out here? And don't think she won't actually try to kill anyone because she most *definitely* would," he said, quickly, like he wanted to just get this conversation over with. "Can we talk about the plan now?"

"Damn," I muttered. "I was just saying." He ignored me

and continued to animatedly tell Jangmi what she needed to do. Her eyes were wide as she tried to process all of the information.

"You think Eset would really try to kill us?" Ash asked me. I shrugged.

"She gets a power trip," Anubys said, overhearing Ash. "She wouldn't mean to. But, it could happen. And that's why I didn't take it."

"Isn't she too far away for you to use your powers anyways?" I asked, crossing my arms.

"It's only for when she's close by. She wouldn't let the creatures wander far from her."

"She doesn't control them though, does she?" Ash asked. Anubys shook his head.

"No, she's not like Lidya. She just resurrects them. But, things can go missing when someone is resurrected. And usually, all that's left at first after someone is raised from the dead is fear and survival. They'll fight anyone in front of them. Which is *why* she would only resurrect someone if you're right there in front of her," Anubys explained. He turned towards me and handed me his sword.

"I've seen the way you move lately during combat training," he said. "You would be more effective if you dual wielded."

"What?"

"Use two swords," he said, pushing his sword into my free hand. "You're in charge of getting as many people out as possible. Oh, and for getting the flag."

"What?" I repeated. This seemed way out of my depth.

"Eset will be coming after our flag, so it should be easy to take theirs, if you avoid her," Anubys mused.

"No, I mean, I don't think that I can..." I let the words drift away. He gave me a quizzical look, and then realization seemed to wash over him.

"Oh, you're one of those people," he muttered, almost under his breath. "I should've known."

"One of—"

"Listen, you're pretty good with a sword. I don't doubt that you'll be able to do it, and you shouldn't doubt yourself either. And your powers are stifled right now because you *stupidly* took that pill, so you shouldn't be afraid of letting loose," he said. This was probably the most annoying I had ever found him to be. I gripped both swords in my hands, hard.

"You're kind of being an asshole," I murmured. He paused for a second before turning towards me. He smirked as he looked down at me, his arms looking more toned in the black armor shirt he was wearing as he crossed them.

"That's not what you were saying last night," he smiled. My jaw dropped. Through my peripheral vision, I could see Jangmi and Ash exchange curious looks.

"We said we'd never talk about it," I said through gritted teeth. He shrugged, smug at my reaction.

"I don't think I ever agreed to that," he said. We stared each other down for a while before Jangmi cleared her throat. I quickly turned away from his gaze at the sound. He turned towards Ash and pointed at the flag, all business once again.

"You're in charge of defending the flag," Anubys said, making a motion with his hands that, I think, was supposed to represent a forcefield. "Also, give me your sword. I've watched you with Zinnia, and you're terrible. I don't even know why they let you hold one." Ash blinked as he gave me a look. He slowly handed Anubys his sword, not breaking eye contact with me. His gaze spoke his unspoken thoughts: *Do something about him.* I sighed inwardly as I made myself move towards him.

"Okay, Anubys," I said, reaching up to grab his shoulders as he wrapped his long fingers around the hilt of the blue sword. I turned him around from Ash who was starting to make a forcefield around the blue flag. I patted Anubys's shoulder in an effort to calm him down as he looked at me, confused.

"What?" he asked, his green eyes softening as they looked at me. I felt myself hold my breath as the memory of his face being inches away from mine came to the forefront of my mind. Every part of me was singing. I was close. Way too close to him. I quickly let go of his shoulders as a smirk started to spread on his lips. He opened them, like he wanted to say something that would most likely embarrass me further, but Jangmi, thankfully, interrupted.

"You know, Agwe is pretty handy with his sword," she said, a single finger on her chin as she looked up in thought. Anubys snickered as Ash's face turned red. She looked at them, her eyebrows furrowed.

"Why is that funny?" she asked.

"I bet he is," is all Anubys said. I hit his shoulder, and he quickly composed himself. "You two are together, aren't you? Just distract him enough until you get him out." It was Jangmi's turn for her face to turn bright red.

"Okay," she whispered under her breath, not denying the relationship that had developed between the two of them.

"Everyone know what their jobs are?" Anubys asked. We all nodded, as we hesitantly looked at each other. If Anubys noticed our indecisiveness, he didn't say anything. He cracked his fingers and then rubbed his neck, a fire in his eyes.

"All right, let's get to it," he said, running into the forest.

"He's probably going to try to find Eset first," I said. Ash nodded his head. I gave him a pitying look as I glanced down at his empty hand.

"Do you need—" Ash shook his head, determination in his eyes.

"I won't need it," he declared. I nodded once, looking at Jangmi.

"Let's go," I suggested. She waved goodbye to Ash, and then we started walking into the woods, in the direction of the yellow flag.

"Do you think Volplie is the one guarding the flag or Agwe?" I asked Jangmi as we walked side by side. I kicked a stick that was in front of me out of the way.

"You don't think Lightning would be guarding the flag?" Jangmi asked. I shook my head.

"I think Eset would take Lightning with her for cannon fodder," I muttered. Then, after seeing Jangmi's horrified face, I added, "And also because he would be able to see the best path to take to the flag and if any of us were coming their way."

"You think little of Eset," Jangmi pointed out.

"You don't?" I asked her. Jangmi shook her head.

"She may realize Lightning has feelings for her, but I don't think she'd use them against him," she said. My eyebrows raised.

"Lightning has feelings for her?" Jangmi giggled.

"You haven't noticed?" she asked. I guess I *kind of* noticed, I thought. But, I didn't think it was to the point where he would be able to be *used* by her.

"I don't know," I said. "I don't think it's like that. Besides, the twins can't care about anything or anyone." Jangmi pursed her lips as she thought about what I said.

"Are you sure about that?" she asked. I stared at her for a moment, trying to understand the weight that was behind her words. But, instead of answering, I turned towards the clearing we were coming upon. The flag was so close.

I motioned towards Jangmi, and she nodded once, determination blooming on her face. We ran towards the flag, hoping to confuse Volplie who was probably the one guarding it. When I saw who was standing in front of the flag, I stopped in my tracks, both swords raised. Eset smiled wildly at me, her eyes almost glowing from glee.

"Oh, I know my brother *so well*," she said, laughing as she spoke. "He thought *I* would be the one after the flag. Oh, I knew it!" She was almost jumping from joy. Volplie stalked out from the other side of the hill the flag was on, in shapeshifted fox form. She looked like herself, but also not like herself. An almost humanoid version of a silver-white fox. She flashed her canines, unnaturally, at us—a sword in her left hand.

"He really needs to think ahead more. Anubys really thought *I* wouldn't count on his thoughts about me? About how I love to win and take all the credit? Ha!" Eset laughed some more, her eyes starting to look crazed as she raised her light-brown arms above her head. Volplie's violet eyes side-eyed her as a cracking sound started to echo in the clearing. Bones started to break the surface of the ground, rising from their graves. I lowered my stance, tightening my grip on the two swords in my hands.

"I'll take care of her," Jangmi whispered from beside me. I looked at her, startled by her resolve. Ice was in her eyes as she started to close them. I heard animal noises from all different directions in the woods, and when Jangmi opened her eyes again, they looked faraway. Like, she was in a different place. She gestured towards Eset, and animals started leaping out of the woods, attacking the humans that Eset was raising from the dead. The dead were starting to regenerate some of their skin and eyes as they stalked towards the person who was attacking them: Jangmi. Eset's laugh echoed as the various animals reached their marks.

"Let's see if you deserve the comparison to me, little one," I heard her say. This was the most joy I had ever seen from her. Jangmi's eyes were fixated on Eset, as she started to walk forwards towards her. I glanced over at Volplie, whose eyes were, in turn, fixated on Jangmi. She was going to take her out of the game in order for no one to be able to attack Eset's creatures.

I ran towards Volplie, striking the dead down with my blue swords, marking them with a blue streak. They would fall, but I knew it was a matter of time before they were up and walking again. At least I was taking their attention off of Jangmi.

My blue sword hit Volplie's yellow one as I reached with the other sword in my hands to stab her in the chest. She evaded it, easily. I heard more sounds of cracking all around us, and watched as Eset laughed maniacally as she easily countered Jangmi's attacks with her sword. She wasn't trying to attack her back, as if she were a cat playing with Jangmi the mouse.

"This isn't good," Volplie muttered, morphing back into her half form. She gave me a worried glance as more dead humans started to form around us.

This must've been a graveyard at some point in the past. Or a battle site. The dead humans didn't know who they were supposed to attack, instead opting to attack whatever was in front of them.

Volplie dropped her sword, opting to use her own limbs for a better defense. I held onto mine and hit the dead before Volplie would jump onto them, in their confusion, and rip their heads off. I tried to swallow the bile that rose into my throat as Volplie jumped from dead human to dead human, ripping their heads off with her elongated snout. Her white ears were pressed against the back of her head as she snarled at the creatures.

I concentrated on the dead whose eyes were focused on me. Some of them were only half formed, and some of them were still bones. I lowered into my stance, and pushed back at them as they clawed at my skin. I hit their heads, their chest, anywhere that I thought would stun them for a moment. *Damn, I wish they gave us real swords*, I thought to myself as I gritted my teeth. I glanced over at Eset and a feeling of uselessness washed over me. The fire I had gotten so used to churning through my bloodstream was now gone, and a part of me would sell my soul if I were able to use it now.

Slowly making my way towards Eset, in order to try and get her out of the game, I felt the cold, empty feeling start to lift from my chest. *Yes,* I thought as I quickly hit the dead creatures coming for me. I jumped over the animals, fighting the dead, as the fire started to melt away my skin. I could feel it, start to feel it come out of me. But, then a cold fist locked around my fire and squeezed it to oblivion.

It was painful, and I gasped for breath as I bent over, a dead human grabbing my hair in the process. He lifted my head up, as he glared at me. This man was fully formed now, fully resurrected. And by the look of him, he looked like he was a soldier at one point. His fury burned in his eyes.

"You think you could destroy us, *mutant?*" he spat the word in my face and I stared at him, my eyebrows knitted together.

"We'll never let you get away with this," he hissed as he pulled back his other fist. I raised my sword, breathless, and hit him in the chest. But, it was as if my blows did nothing to him except pause him for a moment.

"What archaic weapons are you—" he started to sneer. But, then, his eyes went glassy as a silent scream began to appear on his face. His grip on my hair loosened, and I dropped to the ground, pain erupting in my legs at the impact. My eyes searched the clearing for Anubys, but the man in front of me was the only one who was seemingly affected by Anubys's power. Meaning... *he was still too far away.* The man dropped to his knees and then, wordlessly, collapsed.

"Eset, stop this," I heard August's voice say. I glanced over, and at the edge of the woods were August, Lidya, and

Biao. Biao was fighting against the resurrected humans with a real sword, slicing through them easily. With the fully formed ones, blood sprayed across his face.

"Sorry, Silver-Tongue, but you're not in my head," Eset shrugged, her voice almost taunting.

"Kill them," August ordered, and I heard the power that was behind his words.

"Can't. I only can give them life. Didn't you all figure that out by now?" she laughed. I watched as Jangmi finally hit Eset across the chest while she was distracted, making a blue mark appear on her armor. Eset's eyes glanced down at the mark, frozen for a second. Fury flared within her as she glared at Jangmi. With her yellow sword, Eset hit her with a strong force, knocking Jangmi down to the ground. Anger built up in me as I got up, trying to reach my cousin. As I ran towards her, the resurrected humans around me fell to the ground, dead, as if Anubys could see where I was going.

Just as I reached her, the rest of the dead started to scream collectively, and I watched as Anubys entered the clearing, ice in his eyes. He had the same crazed look Eset had on her face a moment ago. But, her face had morphed into fury as she watched the dead humans start to fall to the ground. Her eyes were so fixated on Anubys, that she didn't see me pounce onto her. I dropped the swords and brought her to the ground with my body. We rolled down the hill as she wordlessly screamed in my face.

"What the fuck is *wrong* with you?" I yelled at her as she punched me in the side of my face. The pain startled me for an instant, my eyes seeing stars. But, once I regained my composure, I didn't hold back as I hit her in retaliation.

"*Get up*," August's voice said, near me. Even though my

body fought against the order, I forcibly got up off of Eset. She looked shocked, as if the punch to her face brought her back to reality. The crazed look in her eye was gone, and she looked around, her eyebrows furrowed.

"I went a little too far again, didn't I?" she asked, her eyes meeting Anubys's.

"I knew you would," he said, his voice dead.

"What took you so long anyways?" she retorted, as he helped her up.

"I wanted to win the game and you sent fucking Agwe to the flag," Anubys responded, as if it were obvious. She smiled.

"Did we win?" she asked, looking at Lidya and Biao. Lidya stared at her like she was insane. I felt myself start to pitch forward, in order to hit her again, but a look from Lidya and I couldn't move.

"She's *psychotic*," I felt my mouth say, though it came out slightly muffled as I stood, frozen from Lidya's power. Anubys glanced over at me, and I saw him frown as his eyes flickered towards my cheek. I could feel the bruise that was starting to bloom there. His eyes rove over me, as if checking for more injuries. Hesitantly, his hands reached up, and it looked like he was about to move towards me, but August stood in front of me first. August's warm hands cupped my face as he looked at my bruise.

"I knew we shouldn't have let them use their powers," August muttered to Lidya, though he was still facing me. His fingers grazed over a cut on my hand, and I winced at the slight pain.

"I thought she'd be able to control the ones she resurrected," Lidya grumbled as Biao gave her a disapproving look. Lightning, Agwe, and Ash entered the clearing, the blue flag in Lightning's hands. Their faces were the epitome of shock. Eset clapped from glee, not worried about the bruise that was forming on her jaw.

"We *did* win," she laughed.

CHAPTER TWENTY-SIX

I stabbed the roasted potato with my fork as I glared across the cafeteria at Eset. Anubys was sitting down next to her, whispering heatedly, probably about the exercise from earlier. She looked like she couldn't care less.

"If you glare at her any harder, your eyes will pop out," Lightning mused as he watched me angrily chew the potato I had just stabbed.

"She hit Jangmi," I snapped. "Hard." Lightning's eyebrows raised as he glanced over at Eset.

"I don't think she did it on purpose," he muttered. I let out a dry laugh.

"Yeah, you *would* say that," I said. He furrowed his eyebrows as he glanced over at me, his dark brown eyes searching mine.

"What do you mean by that?" he asked, his voice eerily calm. I didn't say anything further as I continued to stab at the roasted potatoes.

"I'm fine, Zinnia," Jangmi assured, smiling at me from

across the table. She put a small hand on Agwe's shoulder. "Agwe healed me all up."

"Yeah, great," I said, almost sarcastically. Lightning gave me a look as he pointed a bony finger at me, almost in warning.

"You need to chill out," he said, his deep voice not raising a decibel. He, then, focused on his food as if the conversation was over. But, I wasn't done.

"She would've killed us all if it weren't for Anubys not taking that stupid pill," I pointed out. Agwe looked confused as he turned towards Jangmi.

"What pill?" he asked. She waved his words away.

"She wasn't going to kill anyone," Lightning argued. I stared at him, incredulously.

"Are you just blinded by her beauty or something? She's psychotic. Just like her brother," I said, blood rushing to my face as I mentioned Anubys. Immediately, I regretted what I said, but I continued, "She literally can't care about anyone. You know that, right?" Lightning stared at me like he didn't know who I was. He clicked his tongue and looked down at his tray.

"You don't know her," he breathed. I laughed.

"And you think you do?" I said. His hand that rested on the table flexed, and he turned his whole upper body to look at me.

"You think I didn't notice you two were walking around together last night? I see everything. You're completely all right with him, *him* who brings death along with his every step. But, you got problems with his twin sister who faced the same traumatic upbringing? Who are *you* to tell me—"

"She's just using you," I interrupted, not wanting to hear

what Lightning really thought about me. This was the second time I had ever heard him speak more than a couple of sentences in one sitting. He gaped at me, in disappointment and anger. Then, he leaned in, his face so close I could feel his breath.

"If she's using me, what do you think Anubys is doing to *you*?" he almost whispered. My eyes caught Anubys's gaze from behind Lightning's head, and I looked away.

"Okay, let's stop this," August said, appearing seemingly out of nowhere. Lightning just continued to stare at me. It wasn't necessarily a glare, but anger dripped from his eyes. I let August grab my arm, and we left the cafeteria. I could feel Anubys's eyes on me as I walked past him, but I didn't dare meet them. Lightning's words echoed around in my head. *If she's using me, what do you think Anubys is doing to* you? I shook my head. Beware the shadow maker. I already knew not to trust him. And a part of me didn't. But, there was a part of me, a large part, that *wanted* to trust him.

"Eset is a resurrector," August finally spoke as we walked towards the hill that overlooked the camp. My favorite spot. I glanced at him.

"Okay, and?" I said, attitude dripping from my words. August looked quickly at me, amused.

"Sometimes, with resurrectors, at least based on what we know from past resurrectors, they lose a part of themselves as they give life," he said, confirming what I thought. "Based on what we know about her and Anubys's upbringing, she might not be able to think about anyone else's feelings besides her own."

"It was an exercise. She shouldn't have even used it in the first place," I pointed out as we sat down at the base of the tree. His sapphire blue eyes twinkled at me, as if I had said something funny.

"For people who use their powers a lot, it's kind of like a high. We get addicted to using them after a while," he said. "For someone like Eset, she'd jump on the opportunity to use it."

"Are *you* addicted to *your* powers?" I asked, trying to make a point. He stared at me for a moment, and then looked over at the camp. I watched as he clenched his jaw.

"It's a high... for everyone," he said. Then, he gave me a comforting smile. "There's no way around it, unfortunately."

"So, you think I'll get addicted to using mine?" I asked. He shrugged as he leaned back against the tree.

"If you use it enough, you would," he said, matter-of-factly. He stared up at the sky that was bursting into color.

"Do you remember that day? At the swings?" he asked, softly. I scrunched my eyebrows as I tried to remember what he was talking about. August was around me at all times growing up. But, a hazy memory was coming to the forefront of my mind.

"You're called Zero, right?" I remember him asking as I had stared up in awe at him. But, why would I be awed at him speaking to me if we hung out every day? Why would he ask if I were called Zero, if he already knew? I held the side of my head as my temple started to pulsate. He looked over at me, concerned, and moved as if to help me, but I put up a hand.

"I remember," I said, through gritted teeth. "Barely." I thought his eyes looked worried for a moment, but it disappeared so quickly that I didn't know if I imagined it or not.

"It was right before I took the Test," he said, relaxing as I did. "That conversation we had... It helped me a little." I didn't remember the conversation, and I didn't want to try to in order to avoid the impending pain that came with it, but I nodded along as if I did. He gave me a sidelong glance.

"Just to know someone else was the same as me," he muttered.

"I was shocked that everyone forgot about you."

"You must've not taken your pill the next day," he almost laughed. I shrugged.

"I can't remember," I admitted. "But, everyone liked you because of your power, huh?" He looked surprised by my comment and gave me a small smile.

"I can't help it," he said, almost guiltily. "People just seem charmed by me, whether I'm actively using my power or not."

"Did you know you had an ability before failing?" He shook his head.

"No," he answered. "My power isn't something that would be easily noticeable as something... supernatural, I guess. Not like yours." He smiled at me, and I couldn't help but feel like I was the most special person in the world. I looked away from him for a moment.

"Do you ever think about what everyone is doing back home?" I asked, pulling at the grass beneath me. He took a deep breath.

"All the time," he breathed.

"Who was your best friend, in your year?" I pried. August's smile faded from his face.

"I don't want to talk about her," he said. *Her*. For some reason, a pang in my chest appeared. I tried to ignore it.

"Okay," I said. "I don't remember my test, but I see Forest's face in my dreams sometimes. And he has a wound in his chest, like he had been stabbed there. Sometimes, I wonder... If I..." I closed my eyes as I remembered Forest and how he would constantly tease me. June used to say that if love marriages were allowed, Forest and I would've definitely ended up together. I was never sure.

"He was a good friend to you," August said, placing a hand over mine. I glanced up at him, my eyes watering as I tried to smile. A tear spilled over, and August's thumb wiped over my cheek, catching it.

"The Test is necessary, for the Nation's purposes. But, it's... brutal," he muttered. We interlocked fingers in silence as we stared out at the camp.

"Do you think President Eclipse will find this place?" I asked after a moment. I saw August glance at me from my peripheral vision.

"I hope not," he said. "But, it's only a matter of time." I turned towards him.

"What do you mean?" I asked.

"The camp moves every few years, to avoid President Eclipse's forces. But, I've been here for a couple of years now. It's probably time for them to move before another attack happens."

"Another?"

"Well, they call themselves the Shadow Army for a reason," he said. "They've fought President Eclipse's forces a fair amount of times."

"What is our goal?" I asked. The question had been burning in my mind for days. What was the purpose of fighting? There weren't enough of us to take on the whole Nation.

"Their goal?" August asked, knitting his brown eyebrows together. "They want to kill President Eclipse and change how the Nation is run, I guess. But, there's not enough of them to do that." I frowned at August for a moment and then shook the thoughts from my head.

"So you and Anubys went on a midnight walk last night?" August asked, changing the subject. I looked over at him, guilt rising up my throat.

"It wasn't like that. I just had a nightmare and he gets nightmares, too, apparently," I quickly defended myself. He laughed.

"It's not like we're dating," he said, but his eyes burned holes into my face. "Are we?" The question hung in the air.

"I... I don't know," I answered, honestly. I didn't know what I felt for August. I trusted him completely, due to our past together. A part of me liked him a lot. But, some part of me, deep down, was disgusted by him, and I wasn't sure why.

"Well, we don't need to define anything at the end of the world," he muttered, squeezing my hand. *End of the world?* He got up and gave me a sideways smile and then held out his hand. I grabbed it and he easily lifted me off of the ground.

"Biao will probably be pissed if we miss roll call," he said and started to lead the way down the hill. I paused for a moment, staring at his back that looked like it held so much weight on it for some reason. And then, I followed after him.

A face I didn't recognize turned towards me. A smile spread on her face as gold ran down her cheeks, similar to the blood that usually was on my mother's in these dreams.

"Burn them all," she whispered. "Burn them all to the ground." She gripped my shoulders, her eyes completely white.

"Kill them all," she whispered, the words echoing all around me. "You felt the power grow when we consumed them. *Kill them.*" I tried to push her off of me, but she just held on tighter, a crown of fire appearing on her head. And then, I started to recognize her. Her auburn hair was almost floating all around her as she gave me a frightening smile.

"We'll destroy them all," she assured. "For the Nation. All for the Nation." She started to explode, the fire spilling out of her until she was nothing but a living flame. And I screamed as the flames started to burn me alive.

I jolted out of my sleep, frantically checking my limbs for burns as I remembered the feeling of the fire slowly eating at every nerve in my body. Letting out a sigh, I laid back into my pillow, a hand over my face. Another nightmare, except this time, it was myself. *My future self?* Was this another warning from my mother that was sent before her death? A glimpse into my future from my father?

The unnatural smile that was on my face wouldn't leave my mind. It reminded me of Eset's crazed smile from the other day. I tossed and turned, unable to fall asleep. Sitting up, I decided to take a walk. Part of me hoped Anubys would be outside unable to sleep, too. Another part of me hoped I wouldn't have to talk to him again. However, as I opened the door, I saw him leaning against his own cabin, as if he were waiting for me to come outside.

"Why are you just standing there?" I whispered. He smiled as he gestured towards me.

"Couldn't stay away, huh?" he teased, not answering my question. My nose wrinkled as I rolled my eyes.

"Yeah, okay," I said sarcastically. "Like I would ever want to see you again."

"Could've fooled me last night," he said, flashing a mischievous, crooked smile at me as he looked up through his black lashes. He was impossibly beautiful. I felt the heat rise to my face, and I turned quickly. *Why did he keep bringing that up?*

"That *never* happened," I almost demanded.

"Okay," he said, shrugging, but the annoyingly smug smile didn't leave his face. The dimple on his left cheek was more pronounced when he smirked. I resisted the urge to poke it.

"What did August say about you canoodling with me in the middle of the night?" he asked, putting his hands in his pockets. It dulled the magnetic pull only slightly. I laughed.

"Canoodling?" I asked, raising my eyebrows at his choice of words. Also, I didn't want to answer his question. For some reason, I didn't want to talk about August. The thought of him made me want to throw up, now that I was away from him.

"It's a word," he said in response. Then, his face lit up as he tapped my arm with his elbow.

"Hey, I want to show you something that reminded me of you," he said. My heart beat loudly in my chest at those words. I nodded, almost shyly. A mischievous glint appeared in his eyes as he led the way. Eventually, we came upon a pile of ashes from a bonfire. I stared at it, in disbelief.

"This reminded me of you," he said, gesturing towards it with gusto. I blinked.

"A pile of ashes?" I asked.

"Since you seem to burn everything to oblivion, I thought it was fitting," he said, flashing me the biggest grin I've ever seen on his face.

"...fuck you." His grin just got bigger.

"I would if I could," he sighed, dramatically, before turning away. I just rolled my eyes at him.

"That wasn't funny, though," I said, quietly. His hypnotizing eyes glanced over at me, and his grin faded a bit.

"Your nightmare was about *that*? What are the odds?" he said, mostly to himself as he looked up at the sky.

"It was *me*. I had a crown of fire on my head, and I just... I didn't look like me," I muttered. I didn't know why I told him my dreams. Maybe it was because some part of me thought he would understand, thought he was the only one who *could* truly understand. His thick eyebrows raised slightly as he raked a hand through his wavy hair.

"What did you say to yourself in your dream?" he asked, seemingly genuinely curious.

"She was telling me to kill them all. Burn them all to the ground," I didn't mention the part where she reminded me of the feeling I got when I was able to kill someone. The flames of life that I consumed from Rohit, and from... My head started to hurt again.

"Did I... kill Dandelion?" I asked. Anubys raised an eyebrow and then let out a dry chuckle.

"He really did erase it," he mumbled so quietly I wasn't sure if I heard right.

"What? Erase what?" I asked. Anubys's green eyes met

mine, and he stayed still briefly. He looked like he was contemplating something in his mind, and eventually, his mouth opened.

"You killed her," he said, his voice monotone. "She was burned alive." I felt myself freeze, but a part of me deep down knew it already.

"That makes sense," I muttered. He studied me for a minute and then he looked up at the moon again.

"Full moon tomorrow," he said. I furrowed my eyebrows together as I looked up at the moon. I didn't understand why he kept telling me the full moon was almost here.

"You should go to bed," he said, but in a tone that seemed disappointed. He then gave me a glance, a crooked smile on his face. "Before you do something you regret again." I felt myself blush, and I turned away from him quickly, unable to stare into his eyes for a moment longer.

"Thanks for talking to me," I mumbled. His smile faded as he looked at me, as if he were searching for an answer to something in my face.

"Good night," is all he said. I wanted to ask what the words were that he was holding back, but didn't. And I fell asleep dreaming about Anubys's hypnotizing eyes.

CHAPTER TWENTY-SEVEN

"You should talk to Lightning," Jangmi whispered to me, as I continued to pull up the weeds that were threatening to ruin the flowers surrounding it. I scoffed.

"I don't need to talk to him about Eset, of all people," I muttered. Jangmi wore cotton, green gardening gloves as she pulled a weed in front of her. Lidya gave us our day off earlier than usual in the week because of the events that happened yesterday. Although, our "day off" usually consisted of us doing other chores. And currently, we were in charge of taking care of the gardens. The communal gardens where Anubys and I... I shook the memory from my head as I turned my attention onto another victim, pulling the weed out by its roots.

"I've just never seen you two completely ignore each other before," Jangmi said, almost under her breath. At her words, I couldn't help but steal a glance at Lightning who was across the gardens from us. He was next to Ash who was talking animatedly, holding a small shovel in one of his hands he was waving around. Lightning's face was tensed in concentration. I looked back at the dirt in front of me.

"We don't really talk *that* much," I pointed out. Jangmi gave me a look.

"He cares about you," she said, her dark eyes turning towards him. "He watches out for you all of the time. Like he's your big brother, or a protector." Lightning was always there whenever fear was bubbling up in me, asking me if I were okay. And he always made me feel better, just by being there. It was different from the calming feeling August would give me. It was more... natural. I bit the inside of my cheek as I thought about our mini fight from yesterday evening.

"I didn't say anything he should be mad at me about," I said, my voice monotone. I crab walked over to another weed, reaching towards it to grab it.

"He cares about Eset, too," Jangmi sighed, her gaze now on Eset who was sitting in the shade pretending to water a plant. My nose scrunched up in distaste at the sight of her.

"I don't understand how you can—how you *all* can— forgive her so easily after what happened yesterday," I said, taking the garden gloves off.

"What else are we going to do? Be mad at her for the rest of our lives?" Jangmi asked, a small, sad smile on her lips. She shook her head as she focused back on her task, not meeting my eyes. "Besides, I was the one she directly attacked. Shouldn't it only be me who decides whether to forgive her or not? Not you?" I felt myself stiffen at her words that held a little bit of ice behind them. Jangmi was sweet, probably one of the nicest girls I had ever met. But, she reminded me sometimes that just because she was nice did not mean she was weak. I swallowed the bitter lump in my throat from being called out.

"I'm not going to apologize to Lightning. He said some mean things to me, too," I said the last part a little bit more quietly. Jangmi laughed.

"You were the one who told him that Eset is using him," Jangmi remarked. I felt my lips tighten into a line as I dusted the dirt off of my pants.

"Do you really think she's not?" I hissed. Jangmi's eyes widened, and she knitted her eyebrows together as she took off her gardening gloves.

"Zinnia, what do you think Eset is trying to do? She's been in training with us every day for over a month, and nothing has happened. Why do you trust Anubys but not her? They both worked for President Eclipse," Jangmi whispered, confusion creasing her brow.

"I don't trust Anubys," I lied, speaking under my breath. Her confusion only grew.

"You left last night, too," she whispered. "I saw you with him."

"I *don't* trust him," I said, more definitively. "We shouldn't trust either of them. I can't explain *why*, I just... You have to trust—"

"What are you girls talking about?" Eset's voice startled me so much I nearly jumped out of my skin. I turned around, bewildered at her appearing beside me. She pulled on her garden gloves, which were black. *Probably matched the color of her soul*, I couldn't help but think. She smiled slightly as she squatted down to pull out some weeds.

"Me?" she asked, her smile not quite meeting her eyes as

she pulled one out. The force in which she did it, for some reason, made my blood run cold. I ignored Eset and turned slightly towards Jangmi.

"I'm going to go talk to Lightning," I said. Eset seemed to smile to herself.

"You think he wants to talk to you?" she grinned, her green eyes meeting mine. They were so much like Anubys's but also so different. Darker. A darker, more emerald green. Like June's.

"Why wouldn't he want to talk to me?" I asked, crossing my arms. She smirked, her side profile looking exactly like Anubys's. I felt my heart pound as I thought of him.

"Because of what you said about me," she said, fluttering her eyelashes almost innocently. My face contorted into distaste as I walked past her.

"You don't know how I feel about him," her voice cut through the air. I turned around slightly.

"I know you can't care about anyone," I hissed. A small smile appeared on her lips.

"Why do you believe my brother can, then?" she whispered. She and I stared at each other for a moment longer, and then she looked away, breaking the spell that kept me frozen to the spot. I stalked towards Lightning, sitting down in the dirt next to him. He and Ash both held the same expression of bewilderment.

"Why are you sitting here?" Ash asked, after a while of both of them just gaping at me.

"I'm sorry, Lightning. Okay? I'm sorry," I said, turning towards him. He slowly closed his mouth and his face hardened slightly.

"You don't trust my judgment," he said, quietly.

"And, also, no offense Zinnia, but that wasn't *really* an apology," Ash noted. I narrowed my eyes at him, and he sucked in his lips as he turned away.

"He's right," Lightning said, his brown eyes meeting mine. I chewed on the inside of my cheek.

"I'm not sorry for telling you the truth," I muttered. Lightning's gaze turned cold, and he turned away from me, digging a small hole and letting the seed in his hands fall into it.

"I don't like Anubys either," Lightning said, quietly. "I never liked him."

"I know," I said.

"And I don't say anything about how close you have gotten to him," Lightning pointed out, his voice still quiet and in that calm cadence I was used to.

"We're not... really... that close," I stammered, feeling the heat rise to my face. An eyebrow of his just raised as he stared at me.

"We're not," I insisted. Lightning shrugged and continued to dig another small hole.

"I'm not saying I trust Eset," he said slowly. "I don't trust either of them. Something about them is..." He let out a breath. "I just think you give him the benefit of the doubt, and you don't do that for her."

"You just think she's pretty," I muttered. Lightning's eyes turned amused.

"Yeah, she's pretty," he said. His gaze lifted to look up at her who was glaring at the two of us. She ripped a weed out, without breaking eye contact. "But, there's something else about her. Something broken."

"She's not someone you can fix," I whispered to him. He stiffened at my words and then slowly met my gaze.

"Not everyone is a loss cause," he whispered back. I understood how he felt. It was a feeling I knew all too well. We stared at each other in, what felt like, understanding.

"She killed Rohit, not a bunch of spiders that spew fire," Eset cried out, from where she was sitting. She stood up, dusting the dirt off of her dark pants as she gave me a smug smile. I felt my heart drop as I stared at her in horror.

"What... did she say?" Ash said, haltingly. He slowly turned to look at me. I felt the horror and disgust that were on everyone's faces as they looked for me to say something, anything. I licked my lips as my mouth went dry. Rohit's charred body flashed through my mind, and I grabbed my head as it started to hurt.

"I... I..." I stammered. My voice almost sounded hoarse.

"Spiders don't even breathe fire," she said, a hand on her hip. Suddenly, Anubys was at my side as he grabbed my shoulders, trying to help me up.

"You *killed* Rohit?" Ash asked, his face a mixture of anger and terror.

"Anubys?" Lightning said, his eyes looking past me at the person who was next to me, demanding answers.

"No, he—"

"I didn't mean to," I cried out, tears starting to well up in my eyes. "I didn't mean to. There was a spider attacking him, and Anubys couldn't do anything about it and I just... I just..." My hands were trembling, and I stared up into Eset's smug face.

"Why would you tell them?" I asked, my voice small. She just shrugged a shoulder.

"Why would you hide it from us?" Lightning asked, standing up. He towered over me as he looked down with disappointment and... fear.

"I didn't want you guys to—"

"Be afraid of you?" Volplie piped up. I had a sneaking feeling that she knew the whole time. Agwe walked up beside her, glancing over at Jangmi who just looked shell-shocked.

"You *lied* to us," Ash said, tears in his eyes as he narrowed them at me. The tears spilled over as he did, running down his freckled face.

"I didn't... I didn't..." I stuttered. I didn't even know what I wanted to say. What I *could* say.

"You're a monster," Ash said, backing away from me. "How could you pretend to be our friend this whole time when you killed one of us?" *One of us.* His words echoed in my head as I remembered Anubys's warning. *"The moment they find out that you killed one of them, they won't be able to trust you,"* he had said. He was right. Ash shook his head after eyeing me for a while and then walked away.

"Ash," Agwe called after him.

"It's not Zinnia's fault," Anubys said, his hands still holding me up as if I would collapse if he let go. I wondered if he remembered the warning he gave me as well, if it was echoing in his mind, too. "It's mine. I didn't know Agwe could heal people. He was still alive. I should've—"

"You both lied to us," Lightning remarked. His face was cold. He pointed at Anubys. "You, I'm not surprised. *You?*" His finger pointed at me. He shook his head. "No wonder why you were such a mess that day. And *you're* talking about trust?" He clenched his jaw and then opened his mouth as if he wanted to say something more. Then, he shook his head again, patting down his black, tight curls before turning away.

"You should've told us earlier," he hissed to Eset as he passed her. Her face was emotionless at his remark.

"Ash and Rohit really connected the first day," Agwe said, quietly. "He puts flowers at a marker here for Rohit every day." My sight blurred from the tears.

"I didn't know that," I hiccuped. I couldn't see his expression as he turned from me, following the others. Jangmi made a pained expression as she left as well. Volplie didn't look fazed at the information, confirming my fears that she knew from the very beginning.

"Guess it's a good thing this group forgives so easily, huh?" Volplie smirked before turning away. *How did she even* hear *that conversation with Jangmi?* I couldn't help but think.

As she left, I watched Tayen and Lidya heatedly talk about something as they walked by. Mikazuki was with them, and she turned towards the commotion as I felt the tears spill over. Tayen glanced over at us as well, but seemed to chalk it up to teen drama before walking away. Her long, gray braid hitting the small of her back.

"Eset, you didn't need to tell them," Anubys snapped at his sister. She turned her cold face to him, her eyes dead.

"She was about to ruin *everything*," she hissed back at him. Eset's words confused me. I felt Anubys's hands let go of my shoulders as he heatedly whispered towards his sister. And without his support, I felt myself fall to the ground. I stared at the hole Lightning had just dug, coldness settling into every part of my limbs. I felt... empty.

"They were just talking about his feelings for you, *Eset,*" Anubys spat. "I was right here."

"Their trust in her is misplaced, anyways," Eset merely said. She flipped her long, black hair over one shoulder as she turned away.

"Why does she like to play like this?" I heard Anubys mutter under his breath. I felt my hands clench into a fist, collecting dirt as I did.

"I'll kill her," I seethed.

"Well," Anubys said, sitting down next to me, "I don't think *that* would win them back."

"I will, Anubys. I'll *kill* her," I promised. His green eyes seemed to glint with mischief.

"You've changed," he said. "What happened to the girl who didn't want to hurt a fly?" I turned my gaze towards the shrinking back of Eset's. I was never that girl, and he knew it.

"I've already murdered at least three people," I said, meeting his gaze. "That girl's been dead for a while."

CHAPTER TWENTY-EIGHT

"Well," Anubys said, getting up from the ground. He offered me a hand and I grabbed it, letting him pull me up. "I can't really let you kill my sister."

"Why? Because you *care* about her?" I spat. He raised his eyebrows at my tone and smiled to himself.

"For one, yeah, she's my sister. The only family I have left. And for another, she's the one keeping me from dying. If she dies, who knows what will happen to me?" he responded. I didn't know whether he was lying to me or not, but he hadn't lied about his powers once yet. Searching his eyes for a while, I still couldn't figure out if he was lying to me.

"I hate her," I muttered.

"She shouldn't have told everyone. But, honestly, doesn't it feel a *little* better they all know you murdered Rohit?" I blinked.

"Why would it make me feel better?"

"Because you're not lying to them anymore," he said, smiling. "You're not hiding who you really are."

"Because who I really am is a monster, right? A murderous monster? A killing machine? A weapon everyone so desperately wants to use?" I fumed. Anubys held up his hands.

"Hey, I'm not the one you're mad at," he said. I poked him in the chest, angrily.

"*You* are the one who told Eset what really happened," I hissed. Anubys paused for a moment, and then he smirked.

"Okay, you got me there."

"Stop smiling at me, like you find this whole situation funny," I ordered.

"It *is* funny," he said.

"How is this funny? You saw how they all looked at me," I said, gesturing towards where the others went.

"You know what I find funny?" he said, his voice low. He took a step towards me. "You tend to cry in front of them. Big, crocodile tears. But, once they left, you stopped. Immediately." I stared at him, the feeling that I always got whenever I was too honest with him appeared in the back of my throat. The feeling that he knew. That he could understand who—*what*—I was.

"I was *sad*," I insisted. He raised an eyebrow as he leaned back to gaze at all of me.

"Or you're manipulative," he simply said. I felt my face fall as I stared at him in shock.

"What did you say to me?" I whispered.

"You're manipulative, Zinnia. You want everyone to think of you as this good person. This good person who cares so much about everyone and cares about what others think of her. But, I've seen you, when you don't think anyone's watching. You're not as good as you think," he whispered back. He leaned towards my ear. "You *like* the power. You like consuming their life." His breath tickled my neck, and he gave me a lazy smile as he looked me up and down.

"It's not a bad thing," he finished, shrugging a shoulder. I felt my hands ball up into fists at my side as I glared up at him.

"You don't know me," I said, but my voice shook, betraying me. He squinted his eyes slightly as he grinned.

"Don't I, though?" he barely breathed. "Aren't I the only one who really does?" I shuddered as he walked past me. My eyes followed him as he sauntered back towards his cabin. *He doesn't know me*, I promised myself. I tried to keep my hands from trembling as I repeated the lie in my head. *He doesn't know me.*

I tossed and turned in my bunk bed, finally settling on my back to stare up at the ceiling. Anubys's words stayed with me throughout the rest of the day, and I couldn't help but see the image of me from my nightmare every time I closed my eyes. She was the part of me I was afraid of. The part of me who fully embraced her powers. Reveled in it.

I squeezed my eyes shut as I rested my hands over my face. I *was* a good person. Did I kill Rohit? By accident. It was completely by accident because I wasn't able to control my powers. *You still don't know how to control them*, a part of me whispered in the back of my head. *Well, technically,*

Anubys *killed Rohit*, I argued with myself. I turned on my side again.

From across the room, I heard someone quietly getting dressed. Trying to steady my breathing, I stared at the wall in front of me. Quietly, almost imperceptibly so, the door opened and then closed. Quickly, I turned towards the middle of the room, sitting up.

Volplie was sleeping, her short, white hair was tied into two French braids, courtesy of Jangmi, and her limbs were hanging off of the side of the bed. Underneath her, the bed was empty. Frowning, I climbed down the ladder of the bunk, the ladder squeaking as I went. *How did Eset do this so quietly?* I thought to myself.

When I reached the bottom, Jangmi was already sitting up, her black hair in a mess. She rubbed her eyes as she squinted at me.

"What are you doing?" she asked. I gestured towards Eset's empty bed.

"Eset's gone," I whispered. "I'm going to follow her." Jangmi yawned as she looked over at Eset's bed.

"Maybe she's on a midnight walk," she said, her voice slightly curt, as she watched me change my clothes into the black armor we were allowed to wear now, as official members of the Shadow Army. I shook my head in disagreement.

"No, there's something weird going on," I muttered, not meeting her eyes. I could feel the hostility from her, the distrust.

"You *would* think that," Volplie said, her eyes almost glowing in the dark. I jumped slightly at the sound of her voice.

"Do you *not* think it's weird Eset is walking around the camp in the middle of the night? Have you ever seen her do that?" I asked.

"You do that," Jangmi pointed out.

"I've never trusted her," Volplie said, her legs dangling off of the edge of her bed. "I mean, I don't trust you either ever since you killed Rohit..." Jangmi rolled her eyes.

"You don't trust anyone," Jangmi said. Volplie cocked her head to the side as she thought.

"True," she said. "Tayen said it's because of the trauma I went through."

"Trauma?" Jangmi asked, her eyes darting over to Volplie in surprise.

"Yeah, and I guess, passed down trauma from my sister. Though, she's actually, technically, my half—"

"Can we not talk about this right now?" I asked, blowing the hair out of my face. "We need to follow Eset."

"We?" Volplie asked.

"Or... I do," I said, stammering a little. Volplie grinned at me as she jumped off of the bunk. She was in her half form still, returning to it immediately after we weren't required to wear the power-suppressing armor anymore.

"I'll go," she said. "Might as well." She shrugged towards Jangmi who stared at her for a moment, in shock. Jangmi flopped back down on her bed, groaning as she closed her eyes. I had never seen Jangmi so frustrated before.

"Fine," she finally said, her eyes still closed. "Let me get dressed."

It didn't take too long for us to catch up to Eset. We were careful to not make much noise as we walked a distance behind her. Volplie was nearly silent, leading the way so we could make as little noise as possible. But, from the look of it, Eset didn't care if anyone followed her or not. She wasn't sneaking around. Instead, she was openly walking down the street, striding as if she had a purpose. Her wavy, black hair was down around her shoulders, following behind her like a cape of sorts. In her hands, she held a clipboard. My eyes narrowed as I realized it was the clipboard Lidya had used to record our powers from when we first arrived.

"Where do you think she's going?" Jangmi whispered. Volplie glared her into silence as Jangmi's eyes widened at her gaze.

"She's heading towards the edge of the camp," I barely breathed. Volplie directed her anger towards me.

"*Shut up,*" she hissed. While we neared the edge of the camp, Eset walked out into a field where there was nowhere for us to hide. Volplie pushed us behind the last cabin before reaching the field as we peeked our heads out to watch Eset.

She walked up to the bottom of the mountain and looked up towards the top of the cliff. She whistled, the sound resembling the call of a bird, almost exactly. A woman looked down the cliff, her black hair shrouding her face as she stared through the forcefield. She was on a ledge right above where the forcefield started.

"Is that... Is that Ash?" Jangmi whispered in horror. I ripped my gaze from the woman, and I looked over at Eset who was beckoning Ash towards her. A smile played on her lips that resembled Anubys's so much I had to look away.

"Is he awake?" I asked, squinting my eyes at his red-headed self. Volplie stared, her eyes wide as she watched.

"Shh!" she whispered, but with less force than how she was shushing us before. Eset motioned above her and was saying something to Ash. Ash quickly obeyed whatever it was she asked for, raising his arms. In horror, we watched as the forcefield started to come down.

"What is he doing?" Jangmi whispered, her voice catching in her throat. None of us could tear our gaze away from Ash as the forcefield came down around us. The moonlight glinted off of the knife he gripped in his hand.

The woman who was on the ledge right above the forcefield, started to propel down the edge of the cliff. Part of her hair was tied in a braid with rings down it, and they glittered in the moonlight. At the sight, I looked up at the moon. It was a full moon. *Full moon tomorrow,* is what Anubys told me the night before. *Was he a part of this?*

More people started to propel down the edge of the cliffs all around us in the valley. We were trapped. They all wore black cloaks which covered their heads, except for the woman who jumped down once she was far enough. She almost excitedly ran over to Eset, who hugged her immediately. I felt Volplie stiffen next to me.

"Is this an attack?" Jangmi whispered, terror making her voice tremble.

"We need to wake Biao up," I said, starting to straighten up as I looked at the army coming down the mountains around us. Volplie didn't move a muscle, didn't even breathe.

"What is it?" I asked as Jangmi placed a concerned hand on her shoulder. Her eyes were wide as she stared at the woman who was next to Eset. As I squinted, realization washed over at me as I recognized her features. They were slightly similar to Volplie's, but she looked more like me than Volplie did.

"It's Istas," Volplie breathed.

"Who's Istas?" Jangmi asked.

"My older sister," Volplie said. For the first time since I met her, she looked downright terrified.

"Your sister?" I asked. Volplie still didn't move an inch as she carefully watched Istas. Istas flipped a tanned hand towards Ash and immediately, Ash lifted his hand, the knife gripped hard in his palm, and cut his throat. Blood sprayed on the grass in front of him as he collapsed to the ground. I darted forward, as a reflex, wanting to save him even though it was too late. Volplie inhaled sharply as she grabbed my arm and pulled me back, out of sight.

"We need to go," she hissed. Her eyes were darting around wildly as she looked around us.

"Why did Ash... Why did he..." I asked as Jangmi slid to the ground, just staring at her trembling hands.

"We need to *go*," Volplie repeated, trying to pull Jangmi up. She stole a glance back at Istas and took a deep breath.

"Istas found me when I was ten. She was left as an orphan, too, and she heard she had a half sister in the shape of a fox. She wanted me to work with her, with President Eclipse who took her in as a child. She thought she was saving me," Volplie quickly whispered. "She's like Lidya, but she's worse. I've seen what she can do. We need to leave and escape, *now*."

"What do you mean she's like Lidya but worse?" I asked,

my feet unable to move after what I just saw. Volplie focused her unnatural eyes on me.

"She's a commander. Her power. Lidya can make us freeze, can control our bodies. But, I've seen Lidya's powers. It's not as fluid as my sister's. She's not as well trained. Istas... Istas has complete control over her victims. She can make you fight and make you kill anyone she chooses," Volplie explained. "She and Eset work together a lot, since Eset has no control over her creatures."

"You already knew them?" Jangmi asked, her voice almost accusatory but not quite. Her eyes remained unfocused on her hands.

"That's how you knew so much about President Eclipse," I accused. "You worked for her, too." Volplie shook her head, her ears flat on her head as her eyes darted around.

"I didn't work for her. I've just seen... things..." she said. "We don't have time for this. We need to escape before we get caught."

"Escape?" Jangmi said, her eyes suddenly clear. "We need to warn everyone." Volplie stared at her like she was crazy.

"Warn everyone? It's too *late* to warn everyone. Do you not see what's happening?" she asked, gesturing quickly around us.

"An army is descending upon us," I whispered.

"If we want any chance of survival, we need to escape," she whispered.

"I-I can't," Jangmi stuttered. She stood up, her legs shaking as she stared at me. "We are powerful, too. We can save this camp."

"You're delusional," Volplie whispered, but her face looked slightly awed. Volplie peeked back at her sister and then looked around the valley for an escape.

"A noble act," Volplie muttered, almost under her breath. "But, I know a dead man walking when I see one." She transformed fully into a small white-gray fox, and started running away. My heart pounded in my head as I watched her leave. Jangmi grabbed my hands, her eyes pleading up at me.

"Okay, let's get Biao up," I whispered. The alarms that went off the last time when the forcefield went down weren't going off this time. And a horrid thought came to the forefront of my mind. *Maybe the first time was a practice run.*

"We need to warn the boys first," Jangmi begged, pulling my hand in the direction of the cabin where Lightning, Agwe, and Anubys stayed. Though, I had a gnawing feeling Anubys wasn't in their cabin.

"We can't. The most important person who needs to be awake is—"

"Please, Zinnia. I don't know what I would do if something happened to..." she choked on her words as tears started to well up in her eyes. I took a deep breath as I looked at her, and against my better judgment, I nodded my head.

"Fine," I said. "Let's go, quickly." And we both ran as fast as we could towards the cabin across the camp. As we did, I looked for anything that could be a warning as we snuck through the camp, resorting to just throwing rocks through people's windows in their cabins. The noise of shattering glass was just something we would have to endure.

CHAPTER TWENTY-NINE

By the time Jangmi and I arrived at the boys' cabin, the camp was in a full out war. My technique of waking people up seemed to work, and I watched as Biao held a sword in one hand and a gun in the other as he ran past us. Some of the soldiers in the Shadow Army were still not fully healed from the attack on the camp by those mutated creatures. I shuddered as I remembered the black liquid that spilled out of them.

"They're not here!" Jangmi exclaimed after opening the door to the cabin. She paced along the length of the room, looking at each of the beds. Her eyes were wide and quickly filled up with tears. I grabbed her shoulders before she could start completely breaking down.

"It's fine. It's fine," I repeated, over and over at her, trying to desperately convince myself. Maybe Volplie had it right. *We should've escaped while we had the chance.* I chastised myself as quickly as the thought came to the forefront of my mind. I couldn't think like this.

"I'm sure they got out earlier, when people started to make a lot of commotion. Agwe is great with a sword. You know that. He's fine," I assured her. She nodded her head as I talked, trying to convince herself I was right. Then, when I was done talking, she ran out of the cabin. I knew who she was searching for and part of me wanted to tell her to give up on it.

Following her out, I ran into Lidya. She gave me a worried look before beckoning for me to follow her. Her eyes gave me a once-over as I searched for Jangmi. *Goddamn it*, I thought to myself when I couldn't find her anywhere.

"Glad you had the sense to put on the armor. I saw Lightning earlier, and he's just out there wearing his goddamn pajamas," she said, irritation lacing her words. I grabbed her arm, which she twisted in reflex.

"Don't do that," she warned. I put my hands behind my back.

"I'm sorry," I muttered. "You saw Lightning? Did you see Agwe, too?" Lidya glared at me before softening her expression, a silent scream present in her eyes. My eyebrows scrunched together.

"Yeah, I saw the both of them. They were in the armory," she said. "I didn't see Anubys, if that's what you're asking about." I shook my head. I knew he wouldn't be with the others. If Eset helped orchestrate this attack, I knew he was a part of it, too. Anger filled up in me as I remembered what she did to Ash.

"Ash is dead," I said, quietly. My voice almost got lost in the sound of screams nearby. Lidya frowned as she beckoned for me to hurry.

"He's dead?" she asked. Her eyes were back at that terrified expression. It would disappear when she would speak, but come back out when her face was idle.

"There's someone on President Eclipse's army that's like you," I said, warning her. She gave me a quizzical look.

"How do you know this?" she asked.

"Volplie," I answered and her gaze hardened. "Her sister Istas is like you. Volplie said she's worse than you though, better at controlling her powers."

"Really," Lidya said, her expression amused. Her eyes glanced at me, almost like she was screaming. I stared at her, hard, for a moment and then slowly came to a stop, my eyes studying her face.

"Where are we going?" I asked, slowly. Lidya turned around to face me. The sun was starting to rise, and it washed everything in a blue color.

"What do you mean? Biao needs you," she said. "You're hellfire. We need you to help save us." I stared at her for a second longer, trying to study her facial expressions. It was something Lidya *would* say. She wanted to use me as a weapon for the Shadow Army. But, something wasn't right. After she spoke, her eyes, again, seemed to scream at me.

"You're not Lidya," I whispered. A forced smile appeared on Lidya's lips as she darted forward to grab me. I evaded her attack swiftly as I started to run away. My heart was thundering in my ears as I tried to run as fast as I ever did. But, just as I was starting to gain some distance away from her, I felt my body freeze. At the sudden forced stop, I fell face-first into the ground, unable to reach out to even break my fall. Every part of my body ached and at the impact, I saw stars. I heard Lidya's light footsteps come towards me, but I couldn't turn my head to look at her, my face in the dirt. She had complete control over my body.

"Did you *really* think you'd be able to run from me?" Lidya's voice seemed to say, however it was contorted. A tone slightly higher than Lidya's normal voice. I felt her kick me, rolling me over with her foot. She stared down, her curly brown hair slightly obscuring her face.

"You figured it out pretty quickly. I didn't expect it," she said, her eyes wide as she smiled. It was like she was forcing the facial expression onto Lidya's face, and Lidya was in pain for having to obey.

"I was afraid I wasn't going to be able to use this girl's power. It's hard to control people's powers, since it comes from a different place for each person. But, hers is *so* much like mine. It's too bad she won't be able to fully learn how to master it as well as me," Istas said through Lidya's mouth.

"If you're looking for Volplie, she's gone," I managed to get out. Lidya's head was thrown back as she laughed, her body shaking as she did.

"I'm not looking for that girl," she said. "Though, I'm surprised she said anything about me. I was looking for you. How perfect, huh?" Her eyes widened again as she stared down at me.

"If it's me you want, then let them all go," I said, gaining some control over my lips. *Please, just let them all go*, I begged in my mind. Lidya laughed at my suggestion and then reached down to grab my ankle. She lifted it up and started to drag me down the road.

"Sweetheart, we want you *and* we want this camp destroyed," she said, over her shoulder. "It's nothing personal." I watched as a giant boulder fell onto the cabin next to us, dust kicking into my lungs. The rocks on the dirt road dug into my back as I was dragged along. The armor luckily kept my back from being scratched up, but the road wasn't so friendly to my open palms. I couldn't scream, my mouth locked again. But, pain was all I could feel as she pulled me along.

"I'm sorry Lidya," I heard a deep voice say from behind me. Lidya didn't have the chance to look before Lightning sliced her head clean off with his longsword. As her head rolled towards me, I regained control over my body once more.

Lidya's eyes were wide, from shock and fear, and her hand still gripped me. I ripped her hand from my ankle, backing away from her decapitated body. Blood soaked into the dirt road, and I looked up at Lightning who had crimson spots sprinkled on his face. He stared in horror at Lidya's corpse and then doubled over and threw up.

"Thanks," I said, a bit hoarsely after he finished emptying his stomach. He wiped his mouth, smearing blood on his face, and nodded. His dark skin looked ashen at the sight.

"It wasn't Lidya," he said, his voice shaking slightly. I nodded my head in confirmation and placed a hand on his shoulder.

"It wasn't her. There's someone on their side who has the same power as Lidya, but stronger," I explained. He nodded his head and grabbed my wrist, his hand shaking.

"Let's go." We ran from the sight of Lidya's dead body. In the distance, I saw a short girl with chopped black hair dressed in all black. At the sight of Mikazuki, I ran full force towards her, Lightning following after me. She was surrounded by people in black cloaks, but they didn't make a move towards her. Her eyes darted around at each of them, as if she were putting them in a trance. And then quickly, she pulled out a small dagger and slit each one of their throats. They fell to the ground like dominoes.

"Have you seen Jangmi?" I asked, as the last of the soldiers fell. She wiped the dagger on her pants as she looked up at me, her eyes hard.

"Small Shin girl?" Mikazuki asked. I nodded my head. Her face was also splattered with blood. I wondered what mine looked like.

"I saw her run past with an army of animals. I think Tayen wanted her at the front lines," Mikazuki said. "Oh, and I saw the sanpaku kid. He's on their side, in case you wanted to know." *I didn't.* My heart beat faster at the mention of Anubys, but I wasn't surprised. Her face contorted into disgust. Mikazuki let out a dry chuckle as she nodded to herself. She waved the dagger in my face.

"You knew," she muttered. And before I could tell her I had no idea an attack would be happening, she disappeared, running to save a mother and her young daughter.

"Can you find Jangmi?" I asked, turning towards Lightning. His face looked frazzled as he stared at me, eyes wide.

"I-I don't know," he stammered. He was usually the epitome of calm, and it broke my heart to see him like this. "There's a lot of people right now. I..." He took a deep breath and closed his eyes.

"I'll try," he said, his closed eyes twitching slightly. Both of his hands still gripped the longsword, hard. Another boulder fell onto a cabin nearby and screams erupted as it did. Someone was carving out the mountains that surrounded us. We didn't have long before they would start falling all around us, burying this camp in the valley. Lightning's dark eyes opened.

"I found her," he whispered. His eyes met mine. "She's at the front lines. But, she's moving around erratically. I think she's looking for Agwe." I nodded my head in agreement.

"Lead me there," I said. Lightning hesitated for a moment, and I could almost see the thoughts that were going through his head. He didn't necessarily trust me after what happened with Rohit. But, he didn't have a power that would hold its own in the front lines. He needed me, even though I didn't have great control over the hellfire. He could still potentially die if I used it, but he didn't need to know that.

"Okay," he eventually said. He started running towards the direction of Jangmi, and I followed after him.

The journey to the front lines wasn't pretty. Bodies littered the streets, and the dirt road had changed color due to how much blood it had soaked up. Lightning threw up a few more times as we got closer to the front lines.

Tayen was standing in the back, her gray hair was slightly sticking out of her long braid. Above her, she held a floating boulder, which she threw with full force at President Eclipse's army. It would hit a forcefield, bounce off and then hit somewhere else in the camp with a thud. *At least I know who's carving out the mountains now*, I couldn't help but think.

Istas stood near the base of the mountain with Eset next

to her. Creatures of all kinds were raised all around them, fighting the Shadow Army. I saw some woodland creatures, bears, and wolves fighting against the creatures, and I craned my head around, looking for Jangmi.

When my eyes found her, sweat dotted her brow and her black hair was pulled back into a low ponytail. Her arms were raised, and she looked exhausted, like she had been doing this for hours even though it hadn't been that long. I ran towards her, a creature jumping out in front of me. I took a step back, startled. A wolf jumped onto the creature, knocking it down. It looked like the creature from the night where Dandelion... I let my thoughts drift away as I watched as the wolf writhed on the ground, squealing from pain before dropping dead. Anubys. Anubys was somewhere here.

Fury started to rise within me as I walked over the deceased wolf before the creature could get back up and attack me again. Once at Jangmi's side, I wiped her brow as she broke her concentration to look up at me.

"I couldn't find Agwe," she whispered, her voice breaking. I pulled her into my chest for a hug as words escaped me. I didn't know how to comfort her. I didn't know what to say.

Instead, I just watched as Biao cut down creatures with either a wave from his sword or a bullet from his gun. He would fly up to the sky with a burst of air, and then explode in a section of creatures and soldiers.

Jangmi pulled away from me, wiping stray hairs from her forehead as she concentrated again. More woodland creatures scurried down the cliffs of the mountains, meeting the creatures in battle. Suddenly, Devlin grabbed my arm, pulling me away from Jangmi. I gave him a hard look as I tried to figure out if it was really him or not. The arm that wasn't gripping me had been cut clean off, but already he was starting to regenerate it.

"Why are you staring at me like that?" he asked. I stared at him for a second longer, searching his facial expression. His eyes looked normal. Not like they were screaming for help. I relaxed for a minute. He handed me a sword from his belt with his newly regenerated hand and patted me on the shoulder.

"We need more soldiers," he muttered. He glanced over at Eset and then grimaced.

"We need to get rid of *her*, if we have a chance," I glowered. She seemed to feel my hatred as she looked up, meeting my eyes. Her lips twitched into a smile.

"If you can," Devlin said, sighing as he did. He furrowed his eyebrows. "I haven't seen Lidya." I avoided his gaze, and I heard him take a sharp inhale.

"Yeah, I was worried that happened," he whispered, his voice raspy. He took a deep breath and then ran towards the soldiers and creatures. There weren't many soldiers on their side left. Either they didn't bring a lot, they died, or they retreated. I wasn't sure which, but I didn't have time to think about it.

I raised my sword, fixed my eyes on Eset, and started cutting down the creatures that surged towards me. I would be damned if I let my friends die in vain.

CHAPTER THIRTY

Eset fixated her gaze on me, her eyes just as crazed as it was during the training session the other day. She raised her arms and subsequently raised any dead on the ground after being destroyed by the animals. I knew she could just keep bringing them back to life, that it was never-ending. The sight of these gnarled corpses rising and regenerating made my stomach turn. The ones who were previously humans were starting to look more and more like zombies, the more they were raised. A glassy look to their eyes.

Something snapped within my heart as I looked in the faces of some of these creatures who were once human. And when I sliced through them, red blood sprayed onto my armor. With every kill, another part of me hardened. This wasn't natural, this killing. And yet, I was so *good* at it.

Eset was starting to look frustrated that her surge of creatures weren't doing much to deter me, and her eyes darted towards Jangmi. I followed her gaze, and I noticed

Jangmi was looking even more exhausted. Like the life was coming out of her, somehow. When I focused back onto Eset, I watched as she kicked forward a body. Squinting my eyes, I could see it was a fresh corpse. It hadn't even started to rot yet. And then I recognized the shaved black underside on the back of this boy's head as the corpse stood. Eset placed a knife into his hands as she winked at me. *No...*

I took a couple of steps backwards before turning around, trying to make my way towards Jangmi, but one look at her and I knew she had already recognized the body. Her eyes looked faraway as she just stared at the back of his head.

"Agwe!" I heard her shout out his name, her voice hoarse. I turned to look at him and watched as he faced her. Fear was in his eyes, and in horror, my eyes followed as his hand lifted towards his throat, dagger in hand. I jolted forward as I realized what Eset was having Istas do to him. A twinkle was in her eyes as he ran the dagger across his neck. The blood poured out of him, running down his body as he stood there for a second more, the life leaving his eyes. I heard Jangmi's blood curdling scream as he fell to the ground. My balance was compromised as more animals surged forward around me, towards Eset, as if in response to her grief. I watched as Eset laughed as Istas squinted her eyes at the situation. I gripped the sword in my hand until my fingers started to hurt. She also needed to die. They both did.

Eset raised her arms, raising Agwe from the dead once again. And I just heard Jangmi screaming, unable to make out the words, her voice coming closer and closer. Eset kept having Agwe kill himself, and then would raise him again and again. Until, there was nothing left in his eyes. Until all that was left of Agwe was anger and fear. His blood was pooled all around him, his upper half covered in the dark crimson.

"Jangmi, don't," I yelled at her, narrowly missing her arm as she ran past me. Her long black hair whipped out behind her as the wind started to pick up. The sky darkened and when I craned my neck upwards, a horde of different birds were circling over us. In unison, they pointed themselves downwards and the air moved as they came towards the ground. I ducked my head as the birds attacked the different creatures, but many of them were focused on Eset. She looked irritated as the birds picked at her skin, her body regenerating as quickly as the birds attacked, but she seemed to wave them off, almost. The birds were as bothersome as gnats on a summer day. Her gaze was otherwise focused on Agwe who was stalking towards Jangmi.

"It's not Agwe, anymore," I whispered as I tried to get to Jangmi. To help her. I scrambled towards her, waving the birds away as I cut down the creatures around me. *Please*, I begged to any of the old gods. *Please, not her.* Agwe, with an expression of anger I had never seen grace his face before, grabbed her by the neck and lifted her up like a doll. Jangmi didn't even try to struggle as she just stared at the blood-soaked face of her beloved. She hung there, limp, as she took in his face, his features.

I felt the fire inside of me churning. I had gotten close enough that I could just explode, and it would kill anyone in its path. But... I didn't want to hurt Jangmi. *No,* I shook my head. If I didn't do anything, she would die.

I let the fire start to burn through me, expand from me.

Though, just as I felt it start to break free from my body, I felt the cold fist close around it. I could feel my soul scrambling for the last bit of flames, trying to keep it from hiding behind that solid fist. But, the last of the flames were sucked up behind it, causing a sharp pain to travel down my body. I gasped for air as I doubled over from the pain. I looked up, my eyes fixated on Jangmi. Her face was starting to become purple, her eyes were almost popping out, and it didn't look like Agwe was going to stop. His hands just squeezed tighter, no amount of love or affection remained there. *Please*, I prayed. My eyes started to burn, watching her just look at him, and creatures were starting to descend on me. As they scratched my face, I reached down for the sword I had dropped while I felt my fire go out, biting back a sob.

"Let's stop playing, Eset," I heard a familiar voice say behind me, as if an answer to my prayers. I froze as I looked up to see Anubys wearing the same cloak Istas was wearing, the hood around his shoulders. He didn't even look at me as he walked around my body; the creatures that were clawing at me, lifeless at his feet. My eyes followed him as I swallowed the tears that threatened to spill over. Eset scowled as Agwe suddenly fell to the ground. Gray film dulled the brown in his eyes as Jangmi gasped for air. *Thank the Nation,* I couldn't help but think as I watched her chest rise and fall. Agwe's hands had left a red mark on her olive-toned neck, but she was okay. Jangmi still reached towards his corpse. Her cry was guttural.

"The camp is about to be buried," Anubys said, directing his attention towards Istas. "We should go." Istas looked amused as she watched me slowly reach down for my sword, once more. Suddenly, I had no control over my body, my arm still outreached. She almost looked at me, pityingly.

"Fine," she said, waving her hands. "Kill them all." *No!* I cried out. Anubys's green eyes didn't look at me, as if I were invisible, but I begged wordlessly for him to glance at me. To see the plea in my eyes. To at least spare Jangmi. At least Jangmi.

But, he didn't look my way. He didn't even flinch as he raised a hand. And I watched as every living thing collapsed in front of me. Including my cousin. Swiftly and painlessly. *Jangmi*, my thoughts screamed as I watched the life leave her eyes. *Jangmi!* She fell to the ground, her hand falling onto Agwe's.

Every part of me wanted to scream, wanted to rip apart every single person who was standing in front of me. But, I couldn't move, Istas power confining me. I couldn't even cry out loud. All that was shown of my grief was a single tear running down the side of my face.

"Great job with her, August," Eset said, as her eyes lit up at the sight of the person who was walking slowly behind me. *August?*

I watched him with my eyes as he walked past. He glanced down, guilt in his blue eyes, and it made me want to wring his scrawny neck out.

"I was worried she was able to use her powers without your permission," Eset said, laughing a bit as she looked at me. Her eyes were almost taunting. *Without his permission? It was because of* August *I couldn't use my powers?*

"There was no need to worry," August muttered. "She allowed me deep into her head." I *allowed* him? What the fuck was he talking about?

"The map?" Eset demanded, staring at Anubys. Anubys nodded once, sweat dotting his brow. He still refused to meet my gaze, despite my eyes burning into him. I glared at him, directed all my fury towards him. I wished he would look at me, would see what he did to me. He killed her. He killed *everyone.*

However, a part of me let out a sigh of relief as I realized the meaning of his nod. Lightning was alive. At least one of us was still alive.

"Did we get the old maid?" Istas asked, directing her attention towards August. August shook his head, and hung it as he spoke.

"Tayen escaped. With some other members," August said. Istas clicked her tongue as the mountain around us started to shake. It was about to fall apart.

"Guess she didn't trust you as much as you thought she did," she said to August. He hung his head, almost in defeat. Istas gestured towards a small cloaked child, beckoning them closer. The hood shrouded their face as they took a step forward.

"Get us out of here," she said to the child. They nodded their head once as Istas directed her gaze onto me. "And knock her out." August turned towards me, and my glare moved from Anubys to him, instead. He almost shuddered underneath it.

"Sleep," he said with a one word command. As my whole body started to feel heavy with fatigue, my mouth was released.

"I'll drown you in your own blood. *All of you,*" I managed to hiss before I fell to the ground. I struggled against the darkness that threatened to engulf me, but it was fruitless. I heard Istas's bark of a laugh at my comment as I thought about what Anubys had told me yesterday.

"*You're not as good as you think,*" he had said. The words echoed around in my mind as the darkness started to win the battle against me. *He's right,* I thought to myself. After what happened today, I was tired of pretending. *I'm not a good person,* I thought as I clenched my jaw. *And I'm going to make them pay for what they did.*

CHAPTER THIRTY-ONE

When I finally opened my eyes, it was almost as dark as it was when my eyes were shut. From what I could tell, I was in a cell of some sort. Being extra careful around the healing bruise on my cheek, I picked at the dried blood on my face. My head was throbbing behind my eyes, and as they adjusted to the darkness, I looked around my new accommodations. There was a barred door that looked soldered shut. There was a bucket in the corner, which I assumed was where I was supposed to do my business. Tapping a finger to my knee, I realized there wasn't a bed, or a blanket. Just a bucket, and the dirt ground. My whole body was aching as I pushed myself towards the bars.

"Let me out," my voice croaked as I pressed my hot face against the cool metal. I cleared my throat as I tried shouting again.

"Let me *out!*" I yelled, my voice carrying a little further that time. I felt the tears start to freely run down my face as the events that happened at the camp started coming back to me. Jangmi, Ash, Agwe, Lidya, and who knew who else. They were all dead. I searched for the fire that normally churned through me, but it was locked behind that cold, unrelenting fist.

"I'll kill you all," I whispered before repeating the words, louder and louder. Voices whispered all around me as I yelled it out. *You'll kill us all.* My palms thundered on the bars of the door, over and over until I was sure my cut-up hands were bruised as well.

"Zinnia, just stop it," I heard a familiar deep voice sigh. My hands froze mid-air. I turned towards the left wall of my cell, staring at it in disbelief.

"Lightning?" I asked, my voice small.

"Yup," is all he said. I crawled over to where his voice was coming from as I leaned my head against the wall, sobbing.

"Jangmi is dead," I cried, gasping through my sobs. "So is Agwe."

"I figured," he said, quietly, dead-pan. I could hear him more clearly, sitting by the wall. I wondered if he was sitting right up against the other side of it. Swallowing my tears, I took in a shaky breath.

"How long have we been down here?" I asked.

"A few days," Lightning responded. My jaw dropped at his answer, and I shut my eyes. They had me out for a few *days?*

"What happened after...?" The air hitched in my throat. Lightning was quiet for a second.

"I don't remember how we got here," he whispered. "I heard a single word. A command almost. And then, I woke up here shortly later. My guess is we're in the Capital." *The Capital.* The place where no one was allowed to go unless your job required it. And if your job was in the Capital, you never went back to your community again.

"It was August, probably, who put you to sleep," I muttered, my eyes glazing over. He betrayed me. He had betrayed all of us. His blue eyes flashed in my brain as I glowered into the darkness.

"I didn't think August would go against Tayen," Lightning said. "But, then again, I didn't see any of this coming..."

"Anubys and Eset," I almost choked on the words. Lightning stayed silent for a while, as if wanting me to go on. But, I couldn't. I couldn't say what I saw.

"I guessed," Lightning finally said. I moved so my back was against the wall, leaning my head against it. Blood was matted into my hair from the battle, and I could feel the knot press against the back of my skull.

"Why did they leave us alive?" I asked the question that was burning in my throat.

"You're hellfire," Lightning said, matter-of-factly. "They want you in their wheelhouse. Me? I'm not exactly sure, unless President Eclipse wants to find someone."

"Tayen escaped," I said, the thought dawning on me. "Maybe they want you to track her." I heard Lightning shift his weight on the other side of the wall.

"What's the point?" I heard him say, almost under his breath. "What is Tayen going to do? They destroyed her army, that was *barely* an army. What is the point of it all?" I winced hearing his hardened voice.

"This whole Nation doesn't make sense to me," he muttered.

"What do you mean?" I asked.

"The communities. We're split up by race and ethnicity. They're named after... the Senate? The first Senate? *Why* do they matter? Why are they important? Do they represent anything? All I know about Frederick Du Bois was he supported the Nation and was a great warrior, whatever the fuck that means. And that goes for all of the other name-sakes, too. What's so important about being a great warrior? Supporting the Nation, I get. But, a great warrior? Did the first Senate have powers like us? And why is the whole Nation behind a fucking wall?" Lightning was ranting. I didn't say anything. I didn't know where he was going with his monologue.

"And the conditions... The conditions of each community. Some of it is *really* awful. I mean, Adams is plagued with acid rain. Du Bois has terrible pollution. Khaldun is so dangerously hot no one can travel around outside without a cooling suit. But, outside of the Wall, the world is fine. The *Earth* is fine," he said, his voice rising.

"I mean, what is the *point*, Zinnia? Why is the Nation like this? What is it all for?" he asked. "What was Tayen trying to fight against? She never told us. Volplie said there were humans being experimented on, but why? For what? Just... What is it all for?" I closed my eyes as he spoke.

"I don't know, Lightning," I said, quietly. "I wish I knew." All I could think about was what Jangmi had told me about the Nation. That they were trying to hurt humans.

"Something is weird, Zinnia. Something is..." his voice drifted off as we heard footsteps coming down the hall. I pushed against the wall, trying to be as far away from the door as possible. Green eyes peered into the bars of the door.

Anubys, my body almost breathed. Through the bars, he threw an apple in. It rolled onto the ground, close to me.

"You should eat," he whispered. His voice burned me like a brand, and I had to stop myself from crying.

"Fuck you," I snapped. He laughed slightly.

"You'll thank me later," he breathed. And then he walked away, the sound of his footsteps diminishing with every possible second.

"It's a warning," Lightning muttered.

"What?"

"Something's about to happen to you," Lightning said. "You probably should heed it." I stared at the apple for a long time before hunger overtook every part of my body. My hands grabbed it, without my permission, and I ate hungrily, thinking about how much I hated the boy who gave it to me.

Day and night blurred together. They didn't give us meals, as if purposefully trying to starve us. I wasn't sure what time it was down in this dungeon. I didn't know if it had been days or hours since I had seen Anubys. A floating light bobbed in the distance, illuminating part of my accommodations. I squinted at it, not able to make out the figure in front of the bars. The light burned my eyes.

"Take her hand," a voice said. I didn't recognize it, but I crawled over to the bars on the door. My hand reached out towards the cloaked child whose pale one wrapped around it. I tried to peer into their face, but once I attempted to, the area around me started to blur. It was as if I were traveling through space and time at an inhuman speed.

When the world stopped spinning, we were in a completely white room that I immediately dirtied by emptying my stomach.

"What the fuck was that?" I croaked out, still trying to comprehend how I went from inside of my cell to this room. I saw the child smile as the dark cloak still covered the top half of their face.

"Teleportation," the clear voice said, echoing around the room. They waved their hand and disappeared before I could blink. Two more cloaked figures walked in, their heavy steps echoing in my ears. The top half of their faces were also shrouded by the hood of their cloak. I sized the two of them up, wondering if I could take them. But one glance, and I knew I didn't stand a chance. Not in the state I was in.

They stood by the door, which opened again to let in a few more people who wore completely white. They had rubber gloves on their hands and surgical masks on their faces. I scurried backwards until my back hit the wall.

"What do you want with me?" I asked, my voice shrill from panic as they started to grab at my limbs.

"President Eclipse doesn't like to see a mess," one of the women responded. Her eyes crinkled, as if she were smiling at me. And then the people began to undress me. The armor I was wearing, on a pile by my feet.

Despite the situation I was in, I felt ashamed being naked in front of all these people. In an attempt to keep some kind of modesty, I wrapped my arms around my body. And, suddenly, a stream of freezing cold water was being poured onto me as I yelped. I looked around for the source and saw one of them with a hand slightly raised, near their head, as if they were simply thinking. But, I knew they were really using the power they had. I cried out from shock every time the cold water hit my skin, and by the time they were done washing me, I was shivering, badly. My hands were almost blue from the cold.

"Put these on," the same woman said, handing me a set of unblemished, ironed clothes. White, just like everything else in this godsforsaken room. I slipped the clothes on. It fit slightly big on me, and I avoided looking down at my body at all costs. Everything was too noticeable in this lighting. They tied my wet hair into a bun at the nape of my neck, not a hair out of place, and then scurried out of the room. It was as if they were never there to begin with.

"Let's go," one of the cloaked figures grunted, gesturing towards the door. I couldn't hide the shock from my face that they were going to let me walk around on my own voli-tion. Then, I remembered it wasn't like I could do anything to them.

Wiping the expression from my face, I held my head up high as I walked out of the room. I swore I saw one of the figures seem to smirk at my demeanor. They walked me down an equally white hallway until we stopped in front of double doors. The doors opened, almost as soon as I took a step towards them, and the two cloaked figures led me into it.

There were bookcases which spanned the length of the wall and were as tall as the ceiling. The books in the shelves were turned so only the pages of it were shown, instead of their spines. I felt myself swallow as the two figures left the room, closing the double doors behind them.

I was alone, and in the stark whiteness, I felt myself be more self-conscious than ever. I tried to tuck my nonexistent lock of hair behind my ear before realizing it was tied up in a bun. I wasn't sure what I was doing here. All I knew was this *had* to be the office of President Eclipse. I was going to meet the President of the Nation. The thought settled into my stomach like a rock.

Just as I thought of her, the double doors opened to reveal a woman with short white hair and white clothes. She almost wore a lab coat of sorts, that drifted behind her as she moved gracefully into the room. As I stared at her face, my temple started to pound. I put a hand to my head as I rubbed it, squinting at her as a memory came into my mind.

"You're not telling me something," she accused. She grabbed my head and pushed it towards the ground as she leaned towards my ear.

"You must tell me what you know," she hissed. I flinched from her voice.

"We've met before," I managed to get out, wincing at the pain. She smiled, widely. A little too wide for any one person.

"So you remember," she said. She sat down on the surface of her desk as she gestured towards me. "How you have changed."

"What do you want from me?" I asked her, venom in my voice. Her unnerving smile stayed on her lips as her white eyes darted towards my cut up hands, and then back up to my face.

"Your mother sent you a dream," she said. "I want to know what it was."

"It wasn't about you," I spat. "And even if it was, I wouldn't tell you." Almost in a millisecond, the smile on her face was gone. I felt goosebumps dot my skin at the sight.

"You will tell me," she said. "You will tell me all you know, by the end of it." She snapped her fingers, and two more cloaked figures came into the room. My eyes widened as I focused on the one on the left. I would recognize that silhouette anywhere.

"I don't want her to die," President Eclipse said as she coolly passed by Anubys. She went to sit behind her desk, settling in as if she were about to watch a play.

"One more chance, my dear Zinnia," she said, the unnerving smile back on her face. "What was your dream about?" I stared at the hood that hid Anubys's green eyes, and I wondered if he could see me. If he would be able to see the horrors that he was about to inflict on me.

"I can't tell you," I said, holding my chin up, defiantly. She laughed as she gestured towards Anubys and Eset.

"Child, I gave you a chance," she said, her eyes widening. As I watched her, the realization dawned on me. She already knew what my dream was about. But, of course. August saw everything. But, then why...

"Proceed," she ordered. Anubys took a step forward, and as he did, I felt the pain I had seen him inflict upon other creatures. It was unlike any other pain I had felt before.

I didn't realize death would feel like this. So full of sorrow, so cold, so... lonely. I didn't realize it would feel like my bones were slowly breaking constantly until they would turn into dust, that it would feel like my head was exploding and my body was rotting. I thought I had done a great job in not letting the pain show, but I heard the disjointed scream I eventually recognized was my own. Death would be a blessing, at this point. And just as I thought about begging for it, it stopped.

"Thank you, Anubys," President Eclipse said. Anubys took a small step back, but I saw his hands shake as he put them back into his cloak, his blood still calling for me. I gritted my teeth. President Eclipse stepped around her desk, walking towards me. Catching my breath, I placed a hand on the white ground, steadying myself as I tried to stand up.

"Oh, there's no need, child," she responded, waving her hand. "But, I didn't know you would be so loyal to Tayen after a few weeks with her and her crazy bunch." I kept my mouth shut as she leaned down, her white eyes level with mine. And at this proximity, I could swear her skin was actually made of scales.

"*She's a snake,*" Volplie had said. Was she, *literally*?

"Your father, a dear friend of mine, refuses to tell me your future. And August hasn't quite seen that message either. Just the jumbled up dream from your mother, but... Nabi gave you a lot of dreams growing up, didn't she?" she said, her eyes roving over my face. What she was looking for, I wasn't sure.

"She didn't send me any dreams," I panted. It felt like my bones were being reformed even though I knew it had all been in my head. The only other dream I could think of was the image of me. A me I didn't recognize. But, my mother didn't send me that when I was young.

"Beware the shadow maker. Beware the silver-tongue. But, they both work for me? Only two paths, I saw. How would one be different from the other?" she mused as she straightened up. "Nabi always did like to mess with me." Her gaze hardened as she thought about my mom. Then she gave me a cold look, as I finally got myself to my feet.

"Which path would be best?" she asked, glancing over at Anubys who was frozen where he stood.

"Why do you even care about my future?" I barked out. She stared at me, quizzically, and then sat down on her desk, crossing her arms.

"Child, there's something in your future that will cross paths with mine," she said. "Do you not know who your father is?"

"He's an oracle, seer, fortune teller, whatever," I muttered. She smiled that impossibly wide smile again.

"Your father told me when hellfire rears its head, it'll be the end of the Nation or it'll save us all." *You'll kill us all. Save us.*

"Suddenly, your father told me the vision was a lie, after you were born. Not a real vision, he said. Mistook a nightmare for one," she shrugged a shoulder. "I knew then he had created hellfire. I figured an Evolved so amazing would be made from pairing your parents together. I didn't realize my possible demise would show up." She barked out a laugh. Then, her white eyebrows slowly furrowed together as she stared at me for longer.

"You haven't chosen your path yet, I assume," she said. "Perhaps, your mother made sure the vision won't come to you until you decide."

"Or she thought this was stupid and I will choose my own path," I spat. Her lips twitched slightly.

"Winter has never been wrong," she said. "And I *will*

make sure you save this Nation, at the end of this." She stared at me for a moment, and her lips curled back before saying, "Whether I need to break you or not to do it." I steeled my gaze towards her as she tiredly snapped her fingers again. I watched as a man without a hood walked in, and I repressed the urge to widen my eyes. *August.*

"I'm sorry, Zinnia," he muttered, his eyes refusing to meet mine.

"How could you do this? To me? To everyone?" I hissed. President Eclipse acted like I didn't say a word. August's mouth opened and closed, like a fish, looking for the words to say. President Eclipse got up from her desk.

"Remember, dear, you're under my control," she said, mostly to herself. "Love, ha. You stupid, stupid girl." August gave the one word command that brought the heaviness of sleep onto my tired body. The only thought that lingered in my mind was she was right. I *was* a stupid girl. *Trust no one,* were my mother's last words to me. And yet, I trusted a pretty face and the fake, forced charm August had. As I glared up at him, before the darkness consumed my vision, I promised myself I would *never* make that mistake ever again.

CHAPTER THIRTY-TWO

When I finally came to, I groaned as I held my head. Stretching my limbs out as my eyes adjusted to the darkness of my cell, I remembered the pain I felt when President Eclipse ordered Anubys to torture me. My jaw clenched at the memory. I hated him. I hated all of them.

"Zinnia?" I heard Lightning's voice say softly. I crawled over to the wall and leaned my head against the cool stone.

"Yeah, I'm here," I said after some silence. My legs still felt like they were broken. The effects of Anubys being in one's head was... Nothing like I imagined it to be.

"I saw them bring you in. They cleaned you up," he said.

"They tortured me," I muttered. He was silent for a moment.

"Honestly, I wouldn't mind being tortured in exchange for a good bath at this point," he finally said. I was surprised I let myself laugh at the comment. He laughed with me at the ridiculousness of the situation, a deep hearty laugh.

"At least you weren't physically harmed," Lightning mumbled, at the end of his laugh. "From what I saw."

"No," I confirmed. "I wasn't. Just... Mentally, I guess."

"One of her minions?"

"Anubys," I whispered. He was silent. I quickly wiped the angry tear threatening to fall onto my cheek. I didn't want to think about Anubys. I didn't want to think about how I felt the cold tendrils of his power slowly killing me in my brain.

"I just can't comprehend how he was with us, joking with us, *living* with us, and then is suddenly so okay with killing us," I said, filling the silence. Lightning sighed, loudly, as if this was a thought he had been turning over in his head.

"He's been with President Eclipse since he was really young. That's all he's known. That's all they've both known," he said. I scoffed.

"What's August's excuse?" I said. "And don't tell me you're still trying to excuse *her*."

"I'm not trying to excuse any... He gave you an apple the other day. The only food you've been able to eat this whole time. He did it for a reason, and I don't think he did it because he was allowed to," Lightning explained. "He's not... a bad person." The words sounded twisted in Lightning's mouth.

"I thought you hated him."

"I don't hate him. I just don't like him. Or trust him," Lightning said. "But, I don't think he's evil." *Yeah, you weren't the one who was just tortured by him,* I bitterly thought.

I focused my attention onto drawing circles in the dirt ground with my pointer finger. I didn't trust Anubys either, or at least that's what I've told myself. And yet, I felt so betrayed he would hurt me like this, would kill our friends like this. More betrayed by him than by August, who had tricked me into giving him full control of my powers. Maybe, I ended up trusting Anubys a lot more than I wanted to. I shook my head. No, I *knew* I trusted him more than I wanted because I... *"Don't think he did it because he cared about you,"* Eset's words echoed around in my head. *"He's unable to. Neither of us are."* I shut my eyes, trying to practice the meditation techniques Devlin taught us. Breathe in. Breathe out. No thoughts.

"What did she want with you?" Lightning's voice broke my concentration, and I almost choked on my breath.

"Are you okay?" I heard his concern as I went into a coughing fit.

"I'm," I coughed, "fine." I took a deep breath once my airway was open. "She asked me about what my mother sent me, in dreams. She was a dreamer."

"Your nightmares?" he asked.

"Yeah. She has—*had*—the power to send dreams to people. The dream she sent me was... messed up. Confusing. And I realized she's been sending me dreams this whole time," I said, quietly. "My dad, he's an oracle or a seer. He has visions of the future. The dream my mom sent me, Tayen thought it was a warning of some sort."

"That's why you talked to her a lot," Lightning muttered. I nodded my head, even though he couldn't see me.

"I still don't know what it really means. I have two paths I could take. But both seem bad," I said, picking at my nails, nervously.

"Why does she want to know about your future?" he asked, his voice confused.

"She said my father gave her a vision one time. Something about when hellfire comes, it'll either end the Nation or save us all," I whispered. "My mother said something similar in my dream."

"She said you'll end the nation or save us?"

"She said I'll kill them all. And then she begs me to save them," I muttered, shaking my head. I threw a small pebble across the room.

"I don't know," I sighed. "I don't understand any of it."

"It sounds like you have a choice," Lightning pointed out. "A choice we all have in life. Though, not everything is black and white."

"It definitely feels that way," I muttered.

"Are you sure it's okay you're telling me this?" Lightning said after a moment. "There might be cameras or something."

"She already knows about my dream. She just wanted to see if I would tell it to her," I muttered. "*August* had already told her." I heard Lightning take a sharp inhale at the mention of the traitor's name.

"There aren't cameras down here," a familiar voice said near the entrance of my cell. I whipped my head around to see those green eyes that stroke fear and, weirdly enough, relief in me. The hood of his cloak was down, and I could see his face dimly in the darkness. He shrugged slightly.

"There's no need for any of that. She'll find out everything anyways," Anubys said.

"Why are you here?" I hissed, glowering at him. He stared at me, his expression unchanging. He really couldn't care about a soul. His hand searched inside of his cloak, revealing an orange. He tossed it in my direction. I stared at it as it rolled slowly towards me.

"Why?" I repeated, my voice quiet.

"You could die... in those sessions. I don't want you to," he said, his voice low.

"You killed *everyone* I care about," I snapped. I tore my gaze away from the orange and glared at him. I wanted him to feel that every part of me hated him and always would.

"Like you haven't killed your friends before," he muttered.

"What... did you say to me?" I asked, bringing myself to my feet as I marched over to him. "*What* did you just say to me?" He smirked and brought his face closer to the bars of my cell.

"Forest, Rohit, June," he listed the names off. *June?* A part of me broke, wanting to hide away, but I wasn't going to back down. He pretended to think for a moment.

"Oh wait, no, you didn't kill June. You just put her in a coma for probably the rest of her life," Anubys said, his eyes meeting mine once again. I felt my blood still within me. The image of June behind Forest's dead body flashed in my mind. I closed my eyes, wincing at the pain of the partial memory.

"Are you here just to torture me emotionally too?" I whispered, opening my eyes. I saw concern flicker in his, until they turned dead once again. A smile spread on his lips, but it didn't meet his sinister-looking eyes, making him look even more like a predator.

"Eat the orange," he said, nodding his head towards the fruit. "We'll get to play more later." He stared for a moment longer, his eyes roving over me, softening, but I almost felt like throwing up.

"I hate you," I hissed as he turned away. He turned his head over his shoulder, one eye staring at me.

"Yeah, go ahead and keep lying to yourself like that, sweetheart," he said, putting the hood back over his head. I stared at him in horror and then hit the bars in anger as he laughed. My body lowered to the ground as I pressed my face against the metal, watching until I couldn't see his figure anymore.

"We need to get out of here," I muttered, as I selfishly reached for the orange.

"Tell me about it," Lightning responded.

CHAPTER THIRTY-THREE

I didn't know how long I had been down there before the small, cloaked child appeared in front of my cell once again. At some point, they took Lightning, and when he came back, he didn't want to talk. At all. Whatever happened to him up there, it traumatized him deeply.

The little hand stuck through the bars of my cell as I stared at the lower half of the child's face. Their lips were twisted up in concentration, and their neck was tensed. But, it was all I could see.

"Do I have a choice?" I asked, softly. It felt like it had been a while since Anubys brought me that orange, and part of me feared I chased him away from feeding me ever again. The child shook their head as they moved their hand with more urgency.

I guess I could use a bath.

"Fine," I muttered. I took the hand, and the world blurred around me once again. It was less nauseating this time, but it still turned my stomach pretty heavily. When the world stopped moving, we were back in the white room. And just like before, a little army of people walked in to bathe me in order to present me to the President of the Nation.

Except, it wasn't President Eclipse who greeted me this time in that weird office room. It was a man with brown hair the color of sand and circular glasses. He wore the same kind of coat President Eclipse wore, and he rose out of his seat as I was ushered in.

"Zinnia Winterschild of Adams, correct?" he asked, checking a clipboard. His voice had an accent to it that I had only heard once before. There was an elongation in his vowels no one around me ever had. I nodded my head, confused, as I studied him. He put a hand to his chest as he glanced up at me.

"I'm from the Elizabeth Community," he said. *Oh*, I thought, *that's why he had an interesting accent.* Elizabeth, the community's namesake, didn't have a last name, or if she did, she didn't use one. My Instructor had once played an old, hazy video of Elizabeth speaking about the mission of the Nation, and she sounded similarly to this man.

He seemed relaxed, either completely trusting that I wouldn't try to kill him, or he was someone who would be able to take me down in a minute. *Though*, I thought as I measured him up, *he didn't look like someone who knew how to fight.*

"I have a pretty useful power, Zinnia," he said, not looking up from the clipboard as I jumped back, startled.

"I don't know what you mean," I mumbled as I walked into the center of the room. He looked up at me, his hazel eyes boring holes into my face.

"I don't need to fight," he answered, smiling slightly. I frowned. *How did he know I was thinking about that?*

"Because I can read your thoughts, darling," he said. I scowled at him as he put down his clipboard.

"Reading my thoughts doesn't mean you don't need to fight. It just means you have a heads up if I decide to," I snapped. He laughed and nodded.

"Yes, that's true," he said. "But, unfortunately, I'm one of those who has a dual power, much like your mother." My scowl deepened at the mention of my mother.

"Don't talk about her," I hissed. He stared at me curiously.

"Interesting," he said as he checked something off on the clipboard. I craned my head to try and read what he was looking at, but I couldn't see anything from where I was standing.

"Do you know what the other power is?" he asked, his eyes glinting. "The one that keeps me from fighting?" I narrowed mine and shrugged.

"I don't really care all that much," I retorted.

"It's speed," he responded, as if I didn't say anything. "I can read your mind, and I can move faster than you. So, if you *did* try to kill me with this pen, you wouldn't be fast enough." I felt my eyes widen involuntarily in shock at my thought being voiced, and then I looked away.

"Why am I here?" I asked, quietly. "I thought President Eclipse would be..." I let my voice drift off. I didn't know what I wanted to say. I thought she'd be here to torture me again? What an absurd sentence.

"An all around absurd situation indeed," the man responded to my thoughts, turning towards me. He took off his glasses and folded them neatly before placing them onto the desk.

"I'm October," he said. I scoffed.

"She really likes people named after the months," I muttered. October's eyes twinkled at my comment.

"I was wondering how you felt," he said.

"About what, exactly? Basically everyone I know being murdered, being tortured by someone I thought was my friend, being unable to use my powers because of someone I—for some reason—thought I liked? Or are you just inquiring about how I'm adjusting to being in darkness 24/7?" I sneered. His lips twitched, as if he were about to laugh or smile. He was the polar opposite of President Eclipse. Almost genuine.

"I am *very* different from her," he answered my thoughts. "That's what makes us work so well. But, yes. I'm inquiring about how your powers feel."

"Stop reading my thoughts," I said.

"Unfortunately," he said, smiling almost pityingly, "it's not something I can really turn off. You understand." *I don't.* He smirked at my thought.

"Your powers?" he asked, gesturing towards me. I stared at him for a moment, trying to decide if I had the choice to not speak about it or not. His gaze told me that I did not.

"It feels like there's a cold fist around it," I answered, begrudgingly. "Like, someone's hand is around my fire and squeezing it so no air could get through. So the fire can't get through."

"How long have you felt this?" he asked, writing my words down. I winced at how loud the scribbling sounded after being in silence for so long.

"Uh," I said, trying to focus on the question. "It's been like this since I've been captured."

"Before being contained, you could use your powers," he more said than asked.

"No," I answered, shaking my head. "No, I couldn't use them. I was just able to get around it, a little, but the fist would close pretty quickly if it relaxed at all."

"I see," he said.

"Why do you want to know?" I asked.

"Just trying to gauge our new friend's ability," October answered. "Just the strength of it and all that. The fact that he can control your hellfire is pretty impressive in and of itself."

"New friend?"

"August," he said, his eyes meeting mine. "Your friend from Adams."

"He's *not* my friend," I snapped.

"Stay here," he said, ignoring my comment. "Someone will be with you shortly." He flipped the pages he was writing on back onto the clipboard and strode out of the room without a single look back at me.

Something October said disturbed me. August was a *new* friend? So he wasn't working for them this whole time? Only one question remained in my head, a question I needed the answer to: *What made him want to betray everyone in that camp for President Eclipse?*

I heard murmurings outside the door of the office, and I sneaked towards the door in order to hear better. It was unmistakably October's voice.

"She has a lot of anger within her. If we were to allow her to use her power without the silver-tongue, she'd explode. Taking a whole community with her, no doubt," I barely made out what October said.

"We'll break her," President Eclipse's unmistakable drawl pierced through the air. October chuckled.

"I'm not sure it will be as easy as you might think," he said. "She's no Winter." At the mention of my father's name, I slowly backed away from the door. His name sounded so close, as if October was right next to it. Which only meant, President Eclipse was about to enter.

The double doors opened, and President Eclipse strode into the room. She snapped her red-painted fingers impatiently at someone behind her, and I watched as Anubys and Eset walked in. Their hoods were up, but I recognized the smirk on Eset's face and the long, slender fingers of Anubys's hands. Though I wanted to remain stoic, unfazed, by their entrance, the instinct in me took over. I scrambled backwards, in fear, as my body realized what it was going to have to endure again. I bit back a desperate *'please,'* not wanting her to have the satisfaction of how deep my fear went.

"You already know about my dream. What else do you want from me?" I hissed through gritted teeth. President Eclipse just watched me, almost amused. I tried to straighten up, to stop myself from looking smaller than I was, but my body wasn't obeying.

"Winter is being... uncharacteristically defiant," she said, that wide, unnerving smile plastered onto her scaly face. I grimaced at the sight.

"What does that have to do with me?" I snapped. Her smile somehow got bigger.

"Well," she said, circling towards the door, "*You* will help me get the vision out of him." I crossed my arms.

"I'm not helping you with—" I started to protest, but my sentence was cut short as I watched my father walk into the room. He was limping and where his eyes once were, were black empty holes. His right leg was gnarled, as if it had been broken so many times beyond repair. I felt my stomach convulse, wanting to throw up even though nothing was in it.

"He can't see, anymore," President Eclipse smirked, gesturing towards his face. "We thought it might help him *see* better, if you know what I mean." My hands covered my gaping mouth as I just stared at him. His auburn hair, much like mine, was longer than the last time I had seen him. He looked smaller, somehow, instead of the usual towering man I was used to.

"Dad?" I barely whispered. Tears started to form in my eyes, the amber eyes I used to see in my father's face every day. His head lifted, facing my direction as his eyebrows furrowed upwards together.

"Zinnia?" he croaked. He sounded like he hadn't spoken in a while. "Please tell me you're not here." President Eclipse's smile disappeared as she turned towards me.

"Make sure to scream so your father hears the pain he's caused you," she said. Then, she waved her hands towards Anubys, and I swallowed the urge to beg him. There wasn't a way out of this, I knew that. She had starved me, locked up my power—there wasn't a world where I could get away with not being tortured.

I felt Anubys hesitate, but I still didn't look up at him. I was afraid if I did, the plea would slip out of my mouth and I wouldn't be able to stop it. Instead, I stared straight towards my father.

"No matter what she does to me, Dad," I said, a knot appearing in my throat, "Don't give in."

"Anubys," President Eclipse's voice was insistent. Just as she said his name, I felt his cold tendrils start to snake around my body and mind, almost caressing me before breaking me. And even though I tried to keep the screams from coming out, they were almost deafening.

"He tortured you," Lightning said once I had come back to my cell. I nodded, though he couldn't see. It had been a while since Lightning spoke to me.

"I'm guessing he tortured you as well," I muttered. He was quiet. So quiet I could hear the sound of dripping water from down the hall. I curled my legs up into my chest as I felt the tears start to roll down my cheeks.

"They have my dad," I whispered. "They gouged his eyes out." A sob escaped from my lips, and I bit them to keep from making another pathetic sound. My hands curled into fists as I blinked the hot tears away.

"She has my family as well," Lightning said, his voice hard. "She said she'll kill them slowly, one at a time, if I don't do what she asks."

"What is she asking for?" I asked, softly.

"To find Tayen," he said, his voice wearisome. "No one in my family has powers except for me. They don't know what's going on, and... I can't find Tayen. She's either too far away or she's somehow hidden from me, I'm not sure."

"And she doesn't believe you," I assumed.

"She believes me," Lightning grunted. "She just enjoys torturing people." I placed my cheek against the smooth stone that separated Lightning and I.

"She's trying to break us," I muttered. Lightning was quiet.

"I'm afraid she'll be successful," Lightning whispered. "At least, with me." The silence stretched between us. Hoping there weren't any cameras or recording devices down here, I took a deep breath, glancing around in the darkness.

"We need to get out of here, somehow," I whispered.

"Yeah, but how?" his deep voice almost cracked. I took a deep breath as I stared up into the darkness. If I had control over my power completely, I had the semblance of a plan. I had the idea of one, anyway. But, I didn't have control over it because I... *allowed* August to be in my head. I let *him* have control over my power. And without my power, I didn't have a solid enough plan.

"I don't know," I whispered.

"If we cooperate," Lightning muttered, "We'd be able to get out of the cells, our families will be let go..."

"But, we'll be stuck," I finished for him. "We'd be stuck working for her."

"With no way out," he concluded.

"The only way out *is* to work for her," I whispered. I started to mindlessly draw circles into the dirt. "And the only way close to her is to be in her inner circle." My finger stopped moving as an idea came to me. I held my breath, thinking about it. I wouldn't voice it, not yet. Not when I wasn't a hundred percent sure she wasn't listening to us.

"If we were in her inner circle, we'd never be able to leave. We'd never be free," Lightning said, softly. He didn't come to the same conclusion as me. Or if he did, he wasn't going to dare voice it either.

"Right," I answered. "So we have no choice in the matter." Lightning was quiet for a moment.

"None," he said. But, the tone in his voice made me smile a bit. We were on the same page, even if we didn't voice it aloud.

CHAPTER THIRTY-FOUR

"Burn it all. Burn it all to the ground," the girl who had my face whispered to me. She wiped the golden tears off of her face, leaving a shimmery streak across her pale cheek.

"I-I can't. I don't want to," I stammered. The crown made of flame flickered for a moment as she turned her—*my*—eyes towards me, but they were white. As white as President Eclipse's. She gripped my shoulders, her fingers burrowing into them as I yelped out in pain.

"You must burn them all. Kill them all," she said. "Explode. For the Nation. All for the Nation." Her voice was almost detached as her skin started to melt away. Flickering flames replaced it.

"Please," I begged as her hands started to burn me. Her hair rose all around her head like a halo.

"Consume them. Become stronger," she whispered, her voice bouncing off of the walls. "We'll destroy them all." Her smile was the last thing on her face before becoming a raging fire. It consumed me as I screamed, searching for my flame of life. And as the pain intensified, I woke up.

I was shaking on the dirt ground, the room around me as black as the back of my eyelids. I hugged my legs into myself as I recalled the girl who wore a crown of flames from my dreams. *Burn it all. Burn it all to the ground.* I winced as I remembered her words. It was a warning. A warning of who I could become; someone I knew I was capable of becoming.

"Powers are addictive," I reminded myself, remembering what August said. I wondered if that was the reason why he turned on the Shadow Army. If it was because he was too addicted to using his powers in a certain way. I shook the thought out of my head. I didn't want to excuse him for what he did. Ever.

"Zinnia," I heard a far away voice say. I lifted my head at the noise. It was almost like a wail. I crawled over to the bars of my cell as I listened to the voice.

"Zinnia, I'm so sorry," I heard the voice sob. And through the sobs, I recognized the voice of my father.

"It's okay, Dad," I said, hoping my voice would carry itself towards his cell. I heard his sobs pause.

"Zinnia," I heard him say.

"I'm okay," I responded, leaning my forehead against the metal bars. My head was pounding, and I didn't know if it was from the lack of food or from the nightmare I just had.

"You got your mom's dreams, right?" he asked, his whisper snaking through the darkness. I nodded.

"Yes. It was confusing, but I got it," I said.

"I can't tell you anything else. It's your future... I can't..." my father said. *So that's why it was confusing.* I was silent as I closed my eyes, remembering my mother.

"What happened?" I whispered. "To Mom and Happy?" Silence stretched out as I waited for my father to find the words. I heard a gasp, and realized he had started to cry. A part of me morbidly wondered what he looked like crying, now that his eyes were gone. He took a moment before he started to speak.

"When you failed, they came to the house," he said, his voice clear. "They wanted to know what your mother has been telling you throughout the years. If she ever gave any hint as to what they were really up to."

"What do you mean?" I asked, perking up. *What they were really up to?*

"It was important Nabi never told you. If you knew, and they let you go beyond the Wall, you would tell the others in the Rebellion. I told them your mother would never put you in danger like that," my father went on, ignoring my question. "They didn't believe me."

"Why did they think I knew this information? Why did they think Mom told me?" I asked.

"President Eclipse is not just a shapeshifter. She's an Immortal, and someone with great instincts. It's as if... she can smell it on you," my father whispered. At his tone, I shuddered and wrapped my arms around myself. "President Eclipse never worried about your mother stepping out of line. She was broken and had two children she loved more than anything. She wouldn't endanger you. That's what President Eclipse thought. It's also what I told her, over the years."

"But," my father continued, "She met you during your Test. It's abnormal, her coming into the Test to meet the failing citizens. Loyalty is the only thing that is keeping the Nation afloat. She can't afford to have any doubt in what she's doing."

"She came into my Test?" I questioned. My head started to pound as a flicker of a memory forced its way into my head. *"What do you know, Zinnia?" she whispered.* I shook my head. So *that's* where I knew her.

"She wanted to meet the person who was hellfire. The person who was predicted to either help her or destroy her. And she smelled it on you. Something you knew. Something you were hiding from her, subconsciously or consciously. And she realized Nabi must've been desperate. Must've known I would've convinced Eclipse to find the Rebellion camp this year," my father explained. Hearing her name without the title made my skin crawl.

"You convinced her to find the Rebellion camp?" I asked, my voice detached.

"Yes. To save you from certain death when you failed, I convinced her to follow the failed citizens. I saw who would fail months before, and it was the perfect group of kids. A map, a forcefield, a healer. They would be able to help you find and get through to the Rebellion camp," my father said. And as he spoke, I felt a sinking feeling settle itself into the pit of my stomach. It was because of him. It was because of him all of my friends were dead. I closed my eyes in an attempt to dull the pain, but my chest ached at the thought.

"She sent two of her inner circle in with the failed citizens, to report back to her once they had infiltrated the camp. It was too late to go back on her plan and instead kill all of you when she smelled the knowledge on you, not when she thought this was a great plan in finally destroying Tayen. So, she told them to keep an eye on you," my father said. That's why Anubys was always around me, watching me. He was just monitoring me so he could report back to President Eclipse. My hands curled into fists as the fire that was so carefully hidden away, flared.

"She thought Mom told me something, and that's why she killed her?" I asked, quietly. I heard my father's escaped sobs again, and I winced at the sound. I had never heard my father cry before in my life. He was someone I had always seen as being so strong. Someone I could rely on. And here he was, broken beyond repair.

"Your mother wouldn't deny that she sent something to you. She wouldn't deny it or confirm it. I *begged* with Eclipse, on behalf of your mother. Frankly, I begged your mother, too. But, Nabi was just quiet. If she lied, President Eclipse would know. And if she told the truth, and if the truth was that she *did* tell you about the Nation, Eclipse would kill you. So, she stayed silent. And President Eclipse, she... She..." my father's breath hitched, and he was quiet for a moment. He interchangeably used the title and just her name. My eyebrows raised as to the familiarity my father seemingly had with that monster.

My mother's face appeared in my head. The face that resembled my own in structure. The eye shape I inherited from her burned its way through my memory. Tears pricked at my eyes, and I swallowed the lump that threatened to appear in the back of my throat.

"And Happy?" I asked, my voice small. My father was quiet for a long time.

Finally, he whispered, "I don't know… But, I know she's not dead. I still see her future." I let out a breath of relief as I gave a silent thanks to any of the old gods. The Nation didn't have a religion, and nobody practiced any. But, we all knew about the old gods that were in history. *At least one of them had to be real*, is what I desperately thought.

"I'm sorry, Zinnia," my father said. I shook my head.

"I'm fine, Dad," I whispered.

"I don't know how to help you," he said, pushing down a sob. It hurt my heart to hear him like this.

"It's okay, Dad," I whispered, backing away from the bars of my cell. "Get some rest."

"I love you," he whispered back. "And your mother loved you so much." I felt my throat close as tears threatened to spill over. I quickly wiped my eyes with the back of my hand as I leaned against the far wall of the cell. I didn't respond to my father for a long while. What could I even say? He had lost his pride, his strength, his eyes, and his wife. Were there even words to comfort him at this moment?

"I love you, too," I whispered, not knowing if he was able to hear it. It was the only thing I could say, but it didn't ring fully true. A part of me hated him for what he did. For obeying President Eclipse for so long. Even though I knew it was selfish of me to think this, even though I knew he didn't really have a choice, my friends were dead. They were dead and the Rebellion camp, the only thing that could've eventually stopped President Eclipse, was destroyed. And it was because of him. Him and Anubys. And I let the anger eat away any other thought that I had.

To pass the time, all I could think about was the various ways I wanted to kill President Eclipse with and count the dripping of the water from somewhere further down the hall. When I finally reached two thousand drips without any interruption, I heard a tap from the bars on my door. My eyes fluttered open as I heard another drip. Two thousand and one.

"Here," Anubys's eyes were covered by his hood, but his voice was unmistakable. In his hands, he held another orange.

"I realized the apple was probably covered in dirt when you were trying to eat it," his voice was quiet. My eyebrows raised as I recognized the emotion that was coating his tone. Guilt. Anubys, the shadow maker, the grim reaper, felt... guilty.

"An orange, you can peel," he said, shrugging his shoulders. *So that's his reasoning for constantly giving me oranges*, I thought. I lifted myself up and walked over to the barred door. Gingerly, carefully so I didn't touch the palm that called to me, I grabbed the orange from his hand. I lifted the orange in a farewell before I started to peel it.

"Thanks," I said as I turned away and started walking back to the far corner of the cell. The furthest place from the door.

"I'm sorry," he whispered as I was halfway there. I stopped, my back turned towards him.

"I didn't have a choice, Zinnia. I hope you realize that," he whispered. The anger that was so ever present— the anger at hearing my name spoken so softly on his tongue— flared up again as I turned slightly towards him.

"You were watching me. The whole time," I said. "You

were reporting to *her* about me." I watched his veiny hands reach up to his hood, his fingers looping around the fabric. He brought it down, revealing his eyes to me, eyes full of… guilt?

"Don't look at me like that," I seethed. "Don't look at me like you're actually sorry."

"I *am* sorry, Zinnia," he said, his fingers curling around the bars of the door as he leaned forward. His hypnotizing eyes froze me to the spot, to the middle of the cell. I stared at him for a moment longer, the air between us almost electric. Finally, I tore my eyes away from him as I looked down at the orange I had stopped peeling.

"Was it all a lie?" I whispered.

"It wasn't," he responded. "I *had* to report to her about you, but I didn't report to her about everything. I promise. I never told her about your dreams, not after the first one."

"*What* first one?" I snapped. His eyes widened and then realization flooded his face. He sighed as he looked down at the ground.

"Your memories have been tampered with. August removed moments we had together in order for you to place your misguided feelings that you had towards me onto him, so he could control you better," he explained.

"Misguided feelings?" I questioned, my eyebrows furrowed as I looked up at him. Anubys looked flustered as he ran a hand through his wavy, black hair. I remembered how the water droplets in his hair that night looked like starlight. I looked away and popped a piece of the orange into my mouth.

"The best way for a silver-tongue, or a child of Aphrodite, to be able to convince a person with their words is to get inside their head. This is through trust or... love. So, August inserted himself into all your most revered memories, so that you equated him with family, friends, and being love himself. Plus, you had a crush on him as a child, so it was easier for him to do this," Anubys explained. His voice almost seemed small. I just stared at him.

"And he inserted himself into a memory with you? Except, I don't really remember telling August about my dreams," I said, pointedly. Though, I *did* remember him holding my wrist in the middle of the night after a nightmare. My eyebrows furrowed.

"He just erased those parts," Anubys said, darting his eyes away from me. I continued to eat the orange, even though a part of me wanted to crush it in my hands for what I was hearing.

"So, he brainwashed me." The sentence twisted in my mouth.

"Don't act like you didn't know what was going to happen. You *knew* he was going to go into your head," Anubys muttered. I flashed my eyes at him as I walked closer to the barred door.

"I didn't realize he was going to *force* me to feel like I was in love with him," I hissed. A lot of things started to make sense now. Why it felt unnatural. Why I hated holding his hand. And why I felt disgusted by August when he wasn't near me. Anubys raised his hands in defense.

"That feeling of love, he took from the memories of me, you know. Or the buddings of it," he said, smirking. I angrily walked up to the barred door, dropped the orange peel to the ground, and grabbed the bars as I leaned forward.

"I *never* felt anything for *you*," I seethed. He flashed me a crooked smile, his eyes glinting in a way that made me feel relaxed. It was familiar. This. I shook the thought out of my head.

"Why are you *here*?" I fumed. "You couldn't torture me enough in President Eclipse's presence so now you've *actually* resorted to torturing me psychologically?" His smile melted away as that stupid look of guilt appeared in his eyes.

"I'm so—"

"*Don't fucking apologize*, Anubys," I snapped as I let go of the bars. A glimmer of hurt appeared in his eyes as he lowered them. My face softened.

"I already know you can't care about anyone and that this," I gestured towards him, "is all an act. So, just leave me alone." I turned away, and I heard him take a step forward.

"I can't," his voice broke. "I can't... leave you alone." Frowning, I turned towards him. His face looked the most broken I had ever seen it. Part of me ached for him, wanted to comfort him in some way. Another part of me felt smug, felt happy he was hurting as much as I was.

"I didn't want to make you feel... I didn't want to..." he struggled with his words as he anxiously ran another hand through his black hair.

"President Eclipse can't *make* you do anything. You could kill her in a second if you really wanted to," I pointed out. His green eyes met mine.

"You think I haven't thought about that? What do you think would happen if she died? What would happen to the Nation? What would happen to Eset after I..." his voice drifted off. I scoffed. I couldn't care less about his sister.

"So you're just a coward then," I said. He frowned, and

then his jaw clenched. He looked down at the ground and slowly nodded his head.

"Yeah, I guess. I'm a coward," he muttered. "And I'm sorry." His hand was still gripping one of the bars on the cell as he turned away. And some part of me desperately didn't want him to.

"Why do you come and give me food? Why do you look so goddamn guilty for what you've done to me?" the question that burned my throat slipped out. He turned back towards me, his eyebrows furrowed together. He searched the ground for an answer and then took a deep breath. His eyes looked like melted jade as he stared at me. His look made the breath in my lungs still as I stared back at him, waiting.

"All I can do is think about you, Zinnia," he whispered, lowering his gaze. I froze. "You consume me, my every thought, my every waking moment. Every breath, every second, I think of you. You plague my dreams, and it feels like... like I'm *drowning* in you. That I won't be able to get a clear *breath* unless... You know, sometimes, I feel like I'm going crazy. To risk everything—To *want* to risk..." his breath hitched in his throat as he stared up at me, "...I don't know what to do or who I'm supposed to be when I'm around you."

CHAPTER THIRTY-FIVE

I stared at him as my brain tried to process the words that seemed to caress me. His gaze dropped as he stared at the ground.

"Say something," he whispered. I just stared at him, my mind racing.

"Say what?" I asked quietly. His eyes darted back up at me, searching my eyes. I stared blankly back at him as I tried to think. Beware the shadow-maker. Beware the silver-tongue. Both were paths I could go down. They were the only two paths. My future was black and white, as Lightning would put it. The image of Anubys and August holding out their hands flashed through my mind as I stared into his green eyes.

"Say anything," he said, his voice low. I looked back and forth between Anubys and August.

"You've come upon a crossroads of shadows. Two different destinies are laid out before you," voices said within my head. Anubys standing before me, waiting for an answer, seemed to disappear. I turned, in my mind's eye, to look at her. *Hecate*, my body breathed, stilled in fear. She wore a long, dark cloak and had three heads, looking in different directions. One of the heads stared at me, her dark eyes meeting mine.

"I don't know which way is right," I felt myself whisper to the old goddess. She stared, blank-faced at me.

"You'll kill us all. Save us," the heads spoke. "Save the world, or destroy it. You have a choice, but the choice has already been made. You know which path you should take." She stood in front of Anubys and August, both their hands were outstretched.

"I wish you luck, daughter of Nabi," the goddess spoke as I felt myself reach out towards Anubys in my mind's eye, my hand curling around his as he led me down his darkened path. Closing my eyes, I felt my lips thin into a line.

"Fine," I finally said, opening them. I knew exactly what path I wanted to take. His face contorted into confusion as he stared at me, his pale green eyes still resembling melted jade.

"You love me," I said, matter-of-factly. His eyes widened as I assumed his face turned red, though I couldn't see clearly in this darkness.

"I-I didn't say that I... *love* you. I *can't*... love..." his voice faltered, running a hand through his black hair. "I just said that you..."

"That I consume your every thought and that you're drowning in me," I finished for him. His eyes flashed as I recalled his words. "Sounds like love to me." His eyes rolled around again, as he tried to think of something to say. I took a step forward, towards the barred door, and I watched as he took an embarrassed step back.

"If you love me," I cooed, "you'll help me." His eyes studied me for a moment as he froze. I watched his tongue run against the back of his teeth as he thought, and then he took a step forward.

"Help you with what?" his voice was low, but almost threatening. A warning. A part of me panicked at this half-formed idea in my head. But, I had picked my path. There wasn't any going back.

"If you love me," I said, pressing my face against the bars on the door. He took another curious step forward, his face inches away from mine. I took a deep breath as I breathed in his sweet scent.

"If you love me," I repeated, as he raised an eyebrow at my hesitation, "you'll help me kill President Eclipse."

"Are you *crazy?*" Anubys said for the thousandth time as he paced back and forth in front of my cell.

"She sounded pretty serious," Lightning said from his cell. He had heard the whole thing and *obviously* thought it was the most brilliant plan. Anubys pointed his pointer and middle finger at the two of us.

"You're *both* insane," he said.

"Why is it such a crazy idea? You don't like her. I don't like her," I pointed out. Anubys stopped pacing to look at me.

"I never said I don't like her," he said. "I'm *terrified* of her. There's a difference." I rolled my eyes.

"Okay, whatever. You're just a *coward* while Lightning and I hate her for what she's done to our families," I pointed out. Anubys sighed, dramatically.

"You know, I'm *super* sad about what she did to your families. It's terrible. A travesty, really. But, *everyone* goes through their families being tortured and dying at some point," he said, as if it truly were the most normal thing in the world.

"You said you love me," I argued. His jaw dropped.

"I *never* said I love you, Zinnia," he pointed out.

"Eh, sounded like you were confessing your love for her to me," Lightning piped up. Anubys glared at him.

"You weren't even supposed to be—This was supposed to be a private—Oh, whatever. Fine," he muttered. I stared at him, eyes wide. *It was that easy?*

"You're going to help us?" I asked, unable to hide my enthusiasm. Anubys met my gaze, and he tried to hide a smile.

"It's going to be pretty much impossible," he mumbled. "But, yeah. I'll do whatever you ask me to, even if it'll end to your undoing." *My undoing?* He barely breathed the last part, and his words sent shivers down my spine as his hypnotizing eyes met mine.

"Why would it be impossible?" Lightning asked, breaking our gaze. I felt myself take a deep breath the moment Anubys's eyes looked away. *Stop it*, I reprimanded myself. *It's just because he was the first boy to ever say that kind of stuff to you.*

"For one," Anubys said, leaning against the empty cell door across from mine. He looked down the hall, frowning, before continuing. I followed his gaze and then as Anubys relaxed, I let myself look back at him.

"There's October," he finished. The man's face came to the forefront of my mind.

"What about him?" Lightning asked. I mentally kicked myself as I realized.

"He can read your thoughts," I groaned. Anubys pointed at me in confirmation.

"And, he is close to President Eclipse. He's her right hand man," Anubys said. "He can read any thought that is in the forefront of your mind. He can't go beyond that."

"So how do we make sure that he doesn't know what's going on?" I asked.

"By thinking of anything other than what we're planning, since you don't have time to create a mental shield," Anubys said. "When he was around, and I had to stop thinking about you, I would just think of a song. Though my mental shield is pretty strong, just in case, I don't think about anything of importance in front of him."

"Wouldn't he think it's suspicious if we're just recalling a song in our heads?" Lightning asked. I stared at the two of them.

"What's a song?" I asked. Anubys stared at me like I was crazy.

"How do you not know what a fucking song is?" Anubys asked.

"I heard some communities don't have access to music," Lightning mused. *Music?* Anubys sighed loudly as he stared at me and then looked away, like he was too disappointed to meet my gaze.

"Just think of something other than the plan. Like a

nursery rhyme," Lightning said. "But, wouldn't he realize we're trying to cover up our thoughts?"

"A lot of people try to cover up their thoughts around October," Anubys muttered, shrugging a shoulder. "He's used to it by now. And Toasty has met October already, knows what he is, so it's not too weird that she might be trying to cover up her thoughts." *So, we're back to the stupid nicknames,* I inwardly groaned. He stared at me as he pursed his lips.

"A lot of her... workers are here because she eventually forced them to be. Nearly everyone has tried to leave at some point," he said. "Even still, you'll have to be careful in making allies. But, we *will* need allies once the deed is done. It's not just President Eclipse."

"You'll help with that, won't you?" I almost demanded. He smirked.

"I'm at your command," he whispered.

"Please don't do this when I'm standing right here," Lightning commented. His smirk easily turned into his lop-sided grin as he looked over at Lightning.

"The hard part will be killing her. She's an Immortal," Anubys said. He glanced over at me. I knew what he was saying. I would need to explode, burn her to ash all at once in order for her to truly die.

"Like Devlin," Lightning said, more to himself. Anubys nodded.

"She's been here since the Nation began. It will be hard to kill her. And, she can tell when you're hiding something from her," Anubys said, rubbing his temples as he thought.

"It'll be difficult to trick her," he continued. "But, you just have to do things on the spur of the moment. Don't plan it out really. Actually, that would help with October, too, as long as you're not constantly thinking murderous thoughts, *Zinnia.*" He pointedly looked at me. I raised my hands in defense.

"What? I don't think murderous thoughts constantly," I lied. Anubys gave me a look.

"You do," he said. "Even before you were pissed at everyone." I just gaped at him. *How did he know that?*

"So, no plan," Lightning said. Anubys smiled.

"No way to hide anything from her if there's nothing to hide," he smirked.

"Wouldn't we be hiding this conversation from her though?" Lightning asked. Anubys rolled his head side to side as he thought.

"Yes and no," he said. "I'll tell her we had a conversation that convinced Fireball and you to give her your loyalty. But, I can't tell her the contents of the conversation. That explanation will satisfy her and explain why you two feel like you're hiding something."

"So you think it's possible," I said, "to kill her." His smile faded from his face as he gave me a hard look.

"It's a dangerous situation. And we might all be killed," he said. "But, I will help you in any way that I can." He avoided answering my question, and I just nodded in response. He didn't think it would be possible. Even so, I would have to prove him wrong.

"I need my powers back, if we're going to do this," I said. "Full control." Anubys stared at me.

"I know," he said. "And you're not going to like how you get it."

CHAPTER THIRTY-SIX

He was right. I didn't like his idea. It was risky and had the potential to not work at all. But, it was the only option we had to get my powers back from under the control of August. And I tried to remind myself of this as I grabbed the child's hand through the bars of the cell.

I went through the whole process in order to be presentable to President Eclipse for what felt like the upteenth time. The same lady's eyes crinkled at exactly the right times, and the water was as cold as ever. But, I embraced it more than usual. The lady's hands were soft as she twisted my wet hair into a tight, low bun, as if she knew what I was about to go through. The two cloaked men led me down the white official hallways towards her office, and I took a deep breath as I reminded myself that I knew what I was walking into.

Anubys told me my father still hadn't told President Eclipse what she wanted from him. His visions about me, specifically. He had been moved, after that night where we spoke, to one of the isolated rooms, Anubys had said.

I watched as President Eclipse, October, and the twins walked into the room. My father not obeying meant he would have to be broken more, which meant I had to be tortured again. It was the perfect time for us to move forward with the plan in a believable way.

October's eyes roved over me, and I frantically started to think about one of the many nursery rhymes I knew of. *Rock-a-bye baby, on the tree tops…*

"Unfortunately, your father still hasn't told me the information I need from him," President Eclipse said, picking at her blood-painted nails as she looked up at me. The weirdly wide smile was nowhere to be seen on her face.

She snapped her fingers, and two cloaked people walked in with my father hanging between them. He was almost limp, and I saw the bruises on his body. Before he could turn towards me, I looked away, not wanting to see him in his broken state. It felt almost… blasphemous to see my father like this. I curled my hands into fists and forced myself to think of nothing else but the nursery rhyme. *And when the wind blows, the cradle will rock…*

"But, that's why dear October is here with us," President Eclipse said, gesturing towards him. "Your father will think of the vision he's trying so desperately to keep from me, just as he hears your screams. He won't be able to do anything *but* think about it." She smiled a wide smile at me. I glanced over at October.

October's round glasses made his eyes look slightly smaller than they actually were, and those beady eyes were just studying me, intensely. I looked away from him, opting to stare at Anubys's bronzed hands. The hands that were about to kill me.

"No rebuttals today?" she asked me, her head cocking to the side. "Winter will still know you're here from your screams."

"She's too busy concentrating on a nursery rhyme to speak," October said slowly, his eyes briefly leaving my face to look over at President Eclipse.

"Eclipse, please," my father whimpered, her name flitting off his tongue as if it were part of his everyday vocabulary. Her head whipped over to look at him, and I watched as her cold eyes glanced up at one of the cloaked figures. An order. The cloaked man immediately punched my father in the stomach, and I couldn't keep myself from jolting at the sound. I closed my eyes as I continued to drown out the murderous thoughts threatening to spill to the forefront of my mind. *And when the rock breaks, the cradle will fall...*

"It is *always* President Eclipse to you, *Winter*," she spat towards my father as he regained his breath. Her anger was almost palpable and it filled the room. It took everything in me to not shrink away from it. She took a deep breath before turning her attention back towards me.

"Your daughter will at least be useful in proving just how pathetic you are, once and for all," she said, snapping her fingers at Anubys. I watched him raise his hands and saw him hesitate. I looked at his hood, where I thought his eyes might be. I would be okay, I wanted to think—to reassure him and, partly, reassure myself. But, instead, I screamed the nursery rhyme in my brain so loud that October winced slightly.

"Anubys," President Eclipse said, irritated. I watched

him mouth "I'm sorry" before I felt the unbearable pain again. No matter how much I tried, I never was able to keep the screams from leaving my lips. And I watched as my father sobbed on the ground at the sound. His face was contorted into sadness, but it was odd to watch him without eyeballs. It was all I could think about as I felt the cooling feeling of death. The feeling of absoluteness.

"What are you doing?" I heard Eset snap. She grabbed Anubys, but his gaze was set on mine. I watched a smile form on his face.

"What's happening?" President Eclipse demanded, pushing herself off of her desk.

"She's dying," Eset said, urgently as she shook Anubys. "He's stuck in the power." But, I knew better. He was killing me, on purpose.

"Anubys!" I heard a shrill voice say as the world around me went black, the sobs of my father echoing in my ears. And I knew, once the silence filled me, that I was dead.

It felt like I was floating in a sea of darkness, except I didn't have a body anymore. There was a feeling of freedom. Of being lightweight. Gone were the feelings of anger, the feelings of sadness, and all that remained was this overwhelming feeling of calm. A light grew in the middle of the dark sea as I rode the current towards it. As the light grew bigger, someone stood at the entrance of it. And I recognized the face which looked slightly different from mine.

"Mom?" I heard a voice that didn't sound like me say. It sounded more ethereal, somehow.

"Zinnia," she breathed. She looked like my mom, even though I knew we both weren't humans anymore. We were something else. It felt like she hugged me, though she didn't look like she did. And she smiled as she took in my face.

"You will be going back," she said. *Go back?* I felt myself think. *Why would I want to go back when I could feel like this?*

"This feeling goes away," my mother said. "Once you go through the light, you're nothing at all." Being nothing sounded better than being something, with all these responsibilities.

"You *must* go back," my mother said, pushing me backwards. "Remember the dreams I sent you. Be smart, and stay alert. But, most importantly, trust no one." Her gaze was hard as she said the last words. It was a command more so than a warning.

"But first," she reached her arm forwards and grabbed a piece of me that glowed blue as she stuffed it into her pocket, "you can't go back without me taking something." Her eyes that I inherited winked at me as she waved a last goodbye.

"You'll be okay, in the end. You're my daughter," she said, almost proudly.

"Mom," I whispered, my voice echoing all around me. "I miss you." I floated backwards in the sea of darkness, back to where it all began. I started to feel myself fall into it, to drown in it. And I saw my mother's face look towards me, longing in her eyes.

"I miss you, too," her voice seemed to say. And then I was swallowed by the darkness.

I felt myself seem to settle back into my cold body. The sounds around me were muffled, like I was deep underwater as I fought with myself to try and gain control over my body once again. Every part of me desperately tried to fill the coldness, fighting it away with the flame of my life. I heard someone crying and then realized the sounds must be my father, but it sounded too far away. I tried to pull myself away from the feeling of calm, from the dark sea, but still, a part of me was sinking back into it. The relief it gave me was something my soul didn't want to give up.

"She's coming back slower than usual," I heard a muffled voice say. I tried to lean into my ears to hear more clearly, but it felt like I was dragging my feet in my brain. I couldn't fill it up fast enough.

"She wasn't even dead for that long," I heard another irritated voice say. It sounded like Eset.

"She'll be fine." *Anubys*, I felt myself breathe, and the rest of me chased away the last of the chill. I pulled the part of me that was content in the sea of darkness back into my body. And it was like I fell from a great distance as I tried to catch my breath.

My eyes fluttered open, and I could hear just as clearly as I could before death overtook me. I coughed as Anubys helped me sit up. His hood was down and anyone could recognize the concern that was present in his eyes. I felt myself glance over at President Eclipse, and I knew she noticed it, too. Her lips were pursed.

I looked over at my father who had stopped sobbing. A look of desperation was on his face as he tried to understand the situation.

"What happened?" I asked, grabbing Anubys's hand as

he helped me up to my feet. I watched as my father's face relaxed into relief as he heard my voice. He held his shaking hands together as he stayed still on the ground.

"I accidentally killed you," Anubys said, almost sheepishly. He rubbed the back of his head as Eset shot daggers at it. Her hood was down, too.

"*I* brought you back," she said pointedly. It took a minute before I realized she wanted a response as she stared intently at me.

"Thank...you..." I said, slowly. Anubys shared with me a look of disbelief at the audacity of his sister. He dusted off my legs and arms, almost like he was checking if I were still cold anywhere.

"How are you feeling?" he asked. He didn't meet my eyes as he spoke, but I knew what he was asking. I flexed my hands a bit as I felt around within my body. The fire in my blood was there, but I wasn't sure if the fist was still present or not. When I tried to get the fire to flare up, it did, at my command. And just as it did, a flood of memories came back into my head.

"Whoa," Anubys said as I started to collapse. He held me up as I held my head, his hands dusting over me once again, keeping the churning fire at bay. My head was pounding loud, but the image of August watching me in all of my memories disappeared. Anubys was holding my wrist, and the memory of Anubys taking my hand, unmarred by August's face, came to the forefront of my mind as the blood between us started to sing.

"It means we're both just as destructive," I whispered to myself. Anubys's eyes widened as he realized, and he steadied me before letting me go. He gave away his card; I knew it as I stared into President Eclipse's face. But, I wasn't about to reveal mine.

I felt for the hellfire within my blood, and let it heat my body a little. Let it melt away the corpse-like feeling in my limbs and to give my body life. Underneath this skin was pure flame, and I couldn't help but smile a bit. I had my power back, and August was out of my head. For good.

"You lost a part of yourself, when you were brought back," President Eclipse said, her arms crossing over her chest. "How do you feel?" I smiled, a smile that resembled the one that I had seen Eset and Anubys wear before. *If I lost some part of myself, it was a part worth losing*, I felt myself unabashedly think. I knew October heard it, and I knew he would report back to her about it.

"I feel great," I said, my eyes glancing over at October whose beady hazel eyes watched me like a hawk. I smiled at him as my eyes focused back onto President Eclipse. She just looked at my father with utter distaste on her face as she slowly met my gaze. *Down will come baby, cradle and all.*

My smile grew bigger.

CHAPTER THIRTY-SEVEN

"Put her to sleep," President Eclipse demanded once August entered the room. He had the decency to have the hood covering his eyes as he walked up to me. I didn't ever want to see those blue eyes again. I felt myself glare at him, my lips curling upwards as I took in the sight. He looked skinnier, but I couldn't be bothered to care.

"Sleep," he said the word. His voice was like woven silk, and my body relaxed at the command. But, it wasn't completely convincing. He didn't have control over me anymore. He was out of my mind. I stifled a smile as I pretended to fall to the ground, fighting against the sleep.

"Don't hurt my dad," I whispered, closing my eyes as I feigned unconsciousness. I felt for the fire in my body, willing it into a wall of fire around my mind so October couldn't penetrate it. All October would hear was silence, Anubys had told me.

"He won't be able to see what is blocking the thoughts,

and will automatically think you're just sleeping," Anubys said the night before. *Hopefully, he's right*, I thought as I felt someone lift me onto a cot. I waited for them to roll me away, so I could figure out how to escape this prison if need be.

But, instead, I felt a small hand wrap around my fingers. *Great*, I thought sarcastically as the world blurred around me. I fell to the dirt ground of my cell as the child stared at me, the hood still over their face. My stomach churned, but I tried not to move an inch.

"You're not asleep," they said, their quiet voice filling the room. My eyes snapped open as I glared up at them.

"You better not say anything," I hissed. The child's lips pulled back into a smile as they stood in front of me.

"I never snitch," they whispered, wiggling their fingers before disappearing. Their body just seemed to collapse in on itself until it wasn't there anymore.

"I'm guessing it went well," Lightning's voice said, disrupting the silence. I smiled as I looked over at the wall where Lightning's voice came from.

"I have my powers back," I said. "And, I feel more in tune with it than before." I flexed my hand as little sparks flew out of it. My smile widened at the small firework display.

"Do you... *feel* any different?" Lightning asked, his voice low. My eyebrows scrunched together.

"What do you mean?" I asked.

"I mean, Eset said when you come back, you're not yourself," Lightning explained. "Every time you're brought back, something gets taken from you."

"My mom was there," I said. "She only took August out of the equation."

"Are you sure?" There was something in Lightning's voice that annoyed me. I gritted my teeth as the hellfire in my eyes flashed.

"I'm fine," I insisted. Before Lightning could say another word, someone whispered at us in the darkness. I sat up, my heart racing as I looked past the bars at the person standing there.

"Volplie?" I asked, my jaw dropping as I stood up. I walked over to the bars as her eyes glowed at me.

"I'm going to get you two out of here," she said, a smile on her face as she shook a key holder full of iron keys in front of my cell. My eyebrows raised.

"I'm not leaving," I stated, adding, "Plus, the doors are soldered shut." She blinked at me as she glanced down at the door. She looked over at Lightning in the other cell.

"Do *you* want to leave?" she asked.

"I don't know," he muttered. She looked back and forth between us, confusion filling her face.

"I'm sorry," she said, taking a step back so she could look at the both of us, "You two *want* to be in President Eclipse's dungeon?"

"We have a plan," I said, my eyes steeled as I looked at Volplie. She stared at me, before realization flooded her face.

"No," she breathed as she looked at Lightning in disbelief. "Don't tell me—"

"I'm going to kill her," I declared.

"Are you an *idiot*? I didn't peg you for an idiot, Zinnia," Volplie muttered.

"She needs to die. You know it," I said. Volplie rolled her eyes as she looked at Lightning.

"You're condoning this?"

"She has my family hostage," Lightning said softly. Volplie blew a white lock of hair out of her eyes as she narrowed them. She held up the keys that were around her finger.

"I can get them out," she paused, "probably." Then, she insisted, "I'm telling you, you don't want to try and do this. It's not just President Eclipse." I frowned as I remembered Anubys's same words. *What did they mean by that?*

"Anubys is going to help us," I said, leaning away from the metal bars. Her purple-blue eyes widened as her head whipped over to me.

"Anubys?" her voice was small.

"He said he'll help," I said, almost smugly.

"Why?"

"He's in love with her," Lightning said, matter-of-factly. Volplie snorted.

"He didn't say those exact words, but—"

"You're going to trust *Anubys* because he *might* be in love with you? You know he *can't* love, right?" Volplie said, her arms crossing over her chest.

"I'm going to kill her, Volplie. I have to," I said, my voice breaking slightly. Her gaze softened as she chewed on her lip.

"Fine," she said. She looked at Lightning in silence for a moment before dropping her head, her ears lying flat against her head.

"I'll help, too," she muttered. I tried to keep my mouth closed as the seriousness of her words settled into me.

"What?" Lightning said, unable to hide his shock.

"First, I'll report back to Tayen and tell her what's

happening, in case you need back up. Then, I'll let myself get captured. As much as Istas *says* she hates me and wants me dead, she'll do anything to keep me alive. Including begging President Eclipse to let me join her little army," Volplie said, turning into a small white fox. Before either of us could say another word, she bounded away, the keys in her mouth.

"Did she just say she's going to report back to Tayen?" Lightning breathed.

"Guess it's good she came," I whispered.

It felt like it had been days before the child appeared at my cell once again.

"Hello, liar," the child said, smiling at me. I rolled my eyes.

"What is it?" I asked, standing up from the dirt ground. The smile grew wider as they held out a hand towards me. They held out another hand towards Lightning's cell, and I stared at it in confusion.

"Your boyfriend convinced President Eclipse you two are joining her side," the child said. The smile turned taunting.

"I don't have a boyfriend," I muttered. But, I took the hand as I watched Lightning's dark one grab the other.

"This one's going to make you sick," the child laughed as the world melted away.

They were right. Once solid ground was beneath my feet, I emptied my stomach not once, but twice. Lightning did the same. We were back in that impossibly white room as the two large, cloaked men stood there, once again.

"Bye, bye," the child said, twinkling their fingers before collapsing in on themselves until they were no more.

"Remember to think of nursery rhymes," I barely breathed towards Lightning as the group of people in gloves and masks scurried into the room. I turned around as they washed and dressed us, blood rushing to my ears and face in embarrassment at the fact that Lightning was there, too.

"C'mon," one of the cloaked men grunted as the woman finished tying my auburn hair into a bun.

"Perfect," she said, but her hands shook as she pulled them away from me. Her eyes crinkled into a smile, but fear was screaming out in them. The sight made my stomach drop. Who was possibly scarier than President Eclipse?

"A special guest wants to meet you," the other cloaked man smiled, sending shivers down my spine. They led both Lightning and me out of the room, as we exchanged looks, towards President Eclipse's office. The double doors opened and standing there was President Eclipse laughing at someone whose back was turned towards us. His hair was the color of woven sunlight. He turned towards us as the men forced us in. My heart stopped as I stared at his face, tattoos running up the side of his neck. The face I saw every day of my life. The face that was framed in almost every building in the town square of Adams. The face of a member of the first Senate.

"Zinnia, this is Benjamin Adams," President Eclipse said, the ghost of laughter still on her face. "He wanted to meet you."

Benjamin Adams. The man who founded the Adams Community hundreds of years ago. A warrior in the war that supposedly destroyed the world. *He* was standing in front of me.

"How—" but the words hitched in my throat. It wasn't even possible. It couldn't be. My mind raced. How was Benjamin Adams, a member of the first Senate, *still alive*?

-TO BE CONTINUED-

ALSO BY BIANCA K. GRAY

The Celestials: Book 1

Fine

Angst: a collection of poetry

ACKNOWLEDGMENTS

Thank you, first and foremost, to my darling fiancé who supported me while writing this story. You listened to me endlessly talk about this story to you and comforted me through every breakdown that I had about this book. Thank you for being there for me and for listening to each chapter and chapter rewrite that I did, and for giving me your honest thoughts. You are the best partner anyone could ask for and I adore and love you so very much!!

Thank you to my parents for always supporting my dreams. You were the inspiration behind Winter and Nabi, and I appreciate you cultivating my imagination. You two are the reason why I write and why I believe in myself so heavily. I love you two more than life itself!!

Thank you to my beta readers for giving me endlessly valuable advice. I really appreciate the work that you all did, and for giving me much needed constructive criticism. You all made this book better than it was before!! I adore all of you!!

Thank you to the sensitivity readers who were able to give me feedback on my story. Your thoughts and feedback were much needed, and also very validating, so I really appreciate the work that you guys do and for putting a lot of effort into my passion project!!

Thank you so very much to my cover artist Sapro!! Your art is magnificent and I'm so happy that you turned my book into its own work of art. You created exactly what was in my head and I will cherish this book for ages to come!! Can't wait to see what you do with the rest of the series!!

Lastly, thank you to anyone who took the time to buy and read this book. I hope you enjoyed this little story that I created and that it brought happiness into your life. I write because I love it, and I hope you loved it just as much!!